A SECOND CHANCE IN BLUE HAVEN
Copyright © 2023 by Charli Cotner

ISBN 979-8-9864995-4-3

Cover Design by Brittany Evans

Edited by Represent Publishing

A SECOND CHANCE IN
BLUE HAVEN

CHARLI COTNER

Represent
Publishing

"Maybe sometimes love needs a second chance because it wasn't ready the first time around."

Author's Note

Since it still feels like I'm dreaming, I don't know how to articulate what this book means to me. Can someone pinch me? Not really, but really, I'm serious. Regardless of the fact that I do not really wish to be pinched, I wish to express my gratitude to those who have assisted me along the way. As I have shared moments of joy and despair through this book with you all, I am grateful that I have been able to do so. It's almost surreal to realize that I have achieved a goal that I believed was beyond my capabilities. It's an incredible feeling to show that anything is possible with a strong sense of motivation and support.

My writing was inspired by the heaviest season of my life yet, a mama who lost her job while on maternity leave, struggling to find her identity, struggling with postpartum depression, and battling all the in's and out's of not just raising one child, but two. I love my babies, but the transition from 1 to 2 was very hard on me. There were days when I felt like I was drowning and there were times when I did not wish to be earth side because of the worrisome, anxiety, and stress filled days that added up to where I felt as if I would not be able to cope. I know, crazy, right? It's easy to overlook the internal battles that people are facing, as we are only able to see what is presented to us on the surface. No matter what, it is important to remember that everyone's struggles are unique and may be occurring out of our sight.

However, despite that, I have always been prompted to follow certain signs in subtle ways throughout my life. And these certain signs that came and went throughout the years, I knew it was God telling me, "Hey, do this for you. You would do a fantastic job if you just gave it a try." And the final sign came to me on Sept. 9th, 2022. I sat in my office chair, opened a blank document as tears filled my eyes, and I told myself, "This is your life, Charli. You only get one. So what if you fail? At least you are doing something for YOU, not anyone else."

Prior to that day, I had dreamed about these characters constantly. When the book began to unfold in my dreams, I knew I had to put my insecurities aside in order to embrace my destiny. I began writing immediately without hesitation. I felt as though I understood the heart and soul of every character, and soon I was writing with ease and excitement. I felt energized and motivated, as if I had finally begun a journey that was meant for me.

Writing.

Several months later, I made my long-held dream a reality. Through research, dedication, and support, I have been able to achieve it. This book is meant to remind us that while life is full of ups and downs, it is the little moments, people, and dreams that make it all worthwhile. As a result of this accomplishment, I am proud to be able to emphasize that through resilience and optimism, anything is possible. Life is an adventure that we must take on with an open and grateful heart.

Here's to feeling alive, being creative, being ambitious, and making a difference through my words.

Chapter One ♡

Ada

"Ada, get your sweet ass in here. We're ready to go!" Lucy shouts as she enters my room in the penthouse we share. "Damn, girl, you look hot in this," she says as she grabs me from behind.

I stand before the mirror, looking at myself in my last-minute outfit. I rub my hands up and down my skirt. "Are you sure it's not too much?" I ask.

Although I would not normally wear this outfit out, the combination of pieces gives me a sense of confidence and strength. The black leather skirt symbolizes the power and authority I possess as a lawyer, while the ivory bodysuit and boots add a sense of elegance and professionalism. With a dash of sass, this ensemble is a direct reflection of Ada Collins.

A smile spreads across Lucy's face as she says, "Ada Collins, look at you. You are a confident, ambitious, and stunning woman. But you do not need an outfit to demonstrate that; it is all right here," she says, pointing to my heart. "However, you do need some fun every now and then. Besides, you have a killer body in that outfit that's clearly going to attract the attention of every man at the club." She slaps my butt. "Or that tight ass will. Let's go." Lucy may get on my nerves every now and then but she truly is the best hype woman ever.

Taking Lucy's arm, I notice Ashten, our friend, and Lucy's coworker, standing beside us. "Let's go before I have to pee again." She motions to her outfit. "I just went, and this jumpsuit is hard to undo without help, and I'd prefer it in the bedroom, not in the bathroom."

Lucy and I laugh, knowing this is a disaster waiting to happen. Let's just say this isn't Ashten's first go around with jumpsuits.

Despite the fact that it's the end of September and beginning of fall here in New York, I find myself shaking and shivering as we walk on the massive concrete sidewalks.

In the midst of our walk to the club, which is only a few blocks from our penthouse—convenient, I know—I hear someone clearing their throat.

"Ladies, let's have a good time. Let's live it up, we are only young once!"

I look over and see Lucy's eyes laser focused on mine, her words clearly aimed at me.

It's no secret that I am the most introverted member of our group. However, after dealing with the exasperating cases that I handle on a daily basis, I would rather sit in front of our fireplace watching Gilmore Girls for the hundredth time, while shoving my face with some Ben and Jerry's. In my friend mode, however, I put on a brave face to make us all happy, even for a night.

So I say with a playful wink, "I'll definitely try, Luce."

Laughing, she rolls her eyes. "You'll do it, but I'm being serious, Ada. Let's just enjoy each other's company. We don't see each other much anymore, and I really cherish our girls' nights out."

Well okay then, that got sobersided real fast. I nod, knowing what she means: *Ada, you work too much, you're wasting your life. Blah blah blah.* Instead of fighting a losing battle, I let out a silent sigh, "Luce, I hear you loud and clear. Fun Ada coming right up."

The line of eager patrons leads up to the entrance as we approach the club, where the security guard is visible under the bright glow of the 'Envy Lounge Nightclub' sign.

"Girls, let's take a selfie right under the neon sign," Lucy says as she pulls her phone out of her back pocket. "This will be awesome for my Instagram." She grins, anticipating the likes and comments she'll get when the photo is posted.

As we progress at a leisurely pace, I really want to say, 'Is this really necessary?' But I don't since this isn't anything new when around Lucy. She will take photos at every opportunity, as most Social Media Influencers do. After graduating from the University in Fashion, Lucy had brand ambassador positions coming from left and right, but she sealed the deal with two major companies, Chic Logic and Magnolia. She has made tremendous strides since then, and I couldn't be more proud of her.

Moving under the vibrant turquoise and hot pink sign, Lucy squeezes between Ashten and I. "Smile, ladies. This is for Magnolia Boutique." And again, knowing this is a big deal for Lucy, and we proudly support her, I smile and hear her say, "I just know this is going to be one wild night."

"I'm glad someone sees it that way," I say as we walk toward the red velvet ropes, waiting for our turn.

My underhanded comment reaches Ashten, who snorts and surrenders, holding her hands up. "Hey, maybe not wild, but entertainable. Plus, I need a suitable handyman to take home tonight."

I mutter back, "Don't we all."

Music reverberates from the walls as the bouncer waves us in, wearing a dark gray puffer vest and hat that reads 'SECURITY'. Throughout the club, there is an electric atmosphere, with the lights flashing in time with the music and the bass thumping in my chest. Drinks roll rapidly across the tables, sweaty bodies move to the beat on the dance floor, and people try to hear over the banging music.

My phone vibrates in my wallet as we sit in the VIP section, courtesy of the fashion industry, aka Lucy's brand deals. Seeking any excuse to avoid what I am about to read, I reluctantly remove it from my purse. I immediately begin chewing on my inner cheek, already knowing who I am about to deal with: *Emmett.*

As I read his text message, my hands briefly clench around my phone.

> I would like to remind you that we have an important meeting with a potential client concerning mergers and acquisitions.

Right, sir, I already knew this before I left the office today.

I roll my eyes. I am taking on such a big case in my career that I cannot afford to risk anything, and he understands that. What is intended to be a friendly reminder is actually just a last-minute text that gets under my skin. There's a fine line between support and nagging, and he's definitely crossed it.

Knowing I need to end this conversation so I can actually make the best of tonight, I send him a quick reply back.

> Don't worry, sir. I'll be ready as always. See you tomorrow.

Plus, we all know every successful woman needs to cut loose. One night on the town will do no harm; perhaps it will make tomorrow's work worthwhile.

"Ada Collins, who are you texting? It is a girls' night, time to take a break from work," Lucy muses, narrowing her eyes.

She's right; plus, this won't reflect who I am tomorrow. I just want to have a good time with my two besties. My smile returns as I tell the cocktail waitress I want a vodka spritz, my favorite drink whenever we go clubbing. "So . . . why are we here again?" I ask.

Shrugging her shoulders, Lucy turns around. "Nadia from Magnolia mentioned to me at our photo shoot last week that she and her sister went to this club a few weekends ago, so I thought, why not? We are all successful, single, and damn good-looking women."

"I say amen to that sister!" Ashten shouts over the music.

My head tilts back in agreement with my girls, the liquor smoothly flowing down my throat, resulting in a pleasant buzz throughout my body. As the music vibrates the floor, I become more relaxed, loose, and languid. My feet begin to move in my boots as joy filters in, and the beat of the music allows me to let go. Clubs may not be my go-to choice for a night out, but I enjoy the feeling of liberation they bring. There's something special about the combination of listening to great music, the energy of dancing, and the soothing sensation that comes with it.

Several drinks later, the alcohol keeps flowing in my veins like it's on an IV drip. I'm ready for the dance floor, hands in the air, body moving like an uncoiling rope, eyes on fire. Lucy grabs my hand and drags me there before I can say otherwise. "I love this song. Let's dance!" she exclaims.

In moments like these, I am more alive than if I were shouting from the top of a mountain as we begin to jump and dance. The music is a drug that makes my mind buzz with pure ecstasy as my hair bounces along my back and my body moves to the beat.

A few songs in, Ashten joins us. She and Lucy share a look as they both pull me down and whisper in unison: "Wanna play truth or dare?"

Pulling back, I eye them as they start to fall into a fit of giggles. There is always an element of familiarity and knowing on the faces of these two hooligans whenever they wish for some entertainment, such as now.

A sigh emanates from my lips as I ask, "What is with you two always being so gung ho about truth or dare? Isn't drinking the night away with me enough fun?"

Lucy utters with a pouty lip, "Come on, Ada, what kind of fun would that be?"

In a way that is a little too loud, Ashten blurts out, "I'm sorry to cut into this fun conversation, but dance floor, five o'clock."

As we diverge our gazes, the man she's referring to is clearly ogling me. He doesn't look away when I catch him, and I can't help but return the flirtatious gaze. Helplessly, I am drawn to his sexy smirk, and I feel a sudden rush of butterflies as I realize I can't deny the growing intensity between us.

"Ashten, are you talking about the tall guy with sexy brown hair?" Lucy squeals while tugging a little too hard on my forearm.

"Yes, Luce."

"The suit is black, the shirt is white?"

"Yes, Luce."

"Three buttons are undone?"

"Yes," I reply somewhat testily. "He's staring right at us."

"God, damn, that man is a sight for sore eyes."

She definitely is not wrong there. He's certainly a head-turner, with an air of confidence that is hard to ignore.

"Ada, damn girl, go introduce yourself before I do." Lucy urges me to move toward him.

Ashten laughs. "I think I have a better idea. I dare you to walk over there and ask him to dance, perhaps even seal a kiss or two? Give him the flirtatious and charming Ada we all know."

I squish my eyebrows in confusion as I consider her words. Um, okay, not entirely sure who she is referring to. While I may own a penthouse in New York and have a successful career, flirtatious and fun Ada is a rare occurrence these days.

"You never know, maybe something else will come out of it too?" she shrugs.

There you have it, ladies and gentlemen. If these

two aren't trying to get my ass out the door, they are trying to get me involved in a relationship. Yet, I have no time for a relationship, only casual sex.

But being the kind of friend I am, and one who does not back down from a dare, I blow them a kiss as I toss my hair over my shoulders and say, "If you want to get a dare, then you're going to get one."

With her eyebrows wagging, Ashten slaps my butt, pushing me forward a little. "If I was looking to get laid tonight, which I still am, he definitely would be at the top of my list."

In a tone of laughter, Lucy says, "Same girl, same girl. Let me just say that, Ada, honey, if you don't want to walk yourself over there, I would be more than happy to do it for you."

Let yourself dream, Luce. I may have come here unwillingly to blow off some steam, but that doesn't mean it cannot be with some serious eye candy. Plus, I'm Ada Collins, a freaking catch.

I straighten my back, lift my chin, and fluff up my girls in response to my inner voice. My favorite Prada heels—a birthday present for passing the bar association exams—guide me through the crazy crowd. He scans me up and down with his eyes, and I can't help but feel a bit of electricity shooting through my veins.

Okay, maybe tonight won't be as bad as I thought.

His appearance becomes more familiar the closer I approach him.

Do I know him?

Wait, is that—

It couldn't be, could it? I would have recognized him in an instant.

Right?

Even if a decade has passed, one does not simply forget the appearance of someone once loved.

I stop in the middle of the dance floor as I put my hand to my chest, trying to catch my breath. *Ada, it's not him. It has been years since you've last seen him.* As I shake my head, I straighten myself and glance ahead, only to see the incredibly attractive man standing right in front of me; a man who is a stranger, someone who is not *him*.

Inhaling deeply, I let my head drop, uttering a simple prayer of thanks to God. Did I mention he looked like sex on a stick? His tanned skin and bright blue eyes, a reflection of the summer sky, are enough to make me weak in the knees. His broad shoulders and toned body make me think he could easily lift me off the ground and fulfill all my desires. As I bite my bottom lip, I can honestly say that I would undoubtedly allow this man to break some laws in my bed.

Taking a few more steps toward me, he leans in, his lips trailing over my skin as he whispers, "Wanna dance?"

His breath tickles my neck, sending shivers down my spine. "Lead the way," I say.

The smile that graces his face can no doubt destroy an entire population of women, including me. *Hey, vagina, you still intact down there? I know it's been awhile but down, girl. Let's get a feel for him first, yeah?*

Grabbing my hands, he tucks me into his chest as he asks, "Can you guarantee that this will be enjoyable for me?"

I nibble on my bottom lip, giving it a second before responding, I say to him, "Well, let's say I can guarantee that it will be way more pleasant than your last experience."

Raising an eyebrow, his eyes dance with amusement as he says, "Alright, let's see what you got."

With a smirk, he turns me around. My back flush with his chest, and I move my hips right above the spot in which I know he will be inundated with desire. In time with the bass, I raise my arms and interlace my fingers around his neck, making us as physically close as two people can be. His body moves in perfect sync with mine, causing my heart to race.

Damn. He feels good.

While my head is tilted back on his shoulder, I close my eyes and enjoy the sensation of his hands moving freely over my body, triggering a rush of adrenaline throughout my entire body. My connection to him intensifies everything around me, enhancing the ghosting of his fingertips across my skin, the rich, smoky scent of his, which is surprising and refreshing. It is all-consuming and tempting at the same time, which is the perfect combination for a stress-free evening.

As the minutes turn into hours of dancing, drinking, and having a night of exactly what the doctor, or more like my best friends, ordered, I feel Tanner, also known as the man who has been glued to my side all night, grab my hand. Turning us around, we thread through the crowd as I trail behind. We squeeze through a group of people clustered in front of the bar. Standing up on my tiptoes, I lean over the counter, looking for the bartender. Peeking behind me, Tanner is staring at me once again, specifically my ass.

Raising an eyebrow, I ask in curiosity, "Am I

supposed to assume you're an ass man? Or wait, are we both? Ass and tits type?"

A raspy chuckle emanates from his throat as I turn to face him. "You could say I like both—they're both hot, they bring different pleasures, and you got a great set of each on you."

Damn, that was a hot answer. Not going to lie, that comment coming from his mouth was like having my pussy electrocuted with excitement. Before I know it, my hands are around his neck, and his arms are around my waist. I take this moment to touch his neck with my tongue, catching the sweat drops on the surface.

I knew he smelled great, but damn, he tastes just as good, if not better.

This can only mean one thing.

He's a god in bed.

The warmth of his steady gaze dances up to mine, making my heart pound uncontrollably in my chest, and my lips and pussy throb in equal measure. At this moment, I am certain, without a doubt, that we are heading somewhere, possibly without clothing. Rising on my heels, I place my lips against his ear, "Wanna get out of here?"

A smirk appears on Tanner's lips as his eyes go wild with anticipation. "Took you long enough."

Hot damn, Ada, you should thank your lucky stars that you have friends that make you leave your penthouse.

Chapter Two ♡

Ada

Wet kisses down my neck wake me the next morning and let me tell you it's one hell of a way to wake up. With his hand covering my breast, flicking my nipple, I moan and arch my back into him, feeling his erection poking at my bottom.

God, did it always feel this good with *him?*

Ada, you know it does.

Without a thought, barely awake, I snake my hand behind me and grip his shaft. His whole body thrusts forward as it jerks a little. "God, that feels ahhmazing. Please tell me morning sex is your thing."

Hearing an unfamiliar voice, my body freezes. I immediately let go and rotate to face him, wanting to see *him.*

But it isn't *him*; it's a stranger, who is in my penthouse. In my bed.

Shit, it is the guy from last night.

Shit, shit, shit. What is his name, again?

Ada, this isn't your first time having casual sex. Don't over-think it. One step at a time, starting with getting him out of your bed.

Horns honking cause me to jump out of my frozen state. The rumbling of garbage trucks and the shrill of emergency sirens filter in and I forcefully get out of bed. This hangover feels like a balloon under my cranium, slowly being inflated, pressure mounting.

Okay, I'm pretty positive I didn't do that much damage with dancing at the club, did I?

The night's events flash through my mind like a bad movie.

Getting ready with Lucy and Ashten. The club and lights. The dance floor. The brown-haired goddess. His tongue swirled slowly around my nipple, his hand on the other. Whimpering, breathing ragged, trying to angle our bodies closer. Guiding his mouth lower to where I needed it as I softly begged, "Please, Lincoln." I moaned as he grabbed my nipple, his tongue rubbing over the sensitive tip and hungrily sucking it. As he hovered above me, his lips trailing down my body, he gave me that damn smirk that drew me in. He lowered his mouth to pussy, taking long, languid strokes with his tongue that had me crying out, "Lincoln." I grabbed handfuls of his hair, pulling and kneading like a cat. "Oh my God, don't stop, I-I am coming!"

Ada, you didn't?

Oh, but you did, and I think he liked it when you called him that.

Goosebumps scurry up my arms and crawl along my neck as I think about calling this man that.

Why would I be thinking of Lincoln? I've not seen him in years, and I've never called someone that.

"Fuck."

Looking back over my shoulder, I catch sight of the man as he mutters something to me.

Tanner, yes, that's his name.

Score one for one, Ada. Now get him out of here. We have more important matters to take care of, like work.

Shit. Work.

Shit. Emmett.

Shit. Ruth.

Seeing Tanner with all of his limbs entangled in my sheets, I find it difficult to move and groove, but as I gaze upon his chiseled body, which could only have been shaped by the Gods, I feel myself wanting to crawl back under the sheets.

Ada, get it together, I hear my inner voice screaming. *Now is not the time. I repeat: NOW is not the time.*

But the man screams muscle, masculinity, and sex.

Looking away from my bed, I gaze toward my French patio doors. Viewing New York always soothes me; it eases the tension in my shoulders and allows me to relax. From up here, it seems as if time stops completely, as the buildings race toward the soft blue sky and millions of people hurry from one place to another.

The fact that I see this every single day makes me feel like I am living out a dream of mine. It has been said that New York is an excellent place to begin a career as a lawyer, so I moved here.

And they weren't wrong.

The ping of my phone interrupts my serenity. I look down and notice that there is a new message.

ELENA

A glance at my nightstand reveals that it is an hour after I normally wake up. *Shit.* I scramble around my bedroom as I try to put on my underwear and type a reply to Elena, my assistant.

Yeah, you got wasted and had a one-night stand.

Almost rolling my ankle in despair, I look at the strewn clothes from last night; a wave of desire courses through me.

Him, grabbing my breasts as he threw my back to the wall. My hand trembling around his cock. My body pounding with blood. The pleasure of his smooth lips kissing down my narrow torso, dipping his tongue into my navel. His hands pushing my legs apart, licking them as we both teetered on the edge of oblivion.

The thoughts of last night fade from my mind in a blink of an eye as Tanner asks, "Darling, do you mind if I shower?"

Focus, Ada.

I give myself a pep talk by doing a simple clap. *It is not the time for you to dwell on a meaningless hook-up. You have serious matters to deal with, such as your boss yelling at you.*

Tanner sits on my bed with a confused expression on his face.

What is he looking at? Did he say something else?

His eyebrows waggle as he gives me a once-over.

Ugh, now is not the time, dude.

As he aimlessly waves his hands around, he says, "I'll ask again, since you appear a bit unsettled."

"Do you mind if I take a shower, or better yet, we can shower together? Another round might be just what we both need."

Yeah, like four rounds last night wasn't enough.

It is as if I can hear my pussy say, "Down girl."

My face crumples. Truth be told, the sex was good, average at best, and something I needed to get my stress out. However, it wasn't mind-blowing enough to repeat.

Rather than being told I am incompetent by my boss, Emmett, or Ruth, another senior associate at Sullivan & Rothman's and my archenemy, I would rather lose out on another decent orgasm.

As he looks at me, waiting for a response, I smile. *God, this is nothing short of a shitshow.*

I let him down easily and shove my boobs back into my dumb lingerie that should fit better than it does and say, "Sorry, I have a meeting at work today." Pointing back and forth between us, I continue, "So, no shower; you need to get going."

Taking off the covers, he tosses his legs to the side of the bed, along with his swollen cock.

Damn, is that how it was the night before? Thick, girthy, and deeply veined.

Ok, Ada, pick that drool off your lip and focus.

Regardless of how hung the guy is, I have a long list of things to do today. I walk into my ensuite with an attached walk-in closet and begin going through my schedule. Having found clothes, I put on my favorite floral blue poplin midi-dress from Prada, paired with black Jimmy Choo heels. I rush to the bathroom, after seeing my reflection. I make adjustments based on what

I see: brushing my teeth, touching up my makeup, and curling my hair from last night.

Glancing in my mirror, I notice Tanner is still lying naked, but now with his arms stretched out wide behind him. His coy gaze tells me that he might be enjoying this.

What did he think this was? Some sort of role play?

Maybe it was a fantasy kink, and he thought he would fuck a lawyer in a suit?

Wait, does he even know I am a lawyer?

God, last night was such a blur that I don't even remember what was said and what wasn't.

As I turn around, my eyes narrow. "A sloth could move faster than you."

In a matter of seconds, he gives me a glare. Can't say I blame him; I can be a bitch when it comes to my work. I hustle to find some accessories and start throwing his clothes at him.

Having finally gotten his act together, we rush out of my bedroom simultaneously, only to run into Lucy in the kitchen.

Shit. I definitely thought she would be still sleeping.

Rushing him through the kitchen, he starts to blab. "Well, maybe we can meet up again?"

Yeah, not happening.

"Or, you know, at least go for round two?" he asks as I push him into the hallway.

"Thanks, really, but I am good," I say as I slam the door in his face.

Harsh, I know, but how else was I supposed to get rid of the guy?

Letting out a sigh, I push myself off the door, only to see Lucy bite her bottom lip, holding back a laugh.

"Do not say it. I don't have the time, nor do I want to hear you say it."

Suddenly, Lucy starts laughing, a real belly laugh; you know the ones that make your stomach tighten and cramp because you are laughing so loudly. "I wasn't going to speak; your facial expressions were enough to express my thoughts."

Rolling my eyes, I return to my room to gather my work belongings. In response to Luce's words, I shout, "Thank you so much for the moral support, Best Friend! Wait, can I call you that at all? Because best friends are supposed to agree with whatever the other is doing or saying. Let each other make their own mistakes, but be by each other's side when they realize that said mistake."

When I am back in the kitchen, Luce looks up from her phone and shrugs. "What fun is it if I don't say anything?"

The only one who I consider my best friend is Lucy. She's a glass half full, positive, happy person. But she's also a woman who doesn't hold back at all. In spite of the fact that she is brutally honest and will tell you almost everything you don't want to hear, I am willing to put up with her outspoken personality for that very reason, and only that.

While in my freshman year at Hudson University, Lucy and I met. It seems like just yesterday that we attended our mandatory freshman dorm meeting. We were both running late; *shocking, I know, me late?* Anyway, we ran into each other, literally head butting, because we were so frantic we would miss something important.

She glanced at me as we both rubbed our foreheads and she said, "Watch where you are going." Pointing at herself, she continued, "I can't let anything happen to this gorgeous appearance of mine."

I had resisted the urge to roll my eyes. Who says something like that? After I had turned back to her, we both laughed together with huge grins on our faces.

Luce was the only one who helped me through our college years. Whenever I would break down about anything and everything, constantly questioning if I should go through with being a lawyer, she was always there.

What if I am not good enough?

What if I fail?

What if I am judged?

I only trusted her to tell me the truth. "Ada, you're a badass woman who will do great things in life. I can tell based on how determined you are," she pointed to my heart, "but you must decide that for yourself. The what ifs are your insecurities clouding your judgment, Hun. I realize that you think this way because of your upbringing, but you can still be a successful, independent, and thriving woman, no matter what you go through. You need to stop wallowing and start thinking like the powerful and intelligent woman you are."

I followed Lucy's advice every day after that; putting my head down and working my way through college. Four years later, I was Valedictorian, an AP Scholar, and graduated Summa Cum Laude with high honors. Obviously, I achieved any academic achievement I wanted with a healthy dose of competition that eventually allowed me to get into Pennbrook University School of Law.

"Hellooooo . . . earth to Ada!" Lucy looks at me with raised eyebrows. "Where did you go there? You've been staring into space for the past five minutes. I called your name twice."

Pasting on a bright smile, I say, "Sorry, Luce, I got sucked into the past for a second. What did you say?"

Lucy cocks an eyebrow as she says, "I asked you, how was he?" She fans her hand in front of her face and smiles. "He was hot from afar last night, but up close, glory be, girl. He looked like a less hot version of Chris Hemsworth."

Shaking my head, I let out a chuckle. There is something to be said about this girl and her obsession with Chris Hemsworth. I honestly can't comprehend how girls like guys with long hair or buns? That's a hard no for me. Plus, Tanner didn't even have that long of hair. I get it; we women all have different types, and that is not my cup of tea.

As I wait for my response, I bite my lip and carefully select my words. Being a lawyer has taught me to pause and choose my words carefully. The same applies to my best friend. Over the years, she has had a good read on me, and she knows when something is amiss or when I am lying.

So, in a nonchalant shrug, I look at her and say, "He got the job done."

The woman spits out her coffee and clasps her hands to her chest as she looks at me with a sarcastic expression. "I'm wounded. Are you really not going to elaborate on this so-called hook-up with your girl?!"

Shaking her head in disappointment, she continues, "Ada, that guy looked like he had a beefy sampson on him."

I hold back a chuckle as I ask, "Wait, did you just

refer to his dick as a beefy sampson? Where on God's green earth did you come up with a slang like that?"

Lucy gives me a lopsided grin. "Girl, you know me, always in tune with my partners and their fantasies, and one guy loved when I—"

Holding up my hand, I say, "Ok, I don't need the details. I got the picture."

Already running over an hour later than normal for work, I grab my coffee and coat and give her a quick peck on the cheek.

"Sorry, Luce, gotta run, late for work. But, I promise next time at dinner, we can discuss the details that include my non-existent love life."

"I will hold you to that promise, Ada Collins!" she shouts as I close the door behind me.

Chapter Three ♡

Ada

When I walk—more like—jog to the subway for work, I can't help but take in the stunning beauty of the foliage and its changing colors. The vibrant hues of orange, yellow, and red; the crisp and festive air; New York City is special all year round, whether it's holiday fun, blooms of spring, or summer lovin', but nothing can surpass the autumn season.

Despite the cold, my commute is filled with colorful food trucks, sidewalks congested with people of all ages, including businessmen and women, dog walkers, and shoppers carrying heavy bags. As much as I love New York, and this view, it was an adjustment for me at first. The multi-lane traffic, honking cars, non-stop construction noise, being bumped and jarred by pedestrians on the sidewalk, swearing and yelling, and getting lost in a large city I was unfamiliar with. Although, I recognized it as a challenge that I was more than willing to accept.

What I learned is that it's easy to blend in.

No one here questions your morality, background, and you may never see the same person twice. So saying the atmosphere in New York is different from the small town where I grew up isn't an exaggeration. Everyone knew who I was, where I came from, and gossip spread like wildfire, but here I have the freedom to be who I am without fear of judgment. Plus, this city is full of life and spirit, which only energizes me even more; you can literally feel the buzz as you stand on the corner. But as with anything in life, just because something is great does not mean it is perfect.

First, the public transportation systems here are a bitch. The subways are always under repair and delayed. Buses and taxis are subject to all traffic conditions. Gridlock is a real issue, and it could take days or weeks for you to get across a few blocks.

I know, I know, you're probably wondering why are you taking the subway, Ada, when you live in a penthouse in New York?

Easy, it's eco-friendly, duh.

Wait, you didn't think I actually believed in that shit, did you? I mean, I am all for saving the planet, and being more environmentally friendly, but when you are a thriving lawyer in New York, you don't have to take the subway.

But thanks to Nancy, aka my piece of shit vehicle from high school, it broke down months ago and I have yet to get a new car. Sometimes I think, what's the point as I get to observe New York at a slower pace, reminding me of Blue Haven. But then there are also times, like now, where I get a big ol' whiff of what I like to call a backed-up bathroom.

After passing most of the front bench seats and finding a spot right next to the vertical pole that extends from floor to ceiling, I try my best not to make eye contact with any passengers.

As soon as I sit down, I am hit with the putrid odor of vomit. *Come on, people, it's the 20th century, have the decency to put some deodorant on.* In an effort to suppress my gag, I turn toward the smudged glass windows. But it's no use as the scent keeps wafting my way with every movement of the subway.

Stop. Ada, Don't think about it.

The cold tile hits my knees while I scrub leftover vomit from the previous night. I hold my breath with one hand while cleaning with the other, wondering how it came to be like this. When did she get so bad? When did it become more than one drink per night? When's it going to stop?

"Ma'am, can you move?"

I looked up at the so-called person with narrowed eyes, nearly falling into the lap of the person next to me after recalling the past. Clearly wanting me to move over so that she may sit, she nudges her head to the side. Doing so, I grab my phone and open the Mercury app. It gives me a real-time update on where I am on the subway, and what do you know, the universe is not on my side today.

At this rate, it will be close to 10:00 am when we reach the firm. Normally, I am walking through the doors to the firm by 7:00 am, and that's on a good day. I take a quick breath and release it. *Ada, he doesn't scare you, remember he NEEDS you at his firm.*

What feels like hours later, I hear the voice of the speaker announcing my stop. Giving myself the pep talk

I always do before getting off, I stand tall and say, "Another day to kick ass, Ada."

While I say this, I feel as if I cannot quite comprehend that today is different. Today, something major is going to occur; I can feel it in my bones as I walk through the doors of the Sullivan & Rothman Law Firm.

There is a flurry of activity; phones are ringing, voices carry laughter from cubicle to cubicle as office workers gather to talk—it is all the same dreary stuff I hear every time I walk through the front entrance and make my way to my office.

"Ada, you're late! I'm guessing you went out again? Please tell me you found a cute guy to relieve the stress of your day?"

Elena's comment makes me roll my eyes; it is not a recurring issue, it only occurs every time I go out with Ashten and Lucy. My coat and purse are given to Elena to store in my office since I know I will be rushing to the meeting before then. As my right-hand girl, assistant, and partner in crime at work, she's truly incredible and I love her. Most of the time, I dote on her for the amazing work she does. But she is like a tension headache that you know is coming, and you cannot prevent it from occurring. They linger on throughout the day and keep distracting you from everything that needs to be accomplished.

"Ada! Are you even paying attention to what I am saying?! Emmett gets very agitated when meetings begin late, and none of us wish to have to bear the brunt of his unstable emotions because of you."

Relax, woman, I get it.

The girl is being dramatic. I know this isn't the first

time I've been late, but I've worked hard to get here. I'm not that reckless girl anymore. I'm responsible, self-sufficient, and a kickass lawyer who won several cases in her first year of practice.

Beat that, Ruth. That bruiser.

Walking into the meeting with my head held high, I push the doors open just a bit too much. The voices around me stop and take in the doors slamming against the walls behind them.

I clench my fists to my chest, my muscles tensing, as I hear the heavy sigh of Emmett. "Ada, it's so nice of you to join us," he says, sarcasm drips from his mouth.

I glance at Emmett and give him a slight nod and a tight smile. "The pleasure is all mine, sir."

His eyes roll back to the whiteboard as he murmurs, "We will speak after this. Please take a seat."

As I look around the conference table, I find myself sitting beside Ruth, aka Lord Voldemort, who mutters something about my attire to me.

Is it my clothing or my legal skills making her so jealous?

She probably does not even have a single pair of designer clothing in her closet, let alone appropriate lawyer clothing to ensure clients take her seriously. Since we both joined Sullivan & Rothman's three years ago, we have never been close. She has always had it out for me ever since I won the firm's first Senior Associate case in M&A.

Can't say I blame her, but it's pretty simple: don't hate the player, hate the game. The woman has been jealous of my success ever since and is unable to accept a healthy dose of competition from me.

"Ada! Ruth! Are you listening to me at all? I think

you two should listen, considering this may involve you both." Emmett looks at us sternly. "That's if you want it to."

Observing Ruth's look as she lifts her eyebrows at me, I recognize her expression instantly.

Sneering, I raise my own eyebrows. *Game on, Ruth. It takes two to tango.*

Despite Ruth being a sore loser, it won't keep me from competing with her. With my shoulders pulled back, my legs crossed, and my hands resting on the table in front of me, I gaze over at Emmett with eager eyes.

"May we move on to the real reason I called this meeting?" Emmett asks.

The room falls silent as all heads nod in agreement. The last thing we need is Emmett going off on a tangent about other problems at the firm.

"As you all probably know, Mr. Calhoun will be retiring at the end of this month, and Sullivan and Rothman's has an important corporate law case that was brought to my attention last night. Consequently, it would be my pleasure to discuss with you who will oversee this case and perhaps become the next partner."

From across the room, my mouth falls open as I try to process what Emmett just said. Okay, I knew John was retiring, but I had just assumed Tyler, Emmett's favorite employee, would be the next up for partnership.

Ruth gasps as she gives me a playful swat on the side of my arm. "Can you believe this? Me? Next partner?" she asks.

I think she means Ada Collins, next partner at Sullivan and Rothman's.

My eyes are drawn to the group of five of us—some bumping chests, chanting "Next Partner, Next Partner."

"All right, that's enough excitement," Emmett says, gesturing for us to sit down.

A wide grin spreads across my face as I think of the endless possibilities of being a partner. This would be the first time in the firm's history that a senior associate is made partner before six years have passed, and it's within reach of my own two hands.

Yes, I know, as of late, I have been a bit lenient with my working hours, but I am confident that I am capable of taking on this new position and case. Therefore, it is important to remain focused and mentally prepared. Any distractions at this point will not assist me with succeeding.

Just by being given this opportunity, I will be able to prove to the people around me that I am an exceptional attorney and they are well served to have me by their side.

Walking through the halls of Oak Ridge High School, wandering eyes, glaring looks, and whispers follow me. Muttering words surround me. Girls circling in their cliques.

"It's her again. What is she doing back?"

"I thought she went home for the day to take care of that piece of trash mom of hers."

"God, can you imagine what it must feel like to take care of your own mom?"

"In the end, she will never amount to anything and will end up like her mother. Not good enough. Not worthy enough. She will never fit in to do more than be the help."

A throat clears with an "Ahem," and I hear, "Ada. Earth to Ada!"

Elena is peeking through the meeting doors as she

exchanges a concerned look with me. It is understandable; here I was excited about an amazing shot for a new promotion, but not even two seconds later, I likely look like a zombie. My shoulders slumped and my eyes vacant, reliving hell.

My lips curl up together in frustration as I complain under my breath, "It has been so long. Why can't I just let go of it? I have a bright future ahead of me."

Taking a deep breath, I say, "I am sorry, Elena, what were you saying?"

"There is an urgent call on line one in your office."

When Emmett tilts his head toward the doors and Elena, I take that as permission to leave. As I push back my chair and sprint to the door, I can't help but feel myself panic as the thoughts start to take over.

Who would be calling me?

Deadbeat dad?

Tanner? Oh, my gosh, don't tell me he made up some emergency excuse to try and talk to me. Wish I could say this hasn't happened to me, but that would be a lie.

Alcoholic mom?

It's like an instant reaction to clench my jaw when I think about her calling me. God forbid she asks for money once again. It's like ever since Noah gave her an update about my penthouse, career, and everything else, she can't help but play the victim card.

The only other person who comes to mind would be my little brother, Noah.

Noah? Please tell me that he is okay. If anything were to happen to him, I don't think I could—

Nope, no, not today, Ada. Not going there. Nothing happened to Noah.

The moment I enter my office, I begin hyperventilating, breathing shallowly, and clenching and releasing my fists.

Ada, snap out of it; now is the time to be strong.

Yes, I'm sure there is no need to panic. Lucy is probably claiming it is an emergency when she is, in fact, just checking to make sure I made it work.

The sun gliding through my wide glass windows has me taking a deep breath as I squeeze my eyes shut. I block my vision with my forearm, and I walk to my L-shaped desk located in the corner of my room. Taking a seat in my brown leather chair, I wipe my sweaty palms on my dress before whispering into my desk phone, "Hello."

"Ada! Finally, you answered the phone! I have been trying to reach you for over a half an hour!"

I leap out of my chair, my eyes wider than ever. "Oh God, Noah, it is you. Are you okay? Has there been an accident? Do I need to get on a flight to see you? They said it was an emergency." I pace the room, biting my nails as I continue to move back and forth.

"Whoa, whoa, Ada, calm down. It's not me."

Oh, thank God.

I collapse into my chair with relief, letting out a big breath of air that had been holding me back, right as Noah says, "But, it is about Mom."

Just hearing that word, my body instantly tenses, on the verge of springing. In fact, there goes my calm state of mind. Why would Noah call me about our mom? This is Noah, and we rarely speak about our mother unless it is absolutely necessary.

With a heavy sigh, I close my eyes and say, "Noah, why are you calling about Mom? Please tell me she didn't ask you for money? You're still in college and trying to support yourself."

The moment Noah inhales before speaking, I know that he is going to say something important. In spite of my efforts, I cannot help but feel emotional.

My arms shake out to release the pent-up tension just as Noah says, "Ada, mom passed away."

Chapter four 🤍

Lincoln

"St. James! Wake the fuck up!" someone shouts as clothes are thrown at my head.

My eyes dart open as I shoot up from a leather couch and cover them from the sunlight seeping through the basement window blinds. I look for the asshole who the hell thinks it is okay to wake someone up that way.

Immediately my eyes are drawn to the wall of Panther's jerseys, signed posters, and beer glasses with Panther's logos. A foosball table is to my left and a pool table to my right.

Garrett's man cave.

My hangover is in full force and I suddenly feel light-headed and have a pounding headache.

God, what happened last night?

Suddenly, Garrett appears right in front of my face, blocking the bright sun. He grabs the blanket from me and begins folding it. "Man, I've known you for how long, and I didn't know you were a sleep talker," he says.

Flipping him the bird, I rub my hands across my face, trying to clear the fog. "I had no idea I even talked in my sleep."

Turning away from me, he laughs as he eyes the white brick fireplace and tosses the folded blanket into the wire basket beside it.

"Well, now that you know, do you remember what you dreamed about? You seem a bit out of it; although that may have had something to do with the shots you consumed last night."

"Did I say anything that caught your attention?" I ask sarcastically.

"A thing or two about a woman."

The mere thought of that causes my body to tighten. "You heard me talk about a woman?"

Great. God only knows what I may have said. Was it personal? Embarrassing?

As if it doesn't affect me, I reply, "I doubt that."

"Man, you totally were talking about a woman." In an unusually high voice, he continues, "Oh Linc, you're so damn sexy. You know, give it to me like that." His voice switches back. "Don't take it the wrong way, man. I only meant that she seemed like a passionate and eager individual."

There is no doubt that he was right about one thing: I was dreaming about an angel of extraordinary beauty. She had soft blonde highlights that always made her baby blue eyes sparkle when the sun shone upon them. Despite the fact that it's been a decade, I can still remember her perfectly.

I remember how she would smile and crook her finger at me to chase after her, how my legs would automatically follow her every move, how she was like a personal angel and a safe haven to me. Literally, she saved me from all the drama that took place at the St. James' household.

A throat clearing draws my attention, pulling me away from my memories of the past. I observe Garrett across the room as he conceals his smile behind a fist.

The asshole knew exactly the woman I was dreaming about, and although I know it's not ideal to be devoted to the same girl I used to love, what can you do?

I throw a pillow at his head, "Dude, thank God you're married and have two children. At this rate, no woman would ever be foolish enough to pursue you. You're terrible in bed, your impersonations suck, and don't forget, you're a smartass."

He smiles and winks, no doubt thinking the same thing.

Most of the guys I grew up with in Blue Haven have their lives all figured out by this point. Garrett Godson being one of them, and let's just say his life is the complete opposite of mine unless you enjoy bachelorhood. He has a beautiful wife and two amazing children, and thanks to my very generous father, he has the opportunity to work with me in his dream accounting position.

Throwing his hands up, he says, "Hey, now what are you talking about? Women call me by my last name, not my first name, and there's a reason for that. I'm a God in bed; just go ask my wife."

Shaking my head, I laugh. Here we go. It was evidently not the end of that conversation. "You conceited asshole; they call you that because it's your last name."

He chuckles and shrugs. "Maybe, but we all know the real reason; no need to feel jealous, my friend."

Laughing into my water bottle, I walk toward the guest bathroom. He may be a total dimwit, but I still love the guy. Over the years, I have considered Garrett a second brother to me; I have turned to him for all kinds of advice, whether it was about my three younger sisters, my parents, or extensive brother matters.

The moment I enter the bathroom, I am overcome with a dull ache in my chest as Mayra, Garrett's wife, calls out to him.

"Garrett, get your ass up here. I need help with Henry; he's hungry and won't latch onto my breast correctly."

With a chuckle, he says, "Baby, I'll be right there. Remember what the lactation consultant told you: rotate each breast. Once he latches onto one, change to the next."

"No shit, Sherlock; after all, I am the one who is attending all those consultations."

A part of me feels envious of those who are able to experience this bond. Those everyday mundane conversations, the connection that allows for laughing, learning, and sharing lives with one another.

"Baby, I'm just asking you to come help me real quick. I promise we'll do some horizontal hokey pokey later on."

Alright, that is definitely my cue to turn my attention elsewhere. I walk out of the bathroom at the same time that Garrett is adjusting his pants.

"All right, that is my call to leave."

Laughing, he pats me on the back and says, "Yeah, catching up was nice, but I think you should get out while you're ahead. She may need your assistance around the house."

"Got it."

"And Linc?" He grabs me by the shoulder, raising one eyebrow. "Let's not make this a routine, shall we?" He continues, giving me a sympathetic look, "Maybe it is time for you to slow down on drinking and start thinking about settling down? How about asking Sarah in Human Resources out on a date?"

In response, I nod my head in agreement since seeing me happy, with a woman around my arm, would certainly make my friend happier.

He can't be blamed; I want the same thing.

"There is no way to know what is out there unless you try. I know you aren't over, Ada, but man, it has been a decade since you last saw her."

The mere mention of her name causes my heart to race.

What is she doing right this second?

Is she living out a dream of hers?

When will I be able to move on from her?

Maybe Garrett is right. I'm now in my late twenties; it's been over a decade, and it's time to move on and determine whether my hungover behavior indicates a midlife crisis or a desire for companionship.

As we reach the top of the stairs, nothing could have prepared me for what he says next, "Linc, when you fall in love for the first time, your life is forever changed. It is a special experience, both emotionally and physically. The feeling of being loved so deeply by an incredible girl will always remain. However, time goes by, people change, lives change, and it is time that you find someone who can provide you with that same feeling again."

Listening to his words, I close my eyes and feel my thoughts turn inward. I know he has a point, but sometimes I don't see the worth if I know it will never match my previous relationship. Butterflies in the stomach, an overflowing of emotions, comforting and safe, overwhelming, thrilling, and surreal.

Taking a step toward the front door, I softly say, "Maybe you are right. Only time will tell."

Just as I close the door, I feel a slight breeze as fall begins to take hold. Like clockwork, the same soft-spoken, gravelly voice that I hear whenever I leave Garrett's house says, "Hi Lincoln! Over here!"

In the distance, Mrs. Ralston is waving to me from the chairs on her front porch.

"Hello, Mrs. R. Nice to see you again." I smile and wave back.

In Blue Haven, any resident will discover her personality is reflected in her house; the flower boxes, planters, and hanging baskets that always provide a vibrant shade of color. It is her uniqueness that makes her stand out among those around her. Besides being quirky and unique, she has the ability to brighten up any day with a smile.

"If I didn't know any better, I would assume something is going on with how frequently I see you leaving their house early in the morning. But again, what does this old, senile lady know?" she says with a smirk.

A chuckle escapes my lips as I shrug my shoulders. "You know me, Mrs. R. I am quite the scoundrel."

"Oh yes, I know you—" In the midst of her response, my phone rings. Due to my role as Financial

Controller at Legacy Accounting, I have an inkling as to which client it may be.

"I apologize, Mrs. R., but I have to take this; I am running late for work."

As I glance at my phone, it is already 9:30 am. *Shit.*

It is only after Mrs. R. waves goodbye that I hop into my car. As I lower my head on the headrest, I draw a deep breath before answering the phone. "Hello, this is Lincoln St. James."

"Hi Lincoln, this is Patricia from HomeWells Retired Living. I have some unfortunate news to share with you," she says somberly.

My heart races with information to be shared; the seconds turn into minutes that feel like long periods of stillness and silence until I hear, "Mrs. Collins passed away last night."

A feeling of shock and unreality causes my body to become frozen.

When?

But how?

Do her children know?

Was she able to pass away peacefully during her sleep?

I try to cope with the news as I rub my forehead and shake my head.

"Although it may seem shocking to you, Mrs. Collins had you listed as a second emergency contact in case of an emergency. I attempted to reach out to her children, but neither responded, so I contacted you instead."

What could possibly have prevented her children from not answering?

The thought of her death makes my skin tingle. No, this didn't happen, she's mistaken. I refuse to believe that she's gone. There was so much more she wanted out of life, including making amends with her past and her daughter.

"Lincoln, my sincere condolences go out to you for your loss. However, we need to decide how to proceed with her funeral."

There is a deep sense of sorrow in my heart, as I feel sick. I do not know how to arrange a funeral.

"Lincoln, are you there?"

"I'm sorry, Patricia. I'm just trying to take it all in. Don't worry. It will get handled."

"You sure? I can try calling Ada again. She was listed as her first person to contact in case of an emergency."

Ah, so she did attempt to contact Ada. My arms cover in goosebumps as I hear her name being said again. *Let's not go down that rabbit hole again, Linc.*

As I shake my hands, I pull my phone away from my ear and put Patricia on speaker. "If you could give both her children's numbers to me, I will be sure to reach out to them."

I add both Ada and Noah's information to my phone's contacts list. Only to realize Ada's number already appears in my phone, and it is the same number Patricia just mentioned.

"Thanks, Lincoln, I appreciate it. Again, I am sorry for your loss; I know you two were close."

She's right, the two of us were getting close. About a year ago, Mrs. Collins ran into me while bartending at Blue Haven's Safe Harbor, something I do on the side to pass time or help when needed. She had been sober for almost a year when I met her, and over time, she began to open up to me about Ada's past. Hearing things about Ada that I did not understand as a child gutted me to my core.

With the knowledge of what I must do next, I exhale while releasing my hands that are now white due to the strength with which they were gripping the steering wheel. But the question is, how am I going to handle all of this when I do not even have the courage to call her only living daughter after how our relationship ended.

Looking in the rearview mirror, I tell myself, "Lincoln, it is just a phone call."

But is it really a phone call?

It has been twelve years since we have spoken and I know I should call her, but for some reason, I make a cowardly move and go with what seems to be my only option at the moment.

I call Noah.

Chapter five

Ada

"What do you mean Lincoln called you?" My pulse starts to quicken.

Is this some sort of joke?

Unable to stand still, my restless legs propel me across the room as my head spins in response to the news Noah is sharing.

Why would Lincoln call him over me?

You know the answer to that, Ada.

"Ada, I know Lincoln and you did not end on the best of terms, and there is still some resentment between you two, but don't you think it's time to move on?"

The comment makes me roll my eyes. While I understand his point, it can be difficult to move forward when something from the past had such a significant impact on you.

While I think about what to say next, I hold my breath; Noah and I are affected by this in completely different ways.

Sighing, I say, "You're right, Noah. I am sorry for getting upset; this isn't about me or my feelings; it's about Mom. I will board my next flight as soon as possible."

"Meet you at The Crispy Biscuit?"

I smile as I hear the familiar place, and my eyes close as my shoulders relax. I say, "Beat you there."

As I put the phone back on my desk, Emmett comes barging into my office with a steely look on his face.

"Ada, what was all that about?" he asks, pointing toward the conference room. "Being late to an *important* meeting, rude to Ruth, and then having a phone call interrupt the meeting?"

Before I can respond, he blows out a frustrated breath and drops a file on my desk. He begins pacing around the room. "As one of my senior associates, I expect a great deal from you. This is your chance to prove to me that you are capable of handling these responsibilities regardless of what is occurring outside of these doors."

Talk about a slap to the face as I listen to him. I rise from my leather chair, ready to defend myself. Being a corporate lawyer in New York is no joke, especially when you consider the fact that I work 70+ hours each week, which clearly shows if anyone were to take a quick glance at the wall shelf in my office.

It reveals some of the most prestigious awards I have been awarded—On the Rise, Golden Hammer, and Elizabeth Clark Young Lawyers Fellowship.

In any case, this is not the appropriate time or place to bring that up, so instead of becoming defensive, I will use a more subtle response, which might also allow me to take time off for my mother's funeral.

"Emmett, sir, I understand your concern, but you don't need to worry. I know things haven't gone exactly as expected for either of us today, but rest assured, I've got this covered."

Despite his sigh, he nods in agreement, and I continue, "However, I will need to take a week or so off to sort out some things that happened back home."

His eyes narrow as he asks, "Ada, are you really sure that's a good idea?"

Taking a step toward the front of my desk, I lean on it and say, "Sir, there really isn't much of a choice at this time."

"Ada, you are making things very difficult for me right now. You have been off your game and just when I am about to give you one of your most important cases in your career, you have to leave?"

Taking a deep breath and closing my eyes, I let my head fall. If only he were aware of the real reason I am leaving, he might be able to understand.

Ada, just tell him the truth.

As I am about to reply, Emmett adds, "Also, should you forget, this case might lead to you becoming a partner here at the firm. It will no doubt show others and our clients how successful you are in the world of corporate law."

Despite knowing he is correct, I believe going home is the best option, regardless of the relationship between my mother and me. I need to be there for Noah.

As my chin trembles and my arms grasp the crap out of my desk, I move away from it and toward Emmett with all the confidence in the world as I clasp his shoulders, saying, "You're right, sir. I know this news could not have come at a worse time, but I am able to handle it and it should not take more than a week tops."

In response, he nods his head, taking a step back from me and heading toward the door to my office.

I follow behind and say sarcastically, "I know you will miss me greatly, but just think of it as an Ada-free week. Before you know it, everyone will be begging me to come back."

He grunts and opens my door just as his eyes meet mine. "Ada, this is no time for jokes. This is a serious matter and I need a senior associate of the firm who will take on this case and win it, damn it!"

In a state of renewed confidence, I nod in agreement. "Ok, here's what's going to happen. I will take the case file you gave me today, review it, and work on it remotely back home. In the meantime, if I have any questions, I will contact you."

As I push him through the doorway, I say, "Now, if you will excuse me, I must finish some work here before booking my flight home and arranging things."

"Ok, Ada, one week at the most, and if anything changes, please let me know ASAP."

A heavy sigh escapes my lips as I close the door. *All right, Ada, one week to get your shit together.*

I'm not sure how I'm going to figure it out in a week, but I never back down from a challenge. I open my laptop and start researching flights immediately, but am interrupted by a brief rapping on my door. I look up toward my door, hoping someone doesn't need me.

"I assume you're looking for flights," Elena asks, popping in as she raises one brow.

I nod my head.

As she approaches my desk, she hands me a sheet of

paper. "Here is your itinerary for your return home. Your flight departs at 9:00 am tomorrow. I thought that this could give you a sense of peace, knowing it's been all taken care of."

My eyes narrow as I stare at her with puzzlement, wondering how she is aware of my mother's funeral.

"Noah told me what happened."

I force the best smile I can muster as I say, "Thanks, Elena. I'm sure I don't say it enough, but I really appreciate you. With Emmett being on my ass and this new case, if I did not have you, I would have been unable to get everything ready as quickly as I would have liked."

Taking my hand, she gives it a tight squeeze and smiles. "No problem at all. I am always willing to assist when necessary. And Ada?" My eyes meet hers. "You have a lot on your plate right now, so ensure that you rest well before you leave tomorrow morning. It must be difficult for you to leave on these terms, but look at it as a blessing. You will be able to see your brother again and you will be able to take some time off work. I know it is not ideal, but you will be in a better position to come back."

With a smile, I say, "Thanks, Elena. I will try. Thanks again for everything."

"Of course!" she says as she closes my door.

Having successfully regained my office back, I rest my forehead against my glass desk, inhaling deeply, wondering if I will ever catch a break.

Suddenly, I hear another rapid knock at my door. I glance up, knowing that I should allow whoever is on the other side to enter. However, my feet decide to freeze in place as I stay put.

In order to calm myself down, I shout slightly less

loudly, "Not now. Ada is busy. If you would like to leave her a message, write it on a piece of paper and slide it under her door, she will be sure to get back to you. Beeeep."

Just as I am about to lay my head back down on my desk, I hear a rustle. Looking back at the door, I note a small piece of paper. Since I have no choice but to find out what this person wants, I move from my desk and bend down to read the note.

Just let me know you're okay – WB

Of course, the only person who would be so kind as to check on me would be him.

Shit, not now, Ada. My eyes rub together as tears well up from the exhaustion of the morning. Despite the fact that I may be at my emotional limit for the day, I open the door anyway in the hope that comfort may come from a friend on such a hellish day.

Sweeping me into a hug, William, my colleague, grabs my back and whispers in my ear, "Thought I would check in and see if you were okay? With the meeting and knowing what the aftermath might look like with Emmett. Plus, I heard what happened to your mother."

My eyes are filled with confusion as I look up at him.

"I heard you and Elena talking when I was about to knock on your door, thinking you might need a friend."

Nodding, I wipe away my tears as I pull away from the hug. "It's been a rough morning, to say the least," I say as I return to my chair.

An expression of sadness appears on his face as he looks at me.

Really, can everyone stop giving me pity eyes. It's not helping, let alone making me feel better.

Taking a seat on the edge of my desk, he looks directly at me. "Ada, I can't imagine what you are going through, but please know that I am here for you."

A small smile spreads across my face as I think about how blessed I am to have Will in my life. Having first started at this firm together, along with Ruth, I have known him for several years. The best way to describe Will is as the cute neighbor next door. During my twenty-nine years on Earth, I have never met a guy as different as Will. He had a handsome appearance, not necessarily in the conventional sense, but in such a way as to make him stand out among the crowds.

Having blonde wavy hair and grassy green eyes that contrast outstandingly well with his light-toned face, he is the perfect guy for some lucky woman. But not this gal. At the end of the day, he is another one of my best friends.

As the sentiment of his words begin to penetrate my heart and threaten to burst, I wipe away the tears with the back of my hand. While placing my two fingers against my inner eyes, I say, "Thanks, Will, I really appreciate you."

"Always by your side, Ada."

Leaving my desk, I begin to collect the materials I need for a week away from work, including the M&A file Emmett gave me, as I say, "If you do not mind, Will, I need to accomplish a few things before I leave tomorrow."

Taking a look at me, he nods and gives me an

expression of understanding. "Of course, Ada," he says as he walks through my office door and closes it.

❡

Opening the penthouse door, I immediately hear, "Good, you're back."

Out of my peripheral vision, I see Lucy in our kitchen, so I slam the door and remove one of my heels, watching it bounces across the hardwood floor. As one of the newer buildings in our area, our penthouse was modern, but modest in its design. It is so large that when Luce and I first moved in, we did not have the funds to furnish it. We can see the kitchen from the living room, which is surrounded by honey-colored walls and simple framed art on the walls. Several large bookcases are filled with thick lawyer and affirmation books. Topped with colorful throw pillows, there are two brown leather couches positioned in the living room.

The moment I plop down on the couch, Lucy's eyes narrow as she glances at her watch. "Wait, you're home already? Didn't you just get to work a few hours ago?" she asks.

"Yeah, about that," I say as my head sinks back onto the couch.

Closing my eyes for a brief moment, I let out a long sigh and reopen them to see all the unique and different buildings of New York, the skyscrapers, and, of course, our cozy brick stone fireplace.

As Lucy moves toward me, I toss off my other heel, almost hitting her in the process. I cover my mouth, trying not to laugh.

In surrender, she says, "Wow, girl, how about taking

out your anger on somebody else? You look like you are about to rip someone's head off."

I mean, there's a chance that could happen.

I get up from the couch and make my way to the fridge for some much-needed wine. I sigh and say, "Nothing."

The woman shakes her head as she follows behind me. "Nope. Something is amiss. You don't look like the Ada I know. Plus, you are drinking wine, Ada, wine! In the early afternoon, might I add, something you don't do."

Obviously, she notices everything; she's my best friend and can read me like the back of her hand. I shrug a shoulder as I take a sip of my wine. "What do you ever mean?" I ask with a flash of my eyebrows.

She chuckles as she says, "You want to know the truth? Who am I kidding? We know I am going to tell you the truth anyway. Ada, honey, you look like you got hit by a train, and then ran over repeatedly."

Wow, quite a descriptive image. One that I had no idea captured how I looked right now.

"I understand that things are tough and over-whelming at work right now since you are attempting to make partner at the firm, but are you willing to risk your health in order to reach that goal?"

My shoulders slump as I take in what she said. I agree with her, but I have been so close to achieving my dream since I can remember, and to let it slip through my fingers would be devastating, and that's putting it lightly.

A frustrated sigh escapes my lips as I throw my hands in the air. "Ugh, I don't know. Luce, do you still believe that everything happens for a reason?"

"You know, I always have and always will. Why? What's up?"

"I like to believe that everything happens for a reason, but why did *this* have to happen right after I obtained one of the most important cases of my legal career?"

I meet her confused gaze as she says, "Ada, what are you talking about? Just spit it out."

After taking a long pause, I sit down next to her on a barstool and immediately feel my body release some tension.

"Sooo . . . are you going to tell me what's going on at this point?"

While staring blankly at my wine, I let go of a breath I didn't realize I had been holding as I say, "Luce, my mother has passed away."

After hearing a short gasp, Lucy grabs my hand. "Oh my gosh, Ada. I am so sorry. How are you? I'm sure this must be difficult for you."

"Honestly, Luce, I do not know how to feel. Numb. Sad. Relieved?" I hysterically rub my eyes and let out a forced laugh. "Would it be bad if I said this wasn't even the worst part of all of this?"

"What do you mean? Are you attending her funeral?"

"Yes, I need to be there for Noah, but doing so may result in my running into him."

She looks lost as it takes her a moment to figure out who the person I'm referring to is. Taking a deep breath, she exclaims, "Ohhhh, him, him."

Lucy gets up and turns me so that I am facing her directly. "Ada, honey, I want you to understand that love has the power to influence us in both positive and negative ways. Each individual has a unique type of love. There are different types of love for you, such as friendships like ours or relationships like yours and Noah's. Moreover, you may also experience intense feelings of affection for one person. Despite experiencing one heartbreak, you cannot let it tarnish your view of all kinds of love. Loving is an individual decision. You get to choose who you love and let into your life. But remember, without the influence of negative love, we wouldn't get to see how amazing positive love affects us."

"I know you're right, Luce."

Shaking my head, I attempt to prevent tears from falling, but it is of no use because the tears begin to flow down my cheeks as I glance at her. "I know we all experience negative love in life, but at what point is only experiencing negative love sufficient? I believe going back to Blue Haven will destroy me, because that is all I dealt with back there."

Luce lifts my chin and she wipes away the tears. Once again, proving that she is one of the only people who can love me positively aside from Noah.

"Ada, sweetheart, you do not have to prove your excellence or success to Blue Haven, or anyone else, for that matter." She points at my heart. "There is no decrease in value because someone cannot see what you are worth. I know your childhood was difficult, but I believe returning to Blue Haven will provide you with a closure that you did not realize you might have needed."

Even though I understand her point, I find it difficult to understand why returning to a place you dislike must require a great deal of effort when it should be the opposite. Throughout the past few years, I have demonstrated that I am not who the people in that town remember me to be.

Standing up, I start pacing the kitchen. "Luce, how can I face him, or the town, after all these years?" *This is stupid.* I throw my hands up. "I should be over everything. Look at what I have in life and what I have accomplished," I say as I dance around our apartment. "It has been twelve years, Luce, yet I am worried about running into him and returning to Blue Haven."

With a frustrated breath, I slump back into my seat next to her, throwing my head into my hands while grumbling, "Luce, I should be more concerned with planning the funeral of my own mother."

Yeah, that relationship is dead, literally.

"It should be the only thing taking up my thoughts beyond the merger case at the law firm, but it's not."

A sympathetic look crosses Lucy's face. "Ada, sweetie, come here," she says. We both stand up and hug, as Lucy whispers, "You got this, Ada. Don't let the past control your future. Take a few days off, visit Noah, and find closure for your past so that you may move forward with that bright future of yours." Her hands rub over my back as she continues, "This will be good for you, you will see."

After raising my head, I look directly at Lucy and pull my shoulders back. With my hands around her arms, I say confidently, "You're right, Luce. I got this. I am Ada Collins, a bold, charming, and thriving badass New York lawyer. And don't forget a fantastic roommate." I wink at her.

Her eyes twinkle and she gives me a quick wink with a pop of her shoulder. "I guess you're okay."

"Well, I better get packing." I chuckle and smack her ass as I make my way back to my room.

I open the bedroom door and spot my California king bed in the spacious corner next to my French patio doors. I move my sluggish feet toward it as if it were calling my name. The soft, ivory faux fur comforter makes my body go heavy and tired the instant my butt touches it. It is not fair to feel this way, since I have worked all but maybe 4 hours today.

Ada, we both know that your mom passed away, and this has nothing to do with your work.

Argh, I roll my eyes at no one in particular. I know my inner voice is right, but I am not yet ready to accept it. I close my eyes and throw my head back, releasing a large pent-up breath, as I am flooded with thoughts. I honestly do not remember the last time I attended a funeral. I don't think I have? What should I wear for a funeral? So many things to figure out in such a limited time.

Taking this into consideration, I push myself off my bed and head to my walk-in closet. As I glance at my clothes, I realize that going back doesn't have to be the same experience as before.

This time will be different, Ada, as you will be entering Blue Haven as a completely new individual.

Knowing I am not who I once was gives me a sense of pride. I am an independent, courageous woman, who is a money-making attorney; let's not forget who also lives in a freaking penthouse in the middle of New York City!

Rushing to my closet, I start to take down some of my favorite Dolce and Gabbana dresses, along with my favorite black Prada one that I think I will wear to the funeral. One dress sticks out to me like a sore thumb as I pass it. I pick it up off the hanger with my hands, roaming my fingers over it. The shimmering dark Indigo, the feel of it in my hands, recalls distant memories for me.

"Ada, will you please wear this?" Looking down at one of the most expensive pieces of clothing I own, my eyes gloss over. "I thought it would look great on you with the color of your eyes and all."

In the stand-up mirror that leans against my wall, I see Lincoln and my reflection. He stands behind me, coming to wrap an arm around my waist. He places his chin on my shoulder as I look him in the eye.

"I love the dress, Linc, but is it too extravagant? Don't you think it's a little much? I know I need something appropriate for this event, but perhaps not this glamorous? After all, it's just an event . . . don't you like how I am?"

He narrows his eyes before turning me around so that I am facing him. "This has nothing to do with how you look, baby; it's more about my parents. These types of events require certain attire, and I just want to ensure you are at ease when we go."

Great, so he's not doing this out of love for me, but because he's doing it for his parents.

A wave of sadness hits me, but I grin as I give him a hug and whisper, "I'll wear it as long as you promise me a dance."

Laughing, he remarks, "You know I hate dancing. Don't you remember the first time we danced in the parking lot at The Crispy Biscuit?"

A real smile appears on my face this time as I say, "As if I would ever forget it."

I suppress the memory, thinking I was done with

torturing myself, but my body seems to have its own mind. As I take off my clothes, balancing on my now unsteady legs, I walk toward the closet mirrors.

I glance at my reflection and fasten the dress as I take a few steps back to get a good look at myself. I allow the memories to sink in, and I realize that this dress is a symbol of our past, what could have been, and a reminder of why our relationship would never have worked out.

Immediately letting the dress fall to the ground, I rush to take a scalding hot shower. When the water falls onto my body, my shoulders relax and the ground below me blurs with tears. Taking a soft cloth to my face, I gently wipe away the tears and draw my face back into the shower head.

Time to put a stop to these past memories, Ada.

But what if I can't?

What if I will never get over everything that happened?

My conscience is right, but I haven't been back to Blue Haven in over a decade. What will it be like once I return?

Chapter Six ♡

Ada

As the plane touched down on the tarmac, I put away the M&A file I was reviewing over the last two hours of the flight. I feel re-energized by this new case and positive that I will be able to handle it; even remotely. Knowing I should probably update Lucy, I send her a quick text while adding a few exclamation marks to indicate I'm totally fine.

> Hey Lucy, I just landed safely. I am waiting for my rental to arrive so I can go meet Noah!!!

It is only a matter of seconds before her text buzzes.

> You've got this, Ada! I am here if you need me. I love you. Don't forget to check in with me once a day. I want to be sure you are okay.

> You don't have to worry about me, Luce. I'll be just fine. Plus, it's only for a short period.

Putting my phone away, I take my first few steps out of the Valley Airport and inhale the sweet, peppery, almost spicy, fragrance of North Carolina.

It's home.

The specific smell triggers a memory of a time when Noah, Mom, and I used to spend every Sunday at the beach. It was one of my most favorite days of the week, as it was a time when I felt at peace, whether that was because the stress was gone for the day or because the tension in my body was completely released, which almost translated to feeling weightless.

It feels like only yesterday when the sun warmed my cheeks, and the light wind stirred that peppery aroma scent through my nostrils. Mine and Noah's arms were wide open as we ran along the hard, wet sand, doing circles around one another. Mom would always sit on a variety of rocks, admiring us from afar every time we went, smiling and laughing. She was truly happy and content in those moments; she was sober every Sunday, showing Noah and me the love that children should feel from their parents.

In an instant, tears sting my eyes as a hollow ache fills my chest. Looking back on that moment has given me a greater sense of longing for home than I anticipated.

Am I really homesick?

From a place I ran away from?

That has only ever brought me pain?

Using my finger to massage the dull pain in my breastbone, I locate my rental car and make my way eastward. Everything begins to hit me as I start to navigate through the city of Blue Haven. In between wrapping my head around the new case and packing, which, by the way, took much longer than I expected due to my memories haunting me, I'm low on sleep. I am operating on two substantial cups of coffee I consumed this morning.

Despite my fatigue, a shot of adrenaline runs through my veins as I start to recognize the unique things I once remembered about Blue Haven. All the small boutiques, art galleries, antique stores, restaurants and cafes that line the waterfront have now all been renovated. In spite of the nauseous feeling in my stomach, Blue Haven looks different, yet exactly the same.

My heart is pounding and sweat trickles down my body. Boob sweat would be more accurate.

I move my shirt back and forth in an effort to air it out. God, why am I wearing a sweater in these conditions?

Ada, it is fall in Blue Haven.

I was leaving everything behind me when I traveled this route.

It's time to shine, Ada. Time to show the world what you're made of, and that means leaving this shithole forever. You're done with Blue Haven, Lincoln, and even your mom.

Too bad forever only lasted over a decade.

The Crispy Biscuit looms before me, and my heart beats erratically inside my chest.

The place hasn't changed one bit. It remains a run-down diner with a rainbow neon sign that reads 'The

Crispy Biscuit'. Despite the missing shingles on the roof and the rusted red doors, this is still hands down the best place to enjoy breakfast and company.

As I walk toward the doors, I can't help but take languid steps as memories of being here rush through my mind, both too strong and too quickly, as if I am once again seventeen years old.

There is a heavy rainfall surrounding us as I spin my head and close my eyes. Lincoln's soft laugh escapes his throat as he tugs on my hand to rush inside. "Come on, Ada, you're going to make us sick."

As I dance in the rain, a rush of adrenaline liberates me. Although it is freezing outside, warmth infuses my body, allowing me to relax enough to breathe. All I can focus on is the joy of experiencing the moment at hand, showing me that life is much more than unpleasantness and inconvenience.

I remove my hand from Lincoln's and grab him by the shoulders, whispering softly in his ear, "Dance with me, Lincoln."

Taking a second look at me, he raises an eyebrow. "Are you nuts, Ada? It's freezing, and you want to keep dancing in the rain?" he asks.

My cheeky smile spreads across my face as I nod my head. When I close my eyes, I feel his hands go around my waist, making my eyes reopen. My handsome guy is soaked from his sandy blonde hair, something I cannot resist running my hands through. I graze my fingers across his sharp jawline and well-defined lips while he stares at me with dilated pupils.

Stepping closer, I clasp his neck and drops of water slide on our cheeks and neck. Puddles begin to form as the rain becomes heavier. My white dress and ankle socks are completely soaked, but Linc's letterman jacket and his warmth seeping into my skin are the only things that are saving me.

The two of us continue to spin in circles and laugh freely. Being able to watch Lincoln let loose, laughing and dancing with me, makes me feel safe, comforted, loved, adored, and something I want for the rest of my life.

"Come on, Linc, show me your moves. I know you can dance better than this." I give him a pouty lip. "Pretty please, with an Ada on top, that would be even better than a cherry."

His grip tightens on my waist and he flashes me a flirtatious smile. "You're right," he kisses me on the nose, "let's dance; after all, this is technically my first official dance with my girl."

A flutter of excitement takes hold of my stomach as I hear the words, 'my girl'.

His lips are slightly parted with an amused, all-too-knowing smirk. He knows how his words affect me. But before I can respond, I notice a familiar expression in his eyes, one that tells me what he's about to do.

Tickles.

Running around the parking lot, like a chicken with its head cut off, I laugh as I put my head to the sky and enjoy each droplet that falls. I lean my head on his shoulder when he suddenly embraces me from behind. As we gaze over at Hope Bay Beach, the clouds oblige and the rain falls in tiny silver drops against the waves of the water.

"This was our first dance, wasn't it?" I say, sighing.

Lincoln kisses me on the temple. "Our first of many, Ada Collins," he declares.

In the distance, I hear laughter as people pass through the doors, but I am anchored by the memory.

Closing my eyes, I put a hand on my chest in hopes that it will slow down, giving me time to recoup.

Taking a deep breath iiiiin one, two, three, and ooutt one, two, three, I open the rusty red doors. Noah is immediately visible in the corner booth in the back of the restaurant. Seeing him aches my heart. *God, Noah, I have missed you.*

While we have spoken on the phone from time to time, we haven't actually seen each other in person since I dropped him off for college. I remember his excitement at finally being in college, to begin exploring his passions and dreams.

I still remember him as a tall, scrawny individual, but he looks like he has gained some muscle over the past few years. His brown toned hair is still the same with flecked blonde streaks that most likely resulted from the late summer sun. His eyes are olive green like our father's, rather than blue like mine.

Growing up, we never really fought as we got enough of it from our mother, or our parents when our deadbeat dad was actually around. In most cases, when our parents fought, we would visit The Crispy Biscuit. I would grab my hard earned money from the safe box under my bed and rush to get Noah out of his room. After sneaking out of the house, we'd come here at midnight and gorged on waffles and milkshakes.

"Hi!" Noah yells at me, "Ada, over here!"

Glancing at him again, his face is puffy with red eyes, looking utterly exhausted. I stand tall, swallowing the lump in my throat. It's time to support Noah, like I always have.

Laughing and shaking my head, I do a quick look

over my shoulder to observe the tight-knit group of people whispering around me.

That's great, Noah. Let me be the talk of town again. I just arrived.

Ada, stop looking back at your past. You are not the same girl you once were. Do not let them affect you.

Trying to listen to my inner thoughts, I cradle myself in my arms and close my eyes. She's right; I am not the same person they once saw, and it's about time they realize it.

My phone pings right as I reopen my eyes. Glancing at it, I see an incoming text message from Lexie. While in high school, Lexie was one of my closest friends and my partner in crime. We still stay in touch via text even though we separated after graduation. However, I have not heard from her in a few weeks, so I can only guess what she is texting me about.

> Hi Ada! I heard about your mom passing away. I wanted to check in and see how you're doing? Noah told me you were back in town for the funeral. I would love to catch up before you leave town. Would you be up for a coffee date?

The thought of roaming around, getting coffee, and acting as if everything is fine, when really it isn't, creates a gnawing feeling throughout my chest. Since I am in no mood to respond at the moment, I leave the text without responding and begin to walk, practically jogging, to Noah. I put on my big sister's mask as I embrace him in an enormous bear hug and I say, "Bubba, I have missed you so much."

"It's so good to see you, Ada," he says as I sit across from him in the booth.

I smile and say, "You too, bubs."

"It feels like I haven't seen you in forever."

"Well, that's because it's been a while."

"Did you get a haircut? It looks shorter and more sophisticated. Not like Noah I'm used to."

With a chuckle, he runs his fingers through his hair. "Yeah. Someone recently suggested I try shorter hair."

My eyebrows raise. "Hmm, a certain someone. Is that code for a girl?"

Shrugging, he says, "Maybe, maybe not."

Shaking my head, I know it was definitely a woman's influence on his new look. Not that I am complaining, but his new appearance appears to be working in his favor.

Taking a menu from the table, he says, "So, let me know what is happening in your amazing life in New York."

Laughing, I shrug, "Well, New York is New York. Nothing has changed other than the number of pedestrians on the streets." His head shakes as he grins. "Don't get me wrong, I enjoy living in New York," I sigh, "but it is nice to see you again despite these circumstances."

With a nod, he smiles and says, "I'm just glad you were able to take some time off. I missed you."

"Honestly, I am surprised I was able to get time off, as I wasn't sure whether my boss would permit it, given my new case and all. Nevertheless, I just have to get through mom's funeral and then return to work; only should take a week tops."

Noah becomes instantly quiet. He closes his eyes and

by the time he reopens them, he says in a toneless voice, "About that, Ada. It may take longer than a week. I just discovered that Mom wanted to have an estate sale."

What is he talking about?

A rapid pulse throbs in my head and my brows twitch as I ask, "What do you mean by an estate sale? She wants to dispose of the house we grew up in and all our belongings?"

He takes a deep breath and sighs. "Her executor stated that she was uncertain whether either of us would want to inherit the house or anything within, so she wanted it to be given to a worthy recipient."

In disbelief, I let out a forced laugh. I cannot believe what he is saying. Not only have I not heard from her in years, she wants to throw away everything we have grown up with.

That's cause it didn't matter, Ada, not to her at least.

"Surely you're joking, right? This must be some sort of prank?"

Even though I did not expect to inherit my childhood home, it would have been nice to have a say in its disposition.

Taking his eyes off of me, he runs his fingers through his hair and says, "I wish I was."

This is why I left. She didn't care about us at all.

My jaw clenches as my nails rip into the palms of my hands. "Great, just what I needed to hear, Noah. My boss is already upset that I will be away for a week. Imagine if it's for several weeks?"

A bit of sympathy appears in his eyes as he utters, "I'm so sorr—"

Noah is interrupted as I hear, "Oh my gosh! Ada, is that you?" I look up at the woman standing beside me.

My heart fills with joy as her whole face lights up with recognition.

Angel.

Despite looking much older now, she still has the dimple on her right cheek when she smiles. Wrinkles line her forehead, and she has some gray hairs on her head, highlighted by the sun shining through the restaurant blinds. This place and Angel were a safe haven for Noah and me, particularly me. But she became more like a second mother to me, so I sought her advice on everything.

A wide smile spans her face as she says, "Don't just sit there; give me a hug."

Moving toward her, the tightness in my chest is released and is replaced by the warmest hug of my life. "Hi, Angel! It's so good to see you again."

In a soft, compassionate tone, she takes me by the shoulders, "God, it's been so long since I last saw you. Leaving us Blue Haven folks for the big city. How are things going for you? I heard what happened to your mother. I am so sorry to hear that."

Having no idea what to say, I just give her a nonchalant shrug and a forced smile. "I absolutely love New York City."

"That is fantastic, sweety. I am happy for you. Can I get you anything to eat or drink?"

My attention is drawn to Noah, who is staring at me as he nods with a smile.

"I guess that means we will both take a cup of coffee, please."

As if I needed more caffeine, but hey, a girl's gotta do what she gotta do to get through her first day back in Blue Haven.

When Angel leaves the table, Noah grabs my hands and says, "Ada, don't stress out more than you are already. It was important to me to ensure I had everything ready before telling you, and I am sure you will be relieved to know Mom's lawyer told me that she already had all her funeral arrangements ready for when she passed away."

My head spins, trying to comprehend what he said. How did she have the time to make her own funeral arrangements? Did she know she was dying? Who helped her with all of this?

I do my best to listen to Noah as he continues, "I am aware neither of us knows much about funerals, but I know we will have a visitation, funeral ceremony, and a committal service. We just need to get everything in place and make a few phone calls. We still have a few days until the actual funeral, but with the two of us, I know we can get it arranged in a short period of time. The funeral will be at White Willow Memorial Gardens. Therefore, perhaps you can contact them."

In a nod, I tightly close my eyes, holding back the tears that are trying to escape. Reopening my eyes, I look at Noah with a sad smile on my face. "I am grateful that you are taking care of everything, Noah. Just let me know what needs to be done on my end and I will do it."

As I wipe my face, Angel returns to our table with two hot coffees.

Trying to change the subject, I wave my hand in front of me, "Okay, okay, enough sadness. How are things at school? When we talked last time, you said everything was going well with your photography classes."

He lights up at the mention of photography, and his

smiling response makes my heart want to burst. "God, Ada, it has been truly amazing. There are so many things that one can learn from photography that I did not realize until I took my first class."

While I take a sip of my coffee, Noah starts moving his hands from side to side, as he describes one of his favorite aspects of photography.

"First of all, I enjoy being able to share my vision, because it allows me to help myself and others see the world differently. Sometimes, individuals require a new perspective to really see the world around them. I am learning to look around and see things others fail to see. I am learning to convey stories without words. I am learning to appreciate the different lenses I have."

It shouldn't surprise me, but Noah definitely isn't the same Noah I remember. He is growing up into an amazing man, something I know I am missing out on every day, but hearing that he has found his passion in life makes me feel more relaxed. It's now clear to me that, regardless of what we have gone through, we both are pursuing our dreams and that is all I ever wanted.

My hands firmly grip his from across the table. "Noah, I am so incredibly happy for you. It is amazing that you have found such a passion so early in your life, let alone in college. I can tell it makes you happy, and that is all I had hoped for you. I wonder what Mom would think if she was to see us now, living our dreams."

Taking a shaky breath, he says, "Thank you, Ada, and I'm glad to know that you are happy with your life so far. It's all I've wanted for you, too."

"Okay, okay, enough of this emotional nonsense. I can only handle so much in a day, and we just arrived.

By the way, Elena booked our rooms at the Golden Peak Lodge while we were here."

With a nod, he states, "Yep, I already know that. Elena told me."

"Mmhm, of course you do," I say with a pointed stare.

In a flash of redness, he stands up and gives me a wink. "Ready to leave?" he asks.

Chapter Seven 🖤

Lincoln

"Yo, you ready for the meeting?" I glance up from my pile of papers on my desk and see Garrett leaning against it.

"Why are you smiling like that?" I ask.

"What do you mean? Like this?" He points at his face, his cheeks rise and his bright ass white teeth sparkle. "Oh, that smile? Let's just say I had a good night with the wife," he says, wagging his eyebrows excitedly.

In front of my desk, he moves toward a brown leather chair. "Mayra got her sister to watch Georgia for the night, so we made the best of the situation and I am in an excellent mood today."

I roll my eyes. As if I need to hear about his sex life, showing me that mine clearly doesn't exist.

"Of course, if you ever got laid, you would understand what I mean," he says, placing one leg over the other.

With a sharp glance, I grab the stack of papers and begin placing them in a file cabinet. Each file pertains to a specific client at Legacy Accounting, otherwise known as my father's accounting firm.

Do I enjoy handling clients on a daily basis? Not really.

Is this my dream job? No, but it is a job, it is stable.

I have a great assistant and I enjoy working with this idiot next to me, so there isn't much to complain about. Plus, I can't help but feel proud of myself every time I have the opportunity to lead our monthly meetings, as I am about to do now. Getting in front of a group of people, leading the room, and watching their eyes absorb everything I am teaching and sharing with the firm is a dream I once had.

Garrett catches my expression as I close the filing cabinet. "What are you staring at?"

His eyes widen, clearly taken aback by my tone of voice. "Dude, what crawled up your ass? I was only kidding about you not getting laid."

While I know he does not know what is going on and I should inform him, I am hesitant; perhaps it is due to Ada. Garrett always goes on about how I need to let go of Ada, blah blah blah, and can't we just let the past be the past? I may not have forgotten Ada, but I need to move forward. She left me, and that is a feeling and memory I will never forget.

While rubbing the back of my neck with my hand, I glance over at Garrett. "Sorry man, just didn't get a good night of sleep last night. Plus, you know Michael? Our client at The Wine Guys."

"Yeah, I remember him well. That guy never seems to be able to solve any of his own problems."

Despite my desire to roll my eyes at his comment, I

refrain from doing so. I get it, it's annoying as fuck dealing with clients who can't seem to handle the most trivial of problems, but our firm makes money on fixing those said problems, regardless if they are easy or not.

As he rises from his chair, I push him toward my door, because if we do not leave now, we will be late for the meeting.

"Well, it appears that The Wine Guys had some difficulties with their employees and tax management, which means you, lucky fella, get to teach his employees how to manage their taxes properly one day after work hours."

A condescending laugh echoes from his lips as he places a forearm across my body, stopping me in my tracks. "You have to be kidding me? Man, I thought you were serious for a second."

I push his forearm away and turn toward our conference room, looking through the ceiling-to-floor windows of our building. The building isn't particularly big or fancy, just a newer building with solid construction, similar to the firm as a whole.

Walking to these windows is one of my favorite parts of this building when I am stressed or overwhelmed. We have a view of the little shops right next door, and Hope Bay Beach is directly across the street from us. Just steps outside the door, there's a small bridge to the beach where I like to sink my feet in the sand while watching the waves crash.

Reminds me of the times I shared with Ada. The two of us holding hands and discussing our days or futures together.

"You weren't joking, were you?"

Using a little shake of the head, I clear my throat

and force myself to concentrate on the meeting that is occurring in a few minutes. I turn back to Garrett as we approach the conference doors. "I was serious. Michael needs our assistance and there is no better person to help with this kind of work than you. After all, you are the one at our firm who handles all the tax matters."

"Who doesn't know how to handle their own taxes, let alone a CEO," he scoffs.

"I'm sure he knows how to handle it. It's just a matter of finding the time to teach his employees. It is probably easier for him to throw a lot of paperwork at his new staff and leave them to figure it out."

With me hot on his heels, he walks into the conference room. Swinging his leather brown chair toward me, he gives me a quick smirk, pointing his finger directly in my face as he states, "Alright, I will do it, not because you tell me I must do so, but because we know I am the best person to perform the task."

A chuckle escapes my lips as I shake my head. "You are exactly right, my friend."

As my eyes roam around the room, I observe people starting to take their seats. All our eyes are drawn to the whiteboard as Dean, my father, stands by his place at the head of the table.

Garrett leans back in the chair and whispers, "Are you going to tell me exactly what's upsetting you? You and I both know that the Michael situation wouldn't get this big of a rise out of you."

Trying to ignore his pestering, I cut my eyes at him.

Garrett bumps me on the shoulder. "I knew it. Spill, man. What is so bad that you are withholding it from me? Since when do we keep secrets?"

The dude is relentless, and this is not the time nor

place to have a conversation about what's bothering me. But before I can answer him, a stern voice interrupts our conversation from a distance, "Lincoln, Garrett, now is as good a time as any to listen." My father's two eyes bore into us as he narrows his eyebrows.

In a whisper, I say, "I'll let you know later."

"I'm holding you to it," he whispers back.

There is no doubt in my mind that he will. The guy loves gossip and drama almost as much as he loves his wife.

I sit back in my chair as I listen to my father discuss how we will close out this month. He steps toward the whiteboard and writes out 'SEPTEMBER', underlining it numerous times to emphasize how significant his message is about to be. Taking out my black leather bound notebook, I carefully listen to his comments.

"Now that I have everyone's attention, I would like to go over our meeting notes. As you all know, each month we set aside an hour, at most, for us to discuss how the month went, what needs to be done at the end of it, and what lies ahead. But before I dive into all of that, I would like to give a shout out to our employee of the month."

In his characteristic proud tone, which is only evident on rare occasions, he continues, "I know that you are aware of the fact that we are a larger company and some things may go unnoticed. But I believe our employees need to know just how important their contributions are to this organization." He points his arm out in my direction and I turn my chair to take in his line of sight, which is directly across the table from me. It is my pleasure to present the award to Miss Sarah Lineway, Director of Human Resources."

Standing, everyone in the room begins to clap, and some even give her a whistle or two to demonstrate their appreciation.

I feel a nudge in my shoulder as Garrett murmurs, "Told you she was a good one."

Looking at him, he wiggles his eyebrows, as if that will somehow convince me to go out with her. To keep him straight, I elbow him in the ribs as he grunts. Feeling satisfied, I smile and return my gaze to Sarah.

Giving her a once-over, I cannot help but be captivated by how she lights up the room. She has a petite figure, with long hair that gleams in waves across her radiant, porcelain-like skin. Her eyes are framed by black frames and lashes.

Her nose is straight, lips are full and plump, no doubt capable of wrapping themselves around my cock.

A flush spreads across her face as she glances at me, making her cheeks redden. I give her a quick wink, because I can. She keeps her gaze firmly fixed on me and the chaos behind us drops away. Her tongue slides across her lips as she bites her lower lip.

Damn. My cock hardens slightly.

Damnit, Garrett was right. That bastard. Not that I will ever admit it to him, but it has been a long time since I have fucked. Maybe this is the fix I need, and from the looks of her, maybe she needs it as well.

"Sarah, it seems like yesterday when your mother walked through our doors demanding I give you the chance to prove that you are the perfect candidate for the firm. Fresh out of college, ready to take the bull by its horns and prove yourself. It's something I won't ever forget."

A beaming smile spreads across her face as he

continues, "Last thing, I swear," he chuckles. "I promise to never let a day go by where you feel like you do not deserve to be here. It has been a pleasure working with you and you have exceeded all my expectations. Sarah, your work never goes unnoticed; you have been an outstanding asset to our company. Now that is something worth celebrating!" he exclaims proudly.

Laughing heartily, she starts to turn red in the face. *Well, that's adorable.*

As we all sit down, she says to my father, "Thank you very much, sir. It has been a pleasure to work for such a great organization, but don't think that you will be letting me go anytime soon," she says, pointing to my father.

There is a loud chuckle in the room at her response. Can't blame them; she's cute and a bit feisty.

Feeling another jab in my upper arm, I glance over at Garrett and glare at him. "Man, fuck off. I'm gonna have a bruise there by tomorrow."

He grins at me. "Good, maybe it will show you are getting some attention." Pointing to his junk, he continues, "You should see the bruises from yesterday. Now that's worth sharing."

With a hearty laugh, I shake my head from side to side. My best friend, ladies and gentlemen.

"Alright, meathead, get down. None of us want to see you whack your dick around."

The commotion behind us starts to settle down as my father commands the room. Although he appears to have it all together, there is more to him than meets the eye. I remember, from the moment that I was able to understand his business conversations, we did not agree on anything.

Having been his only son, I was destined to be in the business world. From an early age, there had always been high expectations for me. First, in spite of my best efforts, I did attend high school in Blue Haven, but with more distractions than one. Second, I was to attend an Ivy League university, which didn't happen; although I had applied to multiple colleges, including the one that I had planned to attend with Ada: Hudson University.

A wave of nostalgia washes over me as I recall the specific day when Ada and I applied to the university together. I can still remember Ada's horror at the prospect of being accepted to an Ivy League school.

"Ada, come here, sit next to me." I pat the spot next to me on my bed, but she continues to pace my room as she bites her nails.

No doubt her nerves are getting the better of her.

She raises her hands in the air and proclaims, "I can't sit, Lincoln! This is such a big deal right now! What if I don't get in? What if you don't get in? What if neither of us gets it? Then what happens?"

Getting up, I swing my legs off the side of the bed. Holding Ada's hands in my own, I kiss her knuckles. "Relax, baby." Taking a deep breath and exhaling slowly, she closes her eyes. "That's it; release some of that unnecessary stress."

Using my fingers, I gently raise her chin and softly say, "Ada, look at me." Her bright sky blue eyes glisten as our eyes connect. "Regardless of what happens, nothing will separate us. We could be a thousand miles apart, in two different states, for four years, but I would still make us work. Do you want to know why?"

Her eyelashes flutter as she shakes her head.

"You, Ada Collins, are everything to me. Some things can't

survive without air, others can't survive without water, but I can't survive without you."

With glossy eyes, she catches me by the back of my neck and leaps up as her legs wrap around my waist. She sprinkles kisses all around my face, murmuring, "You're right. I sometimes get so caught up in my thoughts and what the future holds that I tend to freak out."

Pulling her head back from mine, I place my forehead on hers. "Ada, it is okay to be afraid of what lies ahead, but know that I will be with you every step of the way."

With a smile on her face, she clings to me like a monkey as we move toward my bed and I throw her on the mattress, making her bounce. "So, what do you say about taking that next step together? Huh?"

While propped up on her elbows, she watches me, her finger curves, indicating that she wants me to come toward her. Taking a step forward, she brings me to her level, biting the lobe of my ear.

Okay, not exactly what I had in mind. But damn, my girl is one feisty girl.

My eyebrows rise as she gives me one of her hearty Ada laughs. "I like that plan, Linc."

Tossing her on top of me, I grab her face and bring it to mine, feeling her breath tingle my lips. "Honestly, Linc, it's a good thing we are applying to the same college, because realistically you weren't involved in the decision anyway. You're stuck with me," she says as one eye closes in a teasing wink.

Little does she realize that her wink is going to get her into trouble with some tickles. "Oh yeah, you think so, do you?" I say.

As she squirms in my hands, a laugh escapes her mouth. "Maybe," she exclaims.

With my hands, I hold her in place as I flip her onto her

back. "Maybe I want you to be stuck with me, ever think of that?"

She wiggles her wrists free, grabbing my face and bringing it to hers as she gives me a quick peck on the lips, "Of course I did, you big goof." She pushes me by the shoulders, and I fall back onto the bed. Peeking over at her, she starts working her way toward the corner desk in my room.

"Where are you going, Ada?"

Her eyes shine like the sun, as she glances at me, making her seem like an angel in my life. She bats her eyelashes as her teeth sink into her lower lip. "Applying for college, silly," she says.

Moving quickly, I grab the laptop and say, "Tsk-tsk, not so fast. This is only happening if we do it together."

The woman crosses her arms as she sticks out her tongue and leaves the desk. When I put the laptop on top of my desk, I grab Ada's hips and pull her into my lap. She squeals and attempts to get away. I squeeze her harder to my chest and say, "You are glued to me as we fill this out together."

After giving me a knowing look, she smiles and kisses my cheek. "Fine, let's do it."

Together, we filled out our Hudson University applications, reading the instructions, providing all of the requested informa-tion, and giving the answers we thought were the most appropriate.

Taking a final look at our applications, Ada turns around and places her forehead against mine. "Are you ready?"

"Not quite, Ada. Close your eyes and breathe for a moment with me."

During the deafening silence, I hear her breathing slow down to a more relaxed pace than it had been a few minutes earlier. We both open our eyes back up at the same time as I kiss her nose. My hand completely wraps around hers as I whisper,

"Remember, Ada, no matter what happens from the moment we submit our applications, we will make it work."

She squeezes my hand back and says, "I know."

With our fingers interlocked, we both press the big red apply button, not knowing what lies ahead of us or how our futures might change.

"Lincoln, I would like you to take charge of the remainder of this meeting." I glance up quickly, my dad is giving me a dazed look of bewilderment.

Oh shit, meeting.

Rising from my chair, I reply, "Of course."

My father passes me, and I give him a forced smile as he pops an eyebrow. I reach behind the podium, grab the paper he left behind, and clear my throat in order to catch the attention of the firm. "Alright, Legacy Accounting, I'll make this quick and harmless as we all have jobs to attend to."

The remainder of the afternoon flew by as I worked on the notes from the meeting and burned through three prospectuses, along with a whole pile of bullshit paperwork that I had been putting off for a few days. Besides following up with some clients, I also organized a business trip for our newer accounts. Each year, we organize a training trip to Chicago for new employees, and a few of us managers participate. This year, Garrett and I will be taking the trip; we took it a few years ago and let me say that it was an unforgettable experience.

After finalizing the business trip, I close my laptop and push myself away from my desk to position my feet on top of it so I can stretch out the discomfort in my legs from sitting all afternoon. Leaning back and placing my head in my palms, I close my eyes for a moment, taking in the silence of the firm.

After barely two seconds, my stomach growls, letting me know that I haven't eaten anything for hours, and my caffeine rush has long since gone.

In response to my exact thoughts, my office door flies open and Garrett walks over, throwing an enormous sandwich on my desk before sinking into the chair across from me. I glance at the sandwich and raise my eyebrows.

"I figured you could use one." He shrugs his shoulders.

With a thankful smile, I drop my legs to the ground and unwrap the sandwich. Taking a big bite, I close my eyes and let out a little moan.

My eyes reopen to find Garrett's eyes widening as he claps and laughs. "It sounded like you were moaning, dude."

I just shrug my shoulders because honestly, who cares if I was moaning. I'm fucking hungry.

"Are you ready to tell me the truth about what is really going on? It looks as though death knocked at our door last night."

If only he knew.

While pushing another bite of the sandwich into my mouth, I say in an unintelligible manner, "Thanks for this, man, I appreciate it, but there is nothing wrong, just too much thinking."

"Linc, isn't overthinking one of your superpowers?"

A superpower? I would call it a flaw.

My sandwich falls on my desk as I rub my face.

Lincoln, just get it over with . . . What do you have to lose by telling him the truth? Garrett's your best friend.

As a measure of honesty rather than joking, I confess, "The other day I heard some unfortunate news, and I was trying to determine how to react." Throwing my hands in the air, I continue, "I've not been used to these types of volatile emotions for quite a while. Do I feel sad? Disappointed? Upset?"

He studies me for a few moments before asking, "Why do I have the feeling this is about a certain woman? Could this be an Angel?"

I glare at Garrett, knowing now isn't the time for jokes. "What makes you think that it's about a woman?" I ask.

Standing up, he eyes my office as he paces the room. "I don't know, man. You just seem off. The other day you were dreaming about some woman, which you have yet to confirm or deny. I feel like you have been trying to keep yourself busier than normal, and then today, you walked into the office all gloomy and pissed, which was not caused by me."

He is right on the mark; I am typically the one people turn to for advice and support, unless it is my own shit I am dealing with.

With a sigh, I push myself out of my chair and walk toward the window in my office's back room. An array of reds, oranges, and yellows fill the sky, reflecting on the waves in the lake.

"St. James, why don't you just spit it out. You have always come to me for advice, whether it was girl advice, brotherly advice, or parental advice. I have always had your back, and this time is no different."

I feel my eyes close as I release a deep breath and

force myself to tell him the truth. "Mrs. Collins passed away."

Over the course of a few minutes, he eventually says, "Shit, man. I am sorry. Clearly, I have no idea what you are going through. However, I do know that everything happens for a reason."

"I think that during the time we spent together, she hinted at things that I had not considered until now, such as the desire to renovate the house, getting financial advice regarding her will and renovations, and telling me about Ada's childhood. When she asked me these questions or did these things, I just felt that it was just to build our friendship, not to prepare me for her death, ya know?"

Turning to face him, he places his hands in his pockets, giving me an unsure look.

I get it; in such situations, it is always awkward and difficult to speak, let alone do anything.

"I know this fucking sucks, Linc, and I wish I could say the right thing, but I can't. All I know is that we grow from the loss of someone close to us, and if she was sick or something worse, there is comfort in knowing she is no longer in pain."

I think about the fact that maybe she is supposed to be where she is at this particular time in her life, and I feel a sense of relief flow through my body.

When Garrett and I hear a knock on the door, we both shout, "Come in."

Sarah peeks inside and asks, "Is this a good time or am I interrupting something?"

With a polite smile, I walk to the door and open it all the way. I motion for her to enter. "Hey Sarah, Garrett and I were just finishing."

He cocks an eyebrow in amusement.

"Not the time, asshole," I mouth as I tilt my head toward the door as a sign for him to leave.

He makes his way out of my office, stopping beside me to lean in close and murmur, "Just think it over. She would be a handy distraction at this time."

Despite my angst-ridden mood, I roll my eyes and let out a laugh at his stupid comment. "You didn't just say that. Please leave my office." Garret laughs back, and I close the door behind him.

My attention is drawn back to Sarah, who smiles at me. I wave my hand for her to take a seat.

"I'd prefer not to sit down, if that's okay with you?"

When I approach the front of my desk, I sit on the edge. "Yes, of course, so what's up?"

"I wanted to see if the business trip to Chicago has been handled? I want to provide the itinerary to our new staff members as soon as possible."

I push myself off my desk until I'm standing directly in front of Sarah. "All handled. I will print it out tonight, so you can give it to them tomorrow."

"Ok, perfect. Great."

She starts to move away from me, but I grab her wrist, pulling her toward me a little. "Oh, and Sarah?" While searching my eyes, she curves her lips into a soft smile. "Would you like to go out with me? Maybe we can go to Scoops for Life one of these nights? Do a little celebration of your outstanding performance."

Inhaling deeply, she bites her bottom lip. "I think I would like that."

With a wink, I follow her to my office door.

After turning to face me again, she adds, "Oh, and Lincoln, since I am the HR director and am responsible for protecting our firm from any foreseeable liabilities, would you say our date is consensual?"

A slow grin spreads across my face as I nod my head in agreement. "I would say so."

She steps up on her tiptoes and kisses my cheek as she murmurs against my ear, "Perfect, can't wait!"

"Same here," I say with a smile.

In the process of closing my door, I see Garrett leaning against his office door, mouthing, "Get it. Get it," with a huge grin.

Smug bastard.

Chapter Eight ♡

Ada

As of yesterday, I remained cooped up in my small 325 square foot lodge room for three days. Three days spent struggling to deal with the reality of my mother's death. Three days spent avoiding everything and anything on my to-do list.

Tears form in my eyes when I think of leaving this confined space. Although I am here, no one really knows I am back in town other than Noah, Angel, and Lexie.

Ada, it does not matter how much you mope around, it will not change how you feel.

I remove my covers as I decide it is time to get going. Standing up from bed, I rub my temples lightly to relieve my ongoing headache.

Don't tell me I am about to get a migraine—it seems to happen whenever I am overly stressed.

Ada, when aren't you stressed.

Despite my inner thoughts, I step back, sitting down

on the edge of my bed as my phone pings with a text message from Lexie. Feeling a twinge of guilt, I know I should have texted her the day I arrived, but I couldn't. And now it's been three days and I am still not sure whether I want to go back into town. As I debate whether or not to reply, another text comes in. I sigh; I do not have any other choice than to get my shit together and stop feeling bad for myself.

When was the last time I even felt bad for myself? I usually control my emotions, and only a few days in Blue Haven have left me trembling in fear.

In an effort to release some of my tension, I close my eyes for a moment and roll my neck in circles. I stand up and walk to the bathroom to prepare for the day. I open my text messages and reread them in order to respond.

LEXIE

Ada! It's Lexie, you know your long lost best friend. It was important to me that you weren't under the impression that I did not exist anymore. Hint this text ;). Anyway, I want to see you and catch up. Maybe ice cream?!

Taking a deep breath and exhaling, I force the air to circulate deeply through my lungs and try to focus on the positive aspects of this situation.

This may be the safest way for me to break out of this little nutshell. Plus, Noah might even be pleased since he's been on my case the last few days, encouraging me to leave this room. I responded immediately to her.

> Hey Lex, I am so sorry! It has been crazy since being back. I would love to catch up, but I have some work and funeral arrangements to make. So how about 7 pm?

> Perfect, let's do it! Meet at our favorite spot?

Scoops of Life. God, I missed that place so much.

> Sounds great, Lex. See you then!

Releasing my phone next to me on the bathroom vanity, I hear a few more pings.

Good grief, people. *Ada, this is what you get for shutting yourself off from the outside world.*

Grabbing my phone, I take a quick look at all the messages.

THE BOSS

> Ada, how are things going?

ARCHNEMESIS

> Ada, it's Ruth. Yes, I had to tell who I was, not sure if you actually had my name in your contacts or if you did maybe it was under something like BFF. Anywho's, I sent you an email in regards to the M&A case, I hadn't heard back yet . . .

BUBBA

> Hey, sis. I wanted to see if you would be able to call Flower Forever today and get White Lilies ordered for the funeral?

BESTIE

> Ada, it's been a couple of days since we last spoke. I wanted to check in on you. Please give me a call, so I know you're okay. Xoxo Luce.

Holding the phone in my hands, I stare down at the screen and immediately tuck it away as I fall to the ground.

You can handle this, Ada. It is just a few tasks. You are used to the daily grind, and you have witnessed a lot more chaos in the past.

Breath iiiiin one, two, three, and ooutt one, two, three. You've got to take it one step at a time.

Pushing myself off the ground and taking a few more deep breaths, I peek in the mirror, seeing my reflection staring back at me. There is no doubt that a drowned rat would look better than me at the moment. The wild strands of hair poking out, the bags beneath my eyes, the red puffy eyes. A sour smell emanates from my armpit, making my nose scrunch up.

Ada, when did you ever allow yourself to become this bad?

I gag a little in my mouth when I smell my armpit again, knowing that is the final straw. Dropping my arms, I step into the tub and rest my forehead against the smooth tile wall as the drum of the water washes away my unwanted emotions.

♡

Surprisingly, the day went by quickly, and I was able to email Ruth back and arrange a meeting with Hamill and Sons for the M&A case to discuss their business objectives. In addition, I ordered my mother's favorite flowers, which I had no idea were her favorite in the first place.

How does Noah know these things and not me? What else don't I know about our mom?

I swallow down the thick lump in my throat and glance at my watch, which indicates that it is 10 minutes until 7:00 pm.

I close my laptop and run into the bathroom. I briefly see myself in the mirror and realize I look like an actual functioning human being. In order for my outfit to match, I grab my black blazer from the back of the door. Black jersey bodysuit from Prada, check, silky cheetah skirt, check, hair curled and make-up applied, check. My confidence instills a smile that just barely lifts the corners of my lips when I take another glance at myself.

Okay, this we can work with. *Calm. Collected. Complacent.*

I move back into my room to retrieve my lipstick when I spot a text highlighted on my phone.

LEXIE

Be there in fifteen. I can't wait Ada, I have missed you so much!

Me too! See you soon!

After taking my purse from the nightstand, I walk

over to my car and head to Scoops of Life, praying the only person I see is Lexie. Yes, I know hopeful thinking, but hey, a woman has to do what she has to do to remain optimistic.

My hands tremble as I turn onto Cherrywood Path. What if everyone stops and stares when they see me like at The Crispy Biscuit? What if I see him?

Feeling like this is a bad idea, I start to push the brake as I put myself in reverse.

WAIT, Ada, do not do this to yourself!

Resting my forehead on the steering wheel, I start to rethink everything. Why did I think it was even a good idea to come back in the first place?

Ada, snap out of it! You know why you came back, Noah, for closure. Let people stare and whisper, it's their loss. They do not realize how extraordinary you are. Keep that head high and show them they are not worth your time.

The subliminal version of me knows what needs to be done. So I put the car in drive. I perform a quick breathing exercise that I learned in New York if I ever felt out of control at any time: *iinn, outt, iiinn, outt.*

The ice cream parlor finally comes into view. I park and turn the car off. Closing my eyes, I allow my thoughts to shut out the world and center myself. Even though the drive to Scoops of Life was not that long, we have entered the poor side of Blue Haven.

Both Lexie and I were raised in this part of town; yes, this *part* of town. The one that rich people and kids avoided at all costs because they did not want to be associated with us. However, one particular boy never treated me that way at all. He could care less about how we grew up or the parents we had, because he loved me. He didn't see rich or poor. He didn't care that I didn't have a father figure and that my mom worked as a server and retail sales clerk. In the end, he saw just me, two people who were entwined with each other.

In love.

After reopening my eyes, I notice a large wooden ice cream cone. It has bright red letters reading 'Scoops for Life'. The top of the ice cream cone is a rainbow of colors, resembling a twisted cone. At the front of the cone are three large glass windows, with a giant chalkboard menu, and eager customers waiting in line to receive assistance. Beyond the parlor, Hope Bay Beach is in the distance, the water still, and the silky, smooth color combination of reds and yellows draw me in.

Although my heart belongs to The Crispy Biscuit, I enjoy Scoops for Life as well, particularly when the sun sets. Whenever I felt overwhelmed in my childhood, I would come here and instantly feel at peace. In fact, Lexie and I met here. Despite the fact that we both lived on this side of town and attended the same school, we did not officially meet until this parlor.

Hearing a knock on my car window, I look over and see Lexie. She's smiling wide, and I hold back my tears as she waves to me.

Dear lord, when did I become such an emotional wreck?

I exit the car, close the door, and stand in front of Lexie. *Iinnn, outt, iiinn, outt.* I exhale deeply.

Catching me completely off guard, Lexie embraces me in a hug, as she whispers, "God, Ada, I have missed you."

And just like that, in the midst of my chaotic emotions, a sense of contempt washes over my body as I hug her back. "I missed you too," I say.

Backing away, she clasps her hands around my face

and stares at me in awe. "You have changed so much, yet you haven't changed a lick. You look amazing, Ada."

A smile tugs at my lips as I look at Lexie, still the same as I remember but a woman now. Her hair is still thick, naturally curly, and hangs just below her shoulders. It is a darker brown with a few blonde highlights. She has a round face with big green eyes that are very appealing at first glance. She is tall and lanky, with a slouch that makes her seem shorter than she actually is. The dress she is wearing is bright red and her shoes are blue canvas.

Shaking my head, I let out a chuckle. "You haven't changed one bit, Lexie Green."

Lexie and I are complete opposites. Her clothing matches her personality, being playful, quirky, and creative, while mine was more calm, sophisticated, and professional.

She smirks as we walk together to the ordering counter. "It's just a matter of maturity. Fashion remains the same." She points at her dress and gives me a wink.

A happy giggle escapes me, making me well aware that this may be the first real giggle I have had since I returned, and it feels nice. "Gosh, I missed you, Lexie. We have so much to catch up on."

"That we do, but first, we say it simultaneously."

"Chocolate chip cookie dough." As we gaze at each other, we laugh, and an unfamiliar soft warmth of happiness fills my chest.

I'm happy living my life the way I am, but it makes me think if I have this type of happiness in New York.

My ears pick up a familiar male voice as we approach the ordering window. "Well, if it isn't Ada Collins! As I live and breathe, my goodness. You are still a sight for sore eyes, darling. You come back to Blue Haven for your old job?"

My throat opens up with a soft laugh as his words give me a sense of calm, helping me realize that maybe I didn't need to be worried about Blue Haven not welcoming me back.

As a kid on this side of the city, Max has always been kind and supportive to me. Putting my elbows on the wooden stand, I lean forward and place my chin in my hands. "Not exactly, but you know me, Max, you and this place have always been ones that I favored."

"Connor!" he yells over the music playing. "Ada, remember my son, Connor?" he asks as a much older Connor approaches the window.

Looking at him, it is obvious that he has changed considerably from the little scrawny blonde boy that was always running around here to a young man who is athletically handsome.

A smile spreads across my face as I wave to him. "Hi Connor, nice to see you again." I'm sure he doesn't remember me, but that's fine with me. He smiles quickly and returns to the kitchen to help the other staff members.

In the midst of placing Lexie and my order, Max smirks all knowingly and asks, "Let me guess, Chocolate Chip Cookie Dough?"

Lexie and I both burst into laughter as we smile at him. How could we not? Max still remembers us as if we were teenagers, despite it being years later. With so much laughter in such a short period of time, my headache has calmed, and I am grateful that I made an effort to come here in the first place.

Without another word, Lexie and I move to a picnic

table outside to sit. This ice cream parlor remains only an outdoor venue; therefore, it's only available during certain seasons. The summer season was the best by far as we basically lived here from the beginning of it until the late fall.

"This place has not changed much, has it?" I ask as I look around, continuing to take everything in. The life-size ice cream building still has the same chipped wooden picnic tables with red checkered tablecloths over them and different assorted flowers as a centerpiece. Porta potties are located along one side of the building.

From across the table, Lexie grabs my hands, smiling. "It hasn't, but what do we need to change? It's perfect just the way it is."

She's got a point.

My hands squeeze around hers. "I am glad I got to see you, Lexie."

Through the window, Max yells, "Table 1!"

Noticing her eyes beginning to appear glossy, I hold my hand up. "Oh no, don't go there. I am already too emotional as it is."

Laughing more like a snort, Lexie nods. "Sorry, couldn't help it!"

In a hurry to get our ice cream, she comes back with some of it on her nose. I smile and point to my nose. "You got something on your nose. Couldn't wait until you sat down, could you?"

"What's the fun in that? You know me, Ada Collins, impatience is one of my best characteristics." She shrugs and licks some ice cream off her cone. "Plus, I have always been the last in our group to eat ice cream, so it is almost a natural instinct for me to eat it as soon as possible."

Laughing, I cannot help but feel a sense of happiness that dances through my mind and brings me back to the best memories we made together here. A group of us always craved something sweet after every home football game we played at Oak Ridge High School. Max would stay open later than normal, and we would pile into Lincoln's bronco to drive here.

I remember the weight of Lincoln's arm around me as I wore his letterman's jacket when we sat on the back tailgate while everyone else sat on the picnic tables looking at Hope Bay Beach. Lincoln knew that I couldn't afford to play sports, nor could I always attend games, since I was working hard to keep my house afloat or dedicated to obtaining an academic scholarship just to attend a decent college. So unfortunately, I sometimes had to miss his games and work here instead, but he always came to see me afterward. He never once made me feel embarrassed about it; he loved me despite all the ugly things happening in my life. But knowing now what I do, apparently it wasn't enough.

Emerging myself from the past, Lexie's eyes bore into me. She raises a brow. "You thinking of anything in particular?" she asks.

Placing the cone in the dish, I fold my hands in front of me and rest them on the picnic table. "The past," I whisper to myself.

In every direction I turn, I am reminded of him, of our memories, of the beach, of this place, of The Crispy Biscuit, of my old home.

Sighing, she eyes me with sympathy. Taking my trembling hands in hers, she says, "That is pretty normal. As someone who lived here until the age of seventeen, it's only natural that you would have a lot of good and bad memories. But sweetheart, right now, in the present time, it is ultimately up to you to determine whether you will let the negative ones override the good ones you still have."

I draw a deep breath and force a smile. I know she is right, and I should be focusing on why I am at Blue Haven rather than reliving the horrors of the past. However, that is easier said than done.

With her elbows on the table, Lexie murmurs, "Last time we spoke, he seemed to be doing really well."

My eyebrows crease. "You still speak with Lincoln?" I ask, surprised.

Well, this is news to me, as Lexie was only ever near Lincoln when I was present.

"It is not a big deal," she shrugs. "We speak every now and then. We only reconnected two years ago when Josh, my fiancé, and he began coaching Little League baseball together.

He's coaching Little League baseball?

There is a bit of sadness in my heart knowing that he is following a dream, and I will be unable to witness it. I still recall how we used to joke around that he would coach our children someday.

Is it crazy that I can still picture mini versions of us running around the bases while he chases them and quizzes them on baseball terminology?

At least one of his dreams came true.

Lexie continues, "Honestly, everyone thought that he would follow you. He was so heartbroken, but something kept him here. I don't know what that reason was, nor do I care to discover it, but I do know one thing: he is completely different from the person you remember."

My eyes roll back. *Yeah okay, I loved Lincoln with all my heart, and if he had reciprocated my love, we wouldn't be where we are today.* Having said that, it does not mean that I do not enjoy my current life, but all those what ifs play in my mind periodically.

I breathe out, "I wish I believed you Lexie, I do, but not everyone knows our history."

Twirling her spoon in her now empty ice cream dish, she asks, "Can I ask you a question? I promise not to bring up this topic in the future."

"Yeah, of course."

"What caused you and Lincoln to break up?"

My heart heaves with the weight of her question. I refrain from fiddling with my ice cream spoon, finding myself speechless, as no one knows the true reason why our relationship ended. As difficult as it was to leave Lincoln, I knew that his mother would never accept me, so I left him first rather than allowing him to leave me and break my heart.

Inhaling, iiiiin one, two, three, and ooutt one, two, three, I respond, "Lex, I think you have an idea of why we broke up."

She shrugged her shoulders. "I know what I heard, but is it the same truth as yours, Ada?"

Most people in Blue Haven believe that we separated due to our different college choices and the distance between us. But the real reason is that loving someone whose family loathes you is not for the faint of heart. Lincoln knew how his mother treated me; he even shielded me from her hatred. The only family members Lincoln had that liked me were his three sisters. Being a dumb and naive girl, I wanted to believe that Lincoln would choose his happiness over the opinions of others, but then I woke up.

My initial thought was that leaving him first would lessen the pain, only to have reality prove me wrong. It didn't hurt less; it hurt more, knowing I had broken both of our hearts.

Releasing my clasped hands, I throw my spoon against the tablecloth, a little too rough, which scatters some leftover ice cream on top. "Does it matter, Lex? It's done and over with. Plus, he is most likely doing well with life right now."

Sighing, she looks down. "I guess so."

We both get up with our dishes and move to the wooden ice cream shaped trash cans that look almost identical to the actual ice cream parlor.

Trying to lighten the mood, I change the subject. "Ok, enough about me and my emotional roller coaster life. How is life treating you? I saw your wedding invitation." A smile spreads across her face as she clasps her hands. "Lex, that's exciting. Isn't it at the end of next month?"

Her whole face lights up. "Gosh, Ada, you've known me since like high school?"

With a laugh, I give her an all-knowing look. "Yes, Lex, high school; don't you remember this place as the first place we met?"

While waving her hand in front of me to dismiss what I had just said, she says, "I have always dreamed of having a fairytale wedding, and now I am experiencing it." Putting her hand to her heart, she says, "I cannot contain my excitement. I am bursting with joy. Planning it all has been challenging, but it is all coming together. In fact, the venue was the first thing Josh and I agreed on. I am sure you saw it on our wedding invitation. Wild Willow Mansion."

My memory of it is vivid, as Lincoln and I had always discussed the possibility of getting married there when we were old enough. The house is a waterfront mansion, specifically a historical landmark for Blue Haven. In addition to offering picturesque views of the beach and colorful flower gardens, the mansion has acres of manicured waterfront grounds, serving as a lovely backdrop in every season, particularly the fall. I can still picture it, the first dance, all our friends, all the love, hope, excitement that place came with for Lincoln and I.

Inadvertently tuning out Lex for a few minutes, I nod my head as she describes her wedding theme. "It will consist of large floral arrangements with vibrant burgundy roses complemented by navy blue and white accents. Wow, now look at who's the emotional one." Using her leftover napkin to wipe her eyes, we both chuckle, and I hug her tightly.

Immediately, she pushes me back with her eyes fixed on me. "Ada, are you able to attend the wedding? I know you did not RSVP, but you are here and all."

As I take a quick look at her, I nibble on my bottom lip.

Shit. How do I even respond to this?

There are two possible outcomes of this conversation:

1. I can rip the bandaid off and tell her I am unable to because of work.
2. I can tell her I will try to get the work off so I am not hurting her feelings at this time.

But how can I say no to her? I am never in Blue Haven as it is, but I also have very limited time off. Maybe I can swing it and make a quick trip back?

"The wedding is a lifelong dream of mine, and you're in Blue Haven." She squeezes my hands, begging, "Please, Ada, I'd love to have you there before you leave me again for the big city."

It is time to rip off the bandage. I take a calming breath before I squeeze her hands back and lean against the trash can. "I know I am back in Blue Haven, Lex, but it will only be for a short period of time. This could make or break my career, and after all the years I have invested in it, I cannot let the opportunity pass me by."

Her gaze turns back to me after a moment, as she briefly closes her eyes.

Way to go, Ada. Seeing her become emotional due to my actions breaks my heart.

"You're right, what was I thinking? There are too many other important things you have to take care of besides attending my stupid wedding."

Now I feel like a terrible friend for choosing work over her, but I have worked so hard on my professional career that making this decision seems almost impossible. My arm loops around hers as we begin the walk back to our cars. The weight of her head presses against my shoulder.

Taking a deep breath, I suggest, "Maybe I can get more time off? Or schedule a weekend trip. Let me talk to my boss and see what he says. If he is okay with it, then I should be able to attend your wedding." Stopping at my car, I point my finger at her. "But only under one condition."

"Oh my God, yes, I will do anything to have you come."

My smile spreads as I hold up one finger. "Do not set me up with a date for your wedding. I would rather go alone. If you are okay with that, I'll try and make it work."

Her happiness streaks through her like a comet as she jumps up and down. When she leans over and takes me in for a quick hug, she's grinning ear to ear, and my chest pounds with joy after our heavy conversation, reviving my spirits.

Lexie holds her hand out in front of her body, waiting patiently for me to shake it. "Do you remember our secret handshake, Ada Collins? The one when if we have a deal or a friendship promise, only this handshake keeps it a secret?"

Laughing, I grab her hand, clasping it in mine, giving her what she wants, our childhood handshake. As we are shaking hands, I see somebody in my peripheral vision.

"Yay! I can't wait," Lexie exclaims when we finish. She walks backward to her own vehicle, as she says, "Call your boss tomorrow, Ada Collins, and let me know if I can include you as a guest. I will be praying," she crosses her middle fingers with her pointers, "hoping for the best outcome."

I chuckle. "I will, I promise."

Once back in her car, she waves goodbye and proceeds on her merry way. I peek over my shoulder one last time to determine whether or not I was seeing things. But my eyes connect with his, making each muscle in my body lock.

This is not happening.

Even though I knew the chances of meeting him were high, it had to happen on the first freaking attempt of me entering town. My heart is erratic inside my chest, and my mind races with Lexie's words: *"He is completely different from the person you remember."*

And she couldn't be more accurate; his golden brown hair on his head is longer than usual; he's wearing a white button-down shirt, with a few buttons undone, and jeans, giving off a sexy businessman's vibe.

Lincoln's piercing blue eyes stare right into my eyes as he catches my admiration. My chest aches seeing this adult version of him, missing out on it.

In the midst of feeling hot and feverish, a woman's voice interrupts our prolonged eye contact. "Lincoln, hurry before it rains!" The woman smiles so brightly and grabs Lincoln's forearm, pulling him toward Scoops for Life. Along with her there is a beautiful autumn-colored golden retriever jumping out of the back of his old bronco.

He still owns that bronco?

He allowed another girl to ride in it?

Cut it out, Ada. It has been over a decade since you last saw him. He has probably had plenty of women in and out of that bronco. She could well be his girlfriend.

A strange expression appears on his face as he lowers his eyebrows and pulls them closer together, making me feel slightly uncomfortable.

How do I even respond to a look like that?

With a brave face, I give him a tight smile and a small wave real quick. He starts to move toward me; his eyes fill with confusion. I quickly get into my car, looking through my windshield while reversing.

He holds up his hand as he keeps advancing toward my car. "Ada, wait!" he yells.

I shake my head repeatedly, fear coursing through my veins. Knowing that if I stayed, I would not want any part of that conversation. The tears finally fall and a sob is released as I drive away.

God, I'm a freaking mess.

Chapter Nine ♡

Lincoln

Atop two tall rocks on Hope Bay Beach, she held her arms out wide, allowing her smile to reach her eyes, wrinkled with crow's feet. With coils of leaf-brown hair and round, bliss-blue eyes, she was bursting with joy. It was a genuine expression of her happiness at that very moment.

But each wrinkle of her's reflected the struggle and survival in her life.

The look on Mrs. Collin's face brings me back to the day when I took this very picture of her. It was after she had completed her addiction treatment program, and she was beginning to talk openly with me about everything—her past, what she wanted with her future, and how she wanted to fix things with Ada.

It will always be one of my favorite memories.

As I stand up from my bed, I turn to my dresser and gaze in the mirror. Seeing tired, dull eyes stare back at me, I run my hand through my hair, noting a week-old growth of beard that should be trimmed, as well as the Armani suit I am wearing—custom tailored, fully lined, and three-buttoned—that still requires ironing.

Blowing a long breath through my nose, I close my eyes. I am unsure which pain is the worse: the shock at what has happened to Mrs. Collins or the agony that I feel at the thought that she will not be able to reconnect with her daughter again. The one thing that she was adamant about, and it was something I wanted for both her and Ada.

Today is not the day for weakness, Lincoln.

In the last decade, I have become proficient at avoiding the loneliness that has more times than not threatened to drag me under. It's a system that involves no-strings attached, throwing myself into work, coaching Little League baseball, and drinking over-priced booze at Safe Harbor. It took a few years to perfect. Just ask Garrett, he won't hesitate to agree, and while I have become skilled at this, I don't know if it's what I want anymore.

After taking one final look at myself in the mirror, I grab the funeral program, fold it in half, and place it inside my suit. Coming from behind, Ginger, my golden retriever, jumps on my bed and wags her tail to get my attention.

When I move toward her, I smile and rub her ears. "Hey, girl." I laugh as she attempts to lick my face, thrilled to see me.

I found Ginger at the Blue Haven Animal Shelter, and I was tempted to take her home that first night I saw her, but I didn't. My mind was continuously flooded with memories of when Ada and I discussed getting a golden retriever for our first dog together. It almost felt like I would have been dishonoring us if I took Ginger in, despite the fact that Ada had left town. But as soon as I knew she wasn't returning home, and I was tired of being lonely, I adopted Ginger.

I kiss the top of Ginger's head one last time and say, "Wish me luck, girl. I'm gonna need it."

Trying to lick me again, I chuckle and shake my head, as I tap my thigh, signaling her to get off the bed. After a moment of hesitation, she jumps off and makes her way directly toward the front door to say goodbye.

Moving along behind her, I'm shaking, feeling a sense of nervousness like I've never known, and I know it's not because of the funeral I am about to attend. As I try to will the nerves off my body, I can't help but think what Garrett said: *"Time goes on, Lincoln; people change, lives change, and it is time for you to do the same."*

He's right; my past cannot dictate my future. I allow a deep breath to escape my body as I reach my front door.

Come on, Lincoln.

My hand hovers over the doorknob as I glance out the glass door windows. The lake sparkles afar, and every part of my body tenses—the twist in my gut, the pain in my neck, the tightness in my chest.

It's now or never.

ADA

After sleeping like shit the night before, I can't help but feel the sadness that weighs me down as I gaze at the memorial in my hand, mesmerized by the photo of my mother. She was beaming with a joyful smile.

Who took this photo? Who got to witness this side of Wren Collins?

When I was a child, I could never imagine her being this happy. It doesn't even look like she missed me when I left. Her beautiful face, encompassed with beauty lines and wrinkles, stared back at the camera—her hands out wide. No one would suspect that the demons were just beneath the surface, waiting to erupt into her life. My childhood was filled with exposure to that side of her on many occasions. But in this photo, she was extremely happy and seemed peaceful . . . without me.

Sharp pricks of unwanted tears sting my eyes and I drop the paper on the bed. The anger, sadness, and frustration at the weakness I feel is too much.

My emotions haven't taken over in years, including the ones I am experiencing now. I've kept them locked down, controlled, but right now they are entirely unmanageable, thanks to being back in Blue Haven, a place I never thought I would ever return to.

As I wipe my tears away, I stand in front of the mirror to finish getting ready. Sadly, I cannot hide from the harsh reality of my reflection. Mirrors lack filters and I appear to be a complete hot mess. My nose runs like a freaking faucet; I have bags under my eyes, red puffy cheeks, and blurry vision as a result of crying.

Being brave, I briefly look at myself once again.

There is no way in hell, Ada, that you will attend your mother's funeral looking as you do.

Doing what I do best, I lock up my emotions and put myself together. My tired face needs a little brightness, so I use some concealer foundation. I cover my blemishes and my under-eye circles, finishing the look with a touch of bright red lipstick on my heart-shaped lips.

A sigh of relief escapes as I step into my silky black stockings matched with my black mid-length skirt from Fendi & Gucci. Keeping the look between formal and casual, I pair it with a cashmere cream sweater and a black collared shirt. Completing it all with my favorite silver hoop earrings and ankle boots.

In front of the mirror, a confident smile plasters its way across my face. *Now, Ada, this is something we can work with.*

New Yorkers are used to going from zero to one hundred in no time. In the city, I am constantly moving. Here, everything moves slower, and I find myself continually needing to slow my pace.

Having finally regained my senses, I roll my shoulders back and stand up straighter, feeling like myself again. I grab a light jacket and scarf for additional warmth just as my phone rings.

Ugh, great timing.

The screen of my phone lights up, revealing six bold letters: Emmett.

Since I have no other option, I pick up the phone and proceed in a courteous, professional, and positive manner. A cheesy smile adorns my face as I attempt to calm my nerves. My heart is pounding and my palms are sweating, but I am determined to make the best out of this conversation.

"Hi, Emmett," I say.

"Hello, Ada. I have texted you several times, but have not heard back. How is the home front going?"

As I fiddle with the fringes on my skirt, I clear my throat. "It's . . . uh . . . fine, sir."

"Ada, are you sure? Why do I get the feeling that you seem uncertain?"

In truth, I am not even sure I am okay; I have been a walking case of frazzled nerves and mental confusion since I stepped back into Blue Haven.

Instead of saying what I really wanted to say, I blurt out in a rush, "Sir, my mother has passed away."

My words are met with a stunned silence, and it's clear that he didn't expect this news. Then, with a loud exhalation accompanied by a low moan, he says, "Why have I only heard about this now? Why did you not inform me about this in the office?"

I should have told him sooner, even if it was to avoid this unnecessary guilt, yet here I am, feeling the weight of my mistake.

"I'm sorry, sir, I w-w-anted t-oo. Trust me, I did. But—"

I am interrupted by a heightened breath as he continues, "But what? Ada, you just got assigned a career changing M&A case, and I need a senior associate who is on top of their game, and right now it's only natural for you to feel all over the place in the wake of such a tragic event. I cannot have a senior associate going through something like this while working on such a crucial case."

Emmett has every right to be upset with me, but could he really take me off the case? I fall back onto my bed, confusion and uneasiness settling in. Throwing my phone next to me, I take a deep breath.

Can anything worse happen? I mean, Jesus, it is evident to the guy that I put a lot of effort into my work. Furthermore, I had just met with him and Ruth the other day, again demonstrating my dedication to this case, regardless of my current circumstances.

I know right now is not the time to battle an

unwinnable fight, so instead of telling my boss off, I sit up and refrain my eyes from rolling. Right now, I just need to remind Emmett how great of an asset I am.

Step by step, Ada.

Being a senior associate, it is pretty evident that this case is the golden ticket to my partnership at the firm. In addition to taking on more responsibility, this type of career change will provide me with an opportunity to gain equity in Sullivan & Rothman's firm, a goal I have been working toward for many years now.

If I don't keep constantly reminding Emmett why I'm the right person for this case, it could end in a blink of an eye. Standing abruptly from my bed, I walk to the mirror. Making eye contact with my reflection, I raise my head and chin simultaneously, while pulling my shoulders back and standing upright.

"Emmett, sir, you do not need to worry. While in Blue Haven, I will handle everything, including the M&A case with Hamill and Sons."

My attempts to convince him don't go far, so I continue, "Emmett, I know you prefer work done at the firm, but you can trust me. Have I let you down before? Does Von Mertz Group sound familiar to you?"

"Yes, Ada. I recall that particular case well. Despite the fact that you have not let me down yet, this is a different type of case. This is a high-profile, more complex case, and attempting to start it remotely would be almost virtually impossible."

"Awe, sir, yes, almost is the keyword here. Never say it can't be done. If anyone is able to balance this M&A case from afar, I'm your girl. To make you feel better, I have already reviewed the file several times since returning home."

With a sigh, I close my eyes and conclude my attempt at persuasion. "Emmett, let me demonstrate this to you. You can rest assured that I will handle this situation with the utmost care and diligence."

Seconds pass into minutes, and I finally hear him clear his throat, clearly ready to respond, so I throw caution to the wind and hope like hell that he will agree with my plan. "Here's what will happen after we end this call and before we meet next. First, once you send over everything to me, I will hop on the meeting I scheduled already with Hamill and Sons to discuss their business objectives. As you are aware, legal issues vary greatly depending on the type of case we are dealing with. Finally, I will develop a road map for them from beginning to end, which will include a timeframe."

A sigh of relief follows his words, "Alright, Ada, I'll give you some time to figure out things back at home, but in the meantime, I trust you to handle the M&A case in the same manner you would here at the firm. No exceptions."

Hot damn, Ada, you did it.

In a moment of pure pride, I pump my fist in the air as I walk toward the ceiling to floor window. I can't help but marvel at Hope Bay Beach: tranquil, serene, and exactly the same today as it was over a decade ago.

With a calming breath, I respond, "No problem, sir. I will provide you with my best efforts."

"Ada, I believe you. Also, Ruth will be assisting more in this case. Since there will only be one new partner at the firm, I believe it is only fair to showcase who will be the best fit for the position through this merger."

Fuuuck.

With a roll of the eyes, I glance at the time. *Shit, there is only half an hour before the funeral.*

"I understand, sir. If I need anything, I will contact you or Ruth."

"Great, and Ada?"

"Yes, sir?"

"I am sorry about your mom."

Hearing his words, a sudden sting of tears rush to my eyes. Closing them, I try to catch my breath as I inhale the fresh scent of Blue Haven from my open window—peppery aroma mixed with a trace of the sap sweet from Hope Bay Beach.

In a quiet voice, I sniffle as I finish the call as quickly as possible, hoping that Emmett will not notice any difference in me. "Thank you, sir. Talk to you soon."

I then grab my belongings from the bed and move to the front door. My hands are trembling as they hover over the doorknob. Glancing out the window once more, I take in the sight of the lake sparkling far beyond, a place that always brings me peace.

Nevertheless, tears fill my eyes as my throat grows tight; feeling every emotion in my body except peace.

Ada, you've got this under control. One step at a time.

Pulling open the doors, I take deep breaths *iiiin one, two, three,* and *ooutt one, two, three.*

It's now or never.

Chapter Ten

Lincoln

It takes me all of about ten minutes to walk to the center of town before I see White Willow Memorial Gardens in the distance. Nervousness shoots through me, knowing who I'm about to see and what's about to happen.

A bump from behind causes me to freeze. The person holds me by the shoulders, gently shaking me. "Hey, man. Thought you might need a friend today."

A sigh of relief escapes my lips as I fall forward. *Garrett.*

The only thing I really need is a shot or two of whiskey to relieve my tension and numb the emotions I am experiencing. But a friend will also do.

With an appreciative smile, I give him a hug and pat him on the back. "Thanks, man. I appreciate you showing up here today even though you didn't have to."

Garrett shakes his head as he shoves my shoulder with his. "St. James, don't be trying to get rid of me just yet; we have the rest of our lives still. You know I will always be here for you and have your back, no matter the situation."

Chuckling, I look up at the sky as the clouds gather. The sky has been postcard-perfect up to now, but as time passes, the gorgeous cocktail-blue shade gradually darkens into gravel-gray. A large cloud cover obscures the golden glow of the sun.

"Come on, man, let's go, before it rains," I say, nudging Garrett.

Our pace speeds up as we reach White Willow Memorial Gardens. A light rain splatter starts when we are halfway across the meadow. We quickly take shelter under an old oak, hoping to survive the shower until the memorial begins. Streams of moisture drip from the leaves and onto my suit. As I wipe away the raindrops from my jacket, I glance over at Garrett. He opens an umbrella, and I raise an eyebrow at him.

A soft chuckle emanates from his chest as he says, "Dude, did you forget that I am always prepared." He positions the umbrella on top of our heads. "I am not only a god in bed, but in all aspects of life. I am coming to your rescue once again, my friend." While laughing at his amusement, he shrugs his shoulders and adds, "I may have also checked the weather prior to coming."

One of us seems to be thinking clearly today.

My throat clenches with sadness and worry as I look around. There are a few families gathered together, along with a large number of dark figures standing to pay their respects to one whom we adore.

My eyes continue to scan the surroundings, and I cannot help but feel on high alert.

Is she here? What if she decided to not show up?

"Boo!"

My attention is caught by a pair of golden brown eyes staring back at me, waiting for a reaction. Unimpressed; I already know who is trying to scare us.

And at a funeral, nonetheless.

Jewels. My youngest sister of three. The creative, outgoing risk-taker.

I roll my eyes. "Ha, ha, ha, you are hilarious."

She shrugs. "Eh, I tried my best."

Jewels stands next to me as I ask, "Jewels, why are you even here? Aren't you supposed to be at college?"

She flashes an eyebrow as she says, "And what? Just let you handle this all by yourself? I wanted to be here for you. We all know Anastasia would blame her pregnancy, and Faye is over in la la land at her new home."

While I appreciate the fact that she is here for me, I also wish that I had been able to handle this day on my own.

My ear is filled with a short gasp. "Wait, is that her?"

Like being drawn by a magnetic force, I follow Jewels' line of sight. *Ada.*

Garrett jolts his shoulder into mine and says, "Oh shit, man, she came. Wasn't sure if she would show up, considering how things ended in Blue Haven."

A swell of lightheadedness rushes into my brain. I can't fucking breathe.

I have to physically hold and grip my nails into the tree trunk to keep myself from running toward her. It doesn't matter that I can't see her face yet. I'd recognize her from a mile away. The first time I saw her at Scoops for Life yesterday, it was like a dream; however, today, seeing her here, it seems, no, it feels real.

Ada's head is downturned, so she nearly collides with Noah's back when they abruptly stop in front of the casket. Jerking her attention up, she searches for what had stalled Noah and her expression becomes dull and somber with a slight tinge of sadness covering it. Tears form in her eyes before streaming down onto her rosy, sunken, puffy cheeks.

Fuck me. This woman, she's even more of a goddess than my brain allowed me to remember.

She's twice as beautiful as before. We were just kids the last time we were together. Of course, she was stunning then, but barely an adult. Now she's a woman in the fullest sense of the world. She's everything I've ever wanted in a woman—soft, yet strong; slender, yet curvy. Feminine and powerful.

Her presence is so overwhelming that it's nearly impossible for me to take my eyes off of her, even if I wanted to. Her mid-length skirt, coat, and a cream sweater are classic and professional, but they do not conceal the mind-blowing curves underneath. She is still breathtakingly beautiful, with her long brown hair flowing in the wind, soft eyes, and plump lips.

Even though she has changed so much, she still resembles my Ada.

Jesus, Linc. She's not yours anymore. You lost that right a long time ago. You haven't seen her in over a decade and you're thinking with your dick. Get your shit together. You're here because of her mother, not a reunion with your one lost love.

Urges slam me from all sides.

Attraction.

Want.

Need.

Shaking my head, I clasp my hands behind my neck and stare at the ground.

Inhaling a deep breath, I close my eyes and attempt to gain control over these fucking feelings.

You got this, Linc.

While running my hand through my hair in an effort to make myself look more presentable, I glance over at Ada, just as she turns her head and our eyes meet.

"Promise me, Linc. Promise me we'll always be together." Meeting her with my pinky, we kiss each other's noses while crossing our fingers together.

"I promise you, Ada. I want nothing more than this for our future."

On the back of my bronco at Hope Bay Beach, it is near midnight and the night sky is perfect; so clear you can almost discern the craters. The moon looms large in the sky, surrounded by an ethereal glow.

I turn to my side and observe her long blonde hair flowing out on the blanket. It moves sideways with the wind and as I breathe in her scent, I can smell every aura coming off her in waves.

Hyacinth and Magnolia leaves.

Bringing my body closer to her, I rest her head on my shoulder while placing my chin on her head and kissing her quickly. I can feel the warmth of her skin through my letterman jacket, and the sensation goes straight to my head.

Damn, she feels good.

Giving her a tight squeeze, I blurt out, "I love you, Ada." Even though we are pretty early on in our relationship, I know that she is it for me.

When she sits up, she places her arms on my chest and turns around. I cup her face with my palm and she relaxes a bit, which reduces the level of my nerves. This was my first time saying that to her, so I wasn't exactly sure what I expected, but it wasn't what she said next.

Leaning forward, she stares at me and her eyes start to flood with tears as I stroke her cheek. She whispers breathlessly, "You know, that is the first time I have heard someone actually mean those three words when they speak them to me." Tears fall on my hand, and suddenly, she sobs. Trembling hands cover her face.

The fact that I had a similar experience to hers in my own life, hearing it from her, puts tears in my own eyes. I can feel the flesh on my chest ripping as I listen to her. Quickly grabbing ahold of her, I roll her on top of me.

She squeals, "Lincoln!" and then relaxes when I wrap my arms around her waist and press my hands against her lower back. Her head lies on my chest as she continues to let it all out. I don't say anything, just wanting to be there for her. Offering my silent support that lets her work through her emotions.

In an instant, her mouth parts, allowing the color to drain from her face. Her eyes widen, and immediately her expression hardens. I cannot blame her. I am the last person she would have expected to be here.

ADA

My heart sinks to my feet. I knew the odds were strong to see him around town, but my mother's funeral? Why? They didn't have a relationship. He's the only one who truly knows how she treated me and made me feel. Could it be he's here for me?

My skin feels as though a million needles are poking

at it. What the hell does he want? I don't need pity; his most of all.

He stands right in front of me, studying me with those piercing blue eyes. Glancing at my hands, I take a deep breath; I pride myself on being courageous, yet here I am, hiding behind Noah like a coward.

I don't think I can do this.

Get yourself together, Ada. Just because you are back in Blue Haven does not mean you are the same girl you once were.

No one can take away my sense of pride as a successful, independent, and strong badass lawyer. Not even the Adonis standing in front of me.

I take a peek toward the casket and see him speaking with a man who looks strangely familiar. You know when you recognize someone but cannot place a name on them?

Yeah, currently happening to me.

In the midst of openly gawking at him, said man gazes in my direction. Everything comes together at that moment.

Garrett.

Somewhat embarrassed by having been caught, I avert my eyes back to the casket.

Garrett is still in Blue Haven? Years later, who would have thought the two notorious high school studs of Blue Haven would still be in our hometown.

Not me, that's for sure.

The sight of them together causes my chest to ache from the memories evoked.

On the roof of the school gymnasium, we used to talk about our individual dreams and goals. Mine always included leaving Blue Haven.

"Ada, it's your turn."

While I glance down at the empty glass beer bottle on the ground, a breeze blows across my hands. The cold immediately causes goosebumps to appear all over my arms. Rubbing them, I look directly at the person who can easily calm my nerves in seconds.

With a mischievous smile, Lincoln raises his eyebrows, making me smile back.

"Come on, babe. It's not a big deal. You know we all had to do it."

But it is a big deal.

With the life I had, the mother and non-existent father, you could say I did not dare to dream often. But for them, it was easy because they had the house, their parents, and the money to pursue whatever they desired without second thoughts.

I may not have money, dreams, goals, or the perfect life, but I have always had one thing that I loved doing and wanted to continue to do. Help others when they are unable to help them-selves. Sort of like myself. There were times, and still are, that I could not help myself or Noah. I couldn't imagine someone else dealing with what I was dealing with, so I decided that a lawyer was fitting. I hadn't told anyone this, not even Noah, yet I blurt it out before I can stop myself.

"I guess my dream would be to attend Hudson University and earn my law degree. Besides helping others, it's also a lucrative profession." With a wink, I add, "Plus, Linc, you know how much I enjoy a challenge."

As he smiles with pride, he says, "I didn't know you wanted to become a lawyer, babe. That's amazing. You would be great at that."

In the midst of my smile, I hear snickering. Two girls across from me are huddled together, laughing and saying things to one another.

"If you got something important to say, Haden and Nicole, then spit it out." Garrett's eyes drill into theirs with a pissed off expression. They stop laughing and roll their eyes at me. "I got you, Collins. Let these bitches be bitches." Garrett looks back at me and winks.

Having never really had anyone stand up for me other than Lincoln, I felt a deep sense of gratitude and happiness. I grin at Garrett and glance back over at Lincoln, who is giving me what I like to call his signature 'St. James' expression, aka sizing me up.

There are no words but one to describe how I feel when I see that one look: loved.

"Ada, do you have anything to say?"

A nudge from an elbow causes me to jump out of my memory. "Psst, Ada," Noah whispers.

I turn toward him as he tilts his head toward Pastor Kelly. A sense of sadness washes over me as I gaze at the coffin in front of me. I shake my head at Noah and Pastor Kelly.

Despite the fact that I have many wonderful memories with her, they are few and far between. Truth be told, I have more dreadful memories with her than happy ones. It's a shame that she chose an addiction over her children, and it is something I choose to not forget. At this point, she is six feet deep in the ground and not one person could persuade me to speak a word about her.

"I'll do it," Noah says as moves toward the podium.

My eyes again become fixed on those blue eyes, causing me to turn quickly away. I knew Lincoln at seventeen and he was handsome, but the adult Lincoln before me, he's so devastatingly handsome I could cry.

The grief of that loss is like a fist squeezing around my heart.

My eyes wander over him—his golden-brown skin from late summer, broad shoulders, and strong legs. He is still slim but there's so much of him. His jaw tightens with a twitch and his hands start to squeeze the memorial pamphlet. The sight of his larger hands sends blood rushing to my ears so loudly it's like I can hear waves crashing inside my head.

I remember like it was yesterday. Him kneeling me over in my bedroom, running those fingers along my body like he had discovered something new. My heart starts to race, and I feel a lump in my throat. My fight-or-flight response is fully alerted at this point.

His name slides softly from my wet lips. "Lincoln?"

An expression of surprise crosses his face as he stares at me. There is an unrelenting hold between his eyes as his gaze moves across my body. His lips are pinched into a flat line, and his chest expands with rapid breathing.

A second stretch of silence lingers in the air, causing my heart to beat rapidly. Taking another step closer to him, his eyebrows shoot up, his face confused.

I halt.

Shit. Shit. Shit.

After taking three giant steps toward me, he clasps his arms around me so tightly that I can smell the distinct scent of spice and musky masculine fragrance that is exclusively his.

I missed this.

When he speaks, his voice is a deep rasp that I want to immerse myself in. "Ada . . . God, Ada. I am so sorry."

Pulling me to his chest, I hear his rapid heartbeat

and labored breathing, and for one second the weight of the world has been lifted off my shoulders. After a moment, I lean back and place my trembling hands on Lincoln's shoulders. As he focuses his attention on my face, I notice everyone around us is staring.

At us.

God, this is too much; without another thought, I listen to my instincts to fight or flee. I look at Noah with a sympathetic look and mouthing the words, "I'm sorry."

As he realizes the reason behind my abrupt departure, he bites his lip, likely to prevent him from speaking in front of the guests. I shake my head and immediately make my way out.

When I run across the meadow, a flood of emotions erupts from within me as I am struck with frosty droplets from the rain. Rain, at one point in my life, meant so much to me; it evoked so many wonderful memories, making me feel hopeful. It served as a reminder that, as humans, we are capable of experiencing beautiful things.

"Ada, stop, wait! Can you just . . . hold on, wait."

Hearing that familiar voice, knowing I can't, I don't look back, not this time.

Chapter Eleven

Ada

Rolling down the windows, the warm afternoon sun kisses my face as I turn onto High Lane Road. In light of yesterday's turn of events, it's difficult not to feel weak.

What even was that? It is not my nature to be cowardly.

In the past, when I encountered similar situations, I avoided confrontation and ran away. But this time, in this situation, I wanted to be different and take on the challenge without avoiding it. However, I allowed myself to be overwhelmed by the situation and it has caused me to experience unnecessary humiliation.

As I bring my car to a halt, I stare at my old house. My knees start bobbing up and down as anxiety grips me.

"Calm down, Ada; it's just a house," I whisper out loud.

Away from the city lights, the traffic, the everyday chaos.

It looks amazing. I don't even recognize the house anymore. The lawn is green and mowed, and the overflowing weeds in the garden have turned into beautiful flowers. The siding and trimming look new and freshly painted. I didn't notice a basketball hoop before, but there's one there now and my favorite porch swing is still intact.

That swing and sitting together before bed are probably the only good memories I have of my father.

I get out of my car, close the door, and stretch out my legs. Walking down the long paved driveway, memories of my childhood flood back.

"Psst . . . Ada! Get up." Hearing a familiar voice with a loud thud that just hit my window, I jump out of bed, only to catch Lincoln throwing yet another rock.

"Lincoln, what are you doing here?" I open my window and see those gentle, deep ocean blue eyes staring at me. Burning with love and care, making me feel instantly calm.

"I came to see my girl, of course."

Shaking my head, I smile lopsidedly, whispering, "You're crazy, you know that?"

God, what a mess he was. But my mess, nonetheless.

"Let me come up, Ada. I have something important to tell you."

My heart leaps with joy as I observe the joy flowing through Linc, making my chest swell. Raising an eyebrow, I ask, "What do you have to tell me, Linc? Can't it wait till morning?"

"No, Ada, it can't."

Holding my breath for a moment, I smile and say, "Fine,

meet me at the front door. BUT be quiet, as Noah's room is right next to it."

I run down the stairs to meet him, barely concealing my excitement. As he opens the door, he grabs me by the waist and pulls me up to where my feet are barely touching the floor.

Putting a finger to his mouth, I whisper, "Shhh, Noah is right there, and my mom is a light sleeper." I squirm in his arms as he pokes me at the sides, and I let out a soft laugh.

"Sorry, I'll be quiet. You finally inviting me into your room for real this time?"

It is possible that I have teased him about coming to my room many times. But tonight feels different.

He places my feet on the ground and I grab his hand, saying, "Come on," as we hurry toward my bedroom.

A warm breath tickles the back of my neck as I close the door behind him. I tense in anticipation. As Lincoln slowly grabs me by the waist, my back hits his rock-hard chest. He begins nibbling and kissing me as his contentment and love sweep over me.

"Now, Mr. St. James, what is so important that you had to sneak over here and ask for access to my home?" I turn around and snake my arms around his neck.

As he makes eye contact with me, he stretches forward, placing his forehead against mine. I can sense the nerves leaving his body as he says, "Well, Miss Collins, I thought you should know I have missed you."

My heart burst with happiness at his words. My attraction for him, and the way I feel when I am around him all the time, are so intense that they scare me.

I drop my hands from his neck and wrap my fingers around his shirt, gently tugging and whispering, "You came all the way here, across town, at 11:00 pm to tell me you missed me? You couldn't just wait till we see each other at school?"

Gazing at me, he says, "Why would I do that? Ada, baby." He points between us. "You and me, it's forever." He grabs my face with both hands. "I never want a day to pass that I do not share with you how much you mean to me, how much I miss you when you are not with me, how much I love you."

He always has a way with words that squeeze my heart, and tonight is no exception.

It's quiet in the room.

Just the two of us.

We're alone.

Not that we haven't been alone before, but never in my bedroom, especially when it's dark with a slight glow from my clock on my nightstand.

In spite of my failure to respond to Lincoln, he grabs my lower back and pulls me toward him. "Come here, baby." He moves us to the wall, pushing my back against it, pinning me with his body. Lincoln has shown me nothing but respect in our intimate relationship, but tonight, in his eyes, I can see nothing more than hunger.

He kisses me so deeply, that I feel its intensity in every nerve of my body. Crushing my tits against his chest, I break away from his greedy lips, and he trails his mouth down the length of my inner neck. Licking and nibbling. I tremble and moan as he kisses me in that sweet spot above my breasts. Watching him, he lifts his head, and our eyes lock. His fingers grab the front of my bra, slowly pulling it downward, leaving my tits completely exposed. He grins mischievously right before his head dips down and he sucks on one of my rock hard nipples. My head falls backward against the wall as my fingers entwine themselves around his hair, tugging as he devours my breasts.

"Yes," I whispered.

My hands travel over his thighs, slowly pulling his zipper down and slipping my hand inside. Wrapping my fingers around his cock evokes a gratified groan of pleasure in his throat. I do it again as I graze the crown with my fingertips, brushing its tip with my thumb, making him groan even louder.

"Ada, keep going."

Listening to him, I try to pull free his boxers and jeans, but he stops me. "Wait, Ada." Taking a deep breath, he places his forehead on mine. Moving my hand over his chest, his heart thuds erratically as he cups my cheeks. "I know this is what I want, but is this what you want?"

I nod to him. I know that he is not a virgin like me, but I want him as badly as I desire my next breath.

"Words, Ada. I need you to tell me what you want."

With both hands clasping his face, I close my eyes; my next words are barely audible against his lips. "I-I want to have sex with you. I am not scared because I know you will take care of me. I love you, Lincoln. I want this more than anything."

Naivety is a gift for the youth, and we decided to let it shield us from the realities of life. Blue Haven used to be one of my favorite places to be. It's small, quiet, beautiful, and secluded. We're surrounded by woods, mountains, and beaches. Even the less wealthy citizens of the town—me, mom, and Noah—got to feel as if we were a part of it all.

I make my way over to the porch swing, remembering sitting there, dreaming of a life here, but little did I know: dreams are lies we feed ourselves.

A life I would have loved until . . . *it never happened.*

This life is better, Ada. It's one you built yourself. One you are in control of. One you don't have to be ashamed of or hide from.

As I sit down on the porch swing, I close my eyes

and rub my temples, feeling a pounding in my head as another headache develops. My heart aches with all these painful memories; I didn't imagine the past would come back to bite me in the ass all at once, let alone so soon.

Suddenly, my phone vibrates in my pocket. I pick it up and read the text message.

BUBBA

Hey sis! I am currently completing a few school assignments and then I will be heading to the house. Will you be there? We only have so much time before the estate sale.

I also wanted to let you know that I understand why you left so quickly from the funeral. Not that I blame you. The tension between you and Lincoln was so thick that I am pretty sure everyone felt it.

Ugh, don't remind me. I'm still recovering from that encounter.

I am already ahead of you, bubba. I am at home now. Concentrate on your studies. I will see you shortly.

Alright, sounds good to me. I'll bring us some pie from the diner to snack on while we sort through the house.

With a chuckle, I shake my head. Noah and his damn sweet tooth. I guess it's true when they say some things never change.

> Ok and make sure mine has extra whipped cream!

> Always do.

Putting my phone back in my pocket, I close my eyes and take a deep breath.

Keep focused, Ada. You only have so much time here, let's make it distraction-free.

I guess it's a good thing I did my research on estate sales, otherwise this could go terribly wrong in a hurry. How hard could it be anyway?

As far as I am concerned, there are only five steps I need to complete, and the Type A Planner in me is eager to start crossing them off my list.

1. Decide what Noah and I want to keep, donate, or sell.
2. Coordinate move outs prior to estate sale.
3. Provide tags with extra information on items around the house.
4. Remove all our personal items.
5. Clear out.

Like I said, piece of cake. If I can manage clients back in New York, then this should be no problem. Having put away my list, I look up at the house where I grew up and make my way to the front door. As I stare down at the doorknob, my hand trembles with nerves and anxiety.

Ada, it's just a house. Move those feet.

When the doorway opens, my body stills. A knot forms in my throat as I whisper, "What is this?"

Taking a moment to recognize that what I am seeing is the home I grew up in, I can't help but be awestruck at my surroundings, as if I was teleported to a brand new house. It's absolutely beautiful, but it doesn't even resemble my childhood home.

First the exterior, now the interior? Who helped her renovate the house? How did she afford these types of renovations?

My fists tighten up and bite into my palms. When did she have time to do these renovations?

Growing up, I always envisioned a home like this, complete with dark hardwood floors, a wide staircase that leads to our rooms, and bright tan walls covered with family pictures.

However, there were no hardwood floors, but rather stained carpet, walls that needed fresh painting, a staircase that had not been completed, and no family photos, since who needs them when you don't actually have a family?

Taking a deep breath, I walk over to the pictures. Letting my fingers brush against the wall, I feel the three large portraits that line the walls. I chuckle when I see the single portrait of Noah with his head thrown back, laughing mid-photo.

Classic Noah.

Then there is a photo of me from high school. I can't help but let my fingers linger on my smiling face.

That smile. It was real.

When did she have the time to blow these up?

Why couldn't we have these hung up when I was living here?

Why did everything change after I left Blue Haven?

I move to the last portrait. Our family one.

A sense of longing, deep and forbidden, takes over. The kind of longing I haven't allowed myself to feel for years. Even though it was from when Noah and I were babies, I can't help but see a *real* family.

A functional one.

Where was *that* family when I needed it?

Mom and Dad were lying down in the grass, looking at one another, as if they had never fought a day in their lives. Noah and I were sitting on top of them, laughing loudly, as if we had just been tickled.

Who even took this photo and why don't I remember it?

Keep moving, Ada, you need this. You need closure.

Inhaling deeply, I rub my temples in order to release some tension, knowing I need closure but also some relief from the emotional turmoil. When I turn toward the kitchen to get a glass of water, I swing an open cabinet door, knowing it's the drinkware, but I only see bowls.

The stainless steel mixing bowl my grandmother left is hanging on the inside of the door and reflects my distorted reflection. Glad some things haven't changed. I take the bowl and clasp it to my chest as I close my eyes. My memory of this bowl brings back fond memories of Mom and I dancing around the kitchen as we baked brownies. I can almost hear the sound of our spoons scraping the last bits of batter from the bowl as we licked it clean.

"I thought you might be here." A deep voice has my eyes opening as I drop the bowl, causing it to clatter.

My hip hits the granite countertop and I leap back from the jab. I flinch as I grab my side in an attempt to stop the pain. "Ouch. Jesus!"

"Sorry," Lincoln says, smiling. "I debated whether to knock before entering, but I remembered I've been here so many times I just walked right in." He shrugs, "Hope that's okay?"

Nodding my head, I reach down and grab the bowl just as a slobber coats my cheek.

What the hell?

The moment I look up, I am struck by a jolt to the kitchen ground. Crossing my forearms in front of me, I attempt to defend myself from the attacker.

"Ginger, down girl, I told you to wait in the bronco." In addition to the slobbering, I am now being assaulted by full-fledged licks.

With a sharp tone, Lincoln snaps his fingers and commands, "Ginger, heal now!"

After returning to her rightful owner, the dog finally frees me, only to take a seat by Lincoln's feet. As I attempt to get myself up, Lincoln beats me to it by sprinting toward me to help me stand. I wave him off, knowing full well I can get myself up, but he remains to be his persistent self.

I sigh heavily and grab his outstretched hand, exuding a tingling sensation throughout my body. I flinch, forcing his hand to tighten around my own.

Did he feel that? *Focus, Ada, it is nothing more than a hand.*

But really, is it just a hand? Won't hurt to take a quick peek. Right?

Okay, yep, the man had some major muscles.

I know what you are thinking, it's just a hand, Ada. But those fingers are capable of a great deal of pleasure and power. Just seeing them sends shivers throughout my body.

Don't forget, that hand had no problem waving goodbye to you.

My eyes travel up right to his ocean blue eyes; they burn with intensity. My lips part, and suddenly, I am taken back to a time where those eyes did strange things to my belly. One glance from him would melt the panties right off any girl, making them feel cherished.

I should know, I was one of those girls. He cherished me, and he was a wonderful boyfriend, but I was just too young and naive to handle any obstacles that came our way.

Standing up, Ginger, the golden retriever, runs toward me, jumping as her paws land on my chest. I rub behind her ears as I say, "You love attention, don't you, girl?"

It was as if a claw had been inserted into my chest as I held Ginger, the type of dog breed Lincoln and I had once discussed getting together. I have always loved dogs, but have avoided getting one because it simply reminded me of *him.*

"Ginger, girl, that's enough." Lincoln pulls Ginger away from me, letting out a chuckle. "Ada, sorry." He points down at my white pants that are splattered with dirty paw prints. "She gets a little too excited when she meets new people."

In a slightly shaky voice, I ask, "What are you doing here?"

"I wanted to talk to you and figured you might be here." As he moves from one foot to another, he rubs his neck. "Ada, when I saw you at Scoops for Life and at your mother's funeral, those weren't my finest hours. I didn't know what to say or what to do. I sort of just froze up."

Yeah, I think we both did.

He moves closer toward me by the island counter in the middle of the kitchen; Ginger follows and lies beside his feet. He crosses his legs and leans his hip on the counter, his casual posture at odds with the apprehension in his eyes.

Finally having the courage to speak my mind, I blurt out, "I appreciate that you have come here, but honestly, you do not have to pretend to care. We have not seen each other in years, and defending your actions is unnecessary. It was a shock to us both."

Moving from the island, he stands up straight, clearly flustered as he scrapes a hand through his thick, golden brown hair. "No, Ada. I mean, yes, but also—" Blowing out a frustrated sigh, he starts to pace as he points at me and says, "You look great, Ada."

I chuckle at how tongue tied he is in this situation. It's not funny but rather awkward because we don't know how to act around each other anymore.

Smiling, I say, "Thank you, Lincoln."

A tight smile is returned to me as he walks toward the kitchen windows, right above the white ceramic sink. His hands rest on the side of the sink as his head falls forward. "Ada, I cared about you. We were friends." Looking at his feet, he says, "I'm sorry."

"For what, exactly? We haven't seen each other for years; what could possibly be your reason for being sorry?"

He lifts a shoulder as he turns around to face me. "Your mom; when I had discovered that she had passed away, I should have called you and informed you of her passing. I should have asked you if you were okay and checked in with you. I am aware that given our history, it would have been the last thing you expected, but I would at least have known you were okay."

I am okay.

I roll my eyes and I step forward, directly in front of him. "I'm fine, and I appreciate your apology, but I did not need your call about my mother's death. Coming for you wouldn't have made a difference. We both know you felt that way because you wanted to ease your guilt about our history, not the history of my mother and I."

Inching closer to me, he sighs, "You're right, and I'm sorry. I really just wanted to know if you were okay? I saw you at the funeral and needed to know."

I am okay.

"I am getting there." And I guess I am. Day by day, little by little, I will get through this and find my way through it, just like I do with everything else in my life.

"That's great to hear, Ada. I know you are only in town for a short time, and I don't want things to become awkward."

"You are right. I will only be here temporarily, but don't worry about it. It was a surprise to both of us to see each other after so many years."

In a muttering tone, Lincoln pats Ginger as he says, "It was, but this is a small town, so we're bound to see each other at some point in time."

"Well, that's a shame," I say while shrugging.

Standing straighter, he raises one eyebrow and asks, "Oh yeah, why's that?"

I may only be here for a little while, but I know that chances of us running into each other are pretty high. So I am hoping that maybe if we can joke with each other, we'll find a way onto neutral ground while I am back in Blue Haven.

Grinning at him, I say, "Well, you were much more charming back then."

Lincoln lets out a deep, rich laugh, making me feel it all the way down to my toes. "You were also much sweeter in the past."

"You were smarter than to say something like that."

He shrugs, giving me a wink. "I was also a seventeen-year-old boy trying to get into your pants."

"Which you did," I reminded him.

"Oftentimes."

I roll my eyes. "Yeah, and if I can remember correctly, you were not—"

"Don't you dare say it, Ada Collins!" He chuckles as he moves closer to me, holding his hands up in surrender. "In my defense, I was only seventeen, as were you, and were both a little terrible."

I hold back a snicker, as I know it was both of us that were bad at it. God, we were just two teenagers fumbling, watching shows to learn what to do, even though it didn't help us out much.

"Yeah, we were, but it helped that we loved each other."

Shit. Did I just say that?

Out loud?

For him to hear?

Lincoln's body becomes rigid, as does mine. Giving me a hard smile, he says, "Yeah, we did love each other, but then you left without a word."

Alrighty then, so that's how it's going to be.

My gaze moves down to my hands and I begin to pick at my nail cuticles. How do you even respond to something like that? It almost sounds like he cared. It almost sounds like he didn't want me to leave Blue

Haven. While I understand, ultimately I am the one suffering. No matter how much time has passed, there is still no closure between us.

Lincoln looks over at me. "I'm sorry, I shouldn't have said that."

My teeth grind together as I glance over at Lincoln. "No, Lincoln. I think you did. You still haven't moved on from your past, and it's clear as day."

Briefly looking down at his feet, looking uncomfortable, he mutters, "Right, okay, well, maybe I should go."

Shit, that didn't sound great.

He starts to move, but before he can, I grab his arm. "Wait, I'm sorry. That came out wrong."

As he shakes his head, he says in a more stern voice, "Ada, it came out as it should have. The truth stings, and I understand that we are grown adults, but there are some memories that are never easy to let go of. No matter how long it has been."

Despite knowing he is right, I choose to ignore my past memories, the good as well as the bad, because it has allowed me to get this far in life.

Independent.

Bold.

Prosperous.

One of the top female attorneys in New York.

Without distractions, including those from my past, none of this would have been possible.

"Come on, Ginger. It's time to leave," he whistles.

There is a sense of familiarity in the air as Ginger flies from the living room across the hardwood floors into the kitchen, following Lincoln into the entryway. Maybe it is my imagination, but it almost appears that she knows this space.. a little too well.

Has she been here before?

Eyeing them as they make their way to the door, I lean my head against the staircase railing. Lincoln glances over his shoulder and gives me a familiar smile that makes a thousand needles to the heart seem far less painful than what he is experiencing.

Ada, what did you just do?

Chapter Twelve

Lincoln

Today is one of those days I should have stayed in bed, but I didn't. Not only did I get woken up at the crack of dawn to go to work on a Saturday, but I found out that our financial analysis was experiencing difficulties; therefore, I got to not only stay and resolve that issue, but I also got to remain there until exactly the moment my next shift started at my other job, 8:00 pm.

It has been a tough couple of days, and seeing Ada the other day at her house only added to it. Everything suddenly feels like it is spiraling down and going completely to shit. Seeing her has brought up some unwanted emotions that I am not quite ready to confront.

The moment I open the door to the Safe Harbor, I am overcome by a wave of familiarity. Nothing unusual; same place, same day, same time. I come here voluntarily nearly every weekend to help out when needed. It is simply another way to pass the time.

The aroma of cigarette smoke hits me immediately. The room is dimly lit, and I recognize Josh, the main bartender, at the polished oak bar countertop, surrounded by alcohol bottles. In response to his wave, I tilt my head to say hello and walk toward the kitchen.

I have a feeling tonight's going to be a good one due to the number of patrons occupying the tables and booths tonight. They're laughing with friends, some hitting on strangers, and others are watching TV, staring into their drinks.

My heart longs for helping out, but I am just not feeling it tonight. Ada shows up in Blue Haven for her mother's funeral, after all this time, and just acts as if our past has never really mattered to her. It is difficult for me to comprehend how one can simply let go of a past as great as ours. It has taken me years to recover from her, but seeing her not only once, but fucking three times, has my heart racing and my emotions strained.

As I attempt to open the silver and black kitchen doors, I almost run into Anna, our youngest server. She is wearing a black shirt with the bar's logo on it and her blonde hair in pigtails, making her appear younger than she is. Despite only being nineteen years old, Anna is one of the sweetest employees at Safe Harbor. I hold the door open politely.

With a shy smile, she turns her head over her shoulder and says, "Thank you, Lincoln."

I give her a wink. "No problem, oh and Anna?" She glances back at me as she holds a tray of drinks. "If you need help tonight, let me know." She nods along to my words as she proceeds back to her assigned tables.

Pulling off my suit jacket, I start to undo my white undershirt, replacing it with my bar shirt. I move my suit into my locker and grab the clean glass tumblers from the dishwasher and place each one on a serving tray. Taking the tray, I move toward the front of the bar, where I spot a particular individual sitting on a wooden stool.

The grin he is strutting stretches from ear to ear as he picks up his scotch and takes a drink. While placing the glass tumblers on the shelf near the row of alcohol bottles, I ask, "What are you doing here, Garrett?"

Turning around, I catch him tilting his head to the right. There is a middle-aged woman standing across the room, chewing on her bottom lip, eyeing me with interest. She has a nice shapely figure with ruby-red hair hanging at her shoulders, and I can tell from just one glimpse that she wants all the attention on her tonight.

Smooth, Garrett. This is the last thing I want to focus on.

After forcing a quick smile on my lips, I abruptly return my attention to Garrett. "What are you doing here?" I ask sternly, my eyes piercing his.

He takes another sip of his scotch and shrugs his shoulders. "I needed a break from the ongoing daddy duties. Man, just wait until you become a father. You will be running to my door even more than you do now."

I roll my eyes. *Okay, sure, since fatherhood is knocking at my door.*

The last time I even thought about my future, let alone having kids or being a father figure, was when I was with Ada. We had everything mapped out: a house in Blue Haven, her own law firm, and myself teaching at the local college, Valley View University.

Sighing, I rest my elbows on the bar counter,

rubbing my head with my hands. Garrett squeezes my shoulder tightly. Looking up, his expression softens. "Plus, I know you have had a rough few days."

He can say that again.

"Yeah, it really has been."

"Lay it on me," he says, raising his hands beside him. "I am here for a couple hours, so you might as well make use of it."

Chuckling, I run my hand through my hair. "Man, I don't even know where to begin or how to express how I feel about all of this," I say, while taking a deep breath.

Putting his scotch on the counter, he leans forward. "Okay, well, what do you even mean by 'all of this'?"

"Ada, her return to Blue Haven, her mother's funeral. It's all very confusing. Not to mention, our encounter at her house made things even more awkward and tense between us. I feel like any time I'm around her, I'm on pins and needles."

His eyebrows furrow as he holds his hands up. "Wait, when did you see her at her house? I thought you had seen her only twice? At Scoops for Life and then her mother's funeral?" he inquires.

Taking a seat, I notice the same redheaded woman I did just a moment ago. She gives a cheeky smile at Garrett.

The bastard looks at her, giving her his famous Godson smile as he wiggles his left ring finger, displaying his wedding band.

Immediately her lips turn down into a scowl as she whispers under her breath, "Asshole."

Trying to hold back my laugh, I bite my bottom lip. He faces toward me with a smug look. Oh, he's definitely enjoyed this. Although he's a taken man, the dude still loves getting hit on; something about how it makes him feel like he's still got it.

Like he needs his ego boosted anymore.

As soon as I finish making the vodka water, I hand it over to the woman. She responds with a loud huff, as if I was the one she was annoyed with in the first place, despite the fact that I had done nothing at all.

Swatting me with the bar towel, Garrett pulls my attention back to him. He holds his scotch glass up in the air, wanting a refill. "Alright, man, tell me what happened with Ada at her house."

I sigh as I grab his glass to make him another drink. "So, I saw Ada at Scoops for Life. We were just getting there when she was leaving, so we caught a glance at one another. Anyway, you know how the funeral went with her running away from me. Then I saw her at her mother's house the other day. I figured she might be there, but I also wanted to check on the house."

"Does she know that you helped her mother renovate the house?"

My head shakes. "No, she is not even aware that her mother and I had a functioning relationship. Part of me isn't even sure if I want her to know. From her point of view, her mother and her had a shit relationship, and here I was having a normal one with the person who was supposed to support, take care, and love her. Ada's childhood was void of such things, and I think if she realized that I had a friendship with her mother, and assisted her in repairing the house, she would be blazing mad."

Stretching his arms behind him, he says, "I mean,

yeah, I get it; however, she was also the one who just up and left everyone, as if they did not exist. What was she thinking would happen? Everyone would stop living? That's bullshit, because we all moved on, or at least I thought everyone did." He flashes an eyebrow at me.

I shake my head. "Yeah, yeah. I hear you."

"Hey Lincoln!" I hear someone say softly. I look to the corner of the bar and Anastasia and Levi, my oldest sister and her husband, are taking seats next to Garrett.

"Hey, what are you doing here?"

A sigh escapes Levi's lips as he rubs the growing belly of my sister and says, "Well, apparently, the baby here wants some greasy food, but I think it's your sister's doing and her being okay with blaming the baby."

Laughing, she nudges him in the ribs and says, "Hey, you said you wanted some fried food as well. After all, it is Saturday, so we can enjoy some bar food together."

Currently, Anastasia is in the second trimester of her first pregnancy and is doing well. Her and Levi's journey has been a long one, as they struggled with a miscarriage two years ago and went through IVF in the past year.

In a chuckle, he asks, "Are you saying I can have some beer as well?"

"Are you on a healthy diet now, Levi?" Garrett asks, shock registering across his face.

He jerks his head at my sister and asks, "Hmm, why don't you tell him what it is that I am doing, dear?"

In spite of the red tint on her cheeks, she shrugs nonchalantly and says, "He eats and drinks what baby and I eat. It's only fair that he goes through what I do."

Garrett's eyes widen as he utters, "Dude, why would you ever agree to such a thing?"

My lips press together to contain a laugh; Garrett wouldn't last in Levi's shoes for a day. Dude pretty much eats cereal for breakfast every day, and no, not the healthy kind.

Mayra's pregnancy was completely different from Anastasia. Garrett and her weren't even actively trying. As I remember, one day at Little League practice, he threw me a baseball saying, *"You're going to be an uncle."* Followed up with him saying, *"Well, you know, not the actual uncle, but I would be cool if it called you Uncle Lincoln."* That day is still vividly etched in my memory. I was so happy for them both, but I also felt unworthy of any good that might come my way.

Having cleared his throat, Levi's features soften as he stares down at my sister with a smile on both their faces. I blink away, feeling a sharpness in my chest.

Do I want what they have?

Would I even be a good husband? A decent father?

I know all too well what it is like to have a bad father. As the only son in the family, I was destined to do and say what my father wanted. He controlled everything about my life until I grew some balls and became frustrated with him. Although there is still some resentment between us, we have tried to maintain civility so that I can work at his firm.

"Yes, I follow her rules, but if it means keeping this little nugget safe and healthy until it is born, I will continue to do so."

"Order 12." I hear a ding from the kitchen window.

Getting up from her stool, Anastasia gets the food ready for them to go.

Garrett pats Levi's shoulder. "Yeah, okay, you got me

there. Your situation is different, and if I was in your guys' shoes, I would do the same thing."

I roll my eyes; he's so full of shit, and Mayra wouldn't make him do that.

As I proceed to the register to process a bar customer's tab, Anastasia approaches me. "Have you talked to Mom?"

My brows narrow. "No. Remember, you do that for me, so I don't have to."

"Sure. Sure. Anyway, she is hosting a family dinner this week, and I was not sure if you were aware of it, but now that you are, I look forward to seeing you there."

Even the mention of my mother makes me tense up. "What makes you think that I will show up?" I ask, crossing my arms over my chest.

She chuckles at my response as she grabs her bag of food. "Because you always do."

She's right about that. No matter what my relationship with my parents is, I'll still show up to make sure we stay civil. My parents and I have gone through a lot in the past and that's where it should stay. It doesn't hurt any less in the present day, but I'd rather move forward and be able to function as a family.

I close the register and turn to look at her. "I will make you a deal." She gives me a questioning glare. "I'll come over and behave at dinner if you make a home-made meal that will feed a dozen crazy boys. I volunteered to help with the Little League banquet, and I chose to do the dinner. It's during our end-of-season game so I want to put my focus on the team, not the food, and we all know you make a great tater tot casserole."

She pauses, so I clasp my hands under my chin and repeat "please."

In response to my request, she moves in as close as her belly allows. She nods as she extends her hand for a handshake and states, "Deal, but I get to choose the food option. I have a serious dislike of tater tots right now, and I cannot stomach even being close to them."

Shaking her hand, I chuckle. "All right, whatever you prepare, Anastasia, I am sure it will be delicious." I wave my hand to shoo her out of the bar. "Now go rest and take care of my niece or nephew."

With a smile on her face, she shakes her head side to side.

"You heard the man. Let's go, babe." Levi puts his arm around her shoulder as he grabs the bag of food from her.

Returning to Garrett, I see an older man chatting with him. "Hey, Lincoln! How are you? I heard that Mrs. Collins passed away. What a tragedy," he says wistfully.

Feeling completely exhausted regarding Mrs. Collins, I rub the back of my neck to release some tightness. "Yeah, it's unfortunate, but I am sure she is in a better place now."

"Yeah, that's true."

Getting up from his bar stool, he strikes the countertop with his palm. "Well, boys, I'd better get home before the Mrs. has me by my own two balls."

Garrett and I look at each other as we laugh. "It was nice to see you, Mr. Donovan."

Of course, *Mr. Dononvan*, an old client of ours. I knew he looked familiar. People come and go in this bar, and in Blue Haven, that sometimes I tend to forget.

"What a nutcase. I cannot believe the man is still alive and moving around."

I shake my head in response to Garrett's comment. In an attempt to suggest that he would like another scotch, he shakes the glass in front of him.

While I grab the bottle of Aberlour behind me, I hear him ask, "Now where were we? Oh, that's right, you were about to tell me the shit that went down between you and Ada."

Turning to give him his drink, I shrug my shoulders. "I mean, I don't have much to say other than she still hates me. We had a moment before Ginger interrupted it, and Ada flipped a switch, basically begging me to leave." I let out a trembling breath. "Shit, man. It was devastating watching her leave all those years ago, but it's almost worse, gut-wrenching, for her to come back here pretending nothing ever happened between us."

Garrett opens his mouth, but then stops short of saying anything.

"Man, just say it."

His voice changes as he shifts in his seat. "You already know she left Blue Haven for an unknown reason and you both still haven't found closure on either side of the relationship. From my point of view, it seems as though there needs to be some sort of closure, at least on yours."

That was the last thing I expected him to say.

Taking one last sip of his drink, he rises from his stool and grabs his jacket. "Linc, dude, how many rela-tionships, let alone dates, have you had since Ada? You cannot move forward into a healthy and stable relation-ship until you get closure. Although I understand she was returning to Blue Haven for her mother's funeral, I think you need to take advantage of this opportunity to try and reconcile things with her as best you can."

Nodding in response to him, he waves goodbye, leaving me to reflect on what he said.

I know he's right, but what if she doesn't want closure?

Chapter Thirteen ♡

Ada

My hand moves slowly over the journal's cover, wiping away dust as I place it on my lap. It has been two days since I returned to my childhood home; honestly, the last thing I wanted to do. I could handle the possibility of running into Lincoln, but packing up the most painful memories of my childhood was a different story.

With a heavy sigh, I release the anxiety running through me as I hover over the date, January 4th, 2010. I lift it with courage, ready to face this challenge. A part of me wishes I could relive the memories, but all I can do is reminisce about the good times I once enjoyed.

My sweaty palms rub against my legs as I pace around the attic, feeling overwhelmed. I close the journal and drop it to the ground, uncertain of whether I am strong enough to do this. This is the journal I kept not only to reread my favorite past memories, but it also reveals a side of me when I was at my most raw and vulnerable; only one person had the opportunity to experience that.

Ada, it's just a journal, nothing more. A half-hearted laugh escapes me.

But it isn't just a journal. These pages contain a rollercoaster ride of childhood memories. I recall my first date with Lincoln, my father's leaving, working at Scoops for Life with Lexie, and my favorite Sunday lake tradition with my mother and Noah. But I also remember my mother's alcoholism, anger, and hurt interspersed with all of the good memories.

Each week, I would reread the entries to be reminded of her love, but right now, I am just over-whelmed by the reminders. In spite of the creaking floorboards underneath my feet, I try to stay focused on something else as opposed to my journal. Growing up, our attic was a safe haven for me sometimes. Whether it was to hide from my mom's emotional instability, my parents' arguments, or just to think alone.

A thick layer of dust fills the room; cobwebs hang from the exposed wooden beams and old antiques, boxes, and toys are covered in white sheets. It almost appears like nothing has changed since I last stepped inside this room.

While the silence surrounding me is utterly deadly, I suddenly find myself standing in front of the Victorian bay windows; a sense of unease in my veins. As I stare out the leaf-shaped windows, I take in the rays of light that pierce through them. Maple trees line our driveway with bright yellow, orange, and fiery red leaves, which cling to their spots on the trees until they fall to the ground.

My stomach churns with excitement viewing the fall

foliage and experiencing the sensation of it again. It's not like New York, where I would have to find a park or even an open bench in order to observe the true colors of fall.

Inhaling deeply, iiiiin one, two, three, and ooutt one, two, three, my breathing slows as I close my eyes.

"Ada, why do you look so panicked?"

I look over at Lexie. "I am not panicked as such, but much more nervous." I start to bite my nails. In the midst of the bright stadium lights, the cool fall weather, and the aroma of cinnamon and apple cider, my nerves start to kick into overdrive. I place my hands beneath my thighs and bounce my legs. "Scouts from all over watch this game. Lincoln's future—our future—hangs in the balance. He wants to go to Hudson University, as do I, and the only way we can go together is with a scholarship."

Lexie's brows draw together in question.

"Well, you know Lincoln's parents are not the biggest fans of us being together, so what will their reactions be when Lincoln tells them he has chosen Hudson University over Duke or UNC, their decisions?"

A sympathetic smile appears on her face.

"Exactly, they'll have a fit and demand he attend the same school as Mr. St. James. His parents' money would never be touched by this scholarship, which would give Lincoln freedom and a full ride to Hudson University."

Lexie looks over carefully, knowing Lincoln and I's future always seems to be a sensitive topic. Grabbing my knee, Lexie says, "Ada, I fully understand your perspective, but perhaps you should allow your two futures to unfold naturally."

Looking more confused than ever, she sighs, "We are only seventeen, and you two are so in love that nothing else matters around you. People say things, people do things, and I feel that you would sacrifice everything for Lincoln."

Yes, I would do anything to be with him, even if it meant dropping everything else.

"Touch Down, Number 15, Lincoln St. James."

Lexie and I turn our heads to the field. Lincoln points his finger at me as the crowd chants, "Lincoln, Lincoln, Lincoln." Smiling at him, a happy hum starts in my chest realizing he chose me to take credit for his touchdown.

He certainly knows how to make a girl feel special.

It takes an instant for my heart to lurch when I see Mrs. St. James frown and press her lips together. Two glaring eyes stare at me intently.

Taking my forearm, Lexie releases my heavy gaze from Mrs. St. James and pulls me to stand. "Come on, Ada, we don't have to sit here and take her scrutiny. Let's just finish the game elsewhere."

Despite my apprehension, I walk out of the stands with Lexie, feeling uneasy with every step.

"How long have you been waiting for me?" Lincoln takes large steps toward me until he lifts me off the ground. When he wraps his arms around me, my body instantly becomes warm from head to toe. "You must be cold, Ada."

I playfully tug on his ear while whispering, "Not too long; it's a good thing you're worth freezing for." He pulls away just slightly and looks me over. He swipes his thumb under my eyes, catching tears and probably no shortage of mascara, which I tried my best to remove earlier. I didn't want him to think anything was wrong, let alone his mother. Not only because I know this will cause problems with his relationship with her, but also because I fear it will create tension between us.

When it comes to Lincoln's family, I am hopeful he will choose me over them, but there are days when I doubt that is possible due to his parents' hatred of me without cause, as well as the fact that his future is already established. Graduate from a private university in North Carolina, major in accounting and minor in business, have him take over his father's business one day. The first time Lincoln told me this, I laughed in his face. At first, I thought he was kidding, but his facial expressions indicated otherwise.

Lincoln lifts my chin, staring down at me. I sigh heavily; lying to him won't work. "Yes, I was crying, and yes, it had to do with your mother, but only because she treats me like garbage. In her mind, I am just the girl on the side of town with an alcoholic mother. How do you think that makes me feel? How can I have a future mother-in-law like that?"

In a flash, his eyes sparkle and he smirks.

"Did I say something funny?"

"You want to get married to me?"

I smile and playfully push his shoulder. "Yeah, you big goof, why else would I put up with you?"

As his stare rests on me for a moment, I am certain that I know what's about to happen: tickles.

Due to the fact that I am ticklish, he believes whenever I joke with him, he can just take advantage of it. I grab his arm and shove him back slightly, saying, "Don't you dare start!"

While the wind slaps me from all sides, I wrap my hands around my arms and rub them to warm myself up. The weather is getting colder; the leaves are falling to the ground, and the temperature is dropping.

Taking my hands and pushing them down to my side, he moves closer to me. "Fine, you're in luck, but this time only."

With a wink, he kisses the top of my head, making me close my eyes as I inhale his fresh post game smell.

Removing his letterman jacket, he waits for me to place both arms in, and then he gives me a tight hug. "Come on, hop in the bronco, let's go meet everyone at Scoops for Life."

"Yo, Adaaaa! AAADDDAAA. Come back to planet earth, Ada."

Blinking several times, I feel wetness in my eyes.

Shit, was I crying? Ada, it was only a flashback.

Peeking behind me, I see a blurry statue as I brush away my tears.

"Ada, what is wrong? What happened? I called your name almost a million times, clearly you were spacing out," Noah asks as he approaches me.

In an effort to clear my vision, I wipe my eyes again and look out of the attic window. I shrug my shoulders. "Frankly, Noah, being back in Blue Haven, at our childhood home, mom's funeral; every day has been a roller coaster of emotions that seems to never end."

It's one thing to relive happy memories, and another thing to have gut-wrenching moments that make me want to return to New York all together.

Noah's features soften, understanding what I'm saying. He may not have experienced the same things I did, but that doesn't mean he can't relate to the struggles I face day in and day out. Despite our age difference, Noah has always been very attentive and supportive.

"I understand, Ada, and I will not pretend to know how you feel or what you are going through, but I know one thing," Noah says as we stand at the top of the attic stairs. His tone changes to a more serious one as he points at me. "I do not know any other individual who is stronger than you. You endured the crap this town threw at you, the shit you were dealt with Mom, and don't even get me started on what Mrs. St. James did to you."

The tears begin to flow again. I nod my head as he continues to speak, "It was your past that helped you become who you are today, even though it was horrible. You became more resilient, stronger, and more independent as a result. It is the people around you who are unable to see that. Given your past, any other person I know would not have stepped back into Blue Haven. They would have said screw the funeral."

A sense of calm permeates my body as I take in Noah's words. How does he always find the right words? How can he always put me at ease?

"While everything has gone against you, Ada, you continue to be a saint, helping your brother as usual. Honestly, I believe one good thing arose from Mom's funeral: we have the opportunity to reunite and relive some of our fond memories. Like this," he holds up a huge seashell and asks, "Remember this gem? We found it on the first day Mom took us to the beach?"

When I take the piece from him, my eyebrows raise in surprise. "Where did you find this?" It is a sandy clear color, with curved lines that still look exactly the same as when we took it from Hope Bay Beach all those years ago.

"I discovered it in a box when I was going through Mom's room downstairs."

"Hey, I was looking at that!" I say as he takes it back.

Grabbing his forearm, I jump to grasp it again as he holds it above his head. The little shit is taller than me *today*. I wore yoga pants with white Nike shoes, which gave me no additional height above him. Taking a deep breath, my eyes narrow at him. I sigh in exasperation. "Okay, okay, I give up."

He lifts his brow, basically asking me, 'Are you sure you are done, because the Ada Collins I know loves a challenge and wouldn't give up so easily.'

"What do you say we blow this popsicle stand and head over to the beach? I think we both could benefit from some Vitamin D, ice cream, and a new view."

He's right.

My body needs a change of scenery right about now; having been packing almost all day has left me extremely exhausted. With the seashell in my hand, I run for the stairs with a freeing laugh escaping my lips.

He chases me down the stairs as I yell back, "Did you just say let's blow this popsicle stand?"

He shrugs. "What's the big deal? A girl in my class always uses it before dismissal. What do you think? Should I use it on my next date?"

I let out a snort as I say, "You should refrain from using that on any date, bubba, if you ever plan on having a wife or girlfriend."

Putting his finger on his chin, considering for a moment, he says, "Yeah, I think you are probably right."

When I am not looking, he grabs the shell from me and runs for the front door. "Asshole." I chuckle and shake my head.

Chapter fourteen ♡

Lincoln

My anxiety increases as I approach my childhood home. This house holds a kaleidoscope of memories, both good and bad. I remember watching the stars on my roof at night with my sisters, having my best friends come over for pool parties, or even sneaking Ada over when my parents attended charity events.

As I step toward the black brick house on a ridge overlooking the Appalachian Mountains, my two feet come to a halt amongst the most gorgeous foliage I have ever seen. A memorable aspect of this house is its tranquility. The heavily wooded driveway of our home was my favorite place to walk whenever I felt stressed, when my parents argued, or whenever I needed to escape for a few minutes.

Opening the sturdy wooden doors, my mother is already waiting for me by the curved oak staircase.

Moving toward me, I tense up as she pulls me in for a hug. "It is good to see you. Your father and I haven't seen you for quite some time. Let's not make that a habit, shall we?"

My mother has short dark brown hair and blue eyes. On the outside, she appears to be a beautiful, strong, intelligent, and fierce woman. However, on the inside, my mother craves attention, control, and power. Having a mother who was always sarcastic, found fault with me, and preferred events over me, was rather depressing, but in the end, it molded me into the person I am today—responsible, loyal, and ambitious.

I roll my eyes and force out, "I miss you, too."

She narrows her eyes and walks away, saying, "Oh, and don't forget to take off your shoes, dear. We just had Martha deep clean our floors today. I would hate to see any dirt accumulate before your siblings arrive."

There may be a day when I will see my parents as kind, loving individuals who do not value material possessions over everything else. However, today is not the day. I peer in my peripheral vision as I remove my boots and notice an enormous belly.

"I was worried you would not make it, but I am so glad you are here. Mother is fretting over everything, including my outfit." Anastasia huffs as she points at her creamy white sweater dress. "Fendi has just released its autumn collection, and Levi said I looked ravishing."

While spinning in a circle, she asks, "Is it too showy? Do I look fat?"

I grasp her by the shoulders and kiss her on the temple. Smiling, I say, "You look as stunning as ever, but who cares if you get fat? You are growing me a future MLB nephew in that belly."

Hitting me upside the head, she says, "It's a girl, Lincoln." She grabs my arm and drags me to the dining room, where Levi sits and looks at her as if to say, 'Help me.'

Kissing me quickly on the cheek, she mouths to him, "Sorry, I'm coming."

"Anastasia, I saw that," my mother states in a clipped manner.

With a tight smile, she says, "Sorry, Mother Dearest."

Glancing at my mother, she's wearing a new outfit, dripping with diamonds and labels. She ignores my father's indiscretions, so he gives her everything she wants. Therefore, she trickles over the ridiculous gifts he returns with on every so-called 'business trip' he makes, proving to her friends that their marriage is an amazing one, while me and my siblings watch in dismay.

In my opinion, the whole thing is utter bullshit.

"Family, Family, what's up my family?"

My gaze is drawn to the glass doors that open into our formal dining room; I see Jewels. Holding back a laugh, I shake my head. Classic Jewels to arrive late as well as appearing to be tipsy. I mean, I am not blaming her for doing so; there are times when I would like to be drunk as a fucking skunk when attending these so-called 'family dinners'.

As Jewels walks toward me, she whispers, "What's the state of things tonight with dear ol' Mom? Happy, Sad, Drunk?"

"Jewels, as a St. James, I expect you to behave better and to not come into our home looking like that." Her tone conveys her disgust as she points to Jewels' yoga pants and bright pink crop top.

Ladies and gentlemen, here is Sheryl St. James belittling one of her children the minute they walk through the door, and she wonders why no child of hers has interest in attending family dinners.

In response, Jewels walks over to our father and says, "Well, Mother, this is what the cool kids are wearing today, and I wanted to wear it too. You will have to deal with what I wear to our weekly dinners if you want me to attend."

"Hello Daddy," she says, kissing him on the cheek. "How was your business trip?"

She rubs her chin, thinking for a moment.

With a chuckle, I shake my head, knowing exactly what she will say next. Jewels may just be the most outspoken person I've ever met. "Where was it? Florida? California? Oh wait, I remember, it was Chicago."

A firm smile appears on his face as he replies, "Hello too, baby girl! Indeed, I was in Chicago, as I was checking things out for our employee trip there in a few weeks. Isn't that right, Lincoln?" He raises an eyebrow, looking for confirmation.

In agreement, I nod and ask Jewels, "Where is Faye?"

She shrugs her shoulders right as Faye takes her seat next to Anastasia.

"Sorry, I'm late. It's hard to get here on time because of traffic." Faye recently relocated to Charlotte for work reasons, which is over an hour from Blue Haven. She is the middle sister, and probably the sweetest and most ambitious one of us all. Anastasia is the motherly one, Faye is the centered one, and of course, Jewels is the youthful and playful one. I love every single one of my sisters in their individual ways.

"Perhaps moving away from Blue Haven wasn't the best move," my mother whispers under her breath. She clicks her fingers, getting our family butler, Jonathan's, attention. "The usual, please, Jonathan. Would anyone else like a beverage?" she asks.

In a wink to him, Jewels says, "I will take a shot or two, Johnny."

"Good try, Jewels. You are not of legal drinking age yet," my mother remarks.

In a voice that only I can hear, Jewels says, "That's what you think."

A smile spreads across my face as I nudge her shoulder. "So, how's college?"

"It's fine," she shrugs, taking an olive and tossing it into her mouth. My eyebrows lift as she takes a hold of my forearm, her eyes gleaming. "Okay, that's a lie; it's amazing! I'm away from our parents, this house; I get to sleep in most days, I party on weekends, and I can do whatever the hell I want. Normally, I dread this day of the week, but ah-mazing sex from college boys makes up for it."

"Really? That is something I didn't need to hear come from my little sister's mouth." I scrunch my nose up in disgust.

Snorting, she pops another olive into her mouth, "Hey, you asked a question, and I answered it."

In a playful gesture, I nudge her in the shoulder and say, "Not exactly the answer I was looking for." I take a sip of my beer and just as I am about to dig into my salad, I hear my mother.

"Lincoln, have you finally put an end to assisting the helpers?"

Uh, what? What the hell is she talking about?

My gaze focuses on her, narrowing my eyes. "What does that mean?" I ask.

She shrugs her shoulders while fiddling with her diamond bracelet. "Oh, like you don't know. I mean, you did help Mrs. Collins with her renovations after all, so I suppose you want to help her children get it ready for the estate sale."

"What are you talking about?" I ask, my mind clouded by confusion.

A huff escapes her, clearly indignant. "I said, they are having—"

Immediately interrupting her, I say, "I know what you meant, Mother. How did you hear about an estate sale?"

This is news to me; Mrs. Collins never told me about an estate sale when we renovated her house. All she ever said was she wanted it to be an acceptable and comforting house if Ada or Noah ever decided they wanted it.

My mother waves her hand in the air. "Oh Lincoln, don't pretend Blue Haven isn't a small town where gossip is prevalent."

Yeah, like you, Mother.

"Plus, some of my girlfriends and I discussed it at the One-2-One program where we volunteer to help young people get their lives back on track." She flashes an eyebrow. "We know who may have needed that, don't we, Lincoln?"

Clearly, she's referring to Ada.

"Lincoln, the house is going to be on the market, and you put all that effort into it. Since you were the one who did all the work, you should be receiving a commission, at the very least," my mother says as takes a swig of her wine.

Despite my attempts to end the conversation, she

continues, "Oh, I also heard that Ada was back in Blue Haven for her mother's funeral." Disbelieving, she says, "I cannot believe she actually came back."

My jaw clenches as anger rises from hearing her speak unkindly of Ada. "That's enough, shouldn't we be pass—"

A quick disgusted snort escapes her mouth when she interrupts me. "She should know by now that this town will never accept her."

My body becomes tense as I tighten my fists. "Is it Blue Haven, or you mother, who does not approve of Ada? Because if I remember correctly, you always seemed to have an issue with her for no particular reason."

Jewels grasps my hand under the table, giving me the support I didn't realize I needed, allowing them to unclench.

"Lincoln, what is the point of being so concerned about something that seems so irrelevant?"

I struggle not to snap and muster every ounce of strength I have as I respond, "Well, let's see, Mother, you continually berate someone who was the most important person in my life, and years have passed, and you are still doing the same thing you always do."

"Lincoln, you cannot possibly still be attached to her," she says with an expression of annoyance.

I focus my attention on Anastasia, who is giving me a sympathetic look. Running my fingers through my hair, I sigh, "Can we please just discuss something else?"

My mother begins to open her mouth again, probably about to say something unpleasant, but Faye bursts out, "I'm pregnant."

Everyone stares at her as my parents shout, "You're what!?"

"Oh my gosh, we're pregnant at the same time?" Anastasia exclaims in excitement.

"Yeah, I guess we are." Faye smiles as she bites her nails.

"Anastasia, you have no business encouraging such behavior!" Our mom glares at Faye. "What were you thinking when you thought about becoming pregnant? You are so level-headed; this is very irresponsible of you."

"A simple congratulations would have sufficed as a response, Mother," she says, rolling her eyes.

The St. James household just became a lot more fun; never a dull moment here.

I am greeted by a sweet, sappy aroma as I drive up to Hope Bay Beach, one of my favorite spots. My father's mistress of the month knocking on the door to our home was the last straw of the night. I removed myself from the entertainment and found myself driving to the one place I could breathe.

As I get out of my bronco, my body starts to decompress. My eyes are drawn to Ginger as I open the passenger door and grab a blanket and bottle of Scotch.

"Come on, Ginger," I say, and she pounces and sniffs, making her presence known.

The cool breeze gently touches my skin while I walk toward the beach. The wind rustles through the pin drop silence, nothing more than a harmonious melody filling my ears as I stand there in awe.

Ginger runs in the opposite direction of me, and I shout at her, "Don't make me use the leash." Unaware of my yell, I begin to run toward her, seeing someone come into my view.

That's strange. Almost as if she arose from my imagination, Ada sits in front of me on a blanket.

Instead of smiling, she scratches behind Ginger's ears in an attempt to gain her attention. "Oh, fancy seeing you here, Ginger. Where is your owner?"

Clearing my throat, I say, "Right here."

Looking over her shoulder, she smiles shyly.

"What are you doing here, Ada?"

Confusion mars her face as she asks, "Me? What are you doing here?"

With a shrug of my shoulders, I reply, "I guess I just needed a break from the St. James dinner. What brought you here?"

With her hands in her lap, she says, "I guess I needed a break, too." She lets out a heavy sigh and continues, "but from packing and going through my old belongings."

I nod in unwavering understanding; my eyes fixed on hers. I can't imagine how she feels, but I am sure it's not easy.

Walking over to her, I ask, "Is there room for two?"

Ada scoots a little to the side as she chuckles, "Of course, it seems like we had the same idea anyways." She points out her wine bottle and the blanket that she is sitting on.

I laugh, pulling out my blanket and sitting next to her. "It appears we were both drawn to a familiar place."

She smiles, curling her legs up into a ball. "I've been

here for quite a while. Noah had found a seashell Mom had given us when she first took us here. He suggested we take a visit down here, and despite my feelings toward her, I felt compelled to be here, to feel her presence. I don't know how to explain this feeling, but when I'm here, I'm at peace. It's nice just letting myself soak up the amazing memories that have taken place here."

"Does returning to Blue Haven feel different for you?" I ask.

Taking in the breathtaking view of the lake, she nods. "Everything feels different, but being here, I don't know, I feel . . . at home."

I lean back on my elbows as the moonlight begins to illuminate the stars, wondering how two kids could be so deeply in love after so many years and just . . . let it go. A yearning glance crosses her face, and my pulse races.

God, she is so beautiful right now.

There is something about her tonight that seems natural. Unfiltered and unforced, as if she is not trying too hard. Her long blonde hair is in a messy bun, and she is dressed in yoga pants and an oversized Blue Haven Raiders sweatshirt. One that looks awfully familiar.

Is it mine?

Giving me a knowing look, her cheeks flush red. Her gaze quickly returns to the sweatshirt as she glances down at it. "Sorry, but I packed only professional clothing, and I wanted something comfortable, so I pulled it out of a box in my room."

I crack a smile as I nudge her in the shoulder. "Don't apologize. I gave you the sweatshirt, didn't I?" I say in a playful tone.

Besides, seeing her in my clothing again causes my body to become all hot and tingly.

Looking at me, she smiles and shifts her weight, bumping her leg into me, sending a tingle down my spine. Blood rushes to my cock.

Shit. Not now, Lincoln.

It is physically painful to sit this close to her, and not be able to grab her the way I want. *The way I used to be able to.*

Suddenly, my gaze latches onto her lips as her tongue slides out and over them, forcing me to shift uncomfortably in my jeans. Biting her bottom lip, she looks down at our hands slightly touching on the blanket. My pinky finger wraps around hers in a familiar manner; one in which we used to seal our promises. A smile tugs at the corner of her mouth, washing away all of tonight's events. Despite my eyes being locked on her, I can't resist the temptation to place my hands on her cheeks. Her pulse thumps under the palm of my hand.

One time.

One touch.

One feel.

It is almost as if the wetness of the lake is hitting my shirt, snapping me out of the moment. Out of my peripheral vision, Ginger runs away, back toward the lake, having the time of her life.

Ada shakes her head, trying to contain her laughter by pressing her lips together.

In full swing, Ginger leaps on me again, and Ada laughs, which in turn causes my own laugh.

"Alright, girl, that's enough." She jumps off me, shaking off her wetness, causing Ada to get wet as well. I hold back a laugh myself, and she smiles, shoving my shoulder.

Leaning back on the blanket, I ask, "What does that mean?" I point at a tattoo of hers I have never seen before.

When she pulls up her sweatshirt, her smooth tan skin makes heat radiate throughout my body. "What, this?" she says as she points to the tattoo above her hip bone.

"Yeah, I didn't know you had a tattoo."

"That's because I didn't get it till college, but it's a Latin phrase. After going through everything I did before leaving Blue Haven, I wanted to remind myself that while there is life, there is always hope. So even when my life back then felt like it was going nowhere, I needed to remember that I was lucky just to be alive. I know it sounds cliche, but I feel like as long as you're still breathing, you have the capability of changing your own life, and I am living proof of that."

Damn. Independent. Sexy. Inspiring.

My heart is tinged with sorrow as I realized that I missed watching her grow into who is today. "Look at you, Ada Collins." I nudge her softly.

A smile spreads across her now flushed face. "Look at what, Lincoln St. James?" she asks.

"Do you remember that one time a group of us were together, and we were sharing our dreams?" She nods her head. "Well, you have achieved your fucking dream. A dream you once wanted, you are now living it. You are successful, you live in New York, you have a great career as a lawyer. You have everything you could possibly desire."

"Not everything," she murmurs.

"What was that?"

"Nothing," she says as she turns to me.

After a brief silence, I ask, "Ada, are you truly happy?"

Taking a deep breath, she asks, "How would you define happiness?"

"Well, it means you're happy with your life as it is and wouldn't change a thing."

She shrugs her shoulders. "I suppose so, if I were in New York, but since I've returned to Blue Haven, I haven't felt a glimmer of happiness up until now."

"And this is the place where you felt it?"

Opening her mouth briefly, she closes it again, before saying, "I felt it just now with . . . you."

Despite my indecision, the beating in my chest grows louder. I need her, yet I know I will never be able to have her. But, at this moment, I realize something is different. I can't keep her, but maybe I can hold her.

The two of us watch each other as we wait for the other to act. My hand reaches out, brushing her cheek. I move slowly, giving her the opportunity to push me away.

Inching closer to her lips, I say, "I have always felt safe with you. I have never been able to let go of you, Ada, regardless of my best efforts."

Her body trembles as she places her hand over my racing heart.

"Ada, do you feel that?"

In a nod of her head, she asks, "What are we doing?"

The distance between our mouths stretches to barely a whisper as I move closer to her. "Whatever we want," I say.

She briefly looks at my lips before her eyes turn a deep shade of blue. "Lincoln, I don't think this is a good idea."

I can't wait for her to tell me it's not a good idea again.

"Ada, I have been looking forward to doing this ever since the moment I saw you again," I whisper, guiding her head toward mine, and kissing her. My tongue glides between our lips, connecting with her mouth.

I'm so done.

While holding her head steady, I control the kiss. I've kissed this girl more than a thousand times. I've experienced her love, passion, and body so many times, but this time feels different. While I know I shouldn't kiss her, and I should stop, I cannot.

She makes soft noises as my fingers sink into her skin with a mind of their own. "Linc," she says softly.

Rolling her over me, I pull her windblown hair from her forehead and whisper, "Ada, I'm right here."

In an instant, her body becomes rigid, as if something clicked within her. Her eyes search everywhere but me, absorbing what's happening. She starts to get up, but I grab her hips, keeping her from getting on her feet. "Wait, Ada, don't go like this."

But as soon as my hands are off her waist, she stands up, wobbly. "I can't do this." She touches her lips. "I can't believe we just did that." Shock colors her tone.

Great going, St. James. Only chance you had to get closure from her and you now have her running for hills. Just fucking fantastic.

She hurriedly grabs her belongings, and as she's about to escape, I grab her hand. With a heavy sigh, she says, "It was a slip-up, Lincoln. These things happen, but it won't happen again." She whispers as she rushes away from me, "I can't go down that road again."

"Ada, can't we talk it out?" I yell back. "I know you think it was a mistake, but there's a reason it happened."

She breathes deeply. "Yeah, it's called an emotional high and I am well acquainted with them." Ginger spies Ada walking to her vehicle and she jumps on her. Ada pets her as she says, "See you around, girl, and stay out of trouble."

The tears in Ada's eyes as she gets into her car tug at my heart, reminding me of the time when she left Blue Haven. Taking a deep breath, I kick a few rocks with my shoe. I run my fingers through my hair, tugging at the ends.

Fuckkk. What the fuck did you just do, Lincoln?

Chapter fifteen ♡

Ada

I awake; his arms are around me, my body tucked within his chest and hips. Not wanting to ruin this moment, I do not move, nor blink. However, I can't help but smile as I gaze at him. When was the last time I woke up like this? Feeling this way?

Touching me reverently and patiently, he leans in, doting kisses all over my neck. I close my eyes and pull myself away, putting my elbows up and taking a long, deep breath as I go in for a much-needed kiss.

Leaning closer, I can feel him. Taste the bourbon from last night. Hear him whisper, "Ada, I am right here."

Feeling as though I am on cloud nine, floating on a euphoric high, I move in one last time, closing the mere distance between us until . . .

Thump.

Shit, what was that? Were we just pushed off the bed by me?

While rubbing my eyes, I examine my surroundings,

including my naked ass on the hardwood floors of my lodge room.

What the hell? Why am I lying on the ground? Where is Lincoln?

Taking a moment to close my eyes, the realization dawns on me. I was fucking dreaming. One that felt so real.

My legs scramble to my feet as I run to the bathroom to grab my robe, slightly freaking out. If I am dreaming about him, about us? What does that mean?

In New York, I would sometimes dream about us, but I was so focused on work that I did not have time to really think about what it meant. Here and now, it's different, and I'm honestly not sure how I feel about that.

But the past is the past, right? It means nothing.

♡

"You what?" Lucy exclaims.

A heavy sigh escapes me as I sit on my bed. "I don't know, Luce, it kind of just happened. One second we were discussing our problems in life, and the next we were making out like hormonal teenagers."

Several moments later, Lucy lets out a breath. "Ada, sweetheart, as hot as last night sounds, when I told you to get closure in Blue Haven, I didn't mean with Lincoln. According to the way you two left things, this situation is already in a precarious state. Are you sure you wish to revisit old feelings before you return to New York?"

My heart rate increases as anxiety overtakes me. I begin to pace the room in an attempt to calm myself.

"Luce, I don't know, maybe. Lincoln and I never got closure, and maybe I should try, but without the kissing part, of course. Although I am not claiming that we will be best friends. If we can cooperate civilly, it won't be the worst thing in the world." I pause. "Right?" I ask, seeking confirmation. I hear clinking and banging noises in the background.

"Are you cooking something, Luce?" Her chuckle grows louder as she says, "Well, I'm hungry since you called me so early."

"God, I'm the worst," I say, feeling guilty. "I didn't even realize what was going on when I called you. I just knew I had to inform someone about it. After last night, I felt . . . " I pause before continuing, "A lot, and right now, in this moment, I am experiencing a combination of emotions: angry, sad, relieved, stressed, literally every emotion a human being can have."

"I need you to take a deep breath for me, Ada." I breathe in, *out one, two, three*, as she continues to speak into my phone. "While this must be a very difficult situation for you, the Ada I know is fiercely determined. I can assure you that you have not reverted to your old ways just because you have been back in Blue Haven for two weeks."

Even though I know she is right, the what ifs are raging in my head. What if the dream meant something? What if the kiss meant something?

Let go of the past, Ada; you are no longer the naive girl you once were. Do not allow anyone to play with your emotions.

Lucy interrupts my inner thoughts when she asks, "Do you remember when you were about to shit your pants on your first day of law school? You kept telling me that you weren't strong enough, you weren't good enough, and that you didn't deserve this, but honey, you deserve this happiness and much more. As I told you that day, you need not conform to a particular mold created by society in order to be perfect, you are perfect in your own way. It was that woman who believed in her abilities and was confident in herself. Ada, you should not depend on Lincoln, Blue Haven, or anyone else to determine your worth. The results of that have already been evident to you." She sighs heavily, continuing, "but if you feel that closure with him could allow you to move forward from your past, then I say go for it."

Do I want that? Do I need closure?

Indecision engulfs me as I move back to my bed. I remove my phone from my ear and scream into my pillow, wanting to just leave the past behind, even if it is only for a day.

I put my phone back to my ear and say, "Lucy, I really appreciate you being here for me, talking to me, telling me how it is, and always giving me good advice. I don't think I could have survived another day here without you."

"Ada, despite the fact that you are a capable, strong woman, who has a clear understanding of who she is today and who she was previously, I believe you would last a whole year without my support. You are handling one of your largest cases remotely while needing to grieve, not just with your mother. Babe, take a day off, if that is what you need, but remember, let Ada be the one to decide what's best."

She's right. Maybe I do need a day off. The past two weeks, I've moved at lightning speed; never taking my eyes off the prize.

But what is the prize? What's my reward at the end of all of this?

With my clients and cases, I usually strive to achieve my end goals.

But what about this? Is it closure with my mom? Closure with Lincoln?

Saying goodbye to a handful of awful memories in my childhood home?

A fresh onslaught of tears envelops me as I sit up. "Luce, thank you so much, and for always telling me that I am enough. That I am worthy of good things in life. I understand being here is confusing to me. I just hope that at the end of all of this, I will be able to achieve whatever it is I am looking for."

When my phone pings, I see a meeting notification and heave a sigh. "Hey Luce, Ruth and Emmett are calling my name, so to speak. I need to let you go. Text me, yeah?"

In a playful tone, she advises, "Of course, and please take a break every once in a while. I know how bitchy you can be if you do not."

A huff escapes my lips. "Hey, that was so uncalled for; we all have our bitchy sides. It's not just me."

"Kidding, Ada," she replies, "I know you don't have the best relationship with Blue Haven, but I'm just telling you that you may never return, so make the most of it, even when it brings back painful memories," she says. "Reliving those hurtful times can sometimes provide us with the necessary tools to overcome the trauma and move on to our true selves."

If anyone were to know my life inside and out, it would be Lucy Davis.

With a much happier sense of calm, I say, "You are

right; I will do my best, and right now, Ada has regained her fiercely independent nature. There are no more wild mood swings. Ada is back to her old self: stable, capable, and level-headed again."

Laughing, Lucy says, "You go, girlfriend. I love you, Ada. Keep me posted."

"Love you too, Luce." I close the call by plopping back on the bed and covering my head with my forearms.

Time to get it together, Ada.

Taking a deep breath, I sit back up and glance in my stand-up mirror. I lift my chin and pull my shoulders back, hearing a voice within me whisper, "Ada, we will get through this, one day at a time. Refocus on the things that matter most."

A sudden ringing sounds in my phone, I briefly look down and see Lincoln's name lit up. I do not need this after spending just a few minutes regaining my focus.

Do not answer the phone. Send it to voicemail.

As I chew on my lip, a second passes before I quickly accept the call, despite my better judgment. "Hello?"

"Good morning, Ada," he says softly.

In a moment of silent reflection, I remind myself that I am in control and that there will be no more roller coaster emotions. "Hi Lincoln, what's up?" I ask in a cool, easy tone.

"Well, I just wanted to apologize for last night," he says in a slowly falling voice. "The emotions got the better of me and I was out of line. I reflected on yesterday. I believe we were so caught up in our nostalgic feelings that we were surprised when it ended. Despite the fact that last night was not what either of us expected, I still enjoyed your company. So maybe we could get together again before you leave?"

The mere thought of him wanting to see me again causes my chest to tighten.

Focus, Ada. Work, estate sale, work, estate sale. No time for reminiscing.

"Honestly, it's no big deal. In fact, Lincoln, everything has already been forgotten, so let's try not to make this awkward anymore," I say quickly.

The phone goes silent; my room becomes quiet, further increasing my level of nervousness.

Shit, should I have said that?

While pacing around my room, I twirl a piece of my hair around my finger. As Lucy had suggested, I could get closure with him while I am back in Blue Haven. Perhaps I should do that, but before I can respond, saying we should get together again, he says in a sorrowful tone, "Oh okay, Ada. I am glad we can move on."

The thought of him sounding so hurt, and by me, no less, makes my heart ache in a way I haven't felt in a long time. Lincoln continues, "Also, I promise that we will not have any awkward moments between us, as long as you can too," he teases.

I smile as his playful behavior dispels the whim-whams that had taken over my body. "The awkward moments are over, Linc. We are both mature adults capable of controlling our emotions."

With a sigh of relief, he says, "That's great. I have a game to attend, but I hope we can catch up before you leave."

"Likewise, good luck today, Linc!"

In just one short phone call with Lincoln, I am

flooded with all of these chaotic emotions, once again making me question everything.

Can I leave without seeing him again?

Should I take him up on his offer and see him again?

Feel his lips on me again?

The touch of my fingers brushes against my lips as I close my eyes. I visualize his signature smirk and he winks, pulling me forcibly into his rock hard chest. His hands wrap around my neck as he guides his mouth over mine, making my body tremble with need; captivating me.

In the blink of an eye, my eyes open and I glance down. My hands frantically move all over my body. I shouldn't be so bothered. But I know I won't find myself in a one-night stand in Blue Haven. So what's the harm of giving myself a hand? Maybe it will help me focus better.

Yes, this will definitely help me.

I stroll over to my nightstand and grab my favorite 'bunny,' aka my vibrator, which I use from time to time, so to deny myself of this would be foolish. Turning it on, I feel the vibration light up my body.

This is what I need.

My shirt and bra slowly fall down as I tease my nipple and let out a moan. My heart starts to race as the sensation of ecstasy radiates throughout my entire body.

"Yesss."

I move my vibrator as it skims across my body. I take a deep breath, anticipating the pleasure that awaits me as I travel to the very wet core.

God, yes, that feels amazing.

The sensation of the vibrator slipping between my lips takes me to an entirely new level.

Oh, this is just what I needed.

I grab one of my nipples, pinching it. Hard.

Awhh, yes, right there..

A noise pings on my laptop, but I continue to ignore it. I am right there. I am teetering on the brink of falling, letting myself go.

I hear the sound again, but this time Siri is playing on my computer. "In five minutes, your meeting with Emmett will begin."

Shit, right now?

I let out a heavy sigh as I toss my vibrator and move from my bed. Grabbing my laptop from the desk in the corner of my room.

In front of me, I open up my email and see that over a dozen emails have been sent in the last 24 hours alone. When I open the first one, it is Ruth's email, notifying me of a meeting that is just minutes away.

Shit. Meeting.

I throw my head into my palms, a yell escapes my lips. Can't a girl get some alone time before she gets bombarded with shit.

Ada, stay calm. Everything will be fine. Get ready real quick. You're used to New York's pace.

Despite my best efforts, I am losing my grip on the present Ada because of my past creeping up on me, which is affecting me more than I care to admit. This is my most challenging case, and I am emotionally bothered by one interaction.

Nonetheless, an amazing one.

I stand up and start browsing through my non-existent wardrobe, selecting an outfit. Ruth will be seeing me, and any weakness she witnesses will be used to her advantage. Taking a glimpse in the mirror, I decide I am capable of doing this. I pick up some dry shampoo and put on light makeup. The moment Ruth's face appears on my laptop, I rush back to my desk and turn on the camera. Her face is affixed with a fake smile. I am almost certain she has Emmett next to her, otherwise she would not be putting on such an act.

"Hello, Ada, I would say nice to see you, but that would be a lie."

My eyes roll back in my head as I grumble, "Hello, thank you, Ruth. You know that my mother passed away not that long ago?"

A slightly guilty-looking smile spreads across her face. "Yeah, I am sorry to hear about that. I can't understand what you're going through, but if looking like a homeless person is helpful to you, it's okay with me."

Almost got a nice sentence out of her. For once, it would be nice to work with a colleague I like on a case.

"Enough bickering, girls," Emmett comments as he joins the meeting. Taking out his leather notepad, he says, "Nice to see you again, Ada. I want to make this quick. Could you please review what you have so far in the merger and acquisition case?"

With a nod of my head, I say, "Yes, sir, just a moment."

Almost falling as I reach across my messy room for my Gucci Diana Laptop Bag, Ruth says, "Ada, where are you staying? That place looks terrible."

"Ruth, we are here for a meeting and not to discuss my living situation. Would it be possible for us to return to the topic of why we are here?"

The woman rolls her eyes as I review my notes.

"As you may have noticed, I have accomplished quite a bit this past week, greater than I would have if I had been at my office," I say confidently, eager to avoid mishaps. In an effort to encourage me to continue, Emmett moves his hands.

"Having discussed Hamill and Sons' business objectives during our last conversation, I have been able to contact them. Tim Hamill explained during our interview that their primary objective was to generate a high return on investment, so he thought merging with another company would be beneficial."

Continuing to flip through my notes, I state, "After knowing the reason for their acquisition, I went ahead and identified their specific objectives and goals. When Tim told me he wanted the merger to be profitable, I asked him what ROI they were striving for, and I included his response in my portfolio for Hamill and Sons.

"Additionally, I promised you the last time we spoke that I would create a roadmap and a timeframe for the entire process, including the four major areas of framework considered by Sullivan & Rothman's in every case, which I have."

In his slightly raised eyebrows, Emmett slowly claps. "Well done, Ada; I didn't think you had the capacity for it, but you seem to accomplish just as much as you would at the firm."

A murderous look crosses Ruth's face as she turns her head toward me.

Raising a finger, he continues, "I would appreciate it if Tim could complete the four main areas of the framework and then Ruth can lay them out in presentation format on my desk."

I nod my head in understanding. "Yes, sir. I have a

meeting with Tim and his sons early next week, so I'll make sure I cover that during the call."

He smiles as he stands and says, "Sounds great, Ada. I will be in touch shortly."

When I wave goodbye to my laptop camera, Ruth remarks, "You really have achieved a lot remotely."

My mouth falls open as I look at her. We stare at each other in silence for a few moments.

Okay, is she serious right now? I can't tell.

"Ada, I am serious. I think we can win this case because of you." Putting her hand on her chest, she flutters her eyelashes. "And since I have already put in so much effort here, I believe Emmett is considering me for the next partner position."

Knew it was too good to be true.

You shouldn't get too comfortable, Ruth. I have worked hard for the last several years to achieve this level of success, and I will not stand aside and watch you take it away.

Instead of saying what I truly want to, I simply paste on a forced smile and say, "While it was nice seeing you, Ruth, I really need to get to work, being the next *real* partner at Sullivan & Rothman's and all." I close my laptop with a shit-eating grin before she has a chance to reply.

Always getting the last word in with Ruth is gratifying. Standing up, I go grab a Diet Coke right as my phone rings, again. The thought of who would be calling me now races through my mind as I rush over to pick it up.

"Hello, this is Ada Collins."

"Surely you already have me programmed into your phone, Ada?" Lexie chuckles.

I laugh. "Sorry, Lex, I am somewhat in work mode at the moment."

"I am just kidding with you; however, I wanted to let you know about the Little League game taking place this afternoon, well, in a few hours, anyway. Think you could possibly join me? They are super fun. Plus, I thought you could use a break from what you are currently doing."

I glance at my watch; it is already early afternoon.

What a whirlwind today has been.

Sighing, I say, "Well, I am actually working right now, but Lincoln informed me that they have a game today."

"What?" Lexie gasps, "You spoke to Lincoln? When? Where?"

A nervous chuckle escapes my lips as I say, "Yeah, well, we sort of had a moment yesterday."

"Wait, what kind of moment are we discussing here?" she asks. After a moment of silence, she shouts, "Did you guys kiss?"

Still staying silent on my end, her voice cracks as she says, "OH MY GOD! You two freaking kissed. Ada Collins and Lincoln St. James freaking kissed. I didn't think I would see the day that would happen again. Scratch, maybe I did a time or two, anyway, DETAILS, I need details, Ada! No wait, don't tell me over the phone. You can tell me when you come to the game with me. That's right, you get but no choice to come with me now that I know about this so-called moment."

Rolling my eyes, I state, "This isn't a big deal."

"Keep telling yourself it wasn't Ada Collins; we both know it was."

Sighing, I say, "Ok, I'll be there. What time does it start?"

"Yay! It begins at 4:00 pm. It's at Beacon Field. You remember that field, don't you?" she asks.

I chuckle. "Yes, Lex, I remember that field. Even though I haven't been to Blue Haven in years, that doesn't mean I have forgotten it."

With a laugh, she says, "I was just checking, Ada. See you soon."

♡

A surge of uneasiness triggers my heart into thumping uncomfortably hard in my chest as I step out of the car. Wiping sweat from my palms, I readjust my baseball cap that reads, 'Blue Haven Haymakers.' Yes, I ran to the local boutique to get a baseball cap specially for this game, and okay, maybe I swapped my regular nude lipstick for something deeper and more sultry.

There's nothing wrong with a girl having to do what she's gotta do. It's not like it's a big deal. Right?

Keep telling yourself that, Ada.

"What are you looking at there?" I jump as I hold my hand over my heart, which continues to race. I glance over at Lexie, whose gaze holds my attention as I become more anxious. Maybe it appears that I am trying too hard?

Let's face it, Ada. It is just Lexie, and she doesn't really care how you look.

With a wink, she remarks, "You look great, Ada. I particularly like your choice of hat and shirt."

In a choking voice, I ask, "Really, you think I look fine? I couldn't decide what to wear."

Laughing, Lexie remarks, "Ada, you are wearing leggings, white converse, a T-shirt with Blue Haven Haymakers on it, and a baseball cap. There's really no point in trying to impress anyone here."

I mean, she's right, but being surrounded by the town of Blue Haven doesn't come with the fondest of memories. Hence, why attending a game like this guarantees me to question my self worth. Even though I know that it is stupid, my entire childhood was characterized by negativity, so it is difficult to let something like that go.

Continuing, she nudges my shoulder, "Unless you are trying to impress a certain someone."

"Shut up." I playfully shove her.

In spite of the increased rate of my pulse with each step, we make our way to the stands. Suddenly, I hear her giggle behind me. I twist to face Lexie. "What's so funny?" Grabbing my butt, looking at it, I ask, "Do I have something on my butt?"

"Ada, did you read the back of your shirt before buying it?" she asks.

"Honestly, no, I didn't have time; I just saw the shirt and bought it. Why?" I ask, clearly confused.

"Sweetheart, you are wearing a shirt that reads, 'I'm here for the coach."

"Oh my god, Lexie, please tell me you are not serious," I say as a flush of heat rises in my face due to humiliation.

Her head shakes. "I'm sorry, but no, it actually says, 'I'm here for the coach'. Unfortunately, there are only two. My fiancé and Lincoln, and everyone in Blue Haven knows that you aren't here for my future hubby."

"I cannot believe this is happening to me," I mutter to myself as I cover my face with my hands.

"Maybe we won't even get noticed if we sit at the back." Lexie grasps my shoulder and pulls me toward the stands, as she whispers, "Ada, don't worry about what others think. You shouldn't care anyway."

Unlike the old Ada, I am determined to keep my chin up and not feel sorry for myself. I refuse to compromise my integrity for the sake of these people.

With a smile, I say, "You're right, I don't care. Let's sit, preferably, in the front row."

In the process of approaching our seats, Lincoln catches my eye, making my heart hiccup. With a little wave, he lets his signature St. James smirk spread across his handsome face. I admire him as he starts running over to the field, decked out in full uniform. My body warms at the thought of the muscles beneath his clothing, the warm bare skin, those powerful legs that could do some damage, or that deep veiny—

"Hi, Lexie," Lincoln says, before turning to me. "Hey, Ada," he says with a wink.

Is it just me, or has his voice become a lot huskier in the past day.

I swallow, crossing one leg over the other to dull the sudden throb from that damn panty-melting grin. God, I knew I should have gotten myself off this morning.

Keep it casual, Ada.

Leaning forward, I laugh and let out a smirk as gravity pulls me toward him. His ocean blue eyes are like a vacuum, sucking me in and for a short period, everything around us is lost in the rush of blood in my ears.

"Lincoln, we need your focus over here!" Lexie's fiancé, Josh, says across the field.

Our eyes briefly diverge for a second before we reconnect and laugh.

My God, the way he laughs, all soft and deep, I forgot how much it made me feel as if I was sinking into a warm bath.

Ada, focus on the important things. Work, estate sale, work, estate sale.

Lincoln's eyes briefly scan me once more, and I can't help but shiver under the intensity of his stare.

When was the last time someone looked at me like this? Like I'm their first meal in days. There is no denying that it is overwhelming, but it is also extremely fucking hot.

While my eyes are completely fixed on him, I suck my lower lip between my teeth. I can't help but let my mind wander. Does he like what he sees? Is he thinking the same things I am?

"Ada, I didn't know you still had team spirit," Lincoln says, bringing me back into the present.

After a small chuckle, more like a snort, I say, "Well, I thought I could support the kids." I shout, "Go Haymakers!" as I throw my first into the air.

Shaking his head, a boyish smile lights up his face. "I saw your shirt, which clearly states the opposite."

Wait, he saw my shirt? How?

My eyes are drawn to the victim, clearly aware that she did something.

Lexie hides her chuckle behind her fists, and I bump her shoulder. She puts her hands up in surrender. "Hey, this was too good an opportunity to let slide. I sent a picture to Josh to show him."

The flush on my face intensifies as I stare daggers at Lexie. This cannot be more embarrassing. My cheeks heat up and my heart races, wishing this moment would be over soon.

Lincoln steps away from the fence, as he says, "Ada, I was just playing with you. Hey, Josh and I are going to the bar after the game. You two should come along."

Before I can even form a coherent thought, Lexie shouts, "Count us in!"

"I am looking forward to it," Lincoln says with a wink as he jogs back onto the field.

My gaze wanders over his broad, toned shoulders as I watch his muscles rip as he runs. His movements are fluid and graceful, illustrating the power and strength of his athletic build.

Mmmk, he's definitely all man.

Lexie chuckles lightly next to me. "You look like you want to devour the poor guy."

I mean, she's not wrong. My memory of last night plays over and over in my mind as if it were a tape recording.

Chapter Sixteen ♡

Ada

The game ended 7-11, with the Blue Haven Haymakers winning! Lincoln had been there to witness the highs and lows of the game, and nothing could have made him prouder as the Haymakers emerged as the victors. His face was beaming with pride as he lifted his team of young boys into the air as they celebrated. I cannot forget the joy that spread across the littles faces. It was a poignant reminder of what sports can bring to a community.

Once it was over, I slipped back to my lodge to freshen up before meeting the crew. The changes weren't drastic; this was not a date. However, I replaced my converse shoes with heel booties, and perhaps I spritzed myself with a little more perfume as well. I felt confident and looked my best, but I was still myself.

It is a couple of minutes before 7 when I receive a text from an unknown number.

> I am at the bar, helping out for a few minutes, but should be free shortly after everyone arrives.

Lincoln.

I add him to my contacts, then reply, "Sounds great. Be there soon."

I never changed my number throughout the years; however, I did block him. He must not have done it on his end.

When I'm ready, I grab my purse and drive leisurely to the bar. As I pass through Blue Haven streets, I take deep, calming breaths. Though, as I approach Safe Harbor, my heart races and my stomach knots.

It's just Lincoln, plus Lexie and Josh. Relax, Ada.

It's hard to relax though. It's only been a few days since I returned to Blue Haven and so much has happened between us.

Would the subject of *our kiss* come up? Me leaving Blue Haven?

"Oh for goodness' sake, Ada," I whisper to myself as I pull open the doors to the bar.

Relax. Just in case though, I text Lexie real quick to see if she was already here.

LEXIE

> Not yet, Josh wanted to take a shower real quick. Should only be 15 - 20 minutes!

Greaaat, so it is just Lincoln and I.

Alone.

The bar is crowded for a Friday evening. People are

in a festive mood, chatting and laughing with one another. Although tonight is lively, it has nothing on the weekends.

My heart aches as I spot the bar counter, the bartender attending to the patrons. I didn't think being here would bring up yet another memory of my mother, but what's new? I remember the Safe Harbor bartenders calling me to pick her up. She was usually so drunk that I was the designated driver more often than I cared to recall.

I spot Lincoln handing an alcoholic beverage and french fries to a customer in my peripheral vision. His enthusiasm and genuine care for the customer is evident as they chat about something.

Hmm, so does he work here or is he just helping out?

After watching him shuffle from table to table, I decide to leave him alone and proceed to find a table for the four of us. As I locate one, a waitress approaches me and hands me a menu.

She smiles as I say, "Thank you. Can I have a beer?"

Nodding, she walks over to the bar and proceeds to bring me one back.

Upon first glance, the beer appears delicious. The color is a rich amber hue, and the foam head is thick and creamy. The aroma is a tantalizing mix of hops, malt, and yeast, while the taste . . . well is amazing, with a balanced hint of sweetness.

I'm more of a vodka girl, but I love a good beer from time to time.

Eyeing the menu, I hear, "What did you think of the game, A?"

Peeking in front of me, I see Lincoln, looking so

damn boyish, with fresh clean hair, and in his post-game outfit: jeans and a button-down shirt.

My mind is screaming at me to take it off him. I wonder if he knows what that nickname does to me. How it makes my stomach flip hearing it coming out of his mouth again.

I bite my lip, watching Lincoln's eyes be drawn to them. In the midst of my pulsating heartbeat and a tingling ache that's coursing through my body, I can honestly say that I have no desire to be anywhere else at this moment.

Lincoln sits in front of me and smirks in an effort to convey that he knows I was just checking him out. "So, what did you think?"

A flush ghosts my cheeks and, under normal circumstances, I would not be embarrassed about checking a man out, but being around Lincoln makes it feel different.

Wrong.

But also thrilling.

A quick drink of beer clears my throat. In a rather high-pitched voice, I say, "It was fun! Linc, you seem to be a natural coach. I enjoyed seeing you in action."

He chuckles as he takes a sip of his beer. "Yeah, it's pretty rewarding to be their coach and witness all the dedication and hard work they put into their games."

Smiling, I say, "I bet. What made you decide to become a coach? I know you always wanted to do it."

His fingers run through his hair as he shrugs and looks away from me. "Honestly, it gave me something to do besides sit in an office from 9 to 5. Although it took me some time to achieve a balance between the two, as soon as I had my first practice with these boys, it became apparent that it was something I had always meant to do."

Our eyes connect. "It felt like I was finally doing something meaningful," he adds, his expression conveying the impact the experience had on him.

I shake my head, knowing exactly how he feels. My career as a lawyer is fulfilling. I'm proud to be able to make a difference in others' lives and that's why I continue to pursue a law career.

But seeing this side of Lincoln, it does something to my insides. Warmth spread through me with a sense of admiration for his compassion and dedication to these boys. Little do they understand that Lincoln is much more than a coach; he will become a role model for them, someone to look up to, who will help shape them into the best versions of themselves.

He leans a little closer to me, his eyes focused on mine. "So, what's Ada Collins been up to over the last several years?"

I shake my head. "Honestly, work."

He raises a brow.

I let out a chuckle. "Yeah, I know, lame, but when you work 70 plus hours a week, it's kinda hard to find other hobbies."

His eyes widen as he practically spits his beer across the table. With a napkin in hand, he wipes up his mess as he says, "Sorry, but 70 hours? Jesus, Ada, that's a lot of time to spend in an office. Don't you think so?"

I pop a shoulder. "I mean, it's fairly common for a lawyer, but it also depends on what sector you're in and how dedicated you are. Working hard and remaining committed to your work is the key to success in this field."

He nods his head in what I assume is acknowledge-ment, so I continue, "For years, I dreamed of becoming a partner at a law firm, so I knew that would mean countless hours in the office. I had to be prepared to make many sacrifices, including my time, in order to achieve my dream."

"Yeah, I get that."

I smile. "So what else do you do besides coach little kids' baseball? Do you work here?"

The man chuckles. "I am quite busy, so I figured what better way to spend my spare time than by volun-teering." While sipping his beer, he continues, "Besides working at my father's accounting firm, I volunteer to coach and I work here, as needed, most Saturdays as a bartender."

"What happened to being a professor?" I ask with a sense of curiosity.

Lincoln's dream was to be a professor at the local college here in Blue Haven. He must have had a good reason for leaving his dream behind, and I'm sure it wasn't an easy decision.

He shrugs. "Life had other plans for me, I guess," he says.

"I get that. Sometimes with life, it feels as though you are going down countless roads without knowing which one is the right one."

The waitress comes over and asks if we want to order something. Lincoln tells her we want fried pickles, and I can't help but smile. Those were always our favorite appetizers to eat here. It's comforting to know that Lincoln hasn't forgotten any of the memories we've shared here.

After she leaves, I look at Lincoln. "Can I ask you something?"

He lifts a brow.

I laugh. "I'll take that as a yes." Trying to calm my nerves, I glance at my beer cup as I run my finger along the rim. "Do you know who did the renovations on my house?"

His eyes narrow.

"I just can't shake the gut feeling that someone helped her, you know? Growing up, we did not have money, and she never expressed any interest in renovating the house, although I wanted it as a child."

"I even asked Noah, and he just shrugged it off. Like it wasn't a big deal. But it sort of is. I mean, what if we wanted to buy the house? Keep it, ya know?" My eyes travel up to Lincoln's. "I get it holds a lot of hurtful memories, but there are amazing ones too."

Amazing ones of us.

As if he is aware of the memories I am referring to, he reaches across the table and squeezes my hand firmly.

Before he has a chance to respond, Lexie chuckles as she takes a seat by me. "We didn't miss out on anything, did we?" she asks suspiciously.

I drop Lincoln's hand. "Nope, perfect timing. We were just discussing the baseball game, right?" I ask, eyeing Lincoln.

He grins mischievously. "Yep, we were just talking about how Ada liked watching me in action."

A loud laugh erupts from my lips, and I kick him in the leg under the table.

"I'll say; you couldn't keep your eyes off him." Lexie whispers.

I shrug unapologetically. The girl is correct. I had no idea baseball coaches got so dirty. In fact, when it came to Little League games, I assumed they were just yelling at the boys to do some sort of baseball play. However, if there is ever a time where I would like to be wrong, it would be now.

Lincoln's actions on the field, whether it was stretching, correcting a little boy's stance, or running with them to a base to cheer them on, left me feeling hot and bothered. He had the whole hot and attractive DILF thing working for him, and let's just say, I was here for it.

Lincoln points to our waitresses, requesting a round of beers for the table.

"To be honest, I was hesitant to do it in the first place, well, because . . . " He glances over at me as his now soft eyes meet mine, causing my chest to become heavy. Rubbing the back of his neck with his hand, he continues, "Anyway, it makes me feel great seeing the boys' eyes light up when I teach them something."

As fun as it was to watch Lincoln look like a natural coach tonight, my heart ached watching him with those kids tonight. When he kneeled down in front of them, at eye level, to speak to, teach, or demonstrate something to them, my mind was brought back to the times when Lincoln and I talked about our future, about how he would be as a father and how he would want to coach our children.

"How about a fun game of Beer Bingo?" Lexie asks, clearly trying to ease the tension that had built since the moment we entered the bar.

Oh God, not this game. If you wanted to get hammered in a flash, this was your go to game. Beer Bingo resembles regular Bingo, but everything is traded out for alcoholic beverages and shots.

With a shrug of my shoulders, I say, "I don't know, Lex. I have a busy morning ahead of me and a hangover is the last thing I need."

A shock shoots through my entire body as Lincoln accidentally brushes his shoe against the side of my leg under the table. "Who says you'll have a hangover?" Lincoln asks, flashing his eyebrows. "Come on, Ada. This will be just a fun round. You still love competitions, don't you?" Lincoln says, sporting a smirk that is more infuriating than charming.

The comment is totally uncalled for and extremely unfair; he knows I'll never back down from a challenge. He's using his old tactics to get a rise out of me.

I arch a brow at him, essentially saying, 'bring it on'. He has not seen me for years; he has no idea how useful my attorney skills are about to play out right now.

Lexie interrupts our stare down as she says, "You're playing, right, Ada?" I nod my head as she continues, "On one condition."

The four of us turn our heads toward Lexie, waiting for her to announce what she had in mind.

Lexie gestures toward Lincoln, then to me, and says, "We will play as long as Lincoln takes Ada home."

"But, I will—"

Lexie cuts in, "You and I both know this game can take a wild turn at any moment. We will play as long as you get a safe ride home. I don't want anything to happen to you."

A sigh escapes my mouth as I concede, knowing I may never be able to play this game with these four again. Besides, it is a harmless ride home anyway; what can possibly go wrong? "Okay, fine, Lincoln can take me home," I say as he smiles over at me.

"Perfect, let's play!" Lexie exclaims as she claps her hands.

I roll my eyes and laugh as I grab the bingo cards from the center of the table.

Taking my two fingers and pointing them toward Lincoln's eyes, I mouth, "Game on."

Shaking his head, I hear his deep chuckle that instantly warms my bones to the core.

Within a blink of an eye, the next hour passes, filled with laughter, heated glances between Lincoln and me, and so much drinking that I am completely tipsy.

"I honestly forgot how much I missed that game," I say, glancing over at Lincoln.

The man watches me in an almost suffocating manner. Touching the rim of his glass to the side of his mouth, he says, "I'm sure you miss many things about Blue Haven."

Maybe he's right—maybe it's a good idea to enjoy Blue Haven to the fullest again.

Since this will be my last time here.

God, it will be, won't it? I never considered it in that manner. I knew when I first left there might be a chance of returning, but now, what is the need to come back?

Mom passed away.

Noah is in college.

The house will be sold by the time I leave.

There really is no reason to, except maybe to visit Lexie, but she can always make the trip to New York to visit me.

In an effort to swallow down the emotion sitting in my throat, I smile and mutter, "Maybe you are right."

Suddenly, a woman walks up to our table and grasps Lincoln's shoulder as she approaches us. "Hi, Linc," she says as she bends down to kiss his cheek.

I quickly glance away, my heart sinking into the pit of my stomach.

A large smile spreads across his face as he looks at her with familiarity.

From an outsider's perspective, it seems like the two of them are a couple. An adorable one at that. I wonder if people ever saw us that way?

Wait, are he and this woman dating?

Oh my God, they probably are!

I don't understand; how could Lincoln let last night happen?!

Maybe I am just overthinking everything?

My mind reels as I attempt to piece together where I have seen her before. It dawns on me as the seconds pass that she was the woman Lincoln was with at Scoops for Life.

She *is* his girlfriend.

Just breathe, Ada; do not allow panic or fear to govern your actions. Here in Blue Haven, emotions do not play a role in the decisions you make.

Trying to stay present, I close my eyes and whisper to myself, "Focus. Work. Estate Sale. Work. Estate Sale."

Breathe in, Ada, onee, twoo, three, out, onee, twoo, three.

Right as I reopen my eyes, feeling a bit more stable than a second ago, I catch Lincoln embracing her as he stands up.

Freaking hell. I can't explain the knotting high in my chest. I shouldn't feel envious of their relationship. Him and I are over. My purpose for being here is to work and to participate in the estate sale.

"Hey, Sarah!" he says.

Her eyes spot me as she scans the table.

Shit. Does she know me?

"And who do we have here?" she asks, raising her eyebrows.

In a nervous smile, I place a piece of my hair behind my ear. There is no doubt that Lincoln's parents are most likely ecstatic with the selection of his girlfriend. The woman is picture perfect. Has all the right curves and doesn't even have any flaws on the outside. She has long, thick brown hair, brownish green eyes; she looks like a fucking Victoria Secret runway model.

Ada Collins, do not even consider comparing yourself to her. You are an attractive, strong, and irreplaceable attorney.

Putting on my most charming smile, I extend my hand to introduce myself. "Hi, I'm Ada Collins."

"Oh yes, Lincoln has told me about you." Her eyes drift over me for a moment before they come to rest on my face.

He has? When? I haven't been back in Blue Haven that long.

Seeing the confusion in my eyes, she continues, "He informed me of your mother's death. I am deeply sorry for your loss. I lost my own mother and I understand how you must be feeling." My hand is taken from the table as she rubs it, in what I assume is support.

Right now, I'm not sure if I should like or hate this girl.

"Seriously, Ada, I am a good listener, if you need some to talk to."

Great, not only is she breathtakingly beautiful, she's got that southern sweetness going on.

Taken aback, it hits me: he told her about my mom? Clearly, gossip spreads like wildfire in Blue Haven, but the fact that he told her face-to-face tugs at my heart-strings. My throat swells and tears flow into my eyes as I turn my gaze to Lexie, who is tightly gripping my hand with a sad smile on her face.

This is exactly what I do not want, for people to feel sorry for me. Lincoln and I are not even dating.

Take a deep breath, Ada.

After inhaling, I turn my head a few times in circles, trying to loosen up my tight muscles. I pull my fingers away from Lexie's, adjusting my chair backward. I stand up in a hurry as I grab my coat from the back of the chair.

"I think I am going to head home. You know, it's been a long day, and tomorrow I'm sure it won't be much better." Facing Sarah again, I say, "It was nice meeting you as well. Maybe we will have the opportunity to catch up before I return to New York."

"Oh, I'd love that, Ada." She smiles warmly.

With one last look at Lincoln, I give him a reassuring smile, trying my best to remain unaffected. "Bye, Lincoln."

There is concern in the outer corners of his eyes, and his lips are pursed together, but he makes no effort to stop me.

Well, guess there's that.

But before I know it, he scrambles to his feet. "Wait, Ada, I'm supposed to take you home." He waits a moment, then approaches me. "Let me at least do that. I'll feel better knowing you got home."

"Don't worry about it, Linc." I pat the back of his shirt, reassuring him that I will be fine without him.

In the process of walking toward the bar's entrance, his hand wraps around my arm, pulling me flush into that rock hard chest of his. His head drops beside my ear and whispers, "Please, Ada."

I close my eyes; his heart beats rapidly against my back. Even after all this time, my presence still affects him just like it does for me. There's electricity in the air, a powerful connection between us that hasn't faltered over the years.

Despite the fact that my heart is racing, I lean deeper into his chest as he whispers, "Ada, it's just a car ride."

He's right. Just a car ride. No big deal.

With a sigh, I realize that if I continue to tell him no, I will only be fighting a losing battle. In an attempt to force the words out, I look at my hands. "Okay, you can drive me home," I murmur softly.

Leaving the bar, we walk over to his Bentley. My eyes widen, marveling at his drastic lifestyle change. I mean, I didn't expect him to drive such a fancy car, but look at his parents. I bet they just love seeing him still drive that old bronco.

Opening the door, he gestures for me to climb in. I smile awkwardly, nervously taking his outstretched hand and step inside.

Damn it, Ada, no more awkwardness.

It's not my fault that the awkwardness has returned between us. Kissing someone who is in a relationship is a definite no for me; therefore, I feel like I don't know how to act around him.

Are hugs still okay?

Ada, no hugs. That may lead to something else.

Right. Could we at least talk? Not intimately, but you know what friends talk about?

I think that'd be fine.

So no kissing. No hugs. Nothing physical altercations. Got it. Should be easy.

After Lincoln leaves the parking lot, I turn to face him and struggle to find the right words. Everything I want to say is stuck in my throat. "Lincoln, I—"

"Ada, wait, let me explain."

"I don't think there is anything to clarify. You and I are simply friends, if you even call us that."

A disappointed look crosses his face before he turns back to the road. "Yeah, I guess that's what we are, just friends." His voice full of sadness. He exhales heavily, the truth of his words settling in the air between us.

I nervously watch the scenery go by and remain in silence for the next ten minutes, thinking of the words that I could have said to make the situation less uncomfortable.

As Lincoln pulls into the lodge, he lets out a sigh before looking at me. "Ada, I am sorry about last night," he says, his voice sincere. Running his hands through his hair, he continues, "But that kiss, Ada, it was like reliving our first kiss all over again." As he gazes into my eyes, I can see the emotion; I can *feel* it. I'm right there with him, reminding me of how strong our feelings used to be for one another.

Suddenly, his fingers wrap around my neck, heat emanating from his body; our faces are now a mere few inches apart. His grip is like a vise, making it hard to breathe and intensifying the already overwhelming need between us.

With his forehead touching mine, he softly says, "God, it meant everything to me." His words resonate in my heart, and I know that he truly means them.

Stay strong, Ada. Don't give in. Just breathe.

While fiddling with my hands, Lincoln grips my chin. "Ada, look at me." He slowly rubs his thumb against my jaw. "Tell me you felt something. Please let me know I am not going crazy." His voice is low and pleading, his eyes sear into mine, begging for a sign that I feel the same.

Suddenly, my heart is pounding, my palms are sweating, and my mouth is dry. As I take a deep breath in and out, I look up into his dark blue eyes. "Yes, I felt it, but that does not mean it can continue." I draw back from his embrace.

"How could it?" I ask condescendingly. "It was a meaningful kiss, but what did you think was going to happen after it was all over? We were supposed to magically get back together? I would relocate back to Blue Haven? It was foolish to think that one kiss could make us forget the past and go back to the way things were," I add firmly.

As he places his head on the headrest, he lets out a low, frustrated groan. "I mean, I don't know. All I know is that you coming back, showing up everywhere in Blue Haven, and feeling all these emotions that have been suppressed for so long . . . I had no idea one moment with you would bring everything back so quickly, but it has."

A million questions dance in his beautiful eyes as he glances over at me and all I want to do is reach over and graze his lips with mine, hoping that I can make the pain disappear, if even for a moment.

No, Ada, we don't want that.

But my body has a mind of its own as I lean toward him, our eyes lock, feeling the electric current flowing between us.

What if it's something I do want?

Lincoln begins to move closer to me, my hand reaches out to his cheek in a desperate attempt to touch him. Feel him. He turns his face into my hand, kissing it, and for a moment, time stands still.

No, no, no, Ada, stay focused on what matters. Work. Estate Sale. Work. Estate Sale.

But what if I just want to get lost in him . . . even for a moment.

The firmness of his grip is complemented by the gentleness of his touch as he circles my wrist and draws me closer. His eyes flash with hunger, and my heart races. I don't know if the reason is because we're in the car and it's dark outside, only the silver rays of the moon illuminating the surroundings; or maybe, it's because he smells so good. Or could it be because I feel lonely, and when I am around him, I start to feel whole again?

I want him so badly.

I want to be.

I want to feel alive.

FOCUS, ADA, screams my inner voice.

"Lincoln," I whisper.

It seems as though time is passing faster and faster as I grapple with what I want while my heart thrums in my chest, hard and heavy. I slide my hands into his thick brown hair, and within a matter of seconds, I launch myself at him. And he doesn't miss a fucking beat.

Our lips move softly together, and he doesn't kiss me like a friend would. He kisses me back with equal fervor. He kisses me like he wants to consume me. My thumb brushes against the stubble on his cheek, reveling in the tiny prickles against my skin. Lincoln groans as his right arm tightens around my back, pulling me closer to him while his left hand moves to the back of my head. He works his tongue between my lips, sending a tingle of pleasure straight to my legs. His hand fists my hair, tilting my head back, and his mouth trails its way down my throat.

"God, Ada, this feels so good," Lincoln growls. "So right."

Taking my lips off his, I straddle him, watching the excitement in his eyes grow as he threads his fingers through my hair. Cradling my head in his hands—his mouth collides with mine once again. My arms entwine around his neck as I press his hips against mine, feeling the bulge in his pants, thick and hard, against my abdomen.

God, imagine what that cock could do.

"Incoming call, Sarah," a woman's voice says from beside me, but I am barely able to hear it over the pounding of my heart.

His hands are like hot brands on my body, squeezing and touching everything, bringing back memories of former times.

"Sarah's calling," the woman repeats.

Suddenly, our kiss comes to a halt when Lincoln lets out a groan and rests his forehead on mine. His breathing is ragged. "Fuck, Ada."

My attention is drawn back to the touch screen, which highlights Sarah's name.

Shit, Shiit, Shi—

How could I forget about Sarah?

How could he?

I scramble back over to the passenger seat and start to gather my belongings.

"Ada, it's not what you think," Lincoln says, grasping

my hand. "I promise I can explain," he adds, his eyes imploring me to believe him.

"I think it is, and I think this was a mistake."

With another groan, he lets go of my hand and drops his head into the palms of his hands.

"Thank you for the ride, Lincoln," I say as I get out of the vehicle and close the door behind me.

With this tension at an all-time high, how far can we go before we travel down a path of destruction we may never return from?

Chapter Seventeen ♡

Ada

The entire night, I was in a state of panic. I tossed and turned in my sleep.

What should I do? Leave Blue Haven early and let Noah handle the estate sale? Tell Sarah that I pretty much dry humped her boyfriend while we made out? Say nothing and carry on as if nothing had happened?

I am left with a decision: stay in Blue Haven and face the consequences of my actions or take the coward's way out and leave town. I haven't made up my mind yet, but I know one thing for sure: I am not about to take the easy way out. I have to face the reality of my choices, no matter how difficult or uncomfortable it might be.

My phone pings next to me as I sit on the rug in my childhood kitchen floor. I'm surrounded by a box to keep, a box to toss, and various kitchen items I have yet to decide on. A frustrated sign erupts from my mouth as I look at the message.

LEXIE

How are you holding up, Ada?

How am I doing? That's a great question.

As a result of sleeping like a bag of shit, I had decided that it would be better to occupy my mind elsewhere, such as work. So I woke at the crack of dawn, put my head down, and began working on the case right away. And as far as I was concerned, the one thing I wanted to accomplish today was to reach an agreement with Hamill and Sons regarding the closure of this case.

After I had worked a while this morning, I finally put my laptop to sleep and took a long shower at the lodge before going out for coffee and blueberry crumble at the diner. Despite the fact that sugar and coffee aren't a healthy breakfast choice, I just needed something to distract me from everything at the moment.

In an effort to push myself off the rug, I stand up and look at my phone once again.

What is Lexie's text even referring to?
How am I holding up with my job working remotely?
How am I holding up with my mom's passing?
How am I adjusting to being back in Blue Haven?
How am I holding up when it comes to Lincoln?

I have been living in a state of chaos since returning to Blue Haven. Everything and nothing feels different since my return. I feel like a decade has passed, and I am back where I was as a teenager. An emotional rollercoaster of confusion, upset, and happiness. Something I managed to conceal well for years. Being a successful attorney in New York shaped me into who I am now, a centered individual.

It wasn't complicated in New York. I commuted to work and home, maybe went out with the girls occasionally, and least of all, I did not second guess myself regarding a man.

Is this merely closure for us both?

Is it just an infatuation from the past?

Or is it something more meaningful and worth exploring again?

He is dating Sarah; how could he want anything more?

Right. Can't forget that little snippet. I would rather deal with Ruth's snarky remarks than this.

Closing my eyes, I take a deep breath iiiiin one, two, three, and ooutt one, two, three. Reopening my texts, I send out a quick reply to Lexie.

Is that supposed to be a trick question?

How about I reword that last message.

How are you holding up on everything you are going through? With your mom, Lincoln, being in Blue Haven, packing the house up for the estate sale?

Even though we chatted about some things currently happening in our lives at the baseball game, she had a knack for understanding me, which makes it feel like no time has passed since our high school days.

> To be honest, I do not know what to say. I want to devote my attention to work, the estate sale, celebrating your wedding, and returning to New York, my safe haven. But I feel like everything is spiraling as each day passes while I am in Blue Haven.

> I understand completely, Ada, and I'm sorry things are so difficult for you right now. If it makes you feel any better, Josh said that Lincoln felt terrible about how the night ended.

Is he regretting our kiss? Does he regret anything he said to me last night?

> Knowing that makes my head spin, honestly the last thing I needed to hear.

Having never been good enough in the past is gut-wrenching, but knowing that the Ada now is no better is even more devastating. Despite all the effort, the fear of not being good enough still lingers.

A pounding throb grows in my head as I move toward the bar stool.

Great, another migraine. I wish I could just get through one day without experiencing any problems.

I feel the weight of a hand on my shoulder, and I jump as Noah says, "Woah, sorry, Ada, didn't mean to scare you." I take a deep breath and turn to face him as his eyes widen. "Ada, you look awful."

"Thank you, Noah," I say, rolling my eyes.

His hand reaches out to grasp my now lukewarm coffee on the island, and he takes a sip. "Shit, this tastes horrible," he remarks. "I guess it's not as fresh as it was probably fifteen minutes ago," he adds with a laugh.

Shrugging my shoulders, I give him a look that suggests he shouldn't have taken a sip of my coffee in the first place.

Putting the mug down, he looks at me. "Sorry, Ada, I didn't mean to imply that you look bad today. It's just you have looked so put together since you have arrived that today you look—"

"Not so put together," I finish for him.

"That is true, but in the circumstances, you are bound to experience it. Your face appears pale, however," he says as touches my forehead. "Dang, Ada, you're on fire. I think you should take your temperature to rule out a fever."

To dismiss the topic, I wave my hand at him. But he does not budge. "Ada, I am serious. I will get the thermometer right now. Stay put." As he walks away, I watch, intrigued. He probably has no idea where it is in this house.

"I found it," Noah says as he runs down the stairs from the entryway.

"How did you know where to locate one of those?"

"We have been cleaning out the house for over a week now," he shrugs. He hands me a thermometer. "Here, take your temperature."

Despite my groaning, I obey his instructions, and the digital screen reads 102.2 degrees Fahrenheit.

Shit, this can't be happening.

With a frustrated sigh, I let my head fall back. "You

have to be kidding me. I have so much to do; I won't be able to finish everything in time to return to New York."

Noah wraps his arm around my neck and he says, "Ada, don't worry, it's okay. It's your body telling you to rest. When have you genuinely taken a break from work or anything else? You deserve a chance to relax and recharge."

Walking away, my eyes roll. Noah—let alone anyone—cannot comprehend the pressure I am under. It seems as though I am carrying the world's weight on my shoulders with this new case, and being in Blue Haven only makes matters worse. It is impossible to avoid a disaster when work stress is combined with emotional distress.

My face flushes with angry tears as I walk to the staircase. My migraine is becoming increasingly severe and more intense with each step I take. I can feel my heart racing as I climb the stairs, my pulse pounding in my ears as I struggle to quell my frustration. As I grip the railing of the staircase, I attempt to stabilize my wobbly legs. Taking a moment to regain my balance, I grasp my head as Noah approaches behind me.

"Ada, what is wrong? What's happening?" he asked.

"My head," I whimper as my eyes close.

Noah grasps my hand. The pain starts coming back so quickly that I clench my teeth and the tears start streaming down my face.

Ada, just keep going.

A few steps further, my legs give out, preparing me for a tumble down the stairs. But suddenly, I am tucked tight against someone's chest. His strong arms support me and I feel safe, the fear of falling suddenly gone.

"Noah?" I whisper to myself. But he doesn't smell like Noah.

I smell a combination of fresh air, spices, and sandalwood. Lincoln's smell fills the air.

It's Lincoln's chest.

I stir but he holds me tighter, his voice quiet. "Whoa, whoa, hold on, Ada. I have you, just relax." His embrace is a protective shield and his words are gentle and calming, a reminder that he wants to be there no matter what, even if I don't have a say in it.

In a concerned voice, Noah says, "I have never seen her like this."

While I am about to say that I am fine, Lincoln lifts me as he climbs the staircase. I keep counting backward as he cradles my head in his chest. The throbbing in my head continues, but it is not as debilitating as it was a few moments ago. Lincoln lowers me slowly onto my childhood bed and hovers over me, gazing at me with such tender eyes, my heart skips a beat. He kisses my forehead, and I realize he is the only one who can make me feel safe and at peace in a moment such as this.

"It wasn't necessary for you to do that," I say.

A wide smile spreads across his face as he says, "Yes, it was. Plus, I wanted to."

As if by magic, I am suddenly aware he is in my bedroom, smiling down at me. His presence is both comforting and unnerving.

What is he doing here? At my house?

I sit up abruptly, my temples stinging with a sharp pain. Grabbing my head, I ask, "Lincoln, what are you doing here?" My voice fills with confusion and surprise.

"Let's take it easy, Tiger," he says, grabbing my hand and sitting down on the bed. "Noah called me to ask if I could help with some heavy lifting. So, here I am, at your beck and call. I'm always willing to lend a hand whenever I'm needed, and this is no exception."

Another pain penetrates my head as I chuckle. "Ow, God, that was painful," I mutter.

Lincoln moves me back to lie down. "How about you let me and Noah handle the heavy items while you rest? You deserve a break, so let us take care of the work."

"No," I croak out.

"Don't argue, Ada, not today. Just let me do this one thing for you," he whispers. He looks at me intently, his eyes pleading, hoping I will grant him this one request.

"Ok, fine, but I will only accept your help today." I sigh, closing my eyes. "Just once," I emphasize. "I will do it myself tomorrow."

A chuckle escapes his lips as he steps toward the doorway. "Deal. Oh, and Ada?" he says. My eyes reconnect with his once again. "I'm glad we came to an agreement," he says with a smirk as he steps out of the room.

Chapter Eighteen ♡

Ada

When I wake up, it is dark outside. The clock on the nightstand says it's just about 5:00 pm. I sit up abruptly; *ow, I hold my head. Bad move, Ada.* At that moment, I realize that I wasted the entire day by sleeping and my heart sinks with a deep sense of guilt.

To find some relief from the pain, I lie back down on my side and try to close my eyes. The pain is still apparent, but it is not as intense as it was a few hours ago.

"How are you feeling?" comes from a deep, male voice from the doorway.

I glance around and spot Lincoln. I can't believe I passed out in front of him. My face flushes with embarrassment.

In order to see him clearly, I turn myself onto my back and find him leaning on the doorframe with his arm raised above his head. I note his signature St. James' smile, along with his dirty cheeks and ruffled hair, indicating that he was working with Noah on the house today.

Warmth instantly fills my chest.

I open my mouth to speak, but he puts a finger to his lips and grins; a gesture that says everything: Don't worry, we took care of it, just rest, Ada.

I finally manage to speak as I say, "The pain has decreased since earlier. Thank you, Linc, for taking such good care of me."

He takes his hand from the doorway and waves it forward, acknowledging that it was not such a big deal. However, he is wrong. It is a huge deal. I will remain eternally grateful for his presence at that time.

He starts walking toward the bed and jumps on the other side of me, making me squeal in the process. Laughter bubbling out of us.

Turning toward him, I blurt out, "Is this weird? This is weird, right? I mean, last time we were in here we—"

In one swift motion, Lincoln turns to his side as he pulls a piece of my hair behind my ear. The tension increases and I anticipate what is to come. My heart beat matches the rhythm of Lincoln's shallow breaths, and the moment seems to stretch on for an eternity.

"The two of us were in love and making love," Lincoln whispers. "Our connection was one of a kind, like a flame that will never die."

Closing my eyes, I feel every inch of my skin awakening to his presence. Reopening my eyes, I'm drawn in and captivated by his ocean blue ones that bore into mine. His gaze speaks to me, wrapping me in a warm embrace that feels like home.

Wrapping my blanket closer around me, my heart hammers as Lincoln holds my jaw steady; his fingers curling around the back of my neck possessively. His touch is like a wave of electricity, sending sparks through my veins.

We both lean toward each other, drawn by an invisible magnet.

Ada, don't do it.

Lincoln says, "I really want to kiss you again."

I've both wanted and avoided this. Equal parts of me are torn apart by desire and fear. I want more than anything to feel his lips on mine and surrender to the moment. Then I can worry about everything else: Sarah, Blue Haven, my work, estate sale.

"Say no, Ada," I whisper to myself, like saying it out loud will give me the restraint I need.

But it doesn't.

Instead, I feel a thrill of anticipation as I nod, eagerly wanting his lips.

In a fraction of a second, his lips finally are on—

"Ada, how are you feeling?"

As if caught in the act of doing something wrong, Lincoln and I separate in an instant. The expression across his face is all I witness, and I feel a pang of guilt for wanting this.

Chuckling, Noah asks, "I hadn't realized you were still here, Lincoln. How are you, Ada? Are you feeling better than you were?"

With a wink, Lincoln looks back at me and remarks, "Our girl is doing just fine."

Our girl.

Lincoln's girl? I am his girl?

No, Ada. Sarah is his girl.

Shaking away the emotions swirling in my head, I breathe deep and remind myself of my strength.

Pushing myself off the bed, I say, "Hello, Noah. Nice of you to check in on me, but I am fine. See?" I say, doing a twirl. I point my finger. "On second thought, I need to take a pee. Please excuse me."

I run to the bathroom that used to be adjacent to my bedroom, but has now been converted into an ensuite.

"Does she seem to be doing better?" Noah asks Lincoln.

Despite the noise from the ceiling fan, the thin walls make the conversation outside sound as if it is happening directly in the room.

It's not like I am purposely eavesdropping.

Lincoln sighs, probably brushing his messy hair with his hand. "I mean, it's Ada. She is strong-willed and will tell you anything to make you feel better about the situation."

I shake my head; he's right. Even though it's been years since we last saw each other, I'm both surprised and touched that he still remembers the old Ada.

You remember the old Lincoln too, Ada.

"Yeah, I sort of figured that. I know she's taking on a lot at work, plus handling this here can't be easy. I think today was a sign that she needed to relax. Her attitude has always been that she has to work herself into the ground if she is to succeed. I am sure this is a result of the way we were raised."

Noah lets out a deep sigh as he continues, "It's time for her to realize that success doesn't have to be achieved at the cost of her wellbeing; she needs to understand that work-life balance is the key to a happier and healthier life."

"I couldn't agree more. And well, I can't imagine what she's been through the last several years, but if today is any indication, she may need you more than you think. I know it seems like your mother's death doesn't affect her, but—" Lincoln pauses and my ringtone fills the silence. "Is that Ada's phone ringing?"

Shit, who would call me at this hour?

In my rush to complete the process of peeing, I almost run into Noah and Lincoln, who stare at me strangely. "Did you see who was calling me?" I ask as I adjust my clothes.

Noah shrugs as Lincoln says, "It said Will."

Will? Why would he be calling me, especially this late at night, not that 5:00 pm is late. Shit, is it about work? The case?

Panic builds as I pick up the phone, hoping for a normal conversation but dreading the alternative.

"Who is Will?" Lincoln asks me.

The air becomes quiet, and Noah claps his hands and says, "Alright, looks like I am outta here. Ada, please keep me updated on how you feel tomorrow."

I nod. "You know I will. Have a good night, Noah. I love you."

Turning to leave, he shouts, "Love you too, you stubborn ass."

A chuckle escapes my lips as I shake my head.

Lincoln mumbles, "Ahem," and I look back at him. He is sitting on the bed with his feet crossed and his hands behind his head. He arches an eyebrow as he says, "So, you going to tell me who Will is? Your boyfriend? Fiancé? Friend?" His eyes narrow slightly as he adds, "Come on, spill the beans. Who is this Will, exactly?"

"A fiancé?" I scoff. "Really?" *That is highly unlikely*, I think to myself.

He shrugs his shoulders, seeming upset for no apparent reason. "I mean, we've seen each other for what, threeish weeks now? I still don't know anything about the present Ada standing right in front of me," he says. "All I know is the Ada from the past, but who is she now?" he continues, emphasizing the question.

After all the years we've known one another, I can't imagine he would think so little of me. As frustrated as I am, I can't help but be disappointed that he would judge me so quickly.

That's a bit rich coming from him, considering he has a girlfriend.

I mean, Ada, you did kiss him, knowing he's with Sarah. His girlfriend.

I stop pacing, looking him dead in the eyes. "First of all, if you had given me the chance to explain, you would have found out Will isn't my boyfriend or fiancé. Not that matters, but he is a coworker. We both work at Sullivan & Rothman Law Firm."

He lets out a relieved sigh and his face softens. "Shit, I'm sorry, Ada. I didn't mean to come off like that."

Nodding my head, I take the silence between Lincoln and me as a sign, and proceed to open the message I received from Will. He did not call me, but he sent a picture. It's a photo of him, with his arms out wide, wearing a bright smile that reaches for his grassy green eyes, and his blonde wavy hair is brushed to the side.

But it isn't his facial features that drawn me in. Zooming in on the background in his photo, it looks awfully familiar. In fact, the scene in the photo is from a place I had visited this morning.

It couldn't be. The missing shingles on the roof . . .

I gasp as I see the big rainbow neon sign that says, 'The Crispy Biscuit'.

Attached to the photo is a message:

I heard that this place serves the most delicious Strawberry Orange milkshakes —I'm hoping it's true!

Something tickles my ear, and I glance over my shoulder to find Lincoln. "So that's Will." His voice is hard, his jaw set in a line; a clear sign of his disapproval.

I glance down to see the photo still displayed on the screen of my phone. *Shit.* I lock the screen on my phone and turn to Lincoln.

Ada, you have nothing to hide, It's not like you are doing anything wrong.

"Yes, that is Will, my *coworker*."

"If he's only a coworker, why is he at The Crispy Biscuit? It's clear that his feelings go beyond professional," he adds, his voice tight with emotion.

"Why are you so concerned, Lincoln? Shouldn't you be with Sarah? Not taking care of me?" I ask stiffly.

He rises from the bed, his eyebrows pinch. "Wait, why does Sarah have anything to do with this? I don't understand," he says, bewildered.

My phone pings again with another incoming text from Will.

Wanna meet me for some milkshakes?

Biting my lip, I start to pace the room again, trying to decide what to say.

> Will! You are in Blue Haven! What the heck?! I would love to get milkshakes, but how about tomorrow? I have been feeling under the weather today and don't want to risk getting you sick.

> 😔 Well . . . Since I am already here, tell me what your favorite food is from here?

> I'm so sorry, Will!! However, I LOVE the Chicken and Dumplings or a good ol' burger and french fries.

> Chicken and Dumplings it is 😔

> Let's catch up tomorrow, and I'll show you around Blue Haven.

"Well, since you're going to be glued to your phone the rest of the night, I will see myself out."

"Hold on, I'm sorry, okay," I say, grabbing Lincoln's wrist. "It's not like I expected Will to show up, and I have no idea why he's here at all. The trip must be related to work since Emmett, my boss, would not approve of him taking time off just to visit a *friend*. But I can't shake the feeling like something is off," I admit, my voice barely above a whisper as I try to figure out why Will would be in Blue Haven.

Lincoln lets out a sigh as he tucks me into his chest. The tension drains out of my body as I allow myself to be comforted by his embrace. Closing my eyes, I breathe in his familiar masculine scent. It is like a balm to my soul, soothing my anxiety away. As if nothing else matters in the world, he continues to hold me close.

After what feels like hours, Lincoln gives me a tight

squeeze and kisses the top of my head. Pulling away, he gives me another kiss on the forehead, and I close my eyes, feeling like I can breathe again.

"Ada, I—" Lincoln and I look at each other with confusion swimming in our eyes when we hear the doorbell ring.

Who would be here?

Noah left. Maybe he forgot something and accidentally locked the door on his way out.

Lincoln tugs on my hand. "Let's find out who it is."

Nodding my head, I follow behind him and continue to hold his hand as we descend the staircase.

"I got it," Noah says as he comes running from the kitchen.

"I thought you left?"

"Nah, I got busy looking through some old comic books. That stuff has to be worth something these days, right?" he enquires, looking toward Lincoln.

Lincoln shrugs his shoulders. "Might be worth checking out."

Noah opens the door, and I see someone who I least expect to: *Will.*

"Hi Ada," Will says with a wide smile as he looks at me on the staircase. Will's eyes drop to mine and Lincoln's intertwined hands. He glances away, his jaw tense, as if he's suddenly aware of how uncomfortable the situation has become.

Observing this, I drop Lincoln's hand like it's on fire.

Will raises his hand, and he holds a clear bag from The Crispy Biscuit. "I brought comfort food, unless you are busy," he says, looking back and forth between Lincoln and I.

"Ok, I definitely am leaving now," Noah says as he

tries to make a quick escape. He glances back at me at the same time he starts to leave. "See you tomorrow, Ada?"

I nod my head. "See you tomorrow, bubba."

"Lincoln, nice seeing you again." Noah shakes Will's hand. "Will, I am Noah, Ada's brother. Sorry for the quick exit, but hopefully we can catch up before you leave back to New York?"

Will shakes his hand as he says, "Yeah, that sounds great. Nice meeting you too, Noah. I have heard only great things about you from your sister."

Noah twists to face me and grins. "As you should." He gives me a wink and whispers, "Good luck."

I mouth, "Thank you," as he closes the door and I walk to Will. "It's so good to see you. I can't believe you're in Blue Haven." I give him a quick hug. "Why are you here?" My brow quirks. "Not that I am not happy to see you because, trust me, seeing a friendly face is exactly what I need."

It is not long before I hear a "pfft" behind me. Turning around, Lincoln shakes his head and shuffles his feet on the hardwood floors. His expression is a mix of frustration and anger.

Good, maybe he should be pissed. He has Sarah anyway. Will being here shouldn't be affecting him the least bit.

Will is about to respond when Lincoln interrupts, "Yeah, why are you in Blue Haven? I believe Ada told you she would see you tomorrow."

I abruptly turn, furious he would say such a thing. He finally makes eye contact and my eyebrows pinch as I glare; he knows exactly what I am saying with that expression alone: *What the hell is your problem?*

Will, being the polite gentleman that he is, just chuckles. "Well, that's a story for another day, but as far as me coming over, Ada and I have a tradition that when one of us is sick, we bring over their favorite food."

Will grins. "Ada, do you remember our first year at Sullivan & Rothman's? We both had just taken on our first big cases as newbies and wanted to impress the shit out of Emmett? We had no idea how much these cases would shape our careers, but we had faith that we'd make an impact." Will eyes twinkle with nostalgia.

For the first time in what seems like days, but is actually only hours, I laugh out loud.

Will continues as he begins to laugh, "Then you came down with that nasty bug, and I went over to the Thai restaurant you loved, and I brought you the Tom Kha Kai soup. And we've been taking care of each other ever since." He smiled, emphasizing the importance of our friendship.

He remembers all of that?

All I can recall is being sick the entire week with my head in the toilet. As I try to avoid making this situation any more awkward or let my emotions get the best of me, I give him a genuine smile and say, "This is really thoughtful of you, Will."

Looking up at Lincoln, Will shrugs his shoulders and says, "Didn't mean to interrupt anything, man. I guess it was an instinct that I had to come bring Ada comfort food; even though it might not have been from her favorite Thai restaurant." With a slight smile on his lips, he adds, "It felt like the right thing to do."

God, who knew he was so intuitive when it came to me. Has he always been like that?

Coming down the stairs, Lincoln walks up behind me and wraps an arm around my neck. My muscles immediately tense, and I give Lincoln a look that says, 'What the hell are you doing?' He is making this situation more uncomfortable than it needs to be, acting all masculine, thinking he needs to mark his territory on me.

Lincoln gives me an apologetic smile and quickly removes his arm from my shoulders. In an attempt to clear his throat, Will glances between us, rubbing the back of his neck awkwardly.

To put an end to this tortuous situation, I turn back to Will, right as he says, "Ada, maybe we can catch up tomorrow?"

I grab onto Will's hand. "Nonsense, stay. You brought me my favorite food while I was sick. I know it's not my favorite Thai food, but we can't break our tradition now, can we?"

Will smiles, squeezing my hand as he says, "Of course not."

A chuckle escapes my lips as I regain my composure. "Plus, Lincoln was just leaving, wasn't he?" I ask with an eyebrow raised. Lincoln's steely gaze penetrates the air, making it clear that he doesn't want to leave.

"Right?" I say again, making sure he heard me the first time.

Lincoln pauses for a moment before nodding and getting ready to leave. With one final kiss on the forehead, he whispers, "Feel better, Ada." Then he turns and leaves the room.

As of this moment, I am not certain whether he truly cares that I am ill or if this is just an act to prove to Will that I am his.

Which I am not. Because Sarah is his.

Are you so sure about that, Ada? The man pretty much swept in like your knight in shining armor today, carrying you up the stairs.

That may be true, and even though he came to my rescue today, I can't forget the other times when I have succeeded without him.

When I hear the door slam behind Lincoln, I look at Will and give him a tight smile. "I think we should go into the living room, light the fireplace, and dig into some comfort food while you explain to me why you are in Blue Haven."

A twinkle appears in his eye as he smiles and interlocks our arms. "Sounds great, Ada."

Chapter Nineteen ♡

Ada

It's one of those days where it is so rainy that it looks like nighttime. The dark clouds and the never-ending rain pouring down seem to mirror my emotions perfectly.

This morning, I had been in and out of a daze throughout my meeting with Ruth and Emmett. I made sure to mention that Will had made it safely to Blue Haven, but Emmett only had an annoying smirk to offer. My temper rose as I tried to figure out if his smirk was a sign of distrust or something else.

I felt like I had been hit by a wave of whiplash from the other day. Emmett had come across as proud of the work I had done on the case, but today it was a complete 180. His condescending attitude indicated that he regarded me as incapable of handling the case, which only increased my determination to prove him wrong.

While Emmett can be an asshole sometimes, I can't say sending Will here to make sure I was 'okay' has been bad. I thought a lawyer like Will, who's a born and raised New Yorker, would hate it here, but from what I've seen during our tour of Blue Haven this afternoon, I think he's really enjoying it. In fact, Will has remarked several times how much he loves the peacefulness and serenity of Blue Haven.

"This is Kardio Work," I say to Will as I introduce him to the local gym.

It is on Ivy Street, the same street I once envisioned opening my law firm on. There is an overwhelming sense of nostalgia in my heart. Driving along this exact street so many times, Lincoln's hand resting on my knee as we discussed our plans for life following graduation . . . I take a deep breath and focus on the present, noting the changes to Ivy Street since the last time I drove down it. It's been years, but the memories linger, reminding me that nothing stays the same forever.

Will laughs and raises his eyebrows. "That's a gym, Ada?"

Even though it is far from pristine, the building still has a certain charm. Inside, the atmosphere is vibrant, with loud music and TVs blaring from the cardio machines. There is a sense of energy in the air as people interact, lifting weights and running on the treadmills.

Rolling my eyes, I nudge Will in the ribs and smirk. "Yes, it is. Perhaps you should check it out while you are here."

When Will winks, a gentle smile appears on his face. It is a smile unlike any I have ever seen from him. More carefree. "Honestly, I may just do that. That way, I can experience Blue Haven to the fullest."

The sound of a loud boom coming from afar causes us to glance up at the sky simultaneously. Amidst the downpour, we can't ignore the thunder that seems to draw nearer with each passing second. It is now time to take cover and quickly run for the diner, heedless of the puddles that threaten to soak us to the bone. Will's white suit pants are the first to bear the brunt of it, leaving him soaked up to his knees.

With his hands up, he halts in the middle of a puddle and lets out a chuckle. "Well shit, guess it's a good thing that I overpacked; there go those pants. Now I'll just have to hope that my other clothes keep me warm and dry."

Biting my lower lip, I try to hide my laughter, but I fail miserably as it slips past my lips. The belly laugh feels like a release, freeing me from all concerns and allowing me to fully appreciate the joy of the moment.

The red rusted doors of The Crispy Biscuit are about to open when we come to a halt and I grab Will's hand. With a mischievous grin, I look at him and ask, "Are you ready to make your milkshake dream come true?"

His smile spreads across his face as he begins to move. I push my arm out and add, "Also, just a heads up, residents of Blue Haven tend to be more friendly than those of New York City, so try to not take anything they say personally."

He acknowledges my advice as he slowly nods his head. "I feel confident I will survive; plus, I have you if I don't." He gives me a wink and says, "Now let's see what the hype is all about." With that, he takes my hand and we walk inside together.

Entering the diner soaking wet, Will and I are greeted by wandering gazes from the residents. The calmness I felt only moments ago comes to a crashing halt. Will must have sensed this because he grasps my hand and squeezes firmly for support. His small gesture brings a wave of comfort over me, and my body instantly relaxes.

"I've got you, Ada."

My smile widens when a young waitress places us in a large red booth in the corner of the restaurant. She seems to have read my mind since this booth is out of the peering eyes of Blue Haven's residents. Maybe they will talk about something else now.

"What a tour that was, huh?" Will says as he runs his hand through his drenched hair.

Trying to resist laughing, I stare at Will. He looks a mess, with his dark blonde hair poking out in every direction. I can't help but smirk at the sight of him; his disheveled appearance isn't usually normal.

"And what are you staring at, Ada?" Will asks.

"I was just thinking about how this day began, and where it led us." I shake my head before grabbing my hair from the side and squeezing out the excess water.

In the middle of my morning meeting with Ruth, Will had called me. I can't say I was sorry, but I was really grateful that it happened. Will's timing was perfect; it gave me a much-needed escape and inter-ruption.

Since I already knew the reason for his presence in Blue Haven, I had been eager to hear from him as to why he had chosen to come. But the moment I brought it up, he shh'd me by putting his finger on my lips and said, I quote, "Let's just have fun today, Ada, let the day take us where it wants."

. . . and we did exactly that.

It really was a fun day. We first started the adventure at the local boutiques where Will insisted on buying his little brother a souvenir. From there, I took him practically everywhere imaginable, which was not a hardship considering Blue Haven has fewer than 5,000 residents.

"And where did that lead us?" he says with a grin.

My arms extend to the side as I smile at him. "Where it wanted us to."

"I would say this is a great way to end our tour, wouldn't you?"

My smile grows as I can't help but feel a flood of emotions as I recall the past. And before I can stop myself, I blurt out a memory to Will.

"As a kid here, I always came to this diner. Angel, one of the servers here, was like my second mother to me. She would brighten up my day by just being a listening ear. More often than not, I would come here after a shitty day to end on a positive note."

Even now, when I come here, Angel gives me the same warm welcome she did when I was younger. I'll never forget the feeling of being truly accepted and welcomed.

Will's features soften, almost making it unbearable to look at him. I can see the hurt in his eyes, yet he holds my gaze with such kindness and understanding.

"To be honest, today was probably the most fun I've had since I returned to Blue Haven," I say with a chuckle. More so, it was special to be able to share this experience with someone who wasn't familiar with my hometown.

"I must have the magic touch," he says as he blushes.

I chuckle, picking up the menu. "So, when will you tell me why you're actually in Blue Haven?" I inquire.

He sighs and lays the menu down as Angel approaches.

"Ada, I'm so glad you're here again!" Angel says. Her gaze moves toward Will, admiring his features with a sense of curiosity. "And who might this handsome young man be?"

A laugh breaks out from me; she is checking him out. Will notices my laughter and gives me a knowing smile.

He extends his hand. "Hi, I'm Will and I work with Ada back in New York."

Angel smiles as she puts her hand on her chest and says, "How awesome that your boyfriend came all the way to Blue Haven to see you. He must really care for you." Her eyes twinkle with joy.

My eyes widen as I spit out my water, hitting Will in the face, practically choking as I do so. His expression is of surprise and amusement.

Angel hits me a few times on the back as she says, "Well, honey, you should have told us so I could make him our tasty Chili Bowls."

Will smiles as he says, "I'd have loved that, but I think we'd love the famous milkshakes. Right, Ada?" He lifts his eyebrows, pausing expectantly, waiting for me to confirm his suggestion. "You know the ones you're always raving about?"

I nod and smile. "Yes, Angel. We would like two Strawberry Orange Milkshakes."

With a wink toward Will, she says, "Ooh darlin', you're going to love our milkshakes. They're what made this diner famous back in the day. One sip and you'll know why!"

The moment she walks away, Will immediately turns his attention to me. "What the hell was that, Ada?"

With a shrug of my shoulders, I grin. "That was a Blue Haven resident, as I warned you before we came in. People here are much . . . friendlier."

"I have to admit, I wasn't expecting that," he chuckles. "I felt like your mother was checking me out just now; it gave me goosebumps. She was more than friendly, if you ask me."

Realizing what he just said, he tightens his lips. "I'm sorry, Ada. I didn't mean . . . I never should have said something like that," he says, voice full of regret.

I laugh half-heartedly, trying to hide the lingering pain in my chest as a reminder of why I am here.

"It is fine, Will, but you should probably get used to it. Some of the women here can be vultures because the town is extremely thin when it comes to men. They will make sure to snatch anyone they can get their hands on!"

Laughing, he says, "I'll keep that in mind the next time I am alone wandering the streets of Blue Haven."

A sense of relief washes over me, listening to Will move on from his last comment.

A heavy sigh escapes his lips while he glances at the rain. "I came here because Emmett asked me to check on you," he admits.

It is like a punch in the stomach having Will confirm what I assumed in this morning's meeting. I guess I was right, after all.

"I see. Although, Emmett is fully aware that I am handling the case just fine remotely," I reply.

"I think he was just trying to make sure you really were doing alright," he says. "There's a big difference between seeing someone in person when they're going through something tough and just hearing them over a video call."

I clench my jaw, turning my gaze toward the windows, my patience wearing thin as I watch the rain patter against the glass.

Who does Emmett think he is?

The death of my mother hasn't affected me at all, and I'm doing just fine.

I am okay.

I do not need anyone's assistance.

Even though we have had a number of meetings recently, no amount of convincing on my part has seemed to make a difference. Emmett clearly doesn't trust me. With frustration boiling over, I force myself to take a deep breath, reminding myself that getting mad at Will won't solve anything.

My gaze returns to Will, right as he says, "But also a selfish part of me wanted to check on you."

Will wanted to come to Blue Haven. Willingingly? But why? After all, Blue Haven is nothing more than a small fishing village—hardly the type of place I'm sure he has dreamed of visiting.

I raise my eyebrows in surprise as he continues, "You know me. I wouldn't let anyone else take care of you. It's you. I'm always there for you." His words are reassuring and heartwarming, reaffirming our bond. "Witnessing how you grew up has given me a chance to learn more about you and your background; it's made me appreciate you even more. Plus, that girl is amazing, right?"

Heat rises in my cheeks as I try to decipher the meaning behind his words.

Is Will flirting with me? Will and I don't flirt?

Angel hands Will and I our frosty tall glass drinks with swirling colors of orange and red. We eagerly reach out and grasp them in anticipation. Will dips his finger in the whipped cream as Angel says, "I made sure to add an extra cherry to yours, honey."

He winks at me with a warm smile, not caring about her bashful flirting. A charming smile spreads across his face as he says, "Thanks, Angel, it's perfect."

She beams with pride and replies, "You're very welcome."

I can't help but grin, holding back a laugh. Will just has such a self-assurance about him. I thought it was because he was a lawyer and all, but we aren't working right now. It's obvious that Will's confidence comes from something deeper than his career; it's a part of his personality, and something I admire.

"Oh holy shit, this is delicious," Will says. His eyes light up as he takes another sip.

"I always say, love is like a milkshake with a brain freeze; it hurts so bad but we always come back for more," Angel says. "It's a cycle of pain and pleasure, but ultimately it's always worth it."

Angel leaves us alone and Will states, "You were definitely right. This milkshake is, without a doubt, the best I have ever tasted."

"I told you so!" I exclaim, pleased to have been right. "I remember this being one of my favorite things as a child. I don't know why, but I feel calm whenever I drink a milkshake. I guess it's the combination of the cold, creamy texture and the sweet taste that makes me feel so content."

Chuckling nervously, I wave my hand in front of my

face. "I apologize, that was dumb of me to say. You probably think I am strange now."

He looks into my eyes with a deep sense of compassion. He softly caresses my face with his hand as he whispers, "Look at me, Ada."

As soon as I do that, my mind calms, my body relaxes, and I feel at ease.

"It wasn't strange. I thought it was kind of cute. Embracing your unique weirdness is something to be proud of; don't let anyone tell you otherwise. It's part of what makes you who you are and it's something to be celebrated. And I just so happen to like who you are, just the way you are. Finding these cute quirky things about you is just the cherry on top."

My face flushes. As tears threaten to spill, I lower my head. My heart is heavy, and my throat feels tight.

Grabbing my chin with his finger, Will raises me to eye level. "Ada, why are you crying?" he asks, rubbing away a tear. His touch is gentle, yet there is an urgency in his voice as he searches for an answer.

A tear runs down my cheek as I sigh. "I don't know why I am crying. I have been feeling extremely emotional since I have been here." Taking a deep breath, I try to soothe my aching heart.

A part of me knows what these tears are for, his words, the way today has turned out due to him. His presence in my life brings a sense of comfort and joy that I had never expected to feel from another man again.

"Well, considering your current situation, that is certainly understandable."

"Yeah, I guess, you're right."

Grabbing my hand, he squeezes it firmly. "If it

makes you feel any better, I'll be here for a few days and can be your shoulder whenever you need it. I'm available 24 hours a day."

I let out a breath, feeling an immediate sense of relief I haven't had in a long time. Will's unwavering support has been a blessing, and one I had taken for granted back in New York.

Perhaps Emmett's decision to send Will to Blue Haven was exactly what I needed. Not only was I able to get away from the stresses of my life for a day, but I was also able to reconnect with Blue Haven and take some time for myself. Exactly what I needed to refocus and recharge.

Chapter Twenty

Lincoln

I've met my fair share of douchebags, and I have no doubt Will is definitely one of them. Maybe it's the way he stood as if he were above everyone that reminded me of my own mother, or maybe it was the way he slicked back his blonde wavy hair, oozing confidence; well, like a lawyer. He had a certain air of superiority that was almost impossible to ignore and made me want to recoil in annoyance.

However, I know the real reason I don't like him.

The way he leered at Ada last night, like she was a juicy steak he hadn't eaten in days. He had a hunger in his eyes that made it clear he wanted her, and it has left me fuming with rage. Irrational loathing isn't something that happens too often to me, but it's definitely getting the better part of me this morning.

I hate it.

I tossed and turned all night, which made my morning at work hell. Constant complaints from my employees led to me yelling at them, and Garrett told me to get my head out of my ass and do something productive. So after pushing through the morning madness and feeling my stress level rise, I took action. A run is the perfect way to clear my head and let go of the pent-up frustration.

My steps falter, causing me to stand for a few moments, my chest heaving as I admire the way the bright lights at Hope Bay Beach make the water shimmer in the distance.

I take a deep breath and slowly exhale as a sense of relief washes over me. I savor the salty air and the surrounding sights. Waves crash and people walk the streets holding umbrellas, while others eagerly await outside Sweet Beat Bakery, the sweet aroma of freshly baked apple crusted cookies filling the air.

My stomach grumbles at the thought of Mrs. Deli's cookies.

It isn't fair of me to take my pent-up frustration out on the employees. So maybe some of Mrs. Deli's cookies can be a peace offering. Plus, I want the employees at the firm to know their hard work doesn't go unnoticed.

As I approach the back of the line, my attention is drawn to a familiar male face.

Will.

I sigh in irritation, wondering just how often our paths will cross now. I had hoped that last night would be the last time I would see him while in Blue Haven, but something tells me that isn't the case.

"Well, aren't you the sweetest thing ever?"

"The man is really something, isn't he, Mrs. Randy?"

"Where are you from? Blue Haven does not have

that many handsome men about. I have a niece, Shelby, and I think you two would get along so well."

A swell of envy rises within me as I watch the local gossip crew of older ladies fawn over him. They act like he is the most charming person here.

God, are women really attracted to assholes?

Spotting me, Will waves. "Hey, Lincoln." He smiles warmly, beckoning me over.

But I don't move a step; instead, I give him a head nod as I say, "Hey, what are you doing at the bakery?"

Laughing, he maneuvers through the throng of old women. "Ada mentioned how much she loves the apple crusted cookies here, and they're a seasonal item, so I decided I would buy her some."

Well, isn't that just sweet.

Rolling my eyes in aggravation, I turn my head away from Will, feeling a pain in my jaw as I clench my teeth. I let a breath out to calm my rising irritation.

Get your shit together, Lincoln; he is just a regular guy. Just because he is from New York doesn't mean he is better.

Looking ahead of me, the line begins to move forward, and we follow the crowd inside.

Will joins me beside me, I say, "Oh nice."

"Lincoln, I—"

Saved by my phone ringing. I turn my back on Will, taking this as a sign to relieve myself from the awkwardness between us.

But that isn't happening as Will looks over my shoulder, clearly trying to see what I'm doing. Obviously, he's never heard the phrase, 'A little privacy, please!'

"Lincoln? Dude, where the hell are you?" Garrett mutters, his voice conveying his frustration. Garrett's face fills my screen as he pulls his large sunglasses over his eyes and waits for a response.

Using my phone's camera, I show him the inside of the bakery. I can't help but feel nostalgic for all the times I've spent here. A variety of doughnuts, muffins wrapped in paper, and cookies are displayed in tall glass cases. The kitchen is bustling with activity, and the air is heavenly with the scent of freshly baked goods. The floor is spotless, and the walls are decorated with vibrant colors, giving the whole place a cozy, inviting feel. The chalkboard near the front counter displays the daily specials, indicating the restaurant's dedication to fresh and updated food. The open doorway to the kitchen allows the customers to watch their favorite baked goods come to fruition.

I smile as I recall the day when I asked Ada to assist me with a cooking course. Even now, I still remember the look of joy on Ada's face when I asked her to join me. It was one of the most memorable moments of my life; a moment of both embarrassment and happiness, and it was made even more enjoyable by the fact that I shared it with someone I loved.

In a flash, I am snapped back to reality by Garrett's words. "I told you to take a break, not the rest of the day off." His eyes widen with excitement. "Wait, are you at Mrs. Deli's? Dude, grab me some donuts. The wife will love me if I bring her some!"

I can't help but chuckle as I say, "I'm on it already, man."

"Anyway, your father has been bugging me for the past couple of hours asking where you are and I am running out of excuses to keep him off your back. Get back to work!"

I chuckle again because it is something that my father would do.

"Come on, man, it's not funny. I am just now getting lunch. Even the interns got to eat before me because your ass isn't back yet, and we both know I'm not the most patient person when I'm hungry," he sighs.

Yeah, nope, he doesn't sound like a child throwing a tantrum to their parents for not getting what they want.

"I'm ordering some Apple Crusted cookies. Would that make you feel better?"

"Uh, duh, I deserve it after covering your ass all morning. Wait, who's that behind you?" He squints his eyes as he tries to get a better look.

Despite my efforts to move my phone quickly away, it isn't enough, as I am left staring at Will's face on my phone.

"Hello, I'm Will, Ada's friend."

"Ada's friend?" Garrett asks with a brow raised. "Well, isn't that something, Lincoln? Ada brought a friend all the way from New York to Blue Haven. You must be a *close* friend to her," he says, his voice dripping with sarcasm.

My eyes roll back as Will laughs. "Yeah, you could say that, but I'm mostly here to make sure she is okay, after her mother's passing and all."

Garrett smiles broadly as he says, "Oh, I see. You are that type of *friend*."

With a playful smile and a sly wink, he says, "I'm trying to break out of the friend zone, if you know what I mean."

What the fuck?

His playful smile extends over to me before he lets out a mischievous grin.

The mere thought of him with her makes my blood boil. I can't seem to shake this terrible sense of jealousy that grips me. What in the actual fuck is the guy trying to play at? This can't be what Ada prefers in men these days, right?

Clearly she has a type, but does it really matter, Lincoln? It's not like she wants you.

Garrett laughs and places his sunglasses on top of his head. "Don't I know it! Good luck doing that. Ada is a tough cookie to crack. Just ask Lincoln," he says with an shit eating grin.

Asshole.

Suddenly, Will turns and stares at me directly, with a look of bewilderment on his face. He seems to be completely taken aback, his eyes wide in shock. His gaze holds mine for a moment before he turns away and shakes his head.

Has Ada never told him about us?

"You and Ada used to date?" Will asks. "I thought you two were just friends."

"Did they date? Pfft, they were fucking love birds, soulmates, two peas in a pod; everyone in Blue Haven thought they were going to end up married and live happily ever after. But that was before Ada decided—"

I clench my teeth. "We get it, Garrett. Is there anything else you need, other than to complain about being hangry?" I ask, attempting to remain calm.

Letting out a chuckle, he says, "I guess your run did not accomplish much, huh? Looks like you're still planning on being a pain in everyone's asses when you return to work. If you have anger management difficulties, you should consider boxing. It might be worth giving it a try—it would be much more productive than constantly being a nuisance."

Jeez, it is only one day. Can't a man have one bad day?

Will's face is in front of my camera again. "I can attest to the fact that it does work. I box in New York." He shrugs. "Every lawyer needs to have a way of coping after a difficult case. Plus, boxing is a great way for me to get in shape and blow off steam," Will proudly declares.

Let's be honest, no one asked for your opinion. Don't just assume that you know what people want or need.

Will stares at me as if he knows what I am thinking and says, "Ada has been with me a few times. I think it's good for her, but she'll argue otherwise. That girl is stubborn when she wants to be."

Since when has Ada enjoyed boxing? I feel a twinge of envy that he gets to share something special with her that I haven't.

"Hmm, Ada, boxing. I bet that's pretty hot, right, Lincoln?" Garrett smirks.

I glare at Garrett, knowing that he is trying to provoke me. "I don't know, Garrett," I respond firmly, "but one thing I can guarantee is that I'm not afraid to take a punch."

"Like you wouldn't believe," Will says with a smirk. "All that sweat, muscles, tight tops, talk about a constant hard on while working out. After all, who could resist all that eye candy?"

"And we're done here. I'll see you in the office," I say as I end the video call. My patience is eroding as I grow more and more frustrated.

A laugh escapes Will's lips. "Seems like a fun dude."

With a forced laugh, I reply, "Yep, I love the guy, but

Garrett can be a handful at times. He means well, but sometimes his enthusiasm gets the best of him."

As Will places his order, he comments, "Oh, by the way, Ada's birthday is coming up in a few days and I was thinking about hosting a party. Think you'll be able to come?"

Taking a second to look at Will, I narrow my eyes. Since when does Ada enjoy having birthday parties thrown for her? She has never been one to make a big fuss over her special day, unless if you count the one time I surprised the hell out of her on her birthday.

Opening her locker, she discovers neon balloons inside. Upon seeing me, she rolls her eyes. She attempts to appear upset, but I know she is truly happy someone is celebrating her. She closes her locker before she struts down the hall toward me.

"Really, Linc, was that necessary?" She scrunches up her nose.

"I couldn't help myself," I reply, smiling. A blush spreads across her cheeks as I place a piece of hair behind her ear. "I wanted the perfect day for my gorgeous girl." I lean in close, letting her feel my breath on her neck as I softly whisper, "But there is one thing to make it even better." I grab her waist and pull her close to me.

Her eyebrows raise as she asks, "Oh yeah, and what is that?"

"This," I say, grasping her hand and yanking her into the science lab.

Glancing around the room, she asks, "What are we doing in the science lab?"

I pick her up from the ground and she lets out a squeal, wrapping her legs around my waist. We move to a corner of the room, out of sight from everyone. I can feel her heart racing against mine as her arms snake around my neck.

My forehead touches hers. "I thought the birthday girl deserved a special treat," I whisper, my lips brushing the shell of her earlobe as I pull her closer to me.

Her hand curls into my hair, tugging at the ends. "I am not opposed to this treatment. I think I can get used to it," she says with a hint of a smile.

A sudden surge of need flushes through me as I force her to the front of my body. Her body softens against my hardness, and it feels so right and good. Her heart-shaped lips meet mine stroke for stroke. She kisses me ruthlessly, her tongue dancing with mine. While the tension builds deep in my stomach, I make a low noise. It feels like a spring winding tighter and tiger-like. We stroke our hands over each other like neither of us can quite convince ourselves to stop. Suddenly, everything seems to stand still in that moment, like the world has come to a complete halt and all that is left is the two of us, forever entwined in that embrace.

I need more.

Want more.

But before that can even happen, Ada pushes on my chest. "Wow, that was—"

The tip of my thumb strokes across her lip as I cup her face, tilting it up. "Amazing?" I smirk.

"Yes," she breathes, her eyes wide and sparkling.

A giggle escapes her lips as she pushes my chest further and looks around the room again; realization dawning on her. Nervously biting her lip, she leans in closer and whispers, "What if someone caught us?" Without skipping a beat, she adds, "I would have gone to the principal's office and you would have been let off the hook?"

Clasping her face with both hands, I kiss her forehead.

"Ada, don't worry. I would have handled that if it had happened. But since it didn't," I add, "let's enjoy the moment."

Her eyes grow serious as she removes her legs from my waist. "You mean it would have been the responsibility of your parents to ensure that their son didn't tarnish his reputation?"

My arms wrap around her and I whisper, "Ada, stop. I will always have your back, no matter what." Knowing what I can do to distract her from that topic, I tickle her sides.

Even though she glares at me, the laugh that comes out of her is infectious, and my mood lightens as I smile back at her.

"Now let's go, so we can finish what we started here later," I say with a wink.

"Stop acting so damn horny." She shoves me in the side.

"It's kind of hard; look at you." I smirk.

"So, what do you say, can you make it?" Will asks, breaking me out of my thoughts.

I look up at Will, my mind racing to process the question, and I reply, "Yeah, I'll come. But are you sure Ada will want a party thrown for her?" My voice is tinged with skepticism as I rub the back of my neck.

He shrugs. "Yeah, I would say that the last few years she seemed to enjoy the parties that I threw for her. But," he continues, "I think that it was my gifts that she appreciated most." He smirks.

What the hell is the dude's problem? Always trying to one up me? Show me that he is the right guy for her?

In spite of my best efforts, my frustration seeps through my pores. There is only so much patience I can muster; my temper is fraying. And let's not get started on the multiple birthday celebrations and gifts he has given her.

Nevertheless, here we are again, another year,

another birthday, something I have missed out on, and Will was able to share with her.

My thoughts wander to the life I could have had with her, a life I could have shared with her, but instead, I am left with envy. We could have shared the kind of love and companionship that others take for granted, but there is only a distant longing for what I can't truly have.

I reply to Will, "Okay, yeah, I'm in. I would love to celebrate Ada's special day." He smiles before turning back to the woman taking his order.

Maybe showing up for this celebration could be an opportunity for me to make up for lost time. And maybe, just maybe, this will give me the closure that I need.

Chapter Twenty-One

Ada

I rest my hands on my hips, staring at my childhood room. All of my stuff either is crammed into boxes from early this morning or still needs attending too. My room, which is on the smaller size, but still uniquely mine, has a built-in bookshelf where I store all of the books I had read throughout my childhood. When I was not running to The Crispy Biscuit, Hope Bay Beach, or even Lincoln, I was cooped up in my room reading, adapting, and learning new lawyer things as well as gaining self-confidence and independence.

I wanted to be able to make my own decisions, to learn how to navigate through life with resilience and strength. I wanted to be able to make an impact in the world and have an impactful career. I wanted to be able to take care of myself and make sure I was financially secure. My room was my haven, my place to learn and to grow.

There is a small desk against the wall facing the

window. *The window.* The one Lincoln threw rocks at, begging to be let into my room. I can still remember the look on his face when I finally opened the front door and welcomed him into my room for the first time. His eyes lit up with excitement and anticipation, and the love I felt was overwhelming.

Growing up in a low-income household often meant having to prioritize needs over wants. As such, extra space for luxury items, such as a large closet, wasn't feasible when there were other more pressing expenses to worry about, like making sure food was on the table.

It is truly mind-blowing that something like that doesn't even require a second thought for me anymore. But growing up, those priorities were perpetually on my mind.

When will we eat?

Is there enough money to cover the electric bill?

Will Mom actually be sober enough when she walks through the door today?

The uncertainty of it all always weighed heavily on my mind.

It's easy to think about the what if's or be in constant fear of not getting your basic needs met. It's why I made a promise to myself to never put myself in that situation as I became an adult. I was, and still am, determined to create a better future for myself.

Was it easy? *Hell no.*

Was it worth all the sacrifices and hard work? *Hell yeah.*

That commitment to myself has made me resourceful and determined, which has enabled me to strive for success and make my dream a reality.

"So, this is Ada Collins' childhood bedroom?" Will

asks, startling me as he slides past me right into my room. "Interesting," he says as he takes a look around.

Will surveys the room with keen interest, his eyes lingering on the things that seemed special to me at one time. The intricate details that make the place neat, from the old photos on the wall to the hand-me-down furniture. He's definitely taking a mental note of every trinket, probably so he can joke around with me later about it all.

A smile spreads across my face as I say, "Nice to see you too, Will; please help yourself into my home."

He lets out a laugh as my hands extend out to the sides as I walk toward him. "This would be Ada 1.0."

Taking a second look around, he smiles. "Hmm, who's this Ada 1.0? I think she's growing on me."

With a shove to his side, I say, "Ha ha, you're funny."

Looking around again, he says, "It's cute and charming, just like you." He winks.

My face flushes immediately.

WAIT, Will thinks I am cute?

Charming? Almost like a cute, charming friend, right?

WAIT, back up. Is he flirting with me, again?

My heart beats faster from nervousness. I'm not sure how to take this—is he just being friendly, or is there something more going on? I breathe in, trying to steady my racing pulse—am I just imagining things, or is there an underlying current to his words?

In New York, he's never exhibited these flirtatious comments.

I sigh. Considering I can't even keep my head straight, maybe I'm just overthinking things. "Yeah, it was okay," I say, shrugging.

The reality of what he sees is simply a mask of what I saw as a child. Despite the changes, the harsh realities of my past still remain, lurking in the shadows of the updated and improved.

Will moves to sit at my desk. "You mentioned your mother wanted you and Noah to have an estate sale?"

I nod my head. "Yeah, that's just what she stated in her will; however, it does sort of hurt that she didn't even consider Noah or I would want the house."

"Well, do you want the house?" he asks, raising his eyebrows.

I shrug my shoulders. "I'm not sure. There are so many good and bad memories associated with this house. But it would have been nice to have had the option, you know?"

My chest stings that Noah and I were overlooked during her decision process. I rub my chest absentmindedly as I try to change the subject.

"I get that. I'm sorry, Ada," Will says in a gentle, yet apologetic tone. "On the bright side, it appears that you have almost completed the packing process," he adds with an over the top smile.

Gazing at Will, his joy is contagious, as if it's translating into a wave of comfort that washes over me.

Moving from my desk, he wraps an arm around my shoulder. "Well, let's get to it. I'm here only for a few more days, so you might want to take advantage of me." With a grin, he looks me in the eyes and adds, "I'm sure you can think of something creative to do with me before I have to leave."

Shock slams into me, my jaw hanging open.

That was definitely flirting, right? There is no way I am imagining this.

My cheeks heat at the insinuation.

No, no way, Ada. His words and what he meant were not misunderstood.

Shaking off the topic, I smile and shake my head. "Well, Noah and I still need to pack up about three rooms. Figured I could do one room, one day at a time. What do you think? This way, I can at least get the housework done, continue on the case, and help Lexie with last-minute wedding arrangements."

Obviously, all the while, I'll be keeping my fingers crossed that I'll be able to make it happen. The Hamill and Sons lawsuit case is a raging nightmare. Not only have they turned down two amazing companies to work with, they are now thinking about working with an entirely different industry when choosing a company.

Do you know how difficult it is to conduct extensive research to merge two companies together?

Fucking hard.

In addition, the situation becomes even more complicated when the so-called merger needs to be completed rather quickly.

Will moves in front of me. He grabs my shoulders and says, "Ada, b r e a t h e."

I closed my eyes briefly and inhale as Will says, "That sounds like an excellent plan, but you are forgetting one very significant detail in that plan of yours."

I look at him in confusion, pausing to consider what I had missed. I am normally on top of my game, but then again, since being in Blue Haven, I have been all over the place.

Will nudges me in the shoulder. "Ada Collins, you did not forget your own birthday."

A small chuckle escapes my lips as I let my head

drop. Relief washes over me as I realize I didn't forget anything significant. "Will, it's my birthday; it's not a big deal." I shrug.

In response, he scoffs, "I mean, it is when you only turn thirty once in your lifetime. You know what happens after you turn thirty?"

Yeah, it's often said that life changes drastically when you turn thirty. This is because it is often seen as a milestone that marks the transition from your twenties to your thirties. It is thought to be a time in your life when you become more mature and have different priorities. But I feel like going from twenty-nine to thirty is going to make absolutely no change in my life, just like every other year.

Walking down the stairs, he says, "Maybe we can have a dirty thirty right here in Blue Haven." His eyebrows wiggle slightly as he adds, "What do you think?"

A glare emanates from my eyes as I say, "You wouldn't."

"You're turning thirty!" he exclaims. "You're entering a new decade in your life, so that's kind of a big fucking deal, Ada."

Despite having very little time to notice my birthday, Will always makes an elaborate celebration for it every year. I should be grateful, and I am, but I also have never been a big fan of celebrating myself other than for my career.

My first course of action once I am in the kitchen is to grab a Diet Coke from the refrigerator. While I should probably just give in to Will, I hesitate before saying yes.

It sounds more fun to just sit on the couch and relax while working and drinking wine.

My inner thoughts all but point out how lame my life is. But, I can't help thinking that it would be even more fun to maybe celebrate my birthday while in Blue Haven one last time.

The event could serve as both a birthday celebration and a farewell party.

Within a few steps, Will comes over to me and picks up a hair strand that has fallen from my forehead. His fingertips linger on my skin as he grabs it. You would think it would send a spark of electricity through me.

But it doesn't.

Only one person can make it happen.

Make my heart hammer in my chest.

Will's hand places my hair behind my ear, causing my heart to race. I feel him move closer to me, leaning into me, as his lips hover just a breath above mine.

But he stops moving just as he whispers, "Let me do this, Ada. Let me celebrate my favorite girl."

Uh, what was that? Could it be just me being cooped up in the house most of the morning that his comments are making me delusional?

Because Will has been on top of his game.

All flirtatious and shit.

And since when have I been *his girl?* Color me shocked.

God, Ada, you must be losing it. Maybe a birthday celebration is just what you need.

I take a calming breath, leaning my forehead against his as I take a moment to process his words before responding, determined not to be overwhelmed by my own thoughts.

"A birthday celebration can happen, as long as it's low key," I whisper.

"You drive a hard bargain, Ada Collins, but that's a deal I can work with. Plus, haven't all my previous birthday celebrations been low key?" While chuckling, I hear a door slam and Noah appears in my peripheral vision.

As if witnessing something inappropriate, Noah covers his eyes with a hand, saying, "Shit, Ada. Sorry. My time is impeccable, isn't it?" He stands awkwardly, unsure of what to say or do.

My laughter grows as I move away from Will and over to Noah.

With his eyes still partially covered, he starts backing up toward the door. "I didn't realize you were busy. I can come back another time."

Continuing to laugh, I grab his hands from his face. "You big goof, we were just talking."

He eyes both Will and I. Clearly unconvinced by my response, he continues to stare at us both skeptically. "Mmmhm, whatever you say," he says. With a hand outstretched, Noah continues, "I'm Noah, Ada's brother. I think we got off to a rocky start the last time we met."

Laughing, Will extends a handshake to Noah. "Will, nice to meet you, Noah. Ada told me all about you."

"Oh she has, has she?" Noah asks with a quirked eyebrow as he turns around to see me.

Will grasps Noah's shoulders. "All good things, man. You have a wonderful sister."

Noah glances back and forth between us, as if we have something to hide. "So what exactly were you two doing? Hmmmm?" he asks.

"We were just discussing Ada's dirty thirty birthday celebration that I am planning."

My cheeks twitch as I chuckle. "Yes, Will insists on organizing my birthday celebration every year."

Noah squints in curiosity. "Every year? I'm pretty certain that every time I call you on your birthday, you tell me you are working?"

With a wink, I say, "That's what I want you to think."

Noah laughs. "I knew you had a wild side."

"Man, if only you knew," Will states.

I gaze at the two men in front of me, my eyes narrow. "That was a joke, Noah; and what exactly does that mean, Will?" I ask sternly.

"Sorry, Ada, I'm just kidding." Will throws his hands up in surrender. "All I was referring to was that you like to go out to the clubs every now and then," Will adds.

Is that supposed to be a crime?

My eyes roll as I start walking toward the dining room. I cannot help but notice the dark gray bay windows, which are frosted by the snow flurries. This type of weather in New York always evokes a sense of nostalgia for me. My desire for those things I once wished for is resurfacing now that I have returned to Blue Haven, leaving me uncertain as to whether I should let them go or embrace them.

"What Will said. I was messing with you, Ada," Noah says as he walks behind me and grabs my shoulder. "You're tense." He starts to rub my shoulders.

I shrug his hands as my agitation increases. I find this topic amusing in no way. "Ha, ha, ha, you two are so funny," I say with a sarcastic tone in my voice.

When will I get a break from people hounding me

about being less stressed? Can they not understand that I enjoy the challenge? My career is my passion and I sometimes have to sacrifice things to be successful. I am dedicated to my work and won't compromise on my goals. I just need some time to unwind and relax, free from the constant reminders to de-stress.

Ada, you know the real reason for their actions and statements. They are concerned about you.

In the distance, I hear footsteps hitting the hardwood floors as I walk back to my room.

Noah grasps my shoulders again, forcing me to face him. "Ada," he says, "I'm sorry, okay. I love and care about you a lot. After seeing you almost hospitalized, I'm worried about your health and safety, and I want to do what I can to help." Noah's concern has me pause. He isn't demanding I rest; instead, he's offering help, reminding me that I am not alone.

"Wait, Ada, you almost had to go to the hospital? Are you okay? What happened?" Will asks in a worried voice as he rushes over to my side and examines me.

Guilt and regret weigh heavily on my mind as concern consumes Will's words, too.

"Yeah, it was actually the day you brought comfort food to her," Noah says.

Will flashes an eyebrow at me. "Ada, why didn't you tell me?"

Cause it's another person to worry. Not only do I not need pity, I don't want it either; it's just another burden to carry along with the feeling of being judged by those familiar faces in Blue Haven.

Taking a deep breath, I say, "Honestly, Will, that was the last thing I wanted to discuss with you. It would've ruined your time here if I brought something up. I want you to be able to have fun here without having to worry about me. You would be overly cautious about everything you said, or we did together."

Will's hand begins to rub my arm up and down, giving me goosebumps. "Mhm, I see," he says. His eyes flash a hint of hurt as he looks away, but he continues to massage my arm with a gentle touch. "Ada, I always worry about you. You know that, right?" he asks. His fingers are soft and gentle, but his words are heavy.

Nodding my head, I take his concern to heart, understanding that he genuinely cares about me and wants what's best for me. "I know you do, I mean, that's what friends are for, right? Having someone to care and worry about you?" I say, squeezing his hand gently in assurance.

Will's expression sours, as if what I said hurt him. Stepping back, he averts his gaze and encloses his lips in a thin line.

Hmm, that's odd.

Or is it, Ada? Look at how the man is looking at you. He finds out you were nearly hospitalized and the first thing he is doing is comforting you.

"Exactly, friends," he murmurs.

Shit, Ada. What did you just do?

Noah steps in to rescue me, per usual. "So when is this party going to take place? I'll be sure to have my plus one ready."

I twist my head suddenly in Noah's direction. "You are bringing a plus one to my birthday party?"

He smirks and raises his shoulders in response.

Well, can't say I expected that.

"Wait, since when do you have a girlfriend?"

He chuckles. "Since . . . I don't know . . . "

I smile, shaking my head. "I can't wait to meet her, you knucklehead," I say while teasing his thick brown hair, just as I used to do as a child.

He gives me a quick glare. "Come on, Ada, not the hair."

"You started it by keeping secrets."

Will snickers beside me. "So, this is what it's like having a sibling?" Will asks as he looks back and forth between Noah and me.

"It's like getting twice the love," I reply, smiling as I mess with his hair again.

My eyes are drawn to Noah, and I make a run back into the kitchen, standing behind the island. Noah rushes into the room with Will, the two of us stare at each other, waiting for the other to take a step forward.

"I see some things never change?"

We all glance over at the entryway, where Lexie is holding Josh's hand. I smile and move toward them, but the presence of another person stops me in my tracks, making it difficult for me to ignore the rat-a-tat of my heart.

Lincoln.

And he's staring directly at me.

My heart beats faster than normal with every step he takes, and I am knocked on my ass. Literally.

What the hell? Did the floor just give way at the worst possible time?

I sit up from the hard tile and my ass starts to tingle in pain.

Great, that's going to leave a nice bruise for later.

Suddenly, my face is covered in slobber as Ginger licks me. I immediately laugh and kiss the top of her head, rubbing her earlobes. "Just my luck," I chuckle, "but I'm glad I got to see you again too, girl."

Lincoln rushes over to me, extending his hand for support. "Ada, I'm so sorry, again," he says, biting his lower lip. Most likely withholding a smile or laugh.

My hand reaches out to him and my smile returns; as soon as our skin touches, our eyes lock and my thighs press together. The warmth of his touch sends a familiar, immediate sensation throughout me. There is electricity in the air, and my racing heart longs to be close to him. The waves of emotions are both comforting and exciting.

Ada, calm down, not now.

As soon as I am upright again, I let out a laugh while my legs wobble around one of the kitchen bar stools. "No worries," I say.

Noah clears his throat as he claps. "Alrighty then, now that Ada is fine, we can move forward with details concerning Ada's party."

Everyone laughs, simmering my stress.

The more time around Lincoln, the harder time I have pushing these emotions that have impacted my body away. Every touch, gaze, sound of his laughter, and waft of his scent, all have me dreaming things I shouldn't. Thinking about things that I shouldn't be.

Yet, I find myself unable to look away, unable to resist the urge of being pulled toward him—a longing to become closer and feel more of what I am experiencing now.

Will moves toward me, placing an arm around my neck. He looks at everyone and says, "Ada's party will be at Parallel 37 around 8:00 pm. I assume everyone can attend, even for a little while?"

Everyone smiles and nods, as Lincoln blurts out, "You know I wouldn't miss it for the world, A."

Lincoln

Ada is gazing at me, like I always imagined she would on every birthday of hers for the rest of our lives, and it all but makes my heart beat faster. I want to stop time and freeze us in place. The smile and happiness radiating from her are the only things keeping me from removing the douchebag who has his arm currently wrapped around her neck. Looking down at her like she's his world. My heart aches to break their connection and wrap her up in a hug that tells her she deserves so much more.

Pfft, newsflash, I was her world once.

Yeah, Lincoln, a long ass time ago. Leave the past where it belongs. Behind you.

But what if I don't want to? Since Ada stepped back into Blue Haven, there has been a whirlwind of emotions inside me, but in the best way. I feel better, sleep better, eat better, and live in the moment rather than wishing the days away. It's reminded me to slow down and enjoy the little moments instead of rushing through life.

Do I love having Ada back in Blue Haven, even for only a little while? *Maybe. Okay, fine, yes I do.*

Do I like seeing her support me at the baseball games I coach? *Absolutely; it means the world to me.*

Do I like seeing her beautiful face light up when she thinks of all our past memories? *Absolutely—I can't help but smile right along with her.*

Am I fooling myself knowing she's going to up and

leave again after Lexie and Josh's wedding? It's not like anything has changed for us. Well, maybe it has, but I still feel bittersweet as I think of the looming goodbye that awaits us both at the end of the wedding. But I'm determined to make the most of the time we have together and find a way to finally move on.

"Okay, perfect, it's settled. We will have everyone join us at Parallel 37 tomorrow night," Will says, breaking me from my thoughts.

"Remember, low key," Ada states, pointing at Will with her index finger.

A grin spreads across the bastard's face as he steps away from her slightly, resting his hip on the island kitchen counter and crossing his ankles. Confidence radiates from him. He extends his finger out to Ada. "Of course, pinky promise."

Her pinky curls around his while she giggles. He bends down and gives her a quick peck on the finger while staring into her eyes.

The heat of my emotions rise watching her with another man, especially in such an intimate way. It's extremely difficult to suppress the hurt and anger.

"I'm holding you to it." Ada grins sheepishly.

"I wouldn't expect anything less, babe," Will says with a wink.

Babe? What in the actual fuck?

I have a sudden urge to lose control. Ready to blow a gasket, I push myself off the kitchen door and start to move toward the two of them, prepared to rip their fingers apart. My chest heaves, my fists clench, and my breathing increases as I approach them; every muscle in my body vibrates with rage. An "ahem" from the corner of the kitchen jolts me back to reality.

Noah clears his throat, and Ada and Will break free from their so-called *promise*. Ada's shoulders plummet, almost like she is relieved by the separation from Will.

Hmm, what's all that about? I remind myself I will need to dig more into that later.

Breathing deep, the tension leaves my body as I appreciate the timing of Noah's interruption.

"My apologies for interrupting this moment of promises," Noah says, while waving his hand between Ada and Will.

A curled fist reaches my mouth, stopping myself from laughing. Those who know Noah well know that was most likely sarcasm coming from him.

Wrapping an arm around Ada's shoulder, he says, "But the more time we spend chatting, the less time we have for packing. Ada and I have only two weeks left before the estate sale."

Noah moves toward an empty packing box on the kitchen table, dropping his arm from Ada's shoulder. "That means we still have work to do, people. So, since there are," he begins counting the people in the room, "uh, six of us. I believe that we can accomplish some serious packing. What do you say? Interested in helping Ada and I?"

With a smug smile, Will replies, "I can definitely help, but Ada already knows that."

She holds his gaze for a moment before turning away, her expression unreadable.

Lexie says, laughing, "That's why we actually came over, and we bought these for you, Ada." She holds what appears to be Mrs. Deli's Apple Crusted cookies on a ceramic plate.

"Looks like you are about to be filled to the brim with those Apple Crusted cookies," Will says to Ada.

Lexie glances over at Will, raising her eyebrows, and he says, "I brought some for Ada too."

"Wait a minute," Noah interrupts, "why does Ada get special treatment here? You guys know I don't live in Blue Haven anymore, right?"

A laugh is heard throughout the room, and then all eyes turn toward me, waiting for my response. I glance toward Ada, waiting for her to give me an inkling that she wants me to stay and help. But all I get is a twitch of her mouth as she twirls her hair around her fingers.

A nervous tell.

She's always had these subtle tellings of when she was nervous, whether anyone picked up on them or not; I know her like the back of my hand. But what is she nervous about?

Me?

Us?

Will?

I take a deep breath, searching for the right words to say, but in this moment, silence speaks louder than words. Maybe it's better to just leave and let my anger settle down.

While the tip of my tongue is poised to utter some lame excuse, it isn't what spills out of my mouth as I try to speak. "Of course, I will stay and help," I say, looking at Ada.

Her mouth curves upward as her head turns slightly downward. I smile, watching her effortlessly move, swaying her hips side to side with every step, making her curvy ass bounce.

I quietly groan to myself. Adjusting my semi-hardened cock, Ada glances over her shoulder and her lips part.

Shit. Just what I need, to look like a hormonal fucking teenager.

As she drags her eyes up my body, she stops at my eyes and licks her lips.

Hot fucking damn. Is this girl trying to make me go crazy?

She looks at me with a smirk of satisfaction on her face, knowing that she is driving me absolutely insane.

Standing by her, my heart beats wildly. It takes all my strength not to throw her over my shoulder, dragging her to where I want to go. I long to feel her body crush against mine and caress her until the sun rises.

Keeping eye contact with me, she grabs the empty packing box on the kitchen table. "Well, let's do it. What are you all waiting for?" she asks.

Laughing, I pick up an empty packing box and join her.

Even years later, Ada is still the same girl I remember, but she's grown up. She's no longer the shy and hesitant young girl she was; instead, she's become a self-assured, sexy, and ambitious woman.

Chapter Twenty-Two ♡

Lincoln

Goddamn, she is beautiful. What is it about her that steals all oxygen from the room whenever she is near me, not to mention the fact that one glance at her sends blood rushing down to my cock.

"Earth to Lincoln." Ada snaps her fingers in my direction.

"Sorry, what?" I refocus my attention on Ada and our surroundings—Ada's childhood bedroom. Her room is her own unique reflection of her personality and interests—something that could not be replicated by anyone else.

We spent the majority of the afternoon packing up one of the three remaining rooms. We finished around 5:00 pm and then ordered pizza as Lexie, Ada, and Noah talked about our favorite past memories together. Will had to excuse himself after packing, as he had work that needed to be attended to. Let's just say he didn't forget to leave with a grand exit, giving

Ada a kiss on the cheek, which once again fueled my anger.

As my eyes take in Ada's room, there are a few things I changed during renovations. The light bulbs were switched to LED lighting to give the room a brighter look and the door hinges were tightened to ensure the door shut securely. The bed was moved to the corner for more space and the nightstand and dresser were repainted to give a fresh look to the room.

But it isn't the stationary items in her room that make it hers. It's the words on her wall—words that inspired her, gave her comfort, or simply drew her smile. I remember the day she was on a stepladder trying to reach a specific spot when I walked in. Her tongue was stuck out a bit as she focused on the project at hand while on tiptoes.

I rest my hip in the doorway and stare at the wall and words already written on it—Courageous, Supportive, Confident, Passionate, Strong, Caring. I watch her finish her writing before clearing my throat. When she steps off the ladder, she smiles shyly at me.

"You are all of those things," I say quietly, my eyes never leaving hers.

With her paintbrush placed to her lips, she observes the progress of her painting.

"What are you doing?" I ask as I move toward her.

The silence consumes us both as we gaze at the wall.

"It was my intention to demonstrate to myself that I am all these things. That I am more than what others think I am. That I am capable of remarkable things in life." As she continues, she turns to me and says, "You know, I could have given up a long time ago, because of all the abuse that I have received

from the people in this town, including my mother. It's not easy being faced with negativity every day, but I have the strength and courage to continue pushing forward and show them what I am made of," she says confidently. "Do you like it?" she asks, twirling her fingers in her hair.

Her nervous tell.

My focus shifts between the wall and Ada, as if I'm captivated by her presence.

My arms wrap around her waist, and I put my chin on her shoulder while staring ahead. "I believe that you are all those things, Ada Collins. Because you know in here," I move my hand to her heart, "that you are all of these things and more."

I want her to understand that it doesn't matter what her external environment looks like or what other people think of her. All that matters is that she knows her worth and trusts her own judgment. She's enough, just as she is.

Leaning her head against my chest, she squeezes my arms tightly. "I love you, Linc. I don't know what I would do without you."

"Good thing you won't have to find out," I whisper as I kiss her head.

"Did you hear me at all?" Ada stands in the closet doorway, holding her hip and lifting her brow.

"Sorry, just got swept back into the past for a moment." She looks around the room, as I say, "There are so many memories within these walls. It's funny how just a few seconds can transport you back in time."

"I know, right? I was just in here thinking about the time I wrote those exact words," she states as she points to the wall.

While rubbing the back of my head, I let out a

chuckle. "Just now, I was thinking of that exact moment."

With a smile, she drops her head, but not before a blush appears on her cheeks.

Is she embarrassed?

"You know, the real reason I put those words on the wall in the first place was because of you."

Me? Not sure if I should take it as a good thing or bad.

"Me?" I ask, moving toward her. "I thought it had to do with your feelings toward your mom and the people of Blue Haven."

She shrugs her shoulders. "Yeah, that's part of it, but you have always spoken these words to me." She pauses, looking into my eyes, her voice fills with warmth and sincerity. "You have always made me feel special, wanted, loved, and cared for, even if it was only for a brief moment. You have always made me feel worth something. I became convinced that I was enough, and that I was worthy of being loved."

I gaze into her eyes, reducing the distance between us. "The words I spoke to you were never for just the moment, Ada. Every time I said them, I meant them."

I meant them with all my heart and soul, and still do.

"I mean, shit, look at you, look at how far you have come. Don't you think you have proved your worth?"

She shrugs. "Yeah, I would like to think so, but I figured maybe putting them on the wall and seeing them every day would make me feel as I did when you said them to me. Knowing I am loved and cared for, and knowing that perhaps what you see in me, I can also see in myself."

I grasp her by the waist. Gently caressing her cheek,

I say, "Ada, you are all these things, plus more." I point to her chest. My gaze lingers on hers as my words reverberate between us. "All along, you always knew that you were capable of whatever you desired, and you made it come true."

She lets out a heavy breath as she leans her forehead against my chest.

"Ada, what's going on? What's wrong? You know you can tell me anything, right?" I rest my chin on top of her head as I rub her back, giving her support the best way I know how at the moment.

Her body instinctively relaxes into mine, and a wave of gratitude washes over me. The voice in her throat catches as she asks, "Why is this so difficult?" She holds back a sob, trying to maintain her composure.

"What do you mean?"

"Everything. Coming back to Blue Haven, attending my mother's funeral, visiting my childhood home, packing things I never planned on keeping, but now I'm reconsidering." She pulls her head off me, staring up at me. "Seeing and being around you."

The truth of her words causes my heart to swell. "Maybe it's so hard because deep down you still care," I tell her, wiping away the wetness from her bottom lip as I speak.

My arms tighten around her, but she pushes me away and begins to pace the room.

"You don't understand what this has been like for me these past few weeks. I'm powerless over anything, and it scares me. The things I see every day are constant reminders of what I once wanted," she says, her voice wavering with emotion.

Watching her wipe another tear from her cheek, I

observe the way she rubs her hand against a word on the wall that reads, 'Lawyer'. Over her shoulder, she turns and says, "Do you know why I wanted to be a lawyer? The honest answer?"

I shake my head as I make my way toward her.

"As a child, I felt powerless, unprotected, and incompetent. I couldn't get my own mother to listen to me when I sought help. Half my life she was drunk off her ass. Therefore, the times when I did want to go to her for help, I just kept it inside myself," she explains, pointing to her heart. "I searched for power everywhere I could, eventually finding it through my career. It was the only means by which I could control my life and ensure my voice was heard.

"My goal was to have my voice heard by those around me, and I never told you this, but when we were in high school, Mrs. Johnson, our guidance counselor, asked me what I wanted to do in college and I replied, 'I want to become a lawyer.' She laughed. She fucking laughed, Lincoln; directly in my face as she asked, 'Are you sure that's a smart move? A four-year university can be expensive, and law school is additional.'"

Ada is hiccupping, stuttering, and sobbing, which tears my heart to pieces. There is a part of me that wants to interrupt her, but I know she has to get this out.

Step by step, inch by inch, I move closer to her, but she extends her hand in front of me, insisting that I remain where I am while she continues to speak.

"I knew at that moment that I would prove everyone around me wrong. I would be one of the best lawyers Blue Haven has ever seen. That was one of the reasons I left Blue Haven so quickly, because I thought it was a sign to get a head start on college. After winter break, I left without saying a word to anyone else apart from Noah.

"I knew that the goodbyes to everyone, including you, would result in me staying and being stuck in a place I hated so much. However, after meeting with our guidance counselor, I realized I needed to put my past behind me and pursue something fulfilling."

I think back to the months before she left. She never once mentioned Mrs. Johnson. Ada could be so vulnerable with me. Noah and I were the only ones she trusted, but despite that, she kept so much hidden. I never knew the real reason why Ada left without even a single goodbye. I had a feeling it might have been because of something someone said or had done, but I never knew for sure. It was always something I'd have to come to terms with. Despite being there at her lowest, I was just another Blue Haven resident when she ran away. Now that she's here, in front of me again, I need to remind her that I'm so much more.

I close the distance between us and tilt Ada's head up. Her nose is red from crying and her eyes are puffy. My gut aches. I hate seeing her so distraught about a past that still haunts her. I understand why one may never get over it, though. Ada pretends that her past doesn't bother her and never did, but by doing so, she is inviting a mess of emotions.

With a heavy heart, I wrap my arms around Ada, feeling her shake as she cries. She's been through so much and needs to work through her pain. I want to be there for her, no matter how long it takes.

"Have you found being a lawyer to be as fulfilling as you had hoped?"

Nodding, her large blue eyes draw me in as she

speaks. "When I am in a courtroom, I come alive," she says with a more calm and happy tone of voice. "You know when people exercise, their bodies release endorphins; well, for me, the endorphins release the moment I enter a courtroom. It is like a drug; the power of the courtroom offers me an adrenaline rush that I can't get anywhere else." Her eyes sparkle with passion.

"Every time I enter, I am reminded of how important my work is and the strength I possess to advocate for those who cannot do so for themselves. It is this feeling of power and euphoria that keeps me continuing to do what I do."

The reasons she gives for becoming a lawyer amaze me. I couldn't be more proud of her even if I tried. She is this successful, independent, and drop dead gorgeous woman who is a fierce advocate in court. It makes me want to drown in those feelings with her. To be as happy in life as she is right now.

But aren't I happy? I have a great job, a nice house, and I'm about to be an uncle. A fucking awesome one at that.

However, these last few weeks with Ada, being near her again, seeing her in Blue Haven, are causing me to question if I was ever really happy after she left over a decade ago.

I may have been content, but never truly fulfilled or joyous until now.

Therefore, the question arises: was I ever truly happy without Ada in my life?

My eyes remain fixed on her as she smiles up at me. I rub her cheek with my thumb as she closes her eyes and relaxes her face into my palm. I love the feeling of her soft skin against my own, and her breath as she exhales in contentment.

God, what I would do to have her smile at me like that because *I am* the one giving her the happiness she's feeling and not her job.

Lincoln, can you hear yourself now? She has moved on and is satisfied with her life. Use this closure in your lives to move forward and you will both be happy.

There is no doubt that my inner self is right. Maybe closure is exactly what she needs. Maybe I should allow her to finish her business here and return to New York. She's better off there than this shit hole that ruined her entire childhood.

My hand drops as I step back; her eyes open and narrow as she considers the situation. The tension between us grows as I wait for her response.

She asks, "Wh–hat's wrong?" in a shaky voice.

I pace the room, running a hand through my hair. "I'm sorry, Ada. I thought I could do this. I really did, but I don't think I can."

She approaches me, stepping toe-to-toe with me in the middle of her bedroom. It's giving me whiplash.

When the door closes, I slam my hard chest against her soft, curvy body in the middle of the night. The love and contentment I sense warm me from within. She nuzzles into my neck, nibbles, and kisses me.

A low groan echoes through my body as my whole body reacts to her touch. My skin tingles with anticipation and elec-tricity as she trails her lips along the length of my neck.

The moment I open my eyes, everything I thought was a dream from the past vanishes in an instant.

Ada is kissing me now.

Wait, Ada is kissing me? What in the actual fuck?

A new groan escapes me as she bites my ear lobe, setting my body ablaze. This sensation only serves to further heighten my pleasure as I lose myself in the moment.

No, this can't be happening, even if I want it to fucking happen.

I gently push her off me and narrow my eyes. "What are you doing?" I ask.

Trying to hide her embarrassment and hurt, she turns her back to me. Her shoulders slowly slump forward, and her breathing becomes shallow and labored as she stares straight ahead.

Shit, way to fucking go, Lincoln.

My hand reaches out to her, facing her toward me. "Ada, shit, I'm sorry. I didn't intend for it to come across that way. I just wasn't expecting that," I say. "I am a mess, and I think both our emotions and our past are getting entangled to the point where neither of us can think clearly."

"Actually, my head is pretty dang clear and I know what I want, even if it is only for a night," she says. "Dammit, Lincoln." Ada walks to her bedroom window, moving away from me. "Can you let go for even just a split second and allow yourself to feel?" She lets out a frustrated sigh and drops her head. "I'm so tired of being stressed and exhausted. I just want to let go of everything, even for just a moment." She turns to look up at me and shakes her head, desperation in her eyes. "Please," she continues, her voice quiet but still holding an intense plea. "Help me to forget. Just for a moment."

I should just walk away now while I have the chance.

Let it end here.

Let us have this closure. Don't let our mixed emotions drown us.

But I can't.

Instead, I take long, powerful strides across the floor. Our eyes meet, and everything in the room stills. The chemistry between us is palpable; the unspoken desire for each other intensifies in the air. My mind is free of consequences or judgments. All I can think of is how I can't help but be pulled in by her gaze and the electricity that is radiating between us. Neither of us know where the night will lead, but we wholeheartedly embrace the unknown.

Ada will leave. I will stay.

We don't have a chance.

I lunge for her at the same moment she reaches for me. I stumble backward as she wraps her legs around my waist, and I slam my body into hers. I move us toward her bed, and for a few minutes, it is nothing but chaos and heat. My hands on her ass. Her soft moans against my lips. My tongue in her mouth. Her tits on my chest. Our movements are primal and desperate, as if we are trying to make up for all the time we spent apart. We move together like a single entity, our hearts and souls intertwined.

The world fades away and all I am aware of is her.

My cock grows harder beneath the heat of her palm as she strokes me over my jeans. It feels both new and familiar to run my hands over her body, skimming every delectable feminine curve. She rolls on top of me, and I feel the connection growing stronger as we continue to explore each other. It reminds me of our previous times together, but yet, this is something completely different.

Ada is sexy as hell, confident in her skin, and damn strong.

She kisses my jawline, letting a moan slip softly against my lips. She is so damn sexy like this, not perfectly put together, just Ada. My heart has been missing this side of her all these years. I thought I had lost her forever when she left, but here she is, all these years later, still with the same warmth and affection. I never thought I'd feel this way again, but when I'm with her, I feel like I'm home. She nips at my ear as she runs her tongue down my neck and into my mouth.

She never knew this, but she was my first kiss. My first real girlfriend. My first love.

While we both mostly spent our adult life pretending we were nothing, our bodies remember otherwise. She moans, and I am tempted to rip off her clothes, but I also want to take in this moment.

"You drive me insane, Ada, and your mouth . . . God, your fucking mouth is everything I remember and more."

Brushing her fingers through my hair, she presses our mouths back together. We kiss, letting our bodies mold as one.

"Don't stop, not this time. Love me again, in the way I know you can." Her plea is full of emotion and desperation.

I love her now; I never stopped.

"No stopping, Ada."

My erection is hard between her legs as she straddles me.

Ada

I've missed this; the way he touches me, bringing me to life in a way that only he can. My sweater and bra lift, his rough calluses touching the skin on my lower back as he pulls them over.

His touch is electric, sending waves of pleasure through me as I let my head fall back. His fingertips run circles around my nipples, sending sparks of pleasure radiating through my body. I arch my back and moan in delight as his hands explore my curves, igniting a fire in my core.

God, this feels so right, too good, and it's everything I want. What I need more than anything right now is to feel him inside me, filling me with everything I didn't know I was missing.

Him.

His tongue runs over my nipple before he grasps it with his mouth, flicking it several times, eliciting a louder and more husky moan from me. He moves to my other nipple, taking it into his mouth and gently biting down.

"God, you feel amazing, Lincoln. It's just like I remember."

Looking into his eyes, I say, "I never thought I would feel this way again."

"Me either, baby. It's like I am finally breathing again."

"Lincoln."

"Ada, no, don't tell me to stop, not now."

I nod my head.

Maybe, if we were somewhere else, I would have the strength, but not here. Not my childhood room, with so many memories of us.

Lincoln rolls over me, staring at me intently while

removing his shirt. "Do you know how many times I wished for this?" he asks.

He did? I would have thought he would have gotten a clean slate once I left. He never once tried to call me or get a hold of me.

I shake my head as tears threaten to flow.

He caresses my cheek and pulls a piece of hair behind my ear. "How often I roll over in bed wishing you were beside me?"

There is a sweetness and tenderness in his words, conveying the audible ache of him missing me.

Something I didn't think was capable of happening.

There is a sense of longing in his touch, a touch that is gentle and comforting.

"Can you imagine how it drives me crazy being in Blue Haven every day, driving past all our spots; what would have been your law firm, or the local college where I should have been teaching? You came back for your mom's funeral, and it drives me insane that I can't just hold you, kiss you, and be with you whenever I want."

He feels that way?

My heart pounds as I grab his hand and move it to my chest. "Linc, please hold me, kiss me, and be with me now. Tonight."

I'm scared, but I know that I want him here with me in this moment.

He nods, and tears stream down my face. He clasps the side of my neck as he kisses me tenderly, and I pray he can feel everything I wish I could convey.

It takes him a moment to pull away from me as he moves his forehead toward mine. "Ada, tell me I am not dreaming. That you are here with me," he says.

"I am here, Linc," I whisper as I press my lips to his in confirmation.

His eyes soften as he traces his lips down the column of my neck to my breasts. He encircles my nipple with his tongue before slipping it into his mouth, lavishing it with warmth. His touch sends shivers down my spine as I moan softly, feeling his gentle caress.

He takes his time, exploring my body with his lips and tongue, each movement eliciting a new wave of pleasure. I thought what we did in the past was hot. However, being older and reunited after so long, and in my childhood bed, where everything reminds me of him, is almost too much.

For years, I tried to ignore the fact that I couldn't breathe without smelling his cologne; I couldn't open my eyes without seeing something that reminds me of him. I never wanted to admit that I felt him everywhere, even in New York.

As he slips his hands down the front of my body to undo my jeans, I unbutton his bottoms in a frenzy. We butt heads as we wrestle to get our pants off and start laughing.

Lincoln rolls me off of him, rising to remove his pants. My breathing is out of control as my eyes roam over his entire body. He glides his pants off and stands in his boxers like a true Adonis. I can't help but bite my bottom lip as I take him in. He truly is breathtaking, and that may not be a manly word, but he is just so sexy. Each muscle is firm. His stomach is all ridges and valleys that my fingers itch to explore.

His broad shoulders and strong arms reach up to his face, where his smirk sends a shiver down my spine. His hair is messy, but it works for him. His eyes, almost a darker blue, seem to see right through me, making me feel exposed and vulnerable.

Lincoln grabs my legs and pulls me to the end of the bed where he removes my jeans and underwear. I have never felt so exposed and liberated at the same time. He is taking his time exploring every bare inch of me, and I can feel the electricity between us.

Sitting up, I tug him onto the bed with me, wrapping my legs around his waist, feeling his cock right at my entrance. Making my body pulse with need.

"Lincoln, I want to feel you inside me."

As he separates himself away from my grip, he makes an incoherent sound of pleasure. "I want that too, but right now, what I want to do the most is make you come on my tongue." His voice is low and deep, and his eyes burn with desire. He kisses my neck and trails further down my body, making me tremble with antici-pation. His warm breath sends a shiver up my spine as he nears my most sensitive area.

My heart pounds in my chest, and my breaths become shallow as he nudges my legs apart. I close my eyes, allowing myself to take in the sensations as he kisses and bites at every inch of my body.

"Baby, open your eyes," he commands.

My head swims as his mouth disappears between my legs. His tongue swipes against my opening, drawing pleasure in a way I haven't felt since . . . him. He licks, tugs, sucks, and teases my clit, pushing me higher and higher. He does it a few times, which makes me want to scream and cry at the same time. I'm panting and holding the sheets in a death grip as my orgasm hits me and I call out his name. Everything is light and blissful; I feel like I am on cloud nine and never want to come down.

His name lingers on my tongue as I drift back to reality, my heart racing from the intensity of the moment; a feeling I never want to forget.

Lincoln crawls up the length of my body, and I stare at him, wondering how the flame between us never died. The spark we once had is still there, if not stronger than before. I eye him as he leans back and pulls his boxers off. My breath catches, admiring his cock. He is magnificent; his cock is thick and long, and everything I remember and have fantasized over the last several years. I wrap my fingers around his shaft, wanting to bring him pleasure, but he grabs my hand and removes it. His gaze meets mine and his eyes are hooded with hunger.

He shakes his head. "That can wait, baby, but being inside you. Feeling your tight heat, can't."

Both of us watch as he aligns himself with me. He slowly slides his cock into me, causing me to gasp and him to groan. His movements become more urgent as I take him in deeper, embracing each surge of pleasure and sharing it in a way we never had before.

"Oh, God, baby, you are so tight," he says, placing his forehead against mine.

Our bodies move in harmony as we continue to look at one another. With every thrust, we become more intertwined and connected. My body responds to his as I wrap my legs tighter around him. I savor every moment, as I know this feeling of pure bliss and connection won't last forever.

Chapter Twenty-Three ♡
Ada

I thought I had a great life back in New York. I have a great career that I love and am damn successful at. I live in the Big Apple; a lot of people can't even say that. Shoot, some people stay in one state their entire lives. I have the best roommate and penthouse suite. I am truly living the dream I once thought I would never have at the age of twenty-nine, or thirty, if you count today, since it's my birthday.

Lying in my childhood bed, it does not seem as though my life back in New York is all that great. As long as I had my work and materialistic belongings by my side, I assumed I would be satisfied. But, in reality, I have discovered that I have been lying to myself. That was all a facade—what I thought would make me happy was really just an escape. True contentment and joy comes from something much deeper than my possessions.

Being back in Blue Haven has me experiencing a

great deal of nostalgia. I am reminded of the good times I had here, of the enjoyable conversations, and of the sweet memories that stayed with me long after I ran away.

There is nothing better than being around Lincoln again, cherishing every moment we share. It only makes me realize how much I have missed him. The longing for him grows with every passing day, and I know that I want to be around him even more than before.

The fact that I am stuck at my firm 70 hours a week, with no socialization, really takes a toll on me. I am missing out on—everything. I thought I could handle it all, but I know that I need more than just a career; I need a sense of belonging and connection and it wasn't until now that I realized what I needed.

Until Blue Haven

Until Lincoln.

Having spent the last month around Lincoln, I've noticed how easy it is to fall back into old habits.

Old habits die hard, they say.

As much as I tried to convince myself that I no longer needed him, that what we had wasn't special, that we were too young and naive . . . last night proved me wrong in ways I never thought possible. It's almost like our connection is meant to be, and that no matter how much time has separated us, it is still there. I can't deny that I still love him, and now I'm questioning why I ever tried to convince myself that I was better off.

But I can't tell him that, can I?

I can't tell him how I am feeling because what if he doesn't feel the same way? What if I put myself on the line again, only to be hurt twice by him?

But what if he has changed?

People can change; therefore, taking another chance and being vulnerable could lead to more.

Something new and exciting

I think there is still a feeling deep inside me that prevents me from telling him. I think a lot of my fear is rooted in the uncertainty of how he will respond. I'm afraid of being vulnerable and of being rejected. I'm also scared of the unknown, of not knowing what this next step will look like for us. Plus, there are the other issues too.

Like he lives in Blue Haven. I live in New York.

Would he even be able to picture himself in New York?

Can I see myself returning to Blue Haven?

His parents' lack of acceptance of me is a heartbreaking reminder of the extent of their disapproval.

Can I even trust him again after what he did to me all those years ago?

How would it look to even move on?

God, Ada, do you hear yourself? How do you know Lincoln even wants anything more than just a good lay. You're a beautiful, successful, independent woman; maybe he just wanted a bite of the forbidden fruit one last time.

Ugh, this is way too much over-analysis for me, especially on my birthday.

Ada, having just entered your dirty thirty era, you should really enjoy your day to the fullest.

This is one thing I can agree on with my inner thoughts. She's usually an annoying little bitch that sits on my shoulder, but today's advice might be helpful. While I do not usually go balls to walls on my day of birth, there is something about being back in Blue Haven that makes me want to fully embrace the day and take advantage of everything that is about to occur.

A sigh escapes my lips as I pull the fluffy down comforter over my head. Closing my eyes, I repeat to myself, "Today is going to be a great day for you, Ada, and your first task is to get dressed in something New York fancy, then get yourself a birthday donut. After all, when you look good, you feel good, and feeling good is an excellent start to your birthday. Then you're going to kick ass on the conference call with Hamill and Sons." To seal the deal, I take a deep breath and let the motivation wash over me.

The sound of my own voice causes me to throw off my comforter and sit up, taking note of the imprint Lincoln has left on the bed. His scent hangs in the air, a reminder of the night before.

While chewing my lip, I shiver as I recall the number of times Lincoln and I continued to go after our first encounter. Although I am, without a doubt, a sexual woman, my sexual experience last night was different on all counts. My appetite was starving and was unable to be satisfied by anyone other than one man, and he succeeded in satisfying my desires. I truly had an unquenchable thirst for Lincoln, and it felt like something I would never be able to get enough of.

My phone pings on the nightstand and I see the name 'BESTIE'. With a quick swipe, I put the phone to my ear. "With whom do I have the pleasure of speaking with?"

Her snicker brings a smile to my face. "Happy Happy birthday. Happy Happy Birthday, Ada! As always, thank you for being older than me."

The coffered ceiling fills my eyes with a gleam of light as I fall back onto my pillow and laugh.

"You're never going to let that go, are you?" I ask.

"Definitely not, girlfriend. I'll always tease you about our age gap because you're a few months older than me."

The fact that she's only four months younger than me does not deter her from rubbing in my face that I'll eventually hit all my gray hairs, wrinkles, and sensory impairments before her.

"Is there anything you plan to do to celebrate this lovely day of yours? Go to any bars? Strip clubs? Casinos?"

With a chuckle, I respond, "There won't be any of that, but Will is throwing me a small party."

After a beat of silence, I hear, "Wait, Will is there? In Blue Haven? Why did I just discover this now?"

Shit, I forgot to mention it to her.

"Sorry, I forgot and became busy with other things. Please forgive me."

She chuckles. "Of course I can, but I still don't understand why Will is in Blue Haven?"

"Emmett sent him to visit me, and before you say anything, that was the only reason he came." I rise from bed and head for the door as I prepare to make my morning cup of coffee.

"Hey, I did not say anything, but I still believe Will has only heart eyes for you. There's something apparent and unmistakable in the way he looks at you. He may not be outwardly expressing his affections for you, but his subtle body language speaks volumes. Will has a strong attraction to you, and it is only a matter of time before you realize it, too."

Is that true?

Even though he has displayed more flirtatious behavior toward me, I just chalked it up to my current situation making him more friendly with me.

There are red roses, happy birthday balloons, a white envelope leaning against a glass vase, and waffles piled high on the kitchen island that interrupt my train of thought. I walk toward the beautiful set-up; the waffle's scent is enveloping me in waves. My heart skirts a beat at my surroundings.

Taking a deep breath, I smell the flavor of blueberries, one of my favorites. It makes my stomach flutter to think that Lincoln still remembers my favorite flavor after all these years.

"Luce, I am sorry, I have to run right now, but I appreciate you calling me."

"Off so soon? We just got on the call. I want to know all the dirt, spill the details of what's been happening since you arrived back home?"

Home

It is a simple word that is simultaneously complex. Could I even call Blue Haven home? Has it ever been my home? Unless Lincoln was around me, it never felt that way. As long as he was by my side, nothing around me mattered, including gossip around town. He made me feel safe, loved, and welcome.

Chuckling, I say, "Well, first of all, I don't have much gossip to share."

Really, Ada? Just like that, you're going to lie to your best friend?

I roll my eyes; you were doing so well inner voice, too bad it didn't last.

"I'll be sure to call you back and update you on anything you want, just another time, yeah?"

"Of course, Ada, I love you. And remember, you deserve the day to yourself, so try to let loose, okay? Perhaps call Will over to help you out with that," she says seductively.

"And that's my cue to hang up, bye Luce," I say with a laugh.

I place my phone on the counter and cannot help but smile. I pick up the envelope and it makes me feel like I'm back in high school. Giddy, happy, excited, and for the first time in a long time, I want to *feel* like this. His gesture has given me hope that I might be able to experience that sensation once again, and I am grateful for that.

Ada, don't get too excited. You will have to return to your life in New York at some point.

I shake my head and I tear open the envelope to discover a letter inside.

Dear Ada, I wish I could express to you what last night meant to me, but I'm sure you know, as you probably feel the same way. OR it's possible I'm completely making an ass of myself and you are experiencing the exact opposite of how I am feeling. Regardless, I just want you to know that last night was truly special for me.

It was special to me too, Linc.

In any case, I enjoyed last night with you,

*and I am looking forward to celebrating your
big day with you tonight. Lawyers like to read a
lot, right?*

Laughing, I let out a sigh. *This man.*

*Because this is the first of many letters you
will receive from me ;). Anyway, I wanted to
keep this short and sweet, until tonight.
Bye-bye butterfly.
Those words have always meant something
to me, Ada, and they always will.
Xoxo, Lincoln*

I close my eyes and hold my hands tight to my chest. I try to recall the last time he said that to me. We were children back then, but he would always say 'bye-bye butterfly' whenever we parted ways. That moment of nostalgia brings a flood of memories. I can still feel the warmth of his hug and the affection of his words.

As he liked to put it, he saw me and got butterflies in his stomach, and butterflies are beautiful, just like me, so he thought of me whenever he saw butterflies.

The guy is really going all out, isn't he?

In the event that this is the first of many letters, what will the others have to say? Will they wreck me too? In anticipation of finding out, I grow anxious in my chest.

Will they be filled with promises of a better tomorrow?

Will it bring me closer to what I'm looking for, or will it simply bring me more confusion?

Whatever the case may be, I cannot wait to find out. I wipe a tear from my cheek as I pick up my phone to text him.

Chapter

Twenty-four ♡

Lincoln

Is she trying to kill me?

Taking a look at my phone, I witness Ada practically topless with a single rose. In an attempt to avoid being affected by the text message, I adjust my pants underneath the conference table of our firm.

> Thank you so much for the sweet letter and the birthday surprise.

> Ugh, Ada, you're killing me.

> Huh? How exactly am I doing that?

> Don't play Miss Innocent. Look at your damn outfit. You could make a guy come by simply wearing it. A lace and satin cami nightdress is a man's dream, did you know that? Fuck, Ada, I can see your peak nipples, you know, the ones you let me suck on all night long.

You're digging yourself a deeper hole here, Lincoln. You shouldn't be saying these things while in a room with a potential client.

I run my hands through my hair quickly, trying to regain focus.

Fuck, fuck, fuccckk.

I wish I could leave this fucking meeting and wank off in my office instead of being trapped here listening to an unbearable client.

> Whoops, I forgot that I was still wearing that outfit! 🙄

I shake my head, letting out a chuckle.

"What was so funny about that?"

When I look up at Dr. Henison, his brows narrow. Garrett's wearing an eat-shitting grin, as if he understands what I am laughing at.

When I turn my attention back to Dr. Henison, Garrett is mouthing, 'ADA, ADA, ADA' in my peripheral vision.

Fucker.

Our client is clearly unaware of the scene taking place behind him, as Garret makes sex gestures with his hands.

"I apologize, sir. I didn't mean to laugh. Let's move forward." I shake my head in dismay. I hand Dr. Henison a few papers. "Maybe you should tell me what services you are interested in."

Dr. Henison rises and moves toward the back of the room. Feeling comfortable doing the same, Garrett and I both walk over to meet him, standing next to the three large glass windows. The man continues to stare; whether it is because he is observing Hope Bay Beach or because he is overthinking his decision. I should try and convince him to choose us for his business before my father confronts me and shows me that I am a complete failure.

"Having already reviewed your services in advance of our follow-up meeting," he turns back to Garrett and me, "and considering we are a new physician clinic in Blue Haven, we need the best we can get. I am confident that you will be able to handle all our accounts efficiently."

We fucking did it.

I exhale deeply, making my body slump, losing its rigid posture. I extend my hand to Dr. Henison as Garrett squeezes my shoulder. "I can promise you will not be disappointed. We look forward to working together."

Shaking my hand, he walks away with a smile, saying, "It was good to see you boys. I look forward to our partnership."

When the doors close, Garrett and I both smile and bump fists together.

With a heavy sigh, Garrett exclaims, "Holy shit. That old bastard almost gave me a heart attack. We have been working with him for how long?"

"Three months, to be precise, though some clients are more challenging than others, especially physicians. There were a couple of seconds when I felt like I couldn't breathe."

"Linc, I knew we had this in the bag," he said, nudging me in the shoulder. "Each client relationship is handled professionally by you, and I know how to celebrate the success of every new client relationship."

I shake my head and laugh. "Well, not tonight, dude. Ada's birthday is today, and Will is throwing her a party. So I will be there."

His eyebrows lift. "So that's what got you all out of sorts?"

"What do you mean by that?"

"There is no doubt that you are jealous that Will is throwing her a party while you are not."

"Let's be clear, he can throw her a birthday party, that's what friends do, but I will take her home after the party," I assert.

With a wide grin, he slams the conference table with a fist. "I knew it. Ada rode the fucking flagpole, didn't she?"

A hearty laugh escapes my lips. "Let's not let the whole firm know all about my sex life, shall we?"

"It was obvious to me that you were distracted when you came into the office. I chalked it up to Will throwing Ada a party."

Suddenly, my eyes narrow. "How did you even know there was a birthday celebration? Half the time, you don't even remember what day it is."

"Aren't most people like that? I often hear people ask, 'What day is it again?' In any case, Will invited me. He must have liked me after seeing me on that Face-Time call of ours," he says with a wink.

I run my fingers through my hair while tugging and squeezing the ends. *Of course he did.* For all we know, he might have invited the whole fucking town.

Despite my nervousness, I open the conference doors, feeling slightly stressed about her upcoming celebration. I take a deep breath and straighten my clothes, determined to stay composed and professional despite the turmoil in my mind.

You have nothing to do with this. Let Will handle it.

On our way to our offices, I turn my attention to Garrett. "Well, let's hope that her celebration remains low key. After all, it was one of the things she stressed to Will."

While rubbing his hands together, Garrett shrugs, clearly anticipating the drama to unfold. "We shall see, won't we?"

Chapter Twenty-five

Ada

For the first time in my life, I promised myself that I would enjoy my birthday, and I did. After I texted Lincoln a thank-you message, I immediately began working.

Today, I wore my favorite Vera Wang dress. Despite its over-the-top glitz and glam, it made me feel alive. I felt powerful, confident, and ready to take on the world. This was reflected in the meeting with Hamill and Sons, as I was able to make informed decisions and present my options regarding which company would be the most suitable fit for them to merge with.

Two company structures were compared and analyzed; the leadership of the company they could potentially merge with was determined and the cultures of the different companies were compared and assessed to determine which one would be most aligned with their own. After evaluating all of the financial costs and positions, we decided to conclude the call. Most people, including lawyers who are not experienced in M&A, fail to realize that transaction costs can impact the entire merger process. It only takes one small blunder for the entire merger to come crashing down.

It had taken me a tremendous amount of effort to ensure the meeting went perfectly, and once it had, I felt such a sense of accomplishment and satisfaction I had never experienced before. My only decision was to treat myself to the local Blue Haven spa, Sunrise Spa, as a way of celebrating the day.

Sunrise Spa, also known as Lexie's business, is really beautiful. She has always been committed to esthetics, and when we first caught up after I returned, she told me about her business endeavors and how she had always dreamed of opening her own business. She had really done her research and knew the industry—from her education to her past experience, she had all the skills and drive to make her business a success. She had strong relationships with the previous tenants, which allowed her to understand the local market, and within a few months, she renovated the building and added her own touches. Before long, she had a full-service spa that included massage therapy, facials, waxing, and manicure and pedicure services.

The place is incredible; the interior design was carefully crafted to make customers feel relaxed and comfortable. The furniture was luxurious, and the décor was up-to-date and stylish. The colors were carefully chosen to create a sense of warmth and tranquility. It is a place where women can go to feel pampered and escape from their everyday stresses.

Exactly why it was the first place I went after a long morning.

As I was receiving my spa treatment, Will called me to inform me of what was going on with tonight's plans. He assured me that everything was going smoothly, so I chose to take advantage of this opportunity to continue enjoying my day, which turned out to be much easier than I anticipated.

I cannot even remember the last time I actually took time out of my day to get my nails, toes, and a facial done, let alone on a weekday. Although I rarely spoil myself, today's decision was the best one I made and something I should prioritize more frequently in the future.

Plus, it had nothing to do with seeing Lincoln tonight, no way.

That's a pretty convincing statement, Ada.

Approaching Parallel 37, one of the fanciest restaurants in Blue Haven, I am unsure of what to expect from my supposed birthday bash. Considering that my only request was to keep it low key, I am hopeful Will kept his word. Though I am both excited and apprehensive about how the evening will unfold.

A heavy sigh escapes me as I rub my hands against my favorite black body dress from Vera Wang. Yes, I changed, but what the heck, a girl can do what she wants when it's her birthday, right?

I knew that it would enhance the color of my eyes and the cut would accentuate my curves. It is a sexy, yet sophisticated dress, and I won't mind if Lincoln's eyes are glued to me tonight. In addition, the dress is so soft and comfortable that I can wear it all night without even realizing I am wearing it.

It is a bit nerve-racking for me to open the solid wooden oak door to the restaurant. I release a shaky breath as I see the hostess standing. I cautiously enter the restaurant, feeling a rush of anticipation.

I can handle this. Nothing bad is going to happen; it's your birthday.

Even though I have never been to this restaurant, when I was younger, I remember it being one of Lincoln's favorite restaurants. He used to rave about the food here, praising the chefs for their exquisite flavors and unique dishes.

My eyes wander, taking in the surroundings. Honestly, this is not the place I would have chosen to celebrate my birthday. I might have gone to a place like this a few times back in New York, but not Blue Haven Ada. Given Will's efforts to continue our tradition, and the fact that he may not have realized this restaurant is so fancy, I should give him the benefit of the doubt.

With benches lining the walls, menus, candlelights, and wine bottles on tables, the dining area is quiet and relaxed. There is a warm atmosphere and a mouthwatering aroma emanating from the kitchen. It is the type of place where people can relax and enjoy one another's company.

My purse vibrates. When I pull my phone out, I see a name on the screen: *Emmett.*

Ugh, can't I catch a break? I don't remember the last time I actually enjoyed celebrating my birthday. My birthday celebrations always revolve around big work victories. But this year, I want to focus on celebrating myself and all I've accomplished in the past year, and just take a break from my career.

Since I have no other choice, I move back toward the lobby where other people are waiting to be seated.

"Hello, Emmett."

Sounding as if he is struggling to breathe, he rushes his words out as he says, "Hello, Ada, we have an urgent matter and I need you to come back tomorrow."

"But I—"

"The last thing I want to hear is any excuses right now. All that matters is that you get yourself on a red eye as soon as possible."

A frustrated breath escapes my lungs as I roll my eyes.

This can't happen, not now.

Not when everything is suddenly falling back into place; plus, the estate sale hasn't even happened nor has Lexie's wedding.

My chest tightens with anxiety as I struggle to understand what is happening. "Can you at least tell me what all the fuss is about?"

Heaving a heavy sigh, he says, "Hamill & Sons are second-guessing their decision to work with us."

"Wait, I thought we had it in the bag." My eyebrows furrow in confusion. "In our meeting this morning, they told me they would send me the remaining paperwork and a working contract. What happened?" I ask, confused.

"Yeah, well, they must have forgotten to mention the fact that they held another meeting today to discuss alternative solutions."

What the hell is going on here? This isn't good, especially for our firm.

My heart falls to the pit of my stomach, realizing my chance of snagging partnership is about to slip through my fingers. I take a deep breath and steel myself with determination, knowing I have one last opportunity to make it happen. "I will get on the next flight I can."

There is nothing but silence on the phone. *What the hell? Did he hang up on me?*

My hands sweat as I pace the lobby. *Shit. Shit. This is bad, and it can't be happening at a worse time . . .*

"Ada, what are you doing here all alone when the party is inside?" I look behind me, and Will is standing in the lobby's doorway. His smile is wide, and he appears overjoyed to see me.

Ada, let's put one foot in front of the other instead of focusing on that. It's your birthday; you have friends and family here celebrating you. Don't fall short of them. Do not let your work circumstances affect tonight. Even though things may be difficult right now, you can still focus on the joy of spending time with your loved ones and celebrating your special day.

Taking a calming breath, I put aside all of my worries and stress and enjoy the moment; it won't last forever.

I smile tightly as I grab Will's arm. "Hello, Will, you look dapper as ever."

With black slacks and a gray button-up shirt accented by a maroon tie, he definitely stands out from the crowd.

His grin spreads across his face as he observes me from head to toe. "Well, I can't let the birthday girl show me up, which I believe you absolutely have done," he says with a low whistle. "You look stunning, Ada." His compliment has me blushing in response.

Laughing, I nudge him on the shoulder as we proceed toward the back of the restaurant. My eyes are drawn down to the outfit on my body. It's a dress I had grabbed when I was packing the rest of my belongings in boxes. I knew right away that it would be appropriate to wear it to a place like Parallel 37. Soft fabric and muted colors added a certain elegance to the restaurant's modern, elegant atmosphere.

And it'll make Lincoln go crazy.

Despite not being short or low cut, it features a one-shouldered design with a side slit that reveals some leg. In addition, I am wearing Ruby Red lipstick. It is an appealing combination that strikes a perfect balance between demure and daring.

"And scrumptious, might I add," he remarks with a wink.

Will is being flirty again. But why? Why with me? Does he want to be more than friends?

I don't think I can handle that.

My smile tightens as my face warms from his comment.

There are no prying eyes on me as we move throughout the restaurant. It's unfamiliar, new, and gives my stomach a tingly sensation.

Euphoric.

Whenever I used to walk into a place in Blue Haven, the attention always landed on me and not always in a positive manner. Maybe it is high time that the town of Blue Haven saw me for more than that girl.

"SURPRISE! HAPPY BIRTHDAY, ADA. HAPPY BIRTHDAY TO YOU!" they all shout.

Observing my surroundings, I relax mentally and physically. The party is definitely low key. In a private room to ourselves, I see a variety of my favorite people, all with smiles across their faces. Lexie, Josh, Max, his son Connor, Angel, Noah, and he's holding his phone up, showing even Luce on FaceTime. Next to him, I see Elena.

I blink a few times to ensure that I am seeing properly. Yep, sure enough, she's still there.

Elena is Blue Haven?

Her arm is wrapped around Noah's as she winks at me.

Okay, something is definitely happening there.

The interaction between them is anything but friendly.

Continuing to glance around the room, I spot in the far corner, looking handsome as ever, Lincoln St. James; and is that Sarah?

I feel lightheaded as the surrounding air thickens. Her presence is surprising; was she invited by Lincoln? As my body instinctively tenses, I am not prepared for that situation.

With her.

With them?

A strong arm wraps around my waist, tightening at my waist. I glance over my shoulder right as Will gives me a quick peck on the cheek. His embrace radiates tenderness and love.

"Happy Birthday, beautiful."

My face immediately flushes from embarrassment. *What is going on with Will tonight?*

I look toward Lincoln, noticing his pissed—no, more like irritated—face.

With fists clenched at his sides, his mouth is a thin, angry slash, and his eyes stare into Will and me. He stands there, a silent force of anger radiating tension, making it hard to breathe.

What's his problem? Is he *jealous?*

What gives him the audacity to feel that way when Sarah is here? Nevertheless, at *my* birthday party.

I mean, isn't she his girlfriend? the little voice inside my head whispers.

God, what if she really is? What does that make me?

I'm fully capable of admitting when I am in the wrong, but am I? I felt like Lincoln wanted what was happening as much as I did. It didn't seem like much in the scheme of things, but I still feel guilty.

I even feel a little remorse.

Walking toward my chair, which has a bright pink banner that reads, 'Birthday girl', I smile and wave to everyone.

I tap my champagne glass a few times to draw everyone's attention as I say, "Now, I will be the first to admit that I do not really enjoy celebrating my birthday; however, something about this year, coupled with my return to Blue Haven, inspired me to do something different. Enjoy it and celebrate it for once. The last several weeks have been a whirlwind, but I do know one thing, being surrounded by you all is truly a blessing." My eyes roam the room. "The love, the support—everything—is greatly appreciated, and thank you for coming tonight, it means the world to me."

"Are you kidding? We would not have missed it for the world," Angel exclaims.

Taking me by the shoulder and hugging me, Elena says, "It is so good to see you, Ada."

I return the embrace, my eyes welling with tears of happiness at seeing another friend. After I squeeze her tightly, I pull back and say, "What are you doing here?" I wave my hand in front of me. "Not that I am not excited to see you, just a little overwhelmed." I chuckle.

As she bites her lip, she shrugs her shoulders. "Well,

Will originally invited me, but Noah kinda sealed the deal."

My eyebrows raise in surprise. "Oh my God, Elena, is there something going on with you and my brother? I don't mean to pry," I say quickly, "but I can definitely tell there's something you're not spilling to me."

She looks down quickly and her face turns bright red, before she says, "I'm not sure. But we have been in contact since you first left Blue Haven for your mother's funeral arrangements, but the conversation kind of escalated from there."

She leans over and grabs my arm. "But don't say anything to him, please? I do not know where this will lead, and I do not want either of us to get hurt."

My lips are sealed, and I nod slowly. "I promise I will stay out of it, but I hope you do not mind me saying that I would not be opposed to you and Noah being together."

Her bright smile spreads across her face as she replies, "Me too, I think. It's just hard. Ya know? He lives in one state and I live in another? How can that be possible?"

With a smile, I say reassuringly, "I understand, but things always seem to work themselves out."

Hugging me, she says, "Happy Birthday, Ada. I am glad I was able to be here and celebrate with you."

As she approaches her chair, I settle into my own, directly between Will and Lincoln. There is an array of Italian food spread across the long table, ranging from appetizers to full courses. The moment we begin to dig into the food, one of my knees is grasped by a firm hand.

I peek over at a smiling Lincoln, who reaches out to

me and hands me a balloon that appears to be black with gold sparkles and reads, 'Dirty Thirty Club.'

"Happy Birthday, pretty girl," he says as he kisses my cheek.

My cheeks redden while my heart skips a beat and my breath catches in my throat. I stare into his eyes. His signature St. James smirk is all it takes for me to be completely under his spell once again, feeling a complex mix of anger, frustration, and desire.

As far as I am concerned, the way I am feeling should not be considered normal. We are not dating. We are friends. That is what we are. We only had sex, not a big deal. Plus, I have to return to New York tomorrow, which should solidify the fact that we will no longer be able to continue whatever it is that we are doing.

My response is a genuine smile, but it feels fake as I say, "Thank you, Lincoln."

Despite my best intentions, it's difficult to let go of the outside world and just enjoy the present moment.

The look of concern he gives me disappears just as quickly as it appeared.

In no time at all, we finish eating, I blow out the candles for my birthday, and everyone packs up to leave.

"See you soon?" Will asks as he hugs me.

Nodding my head, I respond, "I believe so. However, Emmett did call me and specified that he needs me back at the firm by tomorrow."

"Wait, how come?" Will asks. "Is this related to the new merger case?"

"Yes, unfortunately, things are headed south, and he needs me present in order to ensure that everything proceeds as planned."

"I'm sorry, Ada. I know how much time and effort

you have placed into this case. Wanted to become a partner at the firm, but knowing you, you will turn things around and still manage to kick ass."

I smile, and a set of hands wrap around my waist.

Will's eyes widen as he notices Lincoln's hand resting right above my hip bone, and his soft thumb stroking me gently.

My heart races, watching the exchange of unspoken words between them. I have become the center of their attention.

Will's eyes narrow, silently daring Lincoln to cross the line he had drawn, while Lincoln stares back with a heated look, challenging him to make a move. Will steps back, and a wave of relief washes through me.

As I pull myself from Lincoln's hold, I give Will a quick hug and kiss on the cheek. "I really appreciate what you did for me tonight. I know how much you enjoy celebrating this day with me every year, and that means the world to me."

In a tight smile, he says, "Of course, Ada." He then walks out of the restaurant, leaving Lincoln and me alone.

When I turn around, Lincoln is holding something behind his back that was not there before. I raise my eyebrows in question.

"This was going to be given to you later, but I wanted you to have it now." His hand reaches out for me to take a wooden vintage box which says 'LETTERS TO ADA' on the front.

I look up at Lincoln in confusion. "What is this?" I ask.

His gaze is like a sword that cuts through my defenses, leaving me defenseless against his charms. He places a hand on my lower back, guiding me toward the entrance of the restaurant.

The contact of his skin touching mine sends shivers down my spine as I step outside into the frigid night. While we were indoors, a thick layer of snow covered the sidewalks. Snowflakes continue to fall steadily from the sky.

Rubbing his neck, he says, "In that box, there are letters." His voice heavy with emotion as he adds, "About everything that happened after you left."

Chapter Twenty-Six ♡

Ada

Why would he keep these? Why give them to me now? Why continue to write after all these years?

After a long moment of silence, I ask, "Why?"

A frosty breath emanates from his lips as he moves toward me, touching me from top to bottom, forehead to forehead. His intense gaze locks onto mine, and his voice is firm, yet gentle. "Ada, after you left without a word, my whole world came tumbling down. I couldn't eat, sleep; I wondered where you went. Why did you leave? I was so confused to the point that my parents had to put me in therapy. I didn't want to speak, hangout with my friends, or finish senior year. I was completely and utterly devastated the moment you walked out of my life."

As he speaks, tears start to fall down his cheeks. "I felt like my life had been turned upside down and the emotional toll it took on me was unbearable. I had lost my best friend and the person who meant the world to me. Baby, that day I watched you drive away, I felt like my world was falling apart, like I had no control over what was happening. I felt like I'd been thrown into a bottomless pit of despair, and I was unable to get out. The pain and confusion I felt was intolerable, and I couldn't help but crawl into a shell of who I was."

Knowing that he kept this from me makes my heart sink.

He points to the wooden box. "My therapist advised me to write down whatever was on my mind, journal about it, and it helped me move past everything for a while. The purpose of my writing was to clear my mind, to move on, to forget, but deep down, I couldn't do that. Ada, you were my whole world, and I wish you knew just how much you meant to me. How much you still do." He continues, not stopping for a breath, "I wanted to send them to you when I was done with each one, but never could because I had no idea where you went."

"Hudson University," I murmur.

My fingers rub gently across the thick wooden letters, removing the fluffy snow as I try to absorb his words.

How is that possible? Did I just convince myself that he didn't love me or care about me? He didn't stick up for me after what his parents did to me. Does he even know how badly they hurt me? How badly he hurt me?

I shake my head in confusion. "I don't understand how you could feel the way you did after I left. Continue to write letters that were meant for me?"

He grabs my hands. "What do you mean, Ada?"

With a shrug of my shoulders, I let go of his hands

and pace against the blistering snow. I throw my hands up. "I mean, after all this time, you still feel the same way? How is that possible when twelve years ago you made me feel worthless?"

"What are you talking about?" he asks with confusion.

"You don't remember when our last outing was? That time we attended the Living Dreams Foundation event? That was the first time I accompanied you to an extravagant event with your parents."

"Yes, I remember that one, but what does that have to do with any of this?"

Is he really unaware of what transpired that night? Nothing was the same afterward. That night was the catalyst that changed our lives forever, with repercussions that still resonate to this day.

"Well, do you remember when I brought our coats back to the foyer?"

He nods his head.

"Well, after the coats had been hung, I ran to the women's restroom to freshen up and came to a halt as I witnessed the worst thing."

"Ada, no—" His eyes widen with acknowledgement. "Shit, shit, shit," he murmurs. "Ada, that wasn't what the situation looked like."

I let the tears drip down my cheeks and the sorrow wash over me. His touch sends a wave of comfort through me, and I finally release the years of accumulated emotion that had been so tightly wound within me.

"Yes, it was. I caught another girl kissing you, Lincoln. She was fucking kissing you! I witnessed the love of my life, my number one supporter, the person who always had my back on everything, the only one who saw me for . . . me. I saw with my own two eyes, you locking lips with another girl. I was so heartbroken and felt betrayed, like my world was crumbling around me, and I had no control in that situation.

"And then Sarah. My heart ached seeing you in Blue Haven with another girl. It was a familiar sight, a reminder of the past. The universe is sometimes a bitch, since I saw her again tonight. Please tell me you didn't invite her to my birthday party?" I ask, pointing to the restaurant.

"The answer is that Will did that. I am sure someone else in that room told him not to forget to invite her, and she works with me and is friendly with most of those who were here tonight, including you."

Suddenly, my gaze narrows at him. "Friends? We don't even know each other. Last time I saw her, she was rubbing herself all over you in the bar."

"Were you jealous, Ada?" he asks with a sly grin, his eyes glinting with amusement as he raises his eyebrows.

Trying to avoid his damn grin, I lift my head, cross my arms, and stare down the deserted street. The snow has started to fall harder, making it difficult to even keep my eyes open.

Glancing back at him, a sigh escapes my lips. "Maybe?" I say. "I don't know, Lincoln." I try to maintain my calm voice, but there is an underlying sense of uncertainty in my voice.

He grabs my chin, pulling me toward him, so that our eyes meet. In a reassuring voice, he says, "You have no reason to be jealous, Ada. Nothing is going on between Sarah and me. She is a friend, a colleague, a great girl, but she is not the girl for me.

I told her that night after I dropped you off from the

bar, Ada. That moment for me, in the car, kissing you again. It was like the world was giving me a second chance to show me what I have missed out on."

The bar? That was weeks ago.

He knew even then?

My fist moves directly above my heart as I rub it. "Lincoln, all I know is that the pain right here is constant. The first time I saw you again, at Scoops for Life, and then at my mother's funeral. It was like every turn and twist I took, your face was right there. It stopped me dead in my tracks and caused me to over-think every decision that I had been making."

Despite the pain, my heart is still beating fast, and I know why. My eyes close as his forehead touches mine. The touch is like a warm embrace, melting away all of my worries and fears.

Lincoln

Jesus, fucking christ. Is that how she really saw that night at the event? Saw me? Saw us? Have we both been missing the bigger picture here?

My arms go around Ada as I bring her close to my chest, rubbing her back. The Living Dreams Foundation event was an extremely difficult night for both of us. But Jesus fucking christ, is that how she perceived me that night? A cheater?

This cannot be happening.

I knew that Laura, the girl who kissed me, did it solely for my mother. I knew this from the moment she approached me, rubbing her fingers along my arm slowly as she flirted with me.

That girl had one motive: to make Ada turn on me.

Which clearly she succeeded at. I knew it wasn't out of genuine feelings of affection, but instead a cold, calculated move to manipulate the situation.

The reasons why Ada left from the event and Blue Haven were never clear to me, but I had pinned them up to her mother's problems and the gossip around town. That shit was a lot for anyone, especially Ada. As a result of her mother's own actions, she was treated unbearably, and no one gave her any time, apart from me, or so I thought, until she left.

The memory of that night still brings chills to my spine, especially now learning the impact it had on the course of my life.

"Ada, STOP!" I shout, grabbing her arm as she walks back to her car.

Her eyes are filled with tears as she stares at me. I don't understand what's going on.

"I can't keep doing this, Lincoln."

"What do you mean?"

"You, us, your parents, this town," she says, shoving one finger into my chest.

She throws her head back with a scream, "Do you know what it's like to wake up every morning not knowing how the day will pan out? Wondering how your own mother will respond to the day? Will she be sober or drunk? Adversary?

"How it feels to enter Oak Ridge High School? Huh? What will people say about me today? Will I be bullied in the girl's bathroom in the corner by 5th period again? When I walk into a random store in Blue Haven, I have to think twice about what I wear, what I say; my overall appearance is affected by how people treat me. Who wants to live like that? Let alone as

a teenager. However, that didn't matter, did it? Ultimately, I am just like my mother." As she sobs, trying to catch her breath, she says, "I will only be known as her by the people in Blue Haven."

What the hell, I never knew about the bathroom situation.

With a knowing look, she says, "I did not tell you because I did not want you to look at me with pity eyes. Thinking that girl you imagine yourself with can't even stand up for herself. I want to be strong in your eyes, and I can't do that if you're always hovering over me." She continues walking toward her car, "Trying to be my knight and shining armor; I love it, I really do, but I think we need to call it quits."

"Ada, stop, this is nonsense!" I say, grabbing her arm. "I should have been there for you, A," I say, my heart breaking for her as she shakes her head back and forth, tears falling to the ground.

"Please, just let me go."

As she pushes me away, I grab her arm again, lifting her to my chest, wrapping my arms around her. She sobs as I hold her. I kiss the top of her forehead as she pulls away from me once again.

"We have plans, Ada, and you're just going to give them up like that?"

She drops her head to the ground. "We are children, and we will never be able to make our plans work. We both know that we must accept the reality of our situation. I desire to live and feel alive, Lincoln. I am tired of living in this godless town and its foolish judgments. I would like to travel, be adventurous without anyone batting an eye at me because they know my mother. It is imperative that people do not form an opinion about me if I make unwise choices, and I cannot do that with you by my side."

Stepping back, I ask, "Why? Why am I the problem? How am I holding you back?"

In a matter of seconds, she throws her hands up in the air and says, "Because I love you so much that I would do anything to make you happy, even if it meant never leaving you or this town again. It is important that I prove to myself that I am more than just another kid on the other side of the tracks. Show others around me that I am more capable than they realize."

"But we can do it together, Ada." I whisper.

She shakes her head as her face becomes red and swollen. "No, we can't. Can't you see? The world is against us, Linc. Can't you see that Blue Haven, your parents, even the universe doesn't think we belong together, and at some point we have to acknowledge that.

"It's time we accept that we are two different people with two different paths in life to follow," she concludes, her voice soft and resigned.

"So you're just going to leave like that?" I ask. "Leave me?"

She nods her head as tears fill her eyes. "I think it will be for the best, and you will see that too, Linc," she says softly as she gets into her car, leaving the parking lot.

"That wasn't even the cherry on top," Ada says as she pushes me away, startling me out of my memory.

Anxiety fills my heart as I wait for her next words.

"It was your mother coming up behind me as I was witnessing that kiss, whispering in my ear, pointing out every single flaw in me. I continued to watch yours and the girl's mouths come together. At that moment when you were absorbing another female's lips, I wondered, did you feel anything for me? Was I just a side piece? Was your mom right about everything? How I would never be enough for you, that you didn't belong with the trash. How we didn't have a future, and never would, with her being your mother."

I throw my head back in frustration as I let out a loud groan.

"Do you know what it is like to be told that you are not good enough? That you will never amount to anything great? That your possible future mother-in-law would threaten to rob you of everything if her son stayed with you? Married you? So, I made the choice that night to let you go, no matter how much it hurt my heart, because I wanted you to have the world you deserved."

My jaw tightens as I think about my mother threatening Ada. Why hadn't she told me about this? My mother had gone from making snarky remarks to issuing threats. I feel a surge of anger and frustration, wondering why my mother would do such a thing, and Ada not tell me about it.

There is something about Ada's expression that shakes me to my core. It makes me want to slay dragons just for the sake of making it better.

While walking through the snowy ground, I glance back at Ada. "God, Ada, why didn't you tell me she threatened you? I had no idea things had gotten so bad between you two."

Wiping away another tear, she lets out a sigh, and I just want to grab her, hug her, kiss her, and never let her go. I know I can keep her safe and make her feel loved again.

"I knew telling you would prevent us both from

doing what we both needed to do, which was to end things and move on with our lives, and don't you agree that by doing so we have made pretty great lives for ourselves?"

With confidence, she points to herself and says, "I am a thriving New York lawyer! And you're a successful accountant, and Little League baseball coach! Can't you see we are both living healthy, strong, and fulfilling lives?"

"Is that what you think? That I am living my best life?" Shaking my head, I continue, "You're actually a long way from that.

"Ada, fuck." I run my fingers through my hair as I continue, "Ada, every fucking day I crave you by my side, but cannot have you. Walking into my father's firm each day, I think to myself, is this what I really intend to do? I aspired to be a professor, to teach, to share my joy of learning with others. I wanted to inspire young adults to strive for success and ride the ride of life. But how can I accomplish that if I am not even doing it myself? I am a walking robot, going through the motions of life but not really enjoying the blessings that God has given me."

"Linc," she says softly as she bites her lower lip.

As I approach her, I place the box of letters in front of her on the ground. "Baby, if you had informed me that you witnessed Laura kissing me, I would have rectified the situation immediately by stating that I did not care about it. Because of my mother, she came onto me, and it was so abrupt that I did not have time to react. After being kissed, my anger was only exacerbated when I saw my mother smirking. Laura knew I was off limits, but she did not care about it, and when I confronted my mother, she walked away.

"And then I started to panic, looking for you, wondering if you had seen it. But by the time I did see you, you already had your coat on and were walking out the door. I was so confused by why you were leaving, but assumed it had to do with other issues taking place."

While speaking, tears well up in my eyes. "I was heartbroken and shocked. I wanted to know why you left so suddenly. Instead, you gave me a list of reasons why we could not be together and then drove away without saying goodbye."

"Okay, but I—"

While my finger rests on her pink, plump, cold lips, I whisper, "Shhh, I'm not done yet.

"I would also have told you that I wanted to make sure you knew that I was standing by you. I was not willing to let anyone, let alone my own mother's opinions, affect my decisions. Our relationship and our future had to be decided by us. That no obstacle would have stopped me from loving you and wanting to be with you."

She throws up her hands. "I knew you would say that, and that's why I did what I had to do! Can't you see what I did happened to do us both a favor?"

With her voice resolute and eyes unwavering, she says firmly, "It was the right thing to do."

Although she appears confident, I cannot help but feel lost about the reason for her decision. How does she think what she did for us was a favor? All these years have passed by and we haven't spent a moment together?

"We both have great lives, Linc; fulfilling careers, great friends, and we live in nice homes. I mean, we could not have made a better decision that night."

Taking a step back, I state, "There was no 'we' in your decision, Ada. You chose to leave me, this town, and your family."

In a fit of frustration, she mutters, "What does that mean? I did what I had to do to get to where I am now and I refuse to regret my decisions; I wouldn't be where I am if I had done otherwise."

"Baby, I get that, I do, and I couldn't be more proud of you and everything you have accomplished in life."

Pausing for a moment, I continue, "But how do you know? How do you know if you had chosen to stay, maybe you and I could have attended the same university, experienced college together, gotten our degrees together?"

My knuckles scrape across my lips, hesitant if I want to say what I need to.

Fuck it, she needs to know.

"You and I could be married by now. We could live in the same house, have a dog like Ginger, kids. Everything we've ever dreamed of could be happening right now."

"Are you seriously putting all the blame on me? That wasn't an easy decision to make, so don't you dare throw all this on me." She raises her voice to emphasize her point, her tone incredulous. "How can you honestly think this is all my fault?"

She clenches her fists, her voice cracking as she pleads, "Please, don't make me out to be the bad guy here—I did what I thought was right at the time."

Fuck, Lincoln.

She kicks the snow from her shoe as she walks toward me. A pair of narrow, icy eyes pierce through me. Her lips are pressed together in an expression of determination, her jaw set in a hard line.

Taking another step closer, she begins to beat her fists against my chest. "I didn't kiss another girl. I didn't have a mother who threatened you. You didn't have the world throwing signs at you, coming from left and right, saying we needed to go our separate ways." She rests her forehead against my chest and whispers, "It was as if the universe was preventing the inevitable."

I feel the weight of her bitter words. Her eyes accuse me of not being there for her, of failing to comprehend what had been going on.

The truth is now in the air, forcing me to be face-to-face with the reality of our past. I had been in denial for so long, living in a state of blissful ignorance, and I can't hide from it any longer. I have to accept that she was right.

Grabbing her tightly, I tilt her chin upward and say, "God, I'm so fucking sorry, Ada."

Her tension slowly dissipates from her body as I embrace her in my arms. She nuzzles into my chest.

"I promise it won't happen again," I whisper into her hair, determined that this would be the last time I would break her heart.

"Neither what I say nor what I do will take away what I did or did not do. But I would like you to know something, Ada," I say as I grasp her face. "I understand that my words and actions cannot undo the past and make up for any wrongs I have done. However, I want to let you know that I care about you, and . . . "

My heart pauses. "I want more than anything to start over with you, regardless of whether we become friends or more. All I want is you in my life, Ada Collins, and I will take you however it may be."

The warmth of my lips touch her forehead before I gaze into her striking blue eyes. "Ada, I apologize for causing you any pain or hurt," I whisper with tenderness in my voice.

While holding her close, she lets out a sob and slowly lowers her head to my chest. Rubbing her back, she lifts her head so her eyes meet mine as she cries, "God, Linc, I've missed you so much."

My heart swells, and I whisper, "I've missed you too, baby."

Holding her face, I lean in and kiss her deeply. Filling our kiss with passion and sincerity that cannot be adequately expressed by words alone. I want her to understand that I am truly sorry for what occurred, and that I will do whatever it takes to make things right between us.

She separates our lips, catching a breath, and then in a flash, she trails from my forehead to my cheeks, her lips lingering on my neck as if it is her last kiss. She moves on, her kisses growing more passionate and hungry as her mouth travels down my chest. My heart races as her lips explore more of my body; heat radiates out of her. My entire body trembles with anticipation as her passionate touch fills me with a longing to feel even more.

"Let's get out of here, yeah?" I murmur.

With a soft laugh, she asks, "And where are we going?"

Having gently wiped away another tear from her face, I grab her hand as we run through the snow to my car. The snowflakes fall on our faces, and our laughter echoes throughout the night.

Opening the passenger door, she climbs in and looks over at me. I wink at her as I say in a mocking tone, "I guess you will have to wait and see."

She smiles before replying, "I guess I will," with a mischievous glint in her eye.

Chapter Twenty-Seven ♡

Ada

Yes. Yes. Yes.

I keep my eyes closed, wholly focused on all the sensations that grip me. A hand that cups my breast, lips at my neck, and pleasure. Oh, the pleasure—it's every-where. My skin tingles with anticipation as I feel a soft whisper against my ear. Lincoln's body presses against mine; the sensation is electric and there's a deep stirring in my core.

We are lips, tongues, and gasps.

Lincoln pushes me onto my back, his body covering mine as his tongue glides down my stomach. My fingers slide into his thick hair, holding his mouth against my skin. His breath is on my body, hot and urgent, and I know he craves me as much as I crave him. My body quivers with pleasure as his hands explore my curves.

The silence around us is filled with a low groan.

This feels right.

Amazing.

It's perfect.

"Linc," I say impatiently.

"Yes?" He raises his brow as he kisses one inner thigh. With a smirk, he asks, "Do you want me to stop?" before kissing his way down the other side.

I half-laugh, half-pant as he centers his mouth between my legs, using his tongue to lap at my wetness, his nose pushing against my clit. He moves his head side to side, stroking me with his tongue again and again—soft and slow, hard and fast, gentle one minute and greedy the next.

"Oh, God, don't stop," I whimper as I tighten my fingers in his hair. The pleasure builds up inside me as he increases his speed, pushing me closer to the edge.

"A little impatient, aren't we?" he chuckles.

Laughing, I smack him in the shoulder. Never in my life have I experienced such voracious orgasms. Normally, I am a one-trick pony, capable of orgasming only once a day.

Did I fake orgasms?

Sure, maybe. Okay, I have done it in the past, but it didn't take long for me to feel the intense build of my orgasm with Lincoln.

He moves his tongue up to my clit, lashing and flicking, while sliding fingers inside me and pumping in and out. I groan with pleasure; my back arches off the bed. "Lincoln!" I gasp.

As I yell his name, he pumps harder. The intense sensation has me contracting involuntarily, tightening my muscles around his fingers and amplifying the pleasure. He pushes me closer and closer to the edge as his thrusting increases.

In a state of total awe, I failed to notice he went to his nightstand and grabbed a condom. He leans back on the heels of his feet, ripping the condom with his teeth. His hands are steady as he wraps the condom around himself.

"You have no idea how truly stunning you are, Ada," he says, as his gaze is filled with a mixture of longing and heat.

I know he thinks I am beautiful, yet when he actually states it, it causes my stomach to flip; I blush, feeling my cheeks heat, unable to come up with a response that could even begin to convey how I feel.

Lincoln lowers himself onto my body, lining up the broad head of his crown at my entrance. He interlocks his fingers with mine, kissing my lips gently, while our eyes lock; a beat of silence passes before he slowly pushes inside me. He eases in and out, gently.

"Linc," I whisper, digging my nails into his back muscles.

My eyes focus on his as he leans down to kiss my tears cascading down my cheeks. His lips are soothing against my skin and his embrace never falters as he tightens his grip around me.

"I know, baby, I know."

I wrap my legs around his waist, and we move rhythmically back and forth, breathing in tandem, as if our hearts are beating to the same beat, bringing us even closer. I am consumed by Lincoln, our past and present, everything. And it seems like I'm not the only one who is captivated by this moment.

He stares at me, his eyes going soft. The intensity of the moment pushes us over the edge.

"Ada, I lo—"

"I'm gonna . . . " interrupting Lincoln and my thoughts. I don't get to complete the sentence before my body is pulsing around him once again. "Oh, God, Lincoln."

His movements become more and more frantic, pushing us closer and closer to the edge until an explosive climax sends us both over. I cry out in pleasure, the sensation of him filling me, sending us both into a euphoric state of bliss.

His body relaxes as he leans into my neck, our sweat mingling as his breathing slows. "Well . . . " he says as I let out a giggle.

My eyes close as I mutter, "Mhhm."

He pulls away from me and says, "I'll be back."

My eyebrows rise as he points to his dick. "Baby, I need to get rid of this. Don't think for a second that I am done with you yet. We are just getting started."

Watching his damn muscular ass walk to the bathroom, I bite my lip. When he returns, he has a warm towel and I can't help but smile as he washes between my legs. This simple gesture of love and care fills my heart with warmth. When he climbs back into bed, he scoops me onto his chest and holds me close to him. And at this moment, I know I am at *home*.

"That was . . . " Lincoln mutters, staring up at his bedroom ceiling.

Letting out a long breath, I say, "Yeah, it was."

It was so much.

It was amazing and beautiful.

But I can't help but wonder if he was about to confess his love to me?

Did he? Does anyone ever truly get over their first

love? Is that what this is? Us just getting closure in the way we both know how? Or perhaps this is the beginning of something new?

My heart races as I pull my head off his chest and stare at the TV hanging on the wall in front of me, feeling the panic attack roar through my body.

"Ada, what's wrong?" Lincoln asks worriedly.

A beat of silence passes before he pulls me toward his chest and rubs the side of my arms while saying, "Don't panic, baby, just breathe."

I drop my head on his chest and let out a long and shaky sigh.

Grasping my chin, he raises my head to face him. "Ada, please tell me what is going on. Are you alright? What can I do to help you?" he asks as his blue eyes search mine.

I squeeze my eyes shut, tears stinging. I want to say yes right now, but I'm not sure I can. I am being torn in two. On one hand, I feel like we are just causing each other more pain by pretending whatever is happening between us is nonexistent. However, on the other hand, we seem to fit well. The comfort and protection of his arms, his strength, and his heart makes it feel as if I belong here at Blue Haven.

This.

This is what I have been missing.

"Ada, I know you; you're nervous, probably on the verge of a panic attack, if not already there," he says, touching my cheek lightly.

My eyebrows rise.

Taking my finger from my hair, he says, "Well, for one, you tend to twirl your hair with a finger when you're fighting with yourself about something. It's a nervous tick you always have had, even back in high school. Whenever you found yourself in a difficult situation, I could always tell," he concludes, "just by watching you."

My heart beats faster at the thought of him still remembering that little detail about me. With a heavy sigh, I exhale. "I am trying not to overanalyze this. What it means, how I feel, how you feel? What are we doing? Who are we fooling? This," I say, pointing back and forth between us, "it's confusing me."

He grabs my hands and brings them up to his lips, never breaking his gaze as he kisses each of my individual knuckles.

That simple gesture has me melting in a puddle. I have gone so long without the incidental touches, and it isn't until this moment I realize how much I have longed for them.

A brief kiss on the forehead.

Holding hands.

Fingers stroking my cheek.

I am so used to casual sex that I forgot I missed all of this terribly.

"Ada, baby, breathe. Let's enjoy this night together, shall we? Let's not overthink this, and just be here, with me, in this moment. You won't regret it," he says with a smug grin.

I smile as my eyes trail to Lincoln's nightstand. He turns his head and sees the box of letters sitting there.

"What's going through that beautiful head of yours?"

Inhaling deeply, I look him in the eye and decide to

take things one day at a time. Even though I know we cannot erase the past, I remain hopeful that we can make things better now.

In my smug tone, I say, "Besides you and those amazing orgasms you just gave me,"—he shows off that damn smirk of his I love—"I want to read one of your letters."

His eyes widen, as his cheeks turn a little red. "Uh, are you sure we have to do that tonight?" he asks as he scratches his neck. "I figured you would read them on your own time."

Turning around out of his embrace, I give him a cheeky grin. "Is Lincoln St. James nervous to hear me read one of his love letters?"

He starts to tickle my sides, and I laugh softly.

"Awh! No, stop."

His deep voice rings in my ear as he chuckles, "Ada Collins, don't forget I know your greatest weakness."

That damn voice of his. Literally one word from this man's mouth and my entire being melts.

"Quit, no stop," I say, barely able to get out the words as I'm doubled over in laughter.

He rolls us, pinning my wrists above my head as he straddles me. Leaning down, I think he may kiss me for a moment, but then he whispers, "Only if I get to choose the letter."

"Eee, okay, fine, deal," I reply, my voice trembling with anticipation.

Having lost patience after a few minutes, he releases his grip on my wrists, giving me the opportunity to push him off of me, and I try to run for the box of letters.

The moment I grab the box, his arms encircle my

waist, and I squeal, making us both fall onto the bed, laughing. We stay there, catching our breath, my back flush against his chest. Our laughter still echoes in the air as we remain intertwined.

Having finally caught my breath, I feel Lincoln's lips on my ear as he says, "Not so fast."

I start to giggle, and in a playful manner, I wiggle my butt into his dick, knowing that it will make him go crazy, allowing me to let loose.

"Don't think you should play that game, baby." His soft voice sends a chill down my spine, and I find myself desperately wanting his warm touch everywhere.

My body begins to slide over his, and his dick grows harder as I whisper, "Is that a challenge I hear, Linc?" I ask mischievously.

Attempting to turn me around, I quickly grab the box of letters, moving away from him. "Ugh, that's not fair, Ada," he mutters as he purses his lips.

What's unfair is this man could wear any look in the world and still be breathtakingly handsome.

Closing my eyes, I say, "Eeny, meeny, miny, moe, which one is gonna be mine."

Reopening my eyes, I grip the letter tightly with trembling hands and a pounding heart.

Ada

My fingers rub across the letter's words. The one that was meant to be sent to me. My gaze is drawn to Lincoln as he nods his head.

Slowly, I tear it open; the anticipation killing me.

January 1st

Dear Ada,

Today is New Year's Eve. It's a day I pictured in my head over and over again, and one that I would be spending with you. Enjoying it to the fullest. I had the entire day planned for us. I would steal you away from your house, we would go to The Crispy Biscuit for dinner, definitely letting you get more than one milkshake because I know they are your obsession. Then we would dress in our best attire as we took a ride in my Bronco to one of our favorite places, Hope Bay Beach. It would be a night to remember, Ada—the setting sun, the sound of the waves, the fresh crisp air, and the stars that light up the night sky. In the background, we would be playing Just The Way You Are from Bruno Mars, my favorite song that reminds me of you. We could slow dance together, holding each other close, and feeling the love that we share.

A tear trickles down my cheek as I close my eyes, hating that this hurt was caused by no one other than myself.

I did this to him.

To us.

Did you know that my favorite thing to do

was show you much you mean to this world? Mean to me. That day I saw the writing on your wall. I made it my goal to tell you every day how much you meant to me, how beautiful you were, how amazing and talented you were. Worthy of everything this world had to offer and more. I knew that no matter what I said, you would always be the light that lit my life up, and that I would always be there with you, believing in you and supporting you in every way possible.

But apparently, that didn't matter. None of the words I said to you really mattered, did they? Because you're not here, by my side, to celebrate the new year. It was supposed to be our year, Ada, damn it. The one where we graduate together, attend the same university, and start our new journey together, not alone.

In the end, you're out there somewhere, and I'm hiding in my room from the harsh reality that you'll never return. A, I still don't under-stand what happened between us and it is breaking my heart. Where did we go wrong? What did I do wrong? If I had the opportunity to take that night back, I would; I don't want to live in a world where you don't exist.

Come back to me, Butterfly.

Xoxo, Linc

Lincoln

As she reads my letter, tears slide down her face, and I refrain from reaching out to comfort her. I know that she needs this. Needs to know what I went through. That I didn't give up so easily. That every day she was apart from me, it nearly killed me.

I close my eyes and take a deep breath, praying silently that my words bring her the same comfort that my embrace once did.

Reopening my eyes, Ada's connect with mine, her hands trembling as she grasps the letter. I wait a few breaths.

"Linc." She shakes her head, staring at me. Her expression is filled with something I am unable to place my finger on. Sadness? Anger? Fear?

The sight of her in this state breaks my heart to the very core.

Wiping away my tears and shoving down the sadness threatening to take over, I reach out and pull her into my chest. She rushes to catch up with me just as I grab her. We fall back on the bed together as we embrace.

Lying her head on my chest, she says, "I was so lonely, Lincoln. I was hurt and heartbroken, waiting for you to make things better. It was so tempting to call you, just to hear your voice, feel the comfort you could provide. However, I was afraid I would come crawling back if I did. Back then, I did what I thought was best for us, going our separate ways."

My fingers run through my hair as I stare at the ceiling, hesitant to ask a question, but needing to know the answer. "Do you think that it was still the right decision?"

"Yes, I do," she answers without hesitation.

Turning to face me, she places her elbows on my chest as her eyes gaze into mine. "I believe that everything happens for a reason, even if we do not necessarily agree about what that reason is. I would not change anything that has taken place, Linc—my past, us, our breakup—all of it has made me who I am today."

As she slowly slides away from me, she sits upright, still looking at me. "I also believe that your past, no matter how bad, does not define your future. Leaving Blue Haven, you and the people I cared about, was a conscious decision for me. It was clear to me the choices and actions I made starting that very next day would determine who I would ultimately become. It would define who I am. Through my past, I have learned a lot, and I have applied it to my present life to give me the life that I was meant to live."

Letting out a sigh, I put my hands behind my head as I take Ada in. She has a sad smile, but is trying to keep a positive attitude. I'm surprised she told me so much. Previously, she would clam up and lock herself in, and not tell me anything. I had to gyrate her for a long time to figure out why she was acting up. At the moment, I'm really embracing this new version of her.

She is no longer the girl I once knew. She is now a stunning and ambitious woman, one who I have no doubt inspires other young women every day. Throughout her career, she has grown and changed, becoming more self-assured and confident. The way she takes on every challenge with fierce determination and an unwavering spirit is an example of how discipline, hard work, and determination can lead to success.

As I watch her, my heart swells with pride. I couldn't be more proud of her, even if I tried. It's her choices and decisions that've made her this way. Were they hurtful? Hell yeah, but knowing she's living her dream makes them worthwhile.

"Ada, do you know how proud I am of you?"

She bites her lower lip to prevent it from trembling and shakes her head back and forth.

Taking her face in my palm, I move myself off the headboard to sit directly in front of her. "I am so damn proud of you, Ada Collins. Do I care about our past and how it ended? Certainly. Do I wish we could have gotten through the tough days together? Yes, I do. Perhaps maybe figure out our shit with each other? Yes, I wish we could have."

She begins to sob, wiping her eyes with her hands. "I'm so sorry. I'm not proud of the way I handled things between us," she pauses for a moment, her voice trembling, "and I don't expect you to ever forgive me or understand why I had to do what I did.

In an effort to ease her grief, I tilt her chin up and gently wipe away a tear with my thumb. "Ada, I can tell you that every person in the world has a tough choice or a decision that has to be made, and they aren't always easy. Yes, the decision you made hurts, but I understand why you had to make it."

"It kills me to say that I do not regret my choice." She continues to wipe the tears off her cheeks. "I am not saying that to hurt you, but that choice ultimately made me who I am today." She takes a shaky breath and whispers, "The decision I made was difficult, but it was the right one for me. Even though I never wanted to hurt anyone, I'm proud of the fact that I was able to show everyone that I could be a strong, successful individual on my own."

My eyes are drawn to hers as I say, "That you are, baby. Yet you did not have to prove anything to me; I knew you would go far in life, and you have. You should be proud of all your successes and accomplishments; you have achieved so much, and I am extremely damn proud of you."

I continue to look into her glossy eyes. "Ada, all that has transpired between us has already taken place. There is no turning back and changing anything." I take a deep breath and offer a small smile, trying to stay hopeful in the face of her sadness. "But we can make it a fresh beginning, if that's what we both want."

"Can we do that? Can we really move past all of this? Find closure?" Ada asks with tears in her eyes. "Cause that's all I really want, Linc."

I pull her into a hug, nodding my head. "That's all I want, too, baby."

A sigh of relief escapes her lips as she sinks into my arms.

I squeeze her tightly and pull back from her as our eyes meet. "Please stay with me tonight," I say.

Several heartbeats pass before I notice a wide smile across her face, her eyes creasing with delight. I cannot help but smile back, feeling the warmth of her happiness and the moment we have just shared.

I had never felt so alive, free, and content since that moment. Taking me completely by surprise, Ada tackles us both flat onto the edge of the mattress. Making us laugh to the point that she rolls off my stomach, pulling me with her as we tumble to the ground.

Leaning her elbows up against my chest, Ada grins mischievously and says in a teasing tone, "Took you long enough to ask."

Chapter Twenty-Eight

Ada

"Good morning," Lincoln says, leaning against the kitchen island with a mug of coffee, looking so damn fine in his dark navy blue three-piece suit.

My cheeks heat up. "Good morning," because, my GOD, our night last night was everything and more. Closing my eyes, I smile, feeling the warmth linger in my heart.

There was a brief moment of hesitation about what we were doing, that there was nothing more here, that we were simply trying to get closure on the past. My heart, however, knew better, and once I read Lincoln's letter out loud, I knew ending the night the way we did was right. Throughout my life, I have only ever connected with one other soul on an emotional, physical, and intellectual level, and he is standing in front of me.

A smug grin and all.

"What's got you all happy?" I ask.

"Hmm, wouldn't you like to know?" he says as he takes another sip from his coffee, peering over the rim at me.

"Oh, I'm sure I'll find out eventually," I reply, a sly smile playing on my lips.

I walk up to him, placing my hand on his chest. I stand on my toes and give him a kiss on his lips. His arms wrap around my waist, holding me in place. Our mouths collide in a sweet connection. It's not carnal, more like a dreamy kiss that makes your stomach flutter. I linger in the moment, savoring the connection between us that I have so desperately been missing.

Taking the time to tilt my chin up, he presses his mouth to mine for another kiss. "Got any big plans for the day?" he asks.

As I lay my head on his chest, I breathe in his familiar scent. I listen to my heartbeat race along with his, making the most of this moment, knowing it may never happen again.

I would give anything to wake up to this every morning in New York.

Lincoln's affection this whole time I have been in Blue Haven has ripped through me like a gentle but comforting hug. It causes my emotions to ramp up.

The moment he releases me, I take a deep breath, vowing not to let my feelings get out of hand. I am aware of the fact that I have a flight to catch in less than an hour. Elena texted me my flight information when we drove to Lincoln's house last night.

Can I tell him I am leaving? I mean, I am coming back for the wedding in a few days, so I don't have to actually tell him I am leaving.

Won't he know you're gone?

God, why am I so emotional and overanalyzing everything?

Because you know what you're feeling, Ada. You know that last night was much more than closure.

My throat tightens at the thought of leaving him. I cannot help but feel a wave of sadness wash over me as I contemplate the inevitable of saying goodbye.

Dodging his question, I shrug my shoulders.

A phone pings on the counter, interrupting our moment. I look over, seeing it's not mine.

A sigh escapes his lips. "Well, I guess that's my cue now," he says.

Confusion fills my eyes as I stare at him.

"That's Garrett letting me know we leave for the airport in an hour."

My eyebrows raise, still not understanding.

He chuckles. "I guess I should have mentioned I'm heading to Chicago for work. It won't be too long, three days at most."

Considering he's leaving himself, I guess I don't have to tell him I'm leaving.

Right?

We can both leave on the same day, and we'll both be back in time for the wedding.

"I'm going to miss you," he says, pulling me into his arms. "Ada, you have no idea what this last month has been like for me," he whispers.

My heart pounds wildly in my chest. I don't know how to navigate these feelings that I've suppressed for so long. And because of this past month, what I have felt with Lincoln, with being back in Blue Haven, makes navigating those feelings that much more challenging.

Stepping out of his embrace, I head over to the

coffeepot and make myself a cup to calm my racing heart. With my back turned to him, I ask, "And how has it felt for you?"

Taking note of his presence behind me, his lips whispers in my ear, "It felt like heaven." A shiver runs down my spine as I realize that maybe this is the beginning of a new chapter for us.

The nostalgia. A flutter of the heart. A weakening of the knees with every glance.

Ada, focus! There is no time to dwell on your feelings. It's better to sort your emotions out on the plane, or even once back in New York.

Trying not to be too transparent, I lean into him and murmur, "Yeah, I get that."

His face is filled with a sorrowful expression as I turn to look at him, only adding to the pain I was already experiencing.

Does he know that this thing between us is short-lived?

Does he think we could make it work, given our past?

Running his hand through his now untamed hair, he sighs. "Alright, well I better get going, before Garrett has my ass.

"Probably for the best," I force a chuckle.

God, Ada, why are you making this so awkward?

The two of us lean in for a kiss at the same time. Butting heads, we grab our foreheads with laughter. Some tension leaves my body as we look at each other.

"Guess we had the same thought for saying goodbye."

Laughing, I say, "I guess so. Would you like to try that again, maybe with less aggression?" He smiles widely, and before I am able to take another breath, his lips are on mine.

Fuck . . . me.

One touch from him is all it takes to break down my barriers.

Unlike previous kisses, this one is different.

Soft.

In control.

Yearning.

Our lips melding together as though they were made to fit this way. Our past engulfs us, enveloping us in a cocoon of memory.

With a smile, I separate my lips from his. He leans forward, kissing me briefly on the forehead. "One last one for the road," he whispers, pulling back as I catch an adorable wink.

Those words alone make me blush.

Have I mentioned his smirk and wink combination is panty melting worthy? The thought of it alone makes me feel all tingly inside.

Leaving me to my coffee, he starts to walk toward his bedroom, giving me an eye full of his backside. My heart skips a beat as I take in the curves of his body, watching his sexy taut ass move with confidence. Definitely noticing I'm blatantly checking him out, he whips his head around with a smug grin.

He raises a brow. "Ada Collins, were you just eye fucking me?"

The only response I give him is a shrug of the shoulders as I bite my bottom lip.

A hearty laugh escapes him as he continues into his bedroom. "I don't mind if you let your eyes wander, you know? I know you like what you see."

I shake my head, a smile emerging on my lips. "Not to hurt your ego, big guy, but if we allow ourselves to go there, you are likely to miss your flight."

With a suitcase and leather bag in hand, he emerges from his bedroom, looking every bit the businessman he is.

God, is it hot in here or is it just me?

He sets his luggage down, cupping my cheek. "Oh, don't underestimate me, Ada. We both know we can have another go around without me missing my flight." He smiles mischievously, his thumb brushing against my skin.

It is with a playful grin that I shake my head, knowing it to be absolutely true.

As he kisses my forehead, I close my eyes and listen to him whisper, "Why is it so hard to say goodbye, even if it is only for a few days?"

How am I supposed to go back to New York, back to my job, away from him, Blue Haven, everyone here, and pretend nothing happened? If it hurts now, what's it going to be like when I have to officially leave Blue Haven? This goodbye almost has a weight that feels as if we may not see each other again.

"I know, Linc. I feel it too," I say as I squeeze his waist tightly.

After one last kiss, we look at each other, silence enveloping us. The unspoken words linger in the air as he turns and begins to walk to the door. He pauses by the oak side table, grabs a pair of keys, and hangs them from his fingers as he drops his bags and turns to face me. "Lock up when you leave, yeah?"

I give a feeble nod, doing my best to mask the blues weighing me down. A forced smile spreads across my lips. I know I'm not fooling him, but I still playfully joke, "Don't worry—I'll turn the lights off too!"

My heart breaks when I see his somber smile. Is this how it will feel when I have to actually leave?

Ada, this was inevitable. You knew it couldn't last forever, nothing's perfect.

"No need to rush, but when you do leave, just put it under the flower pot outside."

My lips tremble as I stare at him. "Okay," I reply, smiling despite my heavy heart.

"Well, I better get going," he says, picking up his luggage.

I nod my head and let silence fill the air for a few breaths before closing the space between us, until only a few inches separate us. I close my eyes, trying to hold back my tears.

The warm strength of his body against mine again makes me want to confess that I don't want him to leave. To stay with me, but instead, I say, "Be safe, Linc," as my voice wavers. I whisper to myself, "I can't bear the thought of being apart from you," as my heart aches.

He holds me close, his breath warm against my neck, and whispers, "Always, see you soon, Ada girl."

I nod my head.

"Don't miss me too much," he says, walking to the door, his eyes connecting with mine one final time.

A tear rolls down my cheeks as I let out a chuckle. Of course, the man would make a joke to ease this painful goodbye.

God bless this sweet man.

When I follow him to the door, he says, "You didn't think I could leave without seeing that gorgeous smile, did you?"

"Certainly not, silly." I smile as I close the door behind him.

A whisper escapes my lips, "I love you, Linc," as I slide down the door and my tears finally let loose. My heart sinks in two; our final goodbye will tear me apart.

After sitting in the silence of Lincoln's house for God knows how long, I wipe my tears and lift my head high, knowing that I can't let this affect me.

Ada, let's put on your grown up pants and remind your clients that you offer immense value to their company.

Seeing the foyer clock on the wall, I realize I don't have much time until I have to catch my flight back to New York. But knowing this is likely to be my last time here, I start wandering around, admiring the man Lincoln is now. Everything in the house tells the story of his life and his experiences, from the photos on the mantle, the books on the shelves, to the awards in the corner.

I can feel his presence in every room. A deep sense of yearning reminds me of how much I missed out on the person he has become.

Last night, I didn't get much of an opportunity to observe the inside of his house as we were fumbling to get inside and into his bedroom. But I noticed that he does live in a log cabin style house. It's two floors with huge glass windows and a wrap-around porch. With my heart in my throat, I make my way over to the stairs.

This is his life, the one he built without me . . .

In a split second, I am able to visualize our lives together. I can imagine us as husband and wife, laughing, living life to the fullest. Never looking back, never letting the past determine what is to come. Our children giggle around Lincoln and me as we chase them on the front lawn; I can almost feel the warmth of the summer sun and the smell of freshly cut grass as we make memories that will last a lifetime. The moment I hear a knock on the front door, a glimpse of how life might have been with him vanishes.

Observing the jiggle of the doorknob, I crease my eyebrows.

Who would be here? Did Lincoln leave something behind?

Right as I am about to grab the handle, the door flies open, revealing the one person I never expected to see again.

Sheryl. Lincoln's Mother.

The universe is seriously trying to sabotage my day; not only did Lincoln have to leave, but I am now faced with the devil's spawn glaring at me as I contemplate my next course of action.

An eerie silence surrounds us. My fight-or-flight instinct wants me to scream and run away.

Lincoln's mother's face pales. "Ada Collins?" Her voice is barely audible, but it carries a thousand words, a million questions, a lifetime of hurt.

I can almost feel it, the weight of the world pressing down on us in this moment, heavy and oppressive. My heart pounds, my stomach flips, my throat constricts, but I can't speak, I can't move; I can't do anything but stand here and wait for what she has to say next.

Instead, I blurt out, "The one and only."

Her lips part and she sucks in a breath, "Why-y? What are you doing here?"

"I could ask the same of you. Last time I checked, this was Lincoln's house," I say, crossing my arms.

The woman huffs as she moves her hands to her

hips; her chest puffs out and her head is held high. I mimic her pose, refusing to allow her to see my weaknesses.

I will be strong, I think, steeling myself for what is about to unfold before me.

Sheryl closes the door, making her way through the foyer. I follow behind her as she says, "Well, this is an absolute shock. Never thought I would see the day when I saw *you* with my Lincoln. *Again.*"

Oh my God, the nerve of this woman. Years later, it's like nothing has changed.

She's still the same Sheryl St. James, renowned for her sharp tongue and quick wit.

My jaw clenches as I pretend to use my eyes as lasers to strike her rear end, catching it on fire so her ass high-tails it out of Lincoln's house without another word.

After the shit storm of my life the past few weeks, you'd think I would catch a break, but nope, let's add more salt to that wound of Ada's. Also, as old as she is, you would think she'd move on to bigger and better things, instead of focusing on her son's life. Who, by the way, is an adult that is capable of making his own decisions.

Making our way to the kitchen island, I stand there, filled with pain and rage. I take a deep breath, steadying myself as I stare into the eyes of the person who caused my suffering for so long.

She challenges me with a raised brow, her voice stern. "Please do tell, why are you in my son's house, as it looks like he's not here? Do you have Lincoln's permission to be here, or did you just assume it was okay?"

What the fuck?

Who does this woman think she is? Clearly, she hasn't changed, but I have, and she's in for a rude awakening.

"Again, I should be asking you the same question. Does Lincoln just allow you to enter his house whenever you desire?"

Glancing at me, she tilts her head back and laughs off my question. "Looks like you really are different from Ada as a teenager. Feisty, strong, fierce; I didn't think you had it in you, but I also didn't believe it until I saw it with my own two eyes."

Damn right I am.

What's that saying they say, 'The older we get, the wiser we become?'

Well guess what, I have a new saying, 'The older I get, the less I care.'

That includes whatever bullshit comes from this woman's mouth.

"Are you looking for something specific?" I ask as she wanders around Lincoln's kitchen.

"Nothing that you can help me with," she pauses, looking over her shoulder.

I allow my anger to leave my body in a long breath. "Ok, well, if you don't mind, I need to get going, and Lincoln has requested that I lock up. I need to respect his wishes," I say, emphasizing my commitment to being a bigger person.

She waves me off. "Oh honey, I can assure you I can lock up when I leave. Now why don't you run off to where you came from?" With a calculating laugh, she says, "Oh, that's right, the other side of town."

I drop my jaw at her audacity to say such a thing directly to my face.

Are you really surprised by this, Ada? Women like her don't change. It's just a reflection of something she's battling internally and taking out on the world.

"Oh, sweetheart, pull your jaw up. Just because you have a law degree and live in New York, doesn't make you any better for my son. We both know you and Lincoln would never be able to work. Right?" she asks.

Embarrassed, angry, and frustrated, I turn my head away as shame fills my heart. I should be over this, over her words, not letting them affect me so much.

Come on, Ada. Stay strong. Remind yourself that her behavior is a reflection of her, not you. You are so much stronger and better than her. Don't let her words bring you down.

Her bitterness and disapproval glares into me. "You realize I sent my only son to therapy because of you. I had to fork out thousands of dollars for him to attend a facility where he spent countless hours, days, weeks, even months trying to sort out the mess you left behind."

My stomach heaves as I snort, "Because of me?" I say, pointing at myself. "That's really rich coming from you, Sheryl. I left because of you; this town. What choice did I have when every twist and turn I took, I was reminded of the disappointment I was?"

Her eyes narrow at me as I continue, "I left Blue Haven on the night of the Living Dreams Foundation. Remember that one? The one when you chose to stick another girl on Lincoln, only to make me envious and upset. Well, guess what? It really worked. That whole ordeal, along with your scummy comments, made it extremely easy for me to leave that night without a second thought."

Her eyes widen, taken aback by what I said.

"Are you happy about that? Because if anyone sent your son to therapy, it was you and your poor choices. If you would have just accepted me, and let your son be happy, he wouldn't have gone through so much misery. But you still can't see that, can you?"

"Ada, you don't under—"

"No, Sheryl, you do not." I point my finger in her direction as I interrupt her. "You still do not see it, do you? Years later, you are still trying to control your son's life, and he still is not happy."

The woman shakes her head in disbelief, clearly oblivious to what I am saying.

God, how did I ever think Lincoln and I could possibly have a future? A second chance? His mother, family, even the town itself, would never accept us. It's because of this that I had let him go, knowing that I must accept reality, even if it meant leaving my heart behind.

Insecurities creep in and tears threaten to spill over as Lincoln's mother sees right through me.

Throughout my life, I have taught myself to believe that being successful and independent would protect me from being hurt and disappointed. I built up a wall around my heart to protect me from being vulnerable, but I'm starting to think it was all an illusion.

You will never be good enough.
You're that girl from the other side of town. No matter
what you do, you will never amount to anything.
You're just a helpless, naive girl.

In the midst of this reliving nightmare, I hear the front door open.

Now who's here? They better prepare themselves for this lovely reunion.

"Ada, are you still here? I forgot my laptop charger. God knows I need it for the trip." Lincoln laughs as he walks straight into a war zone between his own mother and I. He freezes in place.

"Oh dear, perfect timing. I was just telling Ada that I would be bringing over some toiletry supplies. I know you often forget to restock your home before you travel."

I roll my eyes at the phony shit she is being so blatant about as she goes to hug him. When she pulls him close to her, he looks over her shoulder at me with raised eyebrows.

I can only shake my head in disbelief.

"Glad you were able to come back. I wanted to say goodbye before you left, but it looks like you were already quite occupied with *someone.*" Her voice is laced with disappointment as her gaze focuses on me.

Seriously, petty much?

"Mother," Lincoln says sternly.

She releases Lincoln and then struts toward me, wrapping her arm around my neck.

My brain freezes with her proximity. As she eyes me, the hair on the back of my neck stands. "Lincoln, me and Ada here were just having a little reunion, weren't we, sweetie?" she asks with a fierce gaze.

Distancing myself from her, I shrug her off my shoulders.

This woman has another thing coming if she thinks I'm going to act like the way she just treated me is okay. You better believe I won't tolerate any more disrespect from her.

"Oh, Sheryl, tsk tsk tsk," I say, ensuring that I keep my tone cool and even. "Can't we be adults here? Why not just tell Lincoln the whole truth?" I lift a brow.

"How just now you made me feel like shit? Ashamed of myself? The career and life I have now? Throwing in my face once again that I will never be good enough for your son?"

There is a huff in her laughter.

From the corner of my eye, I see Lincoln stare at his mother, his jaw clenching.

In order to let Lincoln see more of what his mom has done to me, I continue, "Well, newsflash, *Sheryl*, I don't need those reminders, because they're right here," I say, pointing to my head. "I live with them, and my past, every Goddamn day of my life, but what you fail to realize is that people like *you* are the reason for my success. Without your constant criticism, shame, and ruthlessness, I wouldn't have pushed myself to the very peak of my abilities." I throw my hands up as I walk toward Lincoln's bedroom. "And you know what? I have a pretty great life, and I owe it to you, Sheryl. Because without you telling me I was a shameless nobody, that I would never amount to anything, I wouldn't have chosen nor had the guts to get out of Blue Haven. But most importantly, I wouldn't have what I have today: friends who love me and accept me for who I am, family who will be there for me through thick and thin, and a job that I am damn successful at.

"Now, if you will excuse me, I have more important things to attend to," I say, turning into Lincoln's bedroom to collect my belongings.

"Hold on, Ada," Lincoln jogs to me and grabs my forearm, turning me to face him.

I watch his fearful eyes, my heart pounding out of my chest.

This shouldn't hurt this badly; we both knew that we

couldn't be anything more before we started this. The only thing we needed was closure to move forward. And hearing his mother again, the anger and humiliation lacing every word, it makes me feel like that young naive girl again. I refuse to let that girl be broken; I've grown and I'm stronger now. There's no denying the hurt I feel, but it's time to finally close this chapter and move on.

Lincoln's head shakes involuntarily. "Ada, you can't do this," he says, pulling me to his chest. "The spark, the connection, the fire, everything that was once there is still there." He whispers in my ear, "We just got things back to normal between us and I finally feel the closure I needed. Please, tell me you can feel this between us?" He grabs my hand, moves it to his chest, and softly says, "You feel that? It's my heart, Ada; it still beats only for you."

While closing my eyes, I try to focus on not feeling all the pieces of my heart shattering. What I am about to say will change everything.

"Lincoln, we both knew that this wasn't going to happen," I say, pushing back from him. "I live in New York; my life, career, and everything else are located states away from your life. We can't just expect to be able to drop everything and be together after one month."

A heavy sigh leaves Lincoln's throat as he runs his fingers through his hair. "You know, Garrett once said something to me about life and the moments we have. The truth is, Ada, when you first returned to Blue Haven, I selfishly just wanted closure from you, but as we spent more time together, sharing new and old memories, I knew deep in my heart that it couldn't be just that for me. Can't you see, Ada, that no matter how many days, weeks, or months pass, one look at you made me realize I would never want to live without you again?"

He holds me again, and I sink into his embrace. He stares down at me, tenderness filling his gaze. "Can't you see, Ada? I have never stopped loving you. I love you, only you," he whispers, rubbing his thumb across my cheek. His voice is thick with emotion, a reminder of a relationship that has existed between us since day one.

The sound of those three words causes my heart to jolt, and I shake my head. My heart has always been his. I never was able to give it to someone else because they weren't as good as him. But even if that is true, I can't reciprocate those three words back. Doesn't he get it? They hate me. His mother has made it abundantly clear that I'm not welcome. What kind of life, future would that be like? For us, for our children?

I shake my head as I push myself out of his embrace once again. "I-I-I'm sor-ry, I can't do this Lincoln, n-n-not right now."

I gather my clothes, shoes, and purse with my back to him. Despite him reaching for me again, I let my head drop forward, staring at my bare feet.

Suddenly, I breathe out a heavy sigh. "We can't, Lincoln; this would never work between us, can't you see that? I need to do what's best, and that starts with getting my attention back on the M&A case."

Crestfallen, he narrows his eyes at me. "Do you really think that's more important than us?"

I shrug my shoulders. "Honestly, I am not sure. All I know is that it is something I can depend on, something that will never let me down."

He releases me. "So, this is it? You're just going to walk away from this? Me? Us?"

Not sure how to respond, I inhale, feeling the weight of his gaze upon me. "Yes," I say softly. "This is how it has to be."

Shaking his head, he turns his head to the other side of the room.

I throw my hands up. "Lincoln, we have no future. Can't you see that? Your parents hate me, your mother chooses to let me know, time after time, that I am not welcome. What kind of future is that? One that you want?"

"Ada, we're both grown adults here. Does that really matter?"

This sweet, sweet man. He is crazy if he thinks none of that will affect us. How would it not affect our kids? I would never want my children to grow up with me having a hateful relationship with their grandmother.

"We both know it does, Lincoln. I don't want to be the reason you have to choose between your family and me."

"Ada, you won't; can't you just let me worry about them?" He grips my hand, kissing each knuckle, giving my body all the tingles. "I'm not ready to let this go, to see where it takes us." He holds my gaze, the intensity of his blue eyes enough to make me forget our worries about the world.

My eyes linger on him as the silence grows thicker with each passing minute, until I hear my phone start to ring. "It's probably Lexie; she's picking me up," I say, grabbing my phone.

"Why don't you let me drive you?" he asks.

"No, Linc, this is it. I am leaving." I shake my head as I drop my hands from his and move toward my purse.

"Can I at least make sure you get back to the car okay?" he asks, rubbing his neck.

"No, I'm really okay, Lincoln."

While putting on my shoes, I gather the rest of my possessions and head for the door. Entering the foyer, I look out of my peripheral vision, and Sheryl is grinning, broad-shouldered.

Bitch.

Lincoln reaches for my arm one more time. I continue to hold the door handle tightly, as though it were a lifeline, hearing him whisper, "Don't do this, Ada. We can make it work. I promise." His voice weaker, quieter, and sadder with each word.

"Please," he pleads with his blue eyes.

It breaks my heart to imagine what might have been, the future we could have planned together, the children we could have had, but it is better not to dream about what may never happen.

There's no perfect life for me, and it's time I accept that.

My eyes drift back to him one last time as I murmur, "I have to leave, Linc," and close the door behind me.

Chapter Twenty-Nine

Lincoln

This isn't happening. She can't be doing this, not again, not to us. Everything started to feel right again between us, and all it took was a few choice words from my hateful mother to have reality slap us right in the face.

The moment the door closes, I spin on my heels and march toward my mother, who is wearing a self-satisfied grin on her face. As if she is impressed with how this situation played out.

"Are you happy?" I spit out. Anger and revulsion pulse through me with each heartbeat.

Of all the things I expected when I walked back into my house, it was not seeing my mother and Ada.

"Now, Lincoln, calm down. I was doing what was in your best interests."

"No, Mother, you were doing what *you* thought was best for your damn self! Can't you see how every time you interfere with my life, something goes wrong; therefore, I keep building a wall between us." My hands go up. "At this point, we don't even have a relationship, and you're the only one to blame!"

She gasps almost in horror as I finally spill the truth to her after all these years.

Becoming blue in the face, she stomps her foot in protest. "I will not be talked to that way, Lincoln. What I do for my kids is only the best." As she moves toward me, she rubs the side of my arm in a way that she may think is comforting.

Sorry to break it to you, Mother Dearest, it's not.

"I was just trying to show you that you can do much better than her. What about Sarah? She is a nice young lady, one that can give you what you need, what you want."

How dare she say that. She doesn't know what I want. What I need. If she did, she would have known it was Ada all along.

Angry, I push her away from me. I begin to pace, pointing at the door. "You need to leave"

"Linc—"

"GET OUT!" I all but shout at her. I clench my fists and breathe deeply, determined to make my point clear. "And while you're at it, leave the keys to my house," I demand.

"Lincoln, honey, let me just keep the keys. I think you just need a moment to calm down."

"No, I have had enough of this discussion." My voice is firm and low.

In a panic, she grabs her belongings and flees my house like it's on fire.

A frustrated groan escapes my lips as I throw my face into my palms.

God, I don't know why this keeps happening to me. Why can't I have even one moment of happiness?

Garrett bursts through my front door, blowing out a deep sigh.

My face, I'm sure, is stained with defeat, sadness, and anger, all wrapped into one emotion.

"Shit, what happened, Lincoln?" he asks as he touches the base of his neck, looking around in search of answers.

I refuse to say anything, knowing I can't acknowledge that she just up and left.

Again.

I shake my head, grab what I need, and move to the front door, making sure to lock it as I go.

Right as Garrett gets into his BMW, he says, "You know you can talk to me, right? I am always here."

Total silence engulfs us as he puts the car in drive, and we head for the airport.

My mind goes back and forth on whether I really want him involved. He's like a brother to me. We tell everything to each other.

After a heavy sigh, I uttered the word, "Ada."

"What about her? Did she upset you or something?" he asks in confusion, as he narrows his eyes.

"I suppose you could say that," I murmur.

I scrub my hand over my face as I stop fighting myself and tell him the truth. "She fucking left, man. She just up and left, like I meant nothing to her, like this entire month hasn't meant anything to her."

"Fucking hell, Lincoln, shit, man," he says. "Did she tell you why?" he asks.

I mean, she did, but what does it matter? It was like she was almost looking for an excuse to leave again.

My attention is drawn to the cars passing by as I say, "Yeah, also I ran into my mother and Ada in my kitchen. They probably had a heated argument, but I wasn't able to hear as they heard me enter the house."

Shock flashes across Garrett's face as he glances at me.

"Yeah, I know. Tell me about it," I say as I weave my fingers through my hair.

"That's why she just left, right? Because of your mom?"

I sigh. "Pretty much."

"I mean, I am not taking her side, by any means, but do you blame her, Lincoln? She has only gotten rudely repulsed by your family, her mother, and this entire town. Shit, even now, I don't think I could handle that, let alone at seventeen years old."

As he looks at me, he asks, "Linc, did you ever consider that maybe she didn't want to revisit her past? I am sure coming back to Blue Haven was hard for her, and then to see her past right there in front of her eyes again." He sighs. "It probably brought back a lot of bad memories for her."

Frustrated, I say, "I know, dude. I know. I never wanted that for her. I just, shit. I don't know, man; everything is fucking with my head. I thought that she left Blue Haven all those years ago because of everything else that was happening in her life, not just specifically because of my own mother. I know they never saw eye to eye."

"Don't you think that's putting it mildly?" he asks, raising his eyebrows. I glare at him as he shrugs his shoulders. "Oh, come on, you know your mom was, still is, a raging bitch, and not just to Ada. She doesn't deserve a place in your life, but you continue to let her in any way. And yet, she destroys your happiness once again and you're letting it happen, *once again.*"

I clench my fists, staring out the window. I am trying to control my emotions and keep my composure in this difficult situation, even though my instinct is to lash out at him. But I know it's not his fault. He is just telling me what I needed to hear all along.

Taking a few breaths, I slowly uncurl my hands and turn to face him. I have to accept the reality of the situation. "You should have seen Ada laying down the law, no pun intended, with my mother. I was in awe of how much she had changed, a different person, one I wasn't used to seeing."

"That's because she is Lincoln," Garrett says, his voice rising. "She is not that scared, naive, hurt little girl anymore. She is a fucking badass lawyer. She had a shit childhood; she took that and turned her life around, made something of herself, not that she needed to, but you should be proud of her, man."

"Seriously, dude, you don't think I know that? I am fucking proud of her and was going to say that, but you interrupted me. I was so damn proud of her, giving my mother an earful as she stood her ground, showing her that she's more than people realize. I know that's all Ada has wanted in life, to prove her worth, and my mother was at the top of her list."

In a frustrated breath, I say, "I know my mother can see that; I saw her eyes light up when Ada stood firm, telling her all the things that I knew she couldn't handle hearing. It was the best Goddamn thing I have ever seen, and in that moment, I truly thought Ada could handle my mother, that maybe we could have more than just closure between us, but a relationship. Is that so much to ask for? A second chance?" I ask rhetorically.

"Is that what you want? A second chance? To start over, possibly somewhere new?"

With a sigh, I say, "I'm not sure, man. I only know that I want Ada, and I will do whatever it takes to have her back in my life."

For good.

"Yeah?" he says, giving me the smuggest grin I've ever seen.

"Yeah, man; it's all I could imagine when she was around me. It was like a dream of mine coming true when she stepped into my house. Seeing her walk out, in only my shirt, grabbing a coffee, acting as if everything was natural."

Looking back at the road briefly, a smile creeps onto my face as I recall the feelings I experienced this morning. If there was one word to describe it, it would be euphoric. Happiness, contentment, and excitement for the future.

Our future.

"Garrett, all I could think about was, is this what it feels like to be truly happy? The feeling of being content with life? Not having to wonder what ifs, or imagining this feeling each day. In my house, I saw it clearly. Shit, I could even see our children running around; even Ada opening her own law practice, since that has always been her dream, and I would have given anything to make that happen."

"Shit, man, that's deep, but I felt the same way with Mayra, so I can't blame you. What are you going to do about it?"

As we approach the airport parking lot, I sigh deeply.

"Is there anything I can do? She left on her own accords. She showed me what she wanted, and clearly that wasn't me. Shit, she even let my mother have it and she still left me. I can see her running away because my mother brought up her past insecurities, but she stood her ground, Garrett; she showed her who she really is, and to me, I felt like, if she could handle that, she could handle anything.

"I don't know what to think or feel. I just know that there's a bigger reason she left so fast. My mother may have had some doing in it, but I feel like there's something there that she isn't telling me, and the moment she left, without a glance back, solidified things for us, like there was nothing between us on her end."

As we park, Garrett shuts off his car. "Maybe she was able to find closure," he remarks.

Laughing, but with more of a huff, I say, "Yeah, I do not think so. If we both had received closure, she would have left Blue Haven on good terms."

We both open our doors as Garrett says, "Well, clearly, there's a bigger reason for her leaving, a puzzle piece missing to tie everything together." I look over the top of his car as he continues, "And yes, I do think you need to figure it out, but Linc."

Peering over at him, I raise my eyebrows as I wait patiently for him to finish.

"Maybe hold off on getting your girl back, yeah? Maybe this trip will help you two really see things more clearly. Let the dust settle before you decide to approach her again. You know how women are after a fight. Irritable, emotional, and most importantly, you want to go to her when you both have had the time to process everything, really figure out what you want, what you *both* want."

I know he's right, but Ada coming back into my life only to be ripped away again is like a fucking punch to my gut.

I love her so much, more than she knows.

I'm drawn to her. My heart aches, but it's also wary. She may not know it, but she's playing tug-of-war with my heart, ripping and tearing it in every direction. And with all our ups and downs in our lives, Ada loves to run at the first sign of trouble. She runs from me, her problems, from others.

But maybe Garrett is right; maybe I need to let her cool off first, let her decide what she wants.

Me?

Blue Haven?

New York?

Without a doubt, I want a future with her, but she has to decide if she wants one with me.

Chapter Thirty ♡

Ada

To say the last two days have been extremely difficult would be an understatement. I've thrown myself back into work, attempted to concentrate on my case, struggled to sort out my feelings, missed Lincoln, and fought to remember who I am. I thought I was strong enough that no one could break down my walls again, yet it only took a few words from Sheryl to send me spiraling back.

Am I that strong woman that everyone in New York sees? That I've seen?

Do I have what it takes to win over this case?

Am I enough of a loveable person that someone could see a future with me? Not lawyer Ada, but just Ada Collins?

I try my best not to think of him. But it's impossible. Having my work to keep my mind off everything is nice and all, but once the break hits, it just goes out the window and thoughts continue to swirl.

Did he really mean what he said to me? That he loves me? That he wants only me?

As these emotions swell and fill me, I am over-whelmed by the sense of both guilt and relief; I chose to walk away, yet I know I had to in order to remain true to myself.

Doesn't he get it that just because I called his mom out on her bullshit doesn't mean I want her as my mother-in-law? Because daughters and mother-in-laws are supposed to be the closest of friends, have a great relationship, right? Even so, I know that I *need* my relationship with my mother-in-law to be at least thriving.

You only get one mother in life, and I can say mine wasn't the ideal mom. However, if I am about to let another woman, let alone a mother figure, into my life, I need it to be on my terms. I want her to love me for me. I want to spend time shopping with her, enjoy each other's company, and have her love that I am in love with her son. I need her to accept me and my feelings, provide me with the motherly love and advice I have been longing for, and ultimately become an important person in my life—someone I know I can trust and rely on.

I hold back a new set of fresh tears, rubbing my eyes, and letting out a low groan, as this is the last thing I need. My eyes are already puffy from all the crying last night and I haven't been unable to sleep since returning to New York, as evidenced by all the aches in my body. I take a deep breath, steeling myself against the onslaught of emotion that threatens to envelop me. I will not give in to the pain; this time I will fight.

I hear the gurgling sound of mine and Lucy's coffeemaker, clearly telling us we need a new one.

I stretch my body, throw my legs over my bed, and

pull on my slippers and creamy soft cardigan that I wear throughout my apartment.

From the kitchen, Lucy shouts, "Did my coffee wake you?"

"Yeah," I say, my voice sounding as if I had smoked an entire case of cigarettes before going to sleep. "But I knew it was time for me to get ready for work."

She looks over at me as she hands me a cup of coffee. My eyes close and I breathe in the aroma of caramel with notes of roasted almond and maple syrup; Lucy's secret ingredient. When the coffee touches my lips, I groan in satisfaction, feeling almost an ounce better.

Luce chuckles on the bar stool next to me as she says, "Coffee does wonders for the soul."

Nodding my head, a genuine smile spreads across my face as I take one more sip. Maybe today will be better.

A serious expression appears on Lucy's face as she turns toward me.

Or not . . .

It's the expression I've avoided since I got back to New York, and I recognize it all too well. The questions Lexie threw at me were easy to dodge, as I moped the entire way to the airport, nodding or shaking my head in complete silence. When really all I wanted to do was bawl when she glanced at me with a knowing look. I was ready to let it all out, tell her everything. However, it was my own fault for getting attached, for knowing better than to get my heart involved once again.

"Is your heart open to talking about Blue Haven?" she asks, her voice soft but steady.

My mind turns blank as I try to come up with a

reply. I'm not sure if I'm prepared to talk about it yet. I shrug my shoulders. "I don't know if I am ready," I answer quietly, looking around the kitchen away from her.

My bar stool swivels, and I gaze into our living room. With the sun shining through our open wide windows, I am reminded of the city's vibrant energy and why I chose to live here after law school. With its hustle and bustle, constantly changing skyline, and promise of a bright future, the city offers a sense of possibility and excitement. My dreams came true, and I was able to be a part of something greater than myself.

New York gave me that.

In the past, it was a home to me, a safe haven, but somewhere along the way, that changed. I don't know when it altered, but I know deep down that it no longer provides what it once did.

Does it matter if you own a home, a career, money, or a car if you have no one to share it with? Do I even want to be in New York anymore when it doesn't even feel like home to me? How does one even know when a place feels like home?

"Ada, honey, you know you can talk to me, right?" Lucy asks, bringing me out of a haze. Looking at her, a wave of tears brim my eyes. Her sadness echoes mine; it breaks my heart.

"Wha-at if I can't?" I ask, wiping away my tears. When I think of the last month in Blue Haven, I feel so damn paralyzed, frozen. Taking a deep breath, I try to center myself, reminding myself that I have been in tough situations before, but this one is different.

I can't take a deep breath and my muscles tense up, making it difficult to speak or even move. My body overheats, my heart beats rapidly, and confusion consumes my brain as I start to experience a panic attack.

Grabbing my head, I begin to feel that dull thud in my head that always precedes the onset of a migraine.

Shit, not now. I don't have time for this.

Lucy grips my shoulders. "Breathe, Ada, take a few deep breaths for me."

I lift my face from my hands and inhale and exhale three times before blurting out the truth, "I think I am still in love with him, Luce."

She smiles as she rubs my back. "Honey, I could have told you that the day you left for Blue Haven." I raise my eyebrows, making her chuckle. "Ada, ever since I met you, you have never once had a serious boyfriend. You are always having one-night stands, you are always playing it safe, and you keep your heart guarded. In spite of not fully understanding why, I had a feeling it was because of him."

Is she right?

Despite the fact that I was somewhat guarded, which was unattractive to men at times, they always knew my rules. One night, no questions, no strings attached. Just a fun night between two existing people living a lonely world. I wanted nothing to disrupt my focus, like a relationship. My dreams had finally become a reality, so I was not going to let them slip away.

Continuing to look at Lucy, she rubs my back in support.

Thank God for friends like her.

While I was away, did I mention how much I missed her? Because, fuck, I did. She's like a sister I've never had. Even though she annoys me, picks on me, always involves herself in my business, I would not be able to live without her. Honestly, I don't think I could have come back to New York without her. Although I ignored her for the first two days, she was fully aware that something had occurred, so I was left to figure it out until I was ready to share.

"Ada, do you remember what I told you before you left for Blue Haven?"

I shake my head, knowing my mind is so cluttered right now that I can't remember much of anything at this point.

"Well, sweet girl, I said going back to Blue Haven might offer you some closure that you didn't realize you needed."

I nod my head, but I don't feel like I got the closure that I needed, and that makes my heart ache.

I start to grow angry; what was the point of returning to Blue Haven? I usually have a plan and deadline in place, knowing what needs to be handled and avoiding any obstacles at all costs, yet when I first stepped back into Blue Haven, it was as if it all vanished. I guess I went there hoping for something, but now I'm stuck feeling frustrated and disappointed in myself.

"That's the thing, Luce. With the death of my mother and dealing with Lincoln, I never got closure on either. Had I known I would be caught in a tangled web of emotions, I wouldn't have gone."

She eyes me skeptically. "Really? Are you so sure about that? Because regardless of how you feel at the moment, I am certain that the trip did you some good." My eyes fill with confusion as she asks, "Ada, do you want my honest advice?"

I nod because I know her blunt ass will say it anyway.

"I think you're upset because you love him still and it's easier to push him away than to accept getting hurt again. I get it, I do. But the way you feel right now, right here," she says, pointing at my chest, "this isn't going to go away or change on its own. Not until you finally get closure, and Ada," she looks at me as she reiterates her point, "the closure you really need."

With a long sigh, I ask, "Why does it seem that there is no end in sight in this situation?"

Lucy lets out an awkward laugh. "That's because you know what needs to be done. You need to face your feelings, Ada, and put on those large fancy pants you love so much," she says with a wink, "and figure out what the hell you want. Is it New York? Is it Lincoln? Maybe Blue Haven? Shit, maybe even a different career."

She brushes a piece of my hair behind my ear. Our eyes meet, and I feel the weight of her next words. "All that matters at the end of the day is that you are happy; not Lincoln, not Noah, not Emmett, *you*, Ada Collins. That you are happy with the outcome of your life. For so long, you have let others take control of your decisions, outcomes, and life. In the end, it is your life, so now it is your turn to control it."

Having said that, she jumps up off of the bar stool and makes her way to our bedrooms. Glancing over her shoulder, she leans on the door and says, "Promise me one thing, Ada."

My eyebrows rise in anticipation of what she has to say. She takes a moment to think before proceeding, her eyes flitting between mine.

"The next few days are yours to figure out what you want. Only you. Then go for it and know that I am here to support whatever decision you make."

"I promise, Luce," I say in a shaky voice.

Whether or not I acknowledge it fully, Lucy is right; thirty years have flown by in a flash of an eye.

When was the last time I felt truly happy?

I have lived my whole life based on others' opinions of me. Always did what I was told by others. I tried to fit in with the right crowds, applied to the right college, law school, and even became a damn competent and prosperous lawyer. It has been a long, challenging road for me to live up to everyone's expectations of me. At what point do I stop fighting to prove my value, and for whom? And at what price does that truly make me happy? It is only now that I am beginning to realize that proving my worth to others is less important than achieving my own happiness.

So what will that look like?

What will make Ada Collins happy in life?

Chapter Thirty-One

Lincoln

In a flash, another second, minute, hour, day passes. While away for a few days, it was easy to focus on what was needed of me. However, the silence in my house became oppressive as soon as I returned home, following my time in Chicago with Garrett and all the newly hired employees. While I was tired, I did not feel like sleeping. I was hungry, but wasn't in the mood to eat. I was lonely, and the only company I desired was Ada's, which I knew I was unable to obtain.

After almost a week of silence, I am doing my best to hold myself together. I am listening to Garrett's advice and allowing her the space she needs and deserves, but when will it have been long enough?

Feeling anxious, I grab my phone and scroll aimlessly through social media until I see a picture of Ada; I added her. Call me crazy, but I couldn't just let her go, not yet. Scotty T., my pseudonym, is just a normal guy who wanted to follow her.

Shouldn't she know better to add strangers to her social media accounts?

Lincoln, is she really adding a stranger? It's you, for God's sake.

Pulling my comforter off me, I roll to my side as I inhale my sheets and visualize Ada next to me. Have you ever had a dream that was so clear that you knew it was more than just a dream, but rather, a reality? That you knew, deep in your soul, what you saw would eventually come true.

In this very moment, I can visualize waking up to her beautiful self every morning, interlacing our fingers while I kiss her knuckles as she gives me her adorable, tipsy smile. I envision our future children running into our bedroom, jumping on our bed as we tackle them both, bringing out the tickle monster. We'd laugh, and Ada would kiss us all good morning, her warmth radiating and filling us with joy and love, making us feel as if nothing else in the world mattered.

I see it all, everything, and with *her*.

While I pull myself out of bed, knowing I have to get ready for the day, I am unable to understand what the hell is wrong with me.

Did I not try hard enough with her? Maybe she doesn't even want to be with me.

Too fucking bad. You can't be with her, so quit pinning like a teenager.

Just as I am about to yank open the fridge, a knock at the door catches my attention.

"Lincoln St. James, you better open this door right now, or else I will have Levi bust it down with his feet," she chuckles, "we know how sensitive he is to his feet, so please do not make him do that."

Laughing, I shake my head. Only Anastasia would be brave enough to put her husband in harm's way.

As they enter my foyer, Anastasia looks over her shoulder and says, "Well, hello to you, too, older brother. Good to see your handsome face, despite the fact that you look like a shit."

I rub my hands over my face and murmur, "Uh, thanks, sis. Love you too."

She walks to the kitchen island, practically skipping like a damn bunny. She seems all too pleased to be in my presence this early in the morning.

"What did I do to so gratefully have you step into my house at," I look over at my kitchen stove, "7:30 am?"

She shrugs her shoulders as Levi brings a paper bag of what appears to be baked goods from Mrs. Deli's bakery.

This will certainly make up for their early arrival, don't you think?

Putting my hands on my chest, I tilt my head and give Anastasia my best puppy eye look. "Shoot, you really shouldn't have, sis; if this is the reason for your visit, then I approve."

When I attempt to grab a donut, she slaps my hand. "Tsk, tsk, tsk," she says, waving her finger. "Not so fast; this is only for bribes. For every question you answer, I will give you a bite of whatever you choose."

Glancing over at Levi, I roll my eyes. He raises his hands in surrender. "Hey, don't look at me. All she said was to grab some pastries from the bakery, and that we were on a mission today."

I eye Anastasia up and down and rest my fingers on

my chin as I say, "You're kind of looking like Mom; butting into my personal life like this."

The woman huffs. "I'm not sure whether to take that as a compliment or an insult."

"Probably the latter." I shrug.

Her eyes roll back as soon as I hear another knock at my door. *Who the hell would be here now?*

Walking to the foyer, I see two very familiar female faces standing in front of my door. "What the hell, Anastasia. What is this, a fucking intervention?" I yell back toward the kitchen.

Both Faye and Jewels grab my forearms and pull me back toward the kitchen.

"In all honesty," Jewels starts, "if you weren't my brother, I wouldn't even give you the good graces of my presence at this time in the morning. Be glad, Linc, that you are able to see all of this," she says, motioning her hands in the front of her face, "right now."

Almost instinctively, I laugh out loud.

"Yeah, what Jewels said, plus Anastasia bought bagels from the bakery, and me and the little fella here are hungry," Faye says, rubbing her stomach, which now looks as large as a cantaloupe.

How did she get so big? Where the hell have I been all this time?

Lincoln, your focus has been so centered on your own damn world that you have been unable to see what is happening in the outside world.

I feel a slight pang of guilt as I lower my gaze once again to Faye and her baby belly. I should be here for her during this pregnancy. Plus, who knows if Liam, her boyfriend and baby daddy, will take the time to be present since his job always seems to be at the forefront of his mind.

She needs me; everyone needs me. I am the glue that holds this family together.

God, have I really been in my own world the last month?

Taking a seat on the open bar stools in the kitchen, I rub my forehead. Anastasia takes a bite of what appears to be a powdered donut, and says, "I needed back up."

I look over at Levi; he shrugs his shoulders. "Hey man, you know how your sister is. You either are on board with her crazy ideas or will be stuck in the no no zone for God knows how long, and let just say her sexual appetite has increased since being pregnant, so I was going nowhere near the no no zone; she would use sex against me. Do you know how awful that is?!" he says, scrunching his nose.

The feeling is all too familiar to me. Up until recently, I did not have much of an appetite for sexual activity. With Ada, however, I felt insatiable and wanted to spend every moment in bed with her.

Now that's done, over with.

"Thank you for getting me my favorite bagel." Faye grins, grabbing one from the bag.

There is a joyful atmosphere all around me, all my sisters smiling and mingling as they stuff their faces with yummy goodness. I am taken aback by how lucky I am to have these incredible women in my life.

Eyeing the bag of baked goods, I pause. Maybe I should take my chance now. As I reach for the small glazed donut in the bag, I hear what sounds like a low growl. A fucking growl from Anastasia. My eyes travel back up to meet hers. "What do you think you're doing?" she asks, raising a brow.

Holding my hands up, I ask, "Fine, can you at least tell me why you three decided it would be a wise idea to barge into my house this early?"

All three sets of eyes glare into mine. Anastasia seems annoyed, Faye appears calm, and Jewels appears to be excited.

What the fuck is happening here.

"I think you know why we came here, big brother," Jewels says with a wink.

Crossing my arms, I lean back against the kitchen counter. "Why don't you enlighten me?" I ask.

Anastasia throws her hands up in frustration as she says, "Mom, Ada, the shit storm that is currently happening in your life. We are here to talk some sense into you."

What the fuck?

I don't need any advice, let alone from my three younger sisters. My eyebrows flutter in unison. "Me?" I let out a huff of a laugh. "Uh, I think you came to the wrong house, because I can assure you that I don't need your sisterly advice."

I push off the counter and start to pace; my fists clutching at my sides. My jaw is so tight. I think I'm going to crack a tooth, clearly irritated by the entire situation in which I have no control over. "As far as Ada and Mom, that is over and done with. Ada, chose what she wanted, and Mom, well, she does what she does best, fucks everything up."

"You know Mom told us, right?" Anastasia says. "She came to our house, banging on the front door out of frustration because of how you treated her."

"Can't say I'm sorry. She deserved it," I say, rubbing my neck.

Faye moves toward me; she breathes out a sigh. Her stare bores into my eyes, making me feel slightly uncomfortable. "Lincoln, do you think Ada intentionally left or did she feel as though she had no other alternative but to do so?" she asks.

My mind circles around the words. She wanted to leave, I could tell; she wasn't even putting up a fight for us. We aren't teenagers anymore. The least she could have done was sit down and have a normal conversation, talking things out. But no, she had to get up and run, from us, from Blue Haven.

How do I know she wouldn't have just run away if she had stayed? How can I trust her after all this?

My head shakes. "Faye, she left. She said she didn't want a life or future with me."

"Okay, did you tell her that our mother would have to get over it? That you could talk to her."

"Actually, yes, I did. Plus, it seems she's happy to be back in New York, a place she wants to be."

Away from me.

"Why do you say that?" Anastasia asks.

"Well, I saw a picture of her on Instagram. She looked happy, content, and at ease. Plus, she was surrounded by people who want to be around her; they don't cause her stress or make her second guess shit. That's all Blue Haven, her past, our mother, has done to her. It caused her unnecessary stress, made her feel worthless and unhappy. I can't be the reason behind causing that again."

"You have Instagram?" Jewels asks.

I nod. "Well, Scotty T. has Instagram."

"Who the hell is Scotty T.?" my sisters ask in unison.

My head shakes in embarrassment. "I made a fake

profile last week so I could check-in on Ada secretly. You know, make sure she is okay and all, which clearly she is doing just fine."

Without me.

My sisters burst into laughter. "I have to see that profile," Jewels announces.

Anastasia holds out her hand to me, wiggling her fingers as she states, "Well, now we have to see it; it's almost a given. You can't withhold secrets from your sisters. It's a forbidden rule."

I glare at all of them, including Levi, with their fucking smirks. I love the guy, but so much for a stand up brother-in-law. This is a situation I could really use him, have him go to bat for me, but the dude is helpless when it comes to my sister.

"Let's save that for another day, yeah? I'd like a donut anyway." Anastasia slaps my hand again. "What the fuck, Anastasia?"

"Not so fast; this conversation isn't over till I say it is."

"What else could you three possibly want to talk about?" I ask, frustrated.

Faye bites into her bagel as she says calmly, "Help you win Ada back, of course."

I roll my eyes, realizing that they couldn't just come give me pastries and be done with it. "Sorry to break the news. That isn't happening. Like I said, she chose to leave me, us, this." I extend my arms around me.

"How do you know that's what she truly wanted? Did you ask her? Maybe she is unhappy, sad, and moping around just like you are? Have you even reached out to her since you left?" Faye says.

While grabbing my phone, I point to the screen and

say, "See, she looks perfectly happy to me, surrounded by the ones she loves!"

In a sympathetic tone, Faye says, "You left out you."

"Oh wow, who is that handsome chunk of meat?" Jewels says, biting her lip, taking my phone.

I roll my eyes; fucking Will. Of course, that guy is there, right next to her side with his arm around her. Couldn't wait till she returned, so he could have Ada all to himself once again.

Good news, she's fucking yours; clearly not meant to be mine.

"Lincoln, pictures can be deceptive. Maybe she is just having fun with some friends? Maybe they are trying to cheer her up like we are with you?" Faye says.

I shrug my shoulders. "Maybe."

"Definitely wouldn't be opposed to going out with that guy," Jewel says, pointing at Will.

I snatch my phone from them, a bit more aggressive than I probably needed to, but can you blame me? I feel an overwhelming sense of anger and betrayal. I was hurt by the idea that she had moved on without me, and now she is living a life without me in it.

I grab a donut from the bag without giving a damn if I am threatened with my life.

"You know what I think you should do?" Faye says.

"No, please, tell me what should I do?" I ask in a sarcastic tone, which only results in an entire room full of eye rolls.

With a grin on her face, Jewels says, "Go to New York and confess his undying love for Ada?"

"That wasn't exactly what I was thinking, more like showing Ada what she doesn't have but needs, what kind of life she'd miss out on if you weren't there," Faye says.

While clapping her hands, Jewels says, "I love that idea!"

"Yes, that is definitely something we can work with. Maybe, Linc, you should let us handle everything for you," Anastasia says.

Looking at all three of their faces, my eyes widen. "Are you kidding me? I would never let you handle this situation, even if my life was at stake."

An irritated huff erupts from Anastasia as she gets up from the bar stool, wobbling over to me. She places her hands on her hips, pushing her chest out. "We will see about that."

"Anastasia, please don't get involved. I want Ada to be able to process everything on her own."

"What if you wait too long? What if you can't win her back?"

Slowly shaking my head, I let out a small sigh of irritation. "I am going to let her decide that. She chose to leave twelve years ago, and she chose to leave over a week ago. It is her decision whether to remain with me or not. I already know I want a life with her, but I can't convince her that she needs or wants me. She must decide that on her own. Meanwhile, I must respect her wishes."

"Lincoln!" Faye replies in an upset tone, "do you not realize that the reason she left you all those years ago, and recently, was because of our mother, not you. You are choosing to let Ada believe that she isn't worthy enough. That she does not deserve a place in our family, in your life."

"You know, she's right, Lincoln. Ada has always had a spot in our family, but you both didn't see it, even if it was right in front of your faces. You're both adults now, and if our mother can't respect or approve of your relationship, then screw her. You think she approved of Levi right away?" Anastasia says, pointing to him. "No. I never told you guys this, but the first time I introduced him to our parents, Mother thought he was the new butler we were looking to hire. I sat there laughing my ass off as he was blinking in complete shock, and Mom couldn't understand what was going on until I told her who he was.

"I remember it like it was yesterday, she looked at me as she said, 'Why does he look like a butler then?' Bear in mind, he was dressed sort of like one, but again, he was trying to impress her. From that night on, Lincoln, I didn't give two shits about how she felt about Levi. I knew deep in my heart that I loved him, wanted him in my life, to have a future, and that meant dealing with our mother. I stood my ground and made her do the choosing. It was either accept Levi or she would have one less daughter."

"Shut up! You did not say that!" Jewels exclaims, her mouth wide open in surprise.

"Yes, she did, and it was the best day of my life," Levi says, kissing the top of Anastasia's head as he grabs her from behind. "In fact, Lincoln, that was the day I knew your sister and I would never live another day apart. I knew our love was stronger than your mother's opinion of me. Don't get me wrong, your mom still treats me like dog shit," he shrugs, "but I am able to handle her comments about me with impunity."

How did I now know that about him? About Anastasia? It is my responsibility as the oldest to support and protect them, especially from our mother.

Says the guy who didn't protect Ada from his own mother. A slight sting runs through my hair as I pull on its ends. *Shit, shit, shit.*

As my thoughts begin to circle, I pace the kitchen floor, my heart racing a mile a minute. I can feel my stomach sink and my palms sweat, the fear of regret and the unknown overtaking me.

Did I miss my chance with Ada?

What if she doesn't want me anymore?

Can we really have a life together, even with my mother in the picture?

FUCKKKK.

I can't keep living in this unknown, so there's only one way to find out.

Chapter Thirty-Two ♡

Ada

I can still feel his lips on mine. I can still smell his distinctive scent of spice and musky masculine fragrance that was exclusively his. I can still feel his heart beating rapidly when we were close. I can still hear his laugh whenever I joke.

"Hasn't this been a blast so far?" Will says, snapping me out of my thoughts as he wraps an arm around me.

Our firm decided to celebrate our large win by dining at Hickory Fire Eatery. Remember that client of mine? The one who wanted to go with another law firm? Well, ya girl convinced them otherwise.

As we walk along 5th Avenue, I murmur, "Mhmm," feeling nothing but numbness.

It's easy to put on a mask, show others what they want to see. Someone who is happy-go-lucky, someone you can hang out with without bringing them down with your irrational emotions. The truth is, it's really hard to keep such a facade up—to put on a show and pretend to be happy when all you want to do is cry.

That's me, the happy-go-lucky person who should be thrilled that we won over the biggest client and I sealed the deal on being the next partner at Sullivan & Rothman Law Firm, yet, I felt absolutely nothing.

And why the hell not? Good question, I would like to know that for myself.

My time has been devoted to this damn client, attending to their needs 24 hours a day, answering their calls at insane hours, all while ignoring mine; to what end?

Feel prideful?

To feel worthy?

To know I am one of the best damn lawyers in New York?

But I didn't feel any of those in that office this afternoon.

Will every big client feel this way going forward?

Will I be able to share my career highs and lows with anyone?

You know that feeling, the one where goosebumps line up your arms. Your heartbeat is moving a mile a minute. All you can think about is what's going to happen next? That's me, *normally*, but today, being a lawyer, walking into that room, I didn't feel any emotion. It was like this wasn't even the biggest moment of my career, yet it was.

The irony of it all was not lost on me; I knew this should have been a nerve-wracking experience, but instead, all I had wanted was to get from point A to point B as fast as I could.

Maybe it's because being a lawyer isn't everything. The thought itself catches me off guard.

Taking a moment to clear my mind, I peel over at Will as we continue to walk. His eyes are bright, and he is obviously happy, content, and excited about life. He shoots me a smile as he continues to speak about God knows what.

Does that make me a horrible friend?

His lips move, white frost covering every single word. Everything around me seems to be moving at a breakneck speed. I just want to have that small bit of reassurance that I'm doing the right thing, even if it feels like I'm leaving everything I know behind.

"Ada? Hey, are you alright?" Will asks, grabbing my shoulders, stopping us in the middle of the sidewalk.

"Yeah, sorry, I'm just exhausted. The last month has taken a lot out of me, and rushing back to New York to handle this case has only compounded that. I need a few days to recover," I whisper, my voice cracking as tears sting my eyes.

"Aren't you excited that you have won Hamill and Sons over? It's an incredible accomplishment!" he exclaims, throwing his hands into the air, clearly trying to convey his point.

"Of course I am!"

Why don't I feel like I'm on cloud nine then?

As much as I have invested in this case and know it will be a career changer, I still can't seem to get Lincoln out of my thoughts.

What is he doing at this very moment?

Does he miss me as much as I do? Why didn't he try harder for us this time?

Ada, get a grip, he's just a guy.

He's *the* Guy.

I did see a future with him, with us; kids, marriage, everything, and it scares the shit out of me. It's a strange feeling to realize the future you once wanted is now something you are afraid of.

"Okay, here we are," Will says as he points to my and Lucy's penthouse.

Will eyes me with such adoration that I have a hard time voicing it into words. He has been flirtatious all night, let alone in the past few weeks. His expression alone indicates that he intends to make a move.

Doing what I do best, I reach in for a friendly hug, but Will grabs me by the waist. The man is touching me, on the waist, and in a not so friendly manner. My heart thumps uncomfortably hard in my chest as his grip tightens, unsure of what I should do.

I sense that something is about to happen, and it is not going to be good.

"I didn't even get to give you your celebratory gift." I attempt to pull free from his hold, but he tightens his fingers. "Oh, Ada, don't be like that." His voice is firm yet gentle, as he insists, "I want to give it to you."

Oh God, he's going to do it.

The kiss is coming. He steps closer to me, our faces only inches apart.

Lucy was right; he is more interested in me than a friend. And I wait.

Wait for that kiss.

As he bends over and puckers his lips, I can only close my eyes in anticipation. His hot breath hovers right over my ear and makes me shiver. However, it is not in the way I would shiver with a certain someone. Instead, I am filled with a sense of fear and dread.

The tip of his nose suddenly drops to the line of my jaw as it moves across my cheek ever so slightly.

This is it.

Ada, just take the plunge and make it a quick, friendly kiss? Keep it simple and light.

Just as I expect him to plant a kiss on me, he presses the lightest of kisses to my cheek and stands. "Not what you expected . . . " he laughs, and I hear a hint of sarcasm hidden within.

"Uh-h, yee-ah," I attempt to control my obvious stutter. "It definitely wasn't," I reply, letting out a sheepish laugh.

"Well, I can't say I am surprised that you didn't want me to kiss you, but I got the memo real quick. You closed your eyes and your body pretty much went into shock. You were so fucking tense. Honestly, it looked like you were about to kiss Noah. In hindsight, it was clear that the moment was not the right time or place to try anything of that nature."

God, could this be any more embarrassing?

"That bad, huh?" I ask as I glance at him.

In order to avoid laughing, he bites his lip, but we both laugh together as soon as he nods. Clearly attempting to avoid any more awkwardness between us.

"It's alright though," Will continues, taking a deep breath and forcing a smile. "I guess some things just don't work out the way we hope."

Good job, Ada; letting another person down.

In a split second, his eyes return to mine, and I am able to see Lucy through the glass doors over his shoulder.

As she points her finger at Will and me, she is smiling and jumping up and down.

What the fuck?

Rolling my eyes, I know exactly what she is doing . . .

A fucking victory dance

Moving closer to Will, I extend my hand for a friendly hug. Immediately after my head hits Will's shoulder, I wave my hands at Lucy, encouraging her to move her ass along.

Clearly, there is nothing to see here. New York sidewalk, two friends hugging awkwardly.

Lucy waves her fingers, and a cheshire smile crosses her face, and I know an 'I told you so' is just around the corner the moment I step through the door.

Pulling back from Will, I stare at him with tears in my eyes. "Will, I-I didn't mean tt-o," I say. I pace the sidewalk with a frustrated sigh.

God, what the hell is wrong with you, Ada.

I have failed to show Will the respect and kindness he deserves, and I am ashamed of how my actions have caused him pain. I am also overwhelmed with guilt that I am not living up to my own expectations of myself and feel like I am letting everyone in my life down.

Taking my forearms, Will turns me to face him. He lets out a deep sigh, which makes my heart break even more for him. "Ada, breathe. It was only a mistake. One where I thought there was more between us, but there clearly wasn't."

God, why can't I like a guy like Will?

You know why you can't like him, because you love Lincoln.

He's not complicated, doesn't make me doubt my worth, has nothing to do with my past, and God forbid, I bet he probably has a wonderful mother.

All the things I should want in a future partner. Things I need.

But, no, my heart wants to be with Lincoln, the only one it's ever known.

I sigh loudly. "I am sorry for making this so awkward, and I want you to know I never meant to hurt you. If I gave you the impression I intended more, or you felt led on by my actions, I apologize deeply, Will."

I hug him again, hoping with all my heart that we will be able to move on. Whispering in his ear, I say, "I want you to know you are one of my best friends and I couldn't have gotten through the last several years without you by my side, of course, only as a friend."

He erupts in a loud laugh, and I feel the vibration of his laughter as it settles my nerves.

We're going to be okay.

One more time, I squeeze him tight. We scan one another's eyes in anticipation of what lies ahead.

Will extends his hand, as if we are about to strike a deal. "Just friends, Ada Collins. I couldn't be more grateful to have you as one of my best."

A genuine smile appears on my face as I shake his hand. "Friends, Will Parker."

In the end, if all I have is my friends for the rest of my life, I will be just fine.

Ada Collins, you will be hunky-dory.

The apartment door shuts, and I breathe a sigh of relief, but before I know it, I hear, "Is this the right time to tell you . . . I TOLD YOU SO!" Lucy practically screams at me.

Yep. How'd I know that was coming.

With a nod of the head, I exhale a slow breath and

close my eyes in preparation for the inevitable tears to flow.

"Oh honey, come here," Lucy pleads. There is a connection between my eyes and hers. She gives me a knowing look, and I open my mouth, but no words are forthcoming. "It's okay, sweetie, I understand. How about we have a cup of tea and talk about it together?"

My head shakes. "I think I'm just going to call it a night, Luce," I say as I walk back to my bedroom door. "I am tired, anyway; after a long day of work and all."

"Okay, but if you need me, I'm here for you. Always."

"I know, and that's why I love you," I say, closing my door.

A long, exhausting sigh escapes me as I slump into my bed and clutch my pillow close to my chest.

Why does everything feel like it's falling apart? I want to feel whole again, the way I felt only a few weeks ago.

God, I sound like a selfish bitch. I live in a gorgeous penthouse, am an extremely successful lawyer, and have the best friends and support system a woman could ask for.

In your heart, you know there is one thing missing that would truly make you feel whole.

Pushing myself out of bed, I look to the corner of my room. The box of letters stares back at me; I bite my nails. They are taunting me.

Screaming at me to rip them open.

While I realize this will not make me feel better, I am powerless to stop myself. I walk over to the box and aimlessly pick one. When I look down at the one I selected, it is the last thing I expect to see.

To: My Ada Bug
Love: Your Mother

Chapter Thirty-Three ♡

Ada

Sitting cross-legged on my bed, I open the letter and experience a powerful blast of nostalgia.

Dear Ada, do you remember the one time we went to Nana and Papa's house? You and I both just finished making your favorite dessert, Apple Pie Crispy. The leaves still fell from Nana's favorite maple tree, and the smell, well, don't get me started. Our favorite. I will always remember us both taking a big breath as we got it out of the oven, leaning inches from the pie to get a decent smell of the chestnut and cinnamon.

I let out a sad laugh, feeling my tears retreating down my throat as I recall that exact memory. It has been almost fifteen years since that day had happened;

regardless, we did it every fall, and it was my favorite memory of all time. It came crashing down one day. I never knew why, but we all of a sudden stopped, and our lives went downhill from there. I can't tear myself away from the letter now. I have to continue reading it.

Right? There has to be a reason she wrote this to me.

That was probably the last good memory I had before everything fell apart.

You might be wondering what this letter is about or how it got to you? Well, you can thank Lincoln St. James. He's still a great boy, and he's an even better man now.

Lincoln?

Lincoln St. James? Are we talking about the same man here?

Why would she know anything about him growing up, let alone him knowing about this letter?

Enough about that man. The reason I really wanted to write this letter is because it's only days, maybe even hours, before I am taken from this world. A world you exist in, Noah exists in, a world I wish I could continue to exist in, even if it was just to receive your forgiveness before I am gone.

What does she mean, 'taken from this world'? My

eyes continue to scan the letter as they stop on a six letter word, making me nearly fall over breathless.

I have cancer, Ada bug.

My stomach sinks as my heart aches in my chest.

"Mom," I whisper softly, running my fingers over the letter as tears start to blur my vision and wrinkle the paper. I am filled with a mix of emotions—sadness, disbelief, shock, and confusion. This letter changes everything I thought I knew.

What a shocker, right? I am sure you are just as startled as I was. I received the call shortly after making your favorite pie at your grandparents' house that day. The doctors called to inform me that I had lung cancer. According to my exams and x-rays, the cancer had spread from my lungs to adjacent tissue, which was surprising. At that point, I had no other choice but to undergo chemotherapy or live my life until it was my time, and I chose to be a selfish bitch at that time.

Don't shake that head, Ada, I know you are.

I stop shaking my head and let out a heartbroken laugh.

In an effort to avoid burdening anyone, I

chose not to tell anyone about my situation, and with that, I did not receive any support or assistance. Although I am not seeking your sympathy, I would like to explain why your life suddenly turned upside down in a matter of seconds.

It was due to my illness, sweet girl. I never intended to waste the years we had left together by being drunk, emotionally wrecked, addicted to whatever I could find—get my hands on. But you have to know that when I found out I got cancer, the first thing I thought of were my two babies.

Who's going to take them?

Watch them as they grow into wonderful humans?

Who will teach Noah how to kick a soccer ball?

Take pictures of Ada at her first prom?

Show Ada how to bake more desserts?

Growing up, baking new recipes with her was probably my favorite memory of us together.

In my opinion, my parents were not capable of caring for two younger children at their age, and we are both aware your dad and his parents were never really involved in *the family. In that moment, I felt that I had no one else to rely on except myself, and I wasted every single day getting inebriated off my ass. Again, it is not my intention to ask for sympathy, but I felt as though I had the weight of the world on my shoulders and felt that I had no choice but to rely on something that calmed my emotions, provided comfort, and ultimately alleviated the pain I had been experiencing. When I was under the influence of alcohol or a new drug, I felt as though my problems were solved. I know that they weren't, but at that time of my life, it seemed as though they were.*

As I rub my hand against my face, I wipe another tear. The heartbreak I feel still lingers heavily in the air whenever she speaks of our past life. God, if only she had felt like she could have leaned on me, maybe things would have turned out differently?

What if she got chemotherapy? What would our lives look like now?

Would she still be alive?

Would she be there for Noah and me?

Continuing to read, I don't know if I want to let it end. I feel like this is the last thing she will ever give me. This may be the closure I've been longing for; the closure Lucy has been encouraging me to seek.

If there is one thing I want you to take away from this letter, it is that I love you, Ada bug. I never meant to hurt you or Noah. I wanted to live out the rest of my years cheering you two on in anything you did in life. I hope you know that I am doing that now, even if it's from above. I pray that you have gotten every-thing you have wanted out of life, Ada. And just know, sweet girl, it's okay to be scared. We are all humans, and at the end of the day, we all feel that way sometimes. However, getting through our fears, insecurities, and sadness is the most challenging part. I was scared and let it run my life into the ground, literally. You, baby girl, believe it or not, do have the power to take control. Make the leap and take the reins of your life—be bold and daring, and never fear the unknown. Live your life how you want to live it. Not the way you think you're supposed to or how someone else wants you to.

Be true to yourself and live your life in your own unique way.

As my heart swells in my chest, it is as if she could read my mind the way she always did. It is as if she understands me completely.

We're gonna get through this, Ada bug, right? No matter how difficult things get, I want you to know that I am here for you. I truly hope that one day you can find it in your heart to forgive me and move forward without any lingering bitterness.

PS . . . I did leave behind Grandma's recipe book. Lincoln was always a fan of Grandma's baking, so it was no surprise he knew where her recipe book was!

Xoxo Mama Bug.

Dropping the letter on my bed, I jump off and start to pace the room. A sense of panic has begun to unfold, but now it is moving slowly. The shock crawls up my body, and I experience the pain.

My mom had cancer?

Cancer?

Why didn't she tell me?

You know why, Ada. She did not want you to feel as if she was burdening you further with her problems.

My knees hit the carpet, and I whisper, "Oh, Mom," as my last wall withers away. The tears flow.

Is this really the end of it all?

I never got to say goodbye.

Oh, how I wish I could have taken away her pain and given her the comfort she so desperately needed.

Taking a deep breath, I choke back a sob as I try to blink away the sting of fresh tears threatening to spill out again.

It's not that I didn't just get to say goodbye, but she

never got to say goodbye. I just left, acted like it was not that big a deal to leave my dying mother alone.

Ada, don't you dare blame yourself; you didn't know she had cancer.

I know, I know, but that doesn't make me feel any better . . . but I know what might.

Picking up my phone from my nightstand, I scroll through my contacts, stopping immediately on Lincoln.

My lips pull between my teeth as I suddenly feel qualmish. We haven't talked or even texted in the last week.

What if he doesn't answer?

Wait, am I calling him?

Maybe it's safer to just text him.

I nod my head. *Yep, let's just send him a text.*

Opening a new message thread, I hover over his name as I try to figure out what I should say.

> Hey! How's it going? How have you been? I have been great if you are wondering.

Nope, deleting that.

> Hey, Linc. Are doing well? I hope so?

DELETE, DELETE.

> Hey, Lincoln. Did you know my mom had cancer?

You CAN'T say that over text, Ada.

My God, this couldn't be more awkward. A frustrated breath escapes my mouth as I rub my face.

Ada, it's just a fucking text. You're a lawyer, for crying out loud.

Fine, I got this.

> Hey! Lincoln, quick question.

> Do you happen to know where my grandmother's recipe book is?

There, that will work. I hit send and patiently wait approximately two seconds until my phone buzzes by my arm.

> I see you found your mother's letter? 🙂

I draw my eyebrows together in confusion. Obviously he knew about my mother's letter, but the question is: why didn't he tell me about it?

Ada, focus, that's another question for another time.

But before I can respond, my phone vibrates with another incoming text.

> I know what you are thinking. Yes, I did know about your mother's letter, but I hope you know that out of respect I wanted you to find it yourself, instead of me telling you.

Although I want to be upset with him, I feel warmth in my chest. I understand why he did what he did, and for that I can't be angry. I was supposed to find my mom's letter on my own time.

> I understand, Linc. I'm not mad at you. I hope you know that.

> You couldn't stay mad at me even if you tried 😏

A snort of laughter escapes me as I shake my head. In such a moment, Lincoln is the only one who could make me laugh with a joke.

> ANYWAY, it's at the very bottom, hidden in your letter box, under all the other letters.

Before I can respond back, another ping comes in.

> You plan on making me Grandma Ruth's famous Snickerdoodle Cookies?

The box of letters catches my attention as I smile.

> Hmmm . . . maybe . . . let me get back to you on that 🙂

> Thanks, I appreciate it, Linc.

> Of course. Are you still coming to Lexi and Josh's wedding next weekend?

Isn't that the million dollar question? Mom's funeral is over and Noah seems to have handled the estate sale, so there's no need to really go back.

Is there?

Over the last few days, I have asked myself this question repeatedly.

I know it would be best to say goodbye to my childhood home and get the closure I need from Lincoln.

Lucy clearly has voiced to me that she thinks it's something I need to do.

But wouldn't returning make things ten times more difficult for me? To leave again? To say goodbye . . . again?

I don't think my heart can handle it, even right now, as my heart is still hammering through my chest. I let out a deep sigh and respond the best way I know how.

That's not responding at all and doing what I need to do first. My heart and soul require my attention; before I can move forward with my future, I need to let go of this part of my past.

And the closure I have been seeking all along is within my reach.

I let my phone fall to the ground as I run to the corner of my room, where Lincoln told me the recipe book could be found. My smile widens when I remove the dust from the top portion of the title. It reads, 'Nana's Daily Fix Bakery.' When I open the bookmarked page, my heart skitters to a halt.

Rubbing my hand over the page, I whisper, "Hi, Mom," and then, in that moment, I know what we both need.

Chapter Thirty-four

Ada

"Uh, please tell me you do know it's two in the morning, Ada?" Lucy says as she walks alongside the kitchen counter covered in flour, mixing bowls, my KitchenAid mixer, and all the baking utensils even a professional baker would need.

"Yep, it certainly looks like it's that time," I say with a wink, tossing some flour in her direction.

Jumping back, she grabs the kitchen towel and begins to twist it in circles. "Don't make me use this on you."

My chest bulges as I let out a loud laugh. "You know that if you hit me in the ass with that, it will only bounce back at you. Guess having a bubble butt comes in handy, right?"

Lucy's grin cracks in two as she begins to walk toward me. "So, are you going to explain why you are baking at a time when most people are asleep?"

Having found my mother's letter, I wanted to be

agitated. I wanted to be upset. However, I recalled something Lincoln had mentioned to me numerous times during high school.

Don't ask why this was the first thing that came to mind, but it was almost instantly.

"Ada, breathe; you have to let it go, ignore it, don't let this one moment in time ruin the rest of your life.

Give it time, don't compare your situation to them; it's up to you. Only you get the decision to do that, and by letting them get the best of you, it is showing them they have the upper hand. Be that strong girl that I know you are capable of, and when in doubt, stay calm and display the prettiest smile I know that exists."

A smile spreads across my lips. I wouldn't have made it that far in high school without his support every step of the way. He was always present, helping me to keep moving forward, even when I felt like giving up. He gave me the strength to believe in myself, no matter what.

Lucy waves a finger with dough on it. "Earth to Ada! What's up with that smile you're showing?"

A giggle emerges from me. "I have no idea what you are referring to." I shrug my shoulders, looking all but innocent.

As she throws a handful of flour at me, she lets out a laugh, more like a snort. "You're so full of shit."

My shoulders are once again lifted as I wink.

When she turns around to my side, her hand claps my shoulder, and the sympathy reflecting in her gaze catches me by surprise. "Ada, you truly know I am here for you, right?" she asks.

I place my hand on hers as I smile. "Yes, Luce, I

know, and I will always be grateful to have such an encouraging best friend as you. But, I am fine. I feel like I have finally gained closure with my mother, and I am working to achieve the same with Lincoln."

Nodding, she takes another big bite of my dough.

A sigh escapes my lips as I admit, "I know it took me some time to realize it, but it was essential that I close a door in my past, as well as a new one. I was coping with the death of my mother, and the past life that comes with it, having Lincoln and our past mixed into that was so overwhelming that I freaked out."

I continue to knead the dough. "Yes, his mother played a significant role too, as it was what triggered me and caused all of my fears and insecurities to emerge. But I also know that part of me fled back to New York because I was terrified of facing my past, my insecurities, of falling in love again, and the unknown of everything."

Lucy pulls me into her bear hug while whispering to me, "Honey, that is what life is about, forgiving the past, moving forward, falling in love with the love of your life, even if there are risks involved, and being okay with the unknown."

"I know that you have always wanted to control your life because of your childhood, but that is not always the case." With tears in her eyes, she releases her grip and smiles. "But I think it's time to let go. You need to live the life you want, so what does that look like for you?

"What does Ada Collins want in life? Hmmm? Because this smile," she says, pointing to my cheek, "on your face may be due to something or someone." She winks.

My stomach tightens in laughter as I push her away

from me. I reach for some flour on the counter, and she gives me an incredulous look, her eyes widening when she sees the fluff in my hand.

"Don't do it, Ada. You know you don't want to."

Eh, but I really, really fucking want to.

In the midst of flour coating her face, I resist the urge to laugh. She gives me the look of all Lucy's.

Game on.

Shit, shit.

I try to run across the hardwood floor, but fall due to my Christmas fluffy socks. Of course, the only time these wouldn't be necessary.

I look up and Lucy is upside down with flour in her hands.

Yep, you heard that correctly, not just one handful, but two. That little shit.

As soon as she drops the flour on my face, she bursts into a fit of laughter, as if seeing me covered in flour is extremely comical. She pops a hip. "So, you want help with baking or what?"

I nod my head as she grabs my arm and pulls me up, and we do exactly that.

We bake into the wee hours of the morning, and as soon as I close my eyes to rest, my alarm clock goes off. Deciding to do what the new Ada wants to, I shut it off and text Elena that I will be coming in later this afternoon, and to postpone any of my morning meetings.

This. This is what I needed.

To reconnect with my mom.

To reconnect with my past and move forward.

To finally receive the closure I needed.

To find out what Ada Collins really wants in life.

Chapter Thirty-five

Lincoln

Four fucking days. It's been four days since I last heard from Ada. My days have been full of misery, combating sadness, and feeling lonely—something I thought I was content with until she came trotting back into my life. I thought the first time she left me was heartbreaking. This time, however, seeing her leave was excruciating, literally creating a gaping hole in my heart even wider than the first goodbye, making it ache more.

With each passing minute, the distance between us increases, making me worry that I won't see her again. My stomach hurts; I feel like shit, look like hell, and I frankly don't care. I had to all but drag myself to Lexie and Josh's wedding, because did I really want to be surrounded by happiness and love?

Nah, not really, but I was happy; truly for my two friends and wanted to celebrate them, and well, I didn't have a choice. So here I am, standing in the reception hall, while I swipe at my screen, over and over again, flipping through old text messages with Ada, until I settle on one of my most favorite ones.

In the photo, you can see the gift I gave her for her birthday right next to her as she flashes that devious sexy smile into the camera while wearing the damn piece of lingerie she owns.

There is so much love and happiness in her gaze, as well as fierce appreciation and devotion, and that is why my heart keeps telling me to wait for her.

For us.

Our future that I know could be great together.

Just as I'm about to look at more messages, someone steps up behind me. "Dude, do you even know how to be a best man? You're seriously slacking in that department right now. Josh should have made me his best man. God knows I'd be extraordinary at it."

Peeking over my shoulder, I see Garrett's trademark smirk and bouncing eyebrows. He elbows me in the side and asks, "Don't you think?"

"Garrett, hey, honey," Mayra says, her hands full with Henry and his diaper bag. Georgia stands beside them.

"What's up, baby?"

"Please help me for a moment," she says, holding Henry out in front of Garrett.

I look him dead in the eyes. Suppressing a laugh, I mouth, "Yeah, totally a great best man."

He takes Henry, turning once more to me. "You just wait, St. James; when you have children and a wife of your own, you will understand."

As he walks away, I notice the sea of people chatting away in the vast bar. Waiting patiently for the wedding celebrations to begin.

And here I am, patiently, more like praying, that Ada will show.

You know, I had a plan in motion after the day my sisters left my house. Despite their annoying nature, they did manage to talk some sense into me. I fled to my parents' house, telling my mother that either she dealt with mine and Ada's relationship or she was going to lose her one and only son.

If only you could have seen her face that day. Priceless.

She sobbed hysterically, tears streaming down her face, as she expressed her desire to keep me in her life, no matter the cost. I had a heart-to-heart conversation with her, and she shared with me the true reasons she never liked Ada.

In hearing her spill out the truth, it was about as shocking to me as it was for her. Ada was never the issue; it was more about something my mother was struggling with inside herself. I did not know my grandparents or how my parents were raised on either side of my family. My mother told me that she saw so much of Ada in herself, the trauma she endured as a child and what it did to her, that she did not wish for me to be with someone who may have the same experiences.

At the end of the day, Mother Dearest wanted me to be with a better significant other; however, she admitted that she saw a different Ada this time around and was open to accepting our relationship.

Of course, *pending* relationship.

It was my intention to travel to New York, make a grand entrance, and insist that she return. But then I remembered why I had let her go in the first place. She needed space to determine what her needs in life were and what her future was going to be like, with or without me. While standing by and patiently waiting hurts like hell, I do know one thing: letting go to allow her to understand what she wants is important, and if she comes back to me, then it is meant to be.

In 45 minutes' time, I think I am two sheets to the wind, as I fall backward, grasping at the bar counter top to maintain my balance.

"Don't look now, but there is an extremely hot woman checking you out right now," says the bartender.

Kevin, I believe is his name, looks like a surfer from California. He has golden long locks and tanned skin, despite it being winter. *Like, what?*

Scanning the open seated tables, there are a few stragglers, mainly the wedding party, mostly pregaming.

Unfortunately, I cannot say the same for myself. I am unsure of why I felt the need to drink more than I would normally do on such a significant day.

Oh, yeah, that's right. Because the one person I want most is . . .

Well, she's looking right back at me.

I clear my throat as I continue to stare ahead. *Is that Ada?*

I would not be surprised if my eyes are playing tricks on me. It feels like I am living in a surreal dream, where the lines between reality and fantasy are blurred.

"Dude, I instructed you not to look, but hey, do you think I could ask for her number? She sure is attractive."

My eyes never leave the beautiful woman in front of me as I confidently tell Kevin, or whatever the fuck his name is, "She's already taken."

Or is about to be . . .

Ada wraps her hand around a glass of champagne, her eyes not far from mine as she takes a sip.

Being seductive as hell.

As she walks toward me, I feel myself becoming extremely hot.

God, is it that hot in here? Who is fucking blasting the heat?

A shot of desire dips down my stomach when my eyes settle on *her*.

Sweet, holy fuckballs, *that dress.*

With a dress draped in crimson lace, Ada looks as enticing and mouth watering as a candle apple. She's like that forbidden fruit, and all I want to do is fucking devour her.

I hold back a groan as my eyes take in her perfectly hugged curves, the way the lace clings to her waist, and then flows down her luscious thighs before wrapping around her knees. Her sparkling heels complement the two barrettes in her hair, which is styled in wavy curls.

There's an air of confidence in her tonight. However, if I had to guess by the simple rise of her chest, I'd say she's just about as nervous as I am.

Ada

Oh, holy shit, oh shit.

Don't look, don't look, don't you dare look, Ada Collins.

God damn it, but he's in a suit. A full suit. Three piece, denim blue, and my god is it well-fitted.

Hugging his broad shoulders, tapered around his sharp narrow waist.

Holy crap, did I mention those thick, muscular thighs?

I remember those bad boys pinning me to the mattress as he—

I fan my face with two flappy hands.

Ada, stop, you got this.

Damn it, he's grinning. That sexy grin that he knows does things to my lady parts, making them tingle and shit.

I don't know, but I have this intense feeling that I need to mount the man, now. Make up sex is the best sex, isn't that what they say? Or is it hate sex?

Either way, I know what I want, and it's right in front of my eyes.

Only six feet away from me.

Our eyes remain fixed on each other as we walk toward one another.

Lincoln extends his hands and lets out a low whistle. "You're looking absolutely spectacular tonight, Miss Collins."

Well crap, that makes me smile.

I mean, Lexie didn't put me through hell the last several hours for nothing. Right as I returned to Blue Haven, Lexie practically barged into my resort room, requesting I be her maid of honor as her other one went into labor.

Of course, I said yes.

Doing a little twirl for him, I ask, "You think so? Not too much?"

He grabs my hands as his gaze dips down my body. "Absolutely fucking not, Ada; you look insanely beautiful." His intense stare lingers, sending a warm tingle throughout my body. He leans in closer, his voice barely above a whisper. "Don't doubt that."

"You're not looking half bad yourself, Mr. St. James," I say, giving him an extra cheeky smile.

He grows his own grin, causing my blush to intensify. Is it appropriate to blush over a man that you currently have no idea where you stand?

His blue eyes flip to mine, and pain is written all over his face as he whispers, "You're actually here?"

The warmth of his hand cups my cheek, as I say, "Sorta had to be, being maid of honor and all."

"Kind of figured, since the dress and tie matched," he says with a smirk.

That damn St. James smirk. I would die a happy woman if that were the last thing I saw.

And . . . maybe an orgasm or two.

"Yo, we need you, best man! Get your ass in the groom's room, the highness himself is requesting you."

Our eyes are drawn to the hallway as Garrett's eyes widen. "Aww, shit, man, did I interrupt something?" Garrett asks, as he paces the floor.

Lincoln and I burst into a fit of laughter as he freaks out. More like having a panic attack as he whispers God knows what to himself.

A glimmer of hope flickers in Lincoln's eyes as he asks, "Talk later, yeah?"

The final few inches between us close as I rise on my toes, whispering, "Maybe if you're lucky. I heard there are some handsome groomsmen at this wedding."

Lincoln's chest rumbles as he groans, making me laugh. I lean in to kiss him on the cheek, but before I have time to regain my balance, Lincoln wraps an arm around my waist. He tightens his hold on and pulls me even closer, a mischievous smile playing on his lips.

"Don't bet on that, sweetheart. Haven't you heard?

The best man and the maid of honor are always the magic duo at the end of the night."

With a cheeky grin, I move to the table beside us and grab my champagne glass, bringing the rim to my lips. I take a sip of the bubbly liquid, the scent of citrus and sweet fruit filling my nose. I raise an eyebrow. "Let's put it to the test, shall we?"

There is a chuckle in Garrett's voice as he places a hand on Lincoln's shoulder and they walk away. It's pretty clear that he doesn't think that I can hear him say, "Dude, that was so hot to watch. Please tell me we won her over?"

My lips curl into another smile as I shake my head.

Chapter Thirty-Six ♡

Ada

"By the power vested in me, I now proclaim you husband and wife. You may now kiss the bride." Everyone in the room cheers as Lexie and Josh exchange their first kiss as husband and wife. When I gaze across the room, my eyes lock on the most handsome man. A small smile tips the side of his mouth; he gives me a wink, and he extends his arm for me to grasp onto as we walk down the aisle. We make our way through the crowd amidst cheers and laughter, and I savor the moment. The man I love is standing beside me, and I am overjoyed for my best friend.

Lexie's wedding is absolutely breathtaking. I couldn't have asked for a better day for her, except maybe the day when I get married myself. Now that will be a truly unforgettable moment.

Rows of white chairs are set up on the dance floor at the far end of the room with a gold runner between them. A large arch with the letter A, decorated with greenery and burgundy and navy flowers, stands at the head of the aisle in front of massive windows peering outside. Beyond it, the winter landscape of Wild Willow Mansion is visible: white frozen trees, twinkling lights, and Hope Bay Beach.

My mind wanders back to the time when I dreamed of my own wedding to Lincoln, making me a little nostalgic.

My attention is drawn to the reception bar: Drunk In Love, as I make my way along with the bridal party.

Kinda cute, don't you think? Drunk In Love?

Immediately after grabbing my favorite cocktail, a vodka spritz, I feel a shiver of anticipation coursing down my spine as the words, "Dance with me, A?" are whispered into my ear.

Twisting my head over my shoulder, heat rushes up my neck, right to the tips of my ears, as I see Lincoln in all his glory. He has such an adorable grin on his face, making it seem like he's happy and carefree, like a cute puppy. Lincoln sets our drinks down on the bar and displays his signature St. James charm with one hand outstretched.

Did my panties just get soaking wet from one smile?

Yes, yes, they fucking did.

In a shy giggle, I slip my hand into his and let him lead me out onto the dance floor as the chairs are taken down and guests begin gathering around to dance.

"Do you remember the first time we danced together?" Lincoln asks gently as his palm rests on my lower back, and we begin to twirl slowly across the floor. It felt like yesterday, the freezing rain and cold weather, the empty parking lot of The Crispy Biscuit, Lincoln's warm body wrapped around mine.

Kind of like right now, but only years later.

As my eyes are drawn to Lincoln's, I feel the warmth of his gaze, and I respond, "Like it was yesterday."

Lincoln places his chin on top of my head and asks, "Is this okay?"

Moving across the floor, I pull away, my gaze settling on his question, "Is what okay?"

"Us? Dancing? I was-sn't sur-re." He scratches the back of his neck, looking adorable as hell, stuttering over his words. With a nervous laugh, he says, "I was unsure whether you would like to dance with me. I just sort of asked and then grabbed your hand."

I grasp his hand behind his neck, placing it over my chest, feeling my heart beat rapidly.

"I'm more than okay with it, Lincoln." As he smiles, I let out a chuckle. "This is so awkward, isn't it? I tried to be cool earlier, but feel like my efforts failed miserably."

He shrugs his shoulders. "Maybe a little, but you definitely didn't fail, Ada; you were hot as hell at that moment. Plus, it's nice having you in my arms again."

Well shit, there goes my heart again.

Keep it together, Ada. We have to make him work for it.

Yeah, I can maybe keep it together for like 2 seconds before I cave in.

"I know now isn't the time to discuss everything, but can I just say how happy I am that you are here?" Lincoln says, brushing his thumb over my cheekbones, over and over again, causing butterflies in my stomach to flutter.

As soon as I returned to New York from Blue Haven, I wanted to give up so badly. I wanted to convince myself that everything would eventually work out for me if I continued to do what I was doing. But what I didn't realize was that my heart was shattered for all the reasons I didn't understand, and I knew nothing would feel normal or whole again without him.

Lincoln.

My safe place.

My best friend.

While we sway together, the song playing is telling us how important it is to take second chances, how rewarding an amazing future is if you allow it to be.

But is he ready?

What about his mom?

I can tell by the gleam in his eyes that he is nervous and afraid, yet his fingers tangled in mine tell me that he wants to try, so long as I do not run away.

And I don't want to run anymore.

My heart is screaming at me to tell him how I truly feel.

I want to be home, and he's my home.

Whether that's New York or Blue Haven, or some other place, as long as we are together, he needs to know that. Needs to know that I don't care about his mom; I can deal with her, just like I always have.

There is only one thing he needs to understand: I simply wanted some time to get to the bottom of every-thing and reach closure with my past. Although a wedding is not the right place to have this conversation, it is something I feel I must say in my heart, so I blurt out, "I love you, Lincoln St. James."

His eyes flash to mine as I continue, "I think I always have and always will. If I had thought over a month ago, I would be feeling this way, or sharing any of this, I would have called myself crazy. I thought I was over you when I first left, but the truth is, how could I ever be over you? Linc, you're my soulmate, my person, my best friend, and being away from you kills me.

"My time away in New York, away from you, during that entire week, gave me time to reflect on everything. I knew deep down that I couldn't let my insecurities dictate my future. My future with you. I can get over them with time, but what I can't get over is not having you in my life.

"I don't care what others think of me, Linc. I am who I am and people will accept it or not. It's their loss, including your mother. I know I can handle her and won't let her come between us again, even if I have to bite my tongue and not say 'you're a bitch' to her face.

"I also thou—"

I'm cut off by Lincoln's chuckle as he tucks a hair behind my ear, the tip of his fingers skimming my gold barrette. His eyes don't leave mine as he says, "Good, because I don't give a fuck what my mother says either."

Lincoln

"You, uh . . . you . . . " She swipes her tongue across her lower lip before clearing her throat. Her nervousness and stumbling over her words make her look so adorable. "You don't care what your mom thinks?"

I shake my head. "No. Nah. Nada. Never. I told her exactly that when I paid a visit to her house. Gave her an ultimatum; said it was either she accepts our relationship or she won't have a son anymore."

As I observe Ada's shell-shocked expression, my stomach drops.

Shit, did I already mess this up? I thought women loved grand gestures, right?

Maybe I should have waited to tell her?

It might have been better to say, "My mother's opinion is no longer important to me, Ada, only yours."

Yeah, I think that wou—

Ada leaps at me before I can finish. Now, I'm the fucking one shell-shocked.

She has limbs going everywhere, and when I mean everywhere, her legs are wrapped around my waist. Her arms are around my neck, her face close to mine, and our lips lock in a fierce kiss. Her hands cup my neck, then my face, then my shoulders. It's like she can't get enough of touching me. Not that I have a problem with that, but I would prefer it in private.

As I quickly place Ada back on the ground, I rest my palm on her ass. Just making sure it's covered for God's sake.

Grabbing her hand, I move us off the dance floor into a more private area. Resting my forehead against Ada's, I let out a gentle sigh. "Ada, there is no me without you, and the day you left, I knew I wouldn't allow you to run away from me again. We have been through heartache, loss, and pain, and yet we are still standing. I am tired of us battling our pasts, my mother, all the fears and insecurities we have. They might always be there lingering, but it's up to us to push forward. Don't let anything or anyone stop us from being together."

My fingers stroke the side of her face as she looks up at me. "Ada, promise me. Promise me, you won't leave again? Give us a second chance."

Hesitancy flickers in her eyes, and before it can steal

her, I press my lips to hers. She opens for me without a second thought, sinking into my touch, and I wrap my arms around her waist, pulling her close. I memorize the feel of her body against mine, the way I can swallow her whole, the way her skin lights mine ablaze, and I cling to that feeling, the never-ending love, my forever.

Pulling back, a whimper comes from Ada's lips, and I smile. "How about we, uh, finish this, maybe later?" I ask as I look toward the women's bathroom.

"Yeah, later," Ada says as she bites her bottom lip.

"Later is probably for the best." I grab her hand and drag her toward the bathroom.

Nodding, she says, "You're right. We have all the time in the world."

Awh fuck it . . .

I move us into the bathroom and lock it, for safety precautions, of course, as Ada pulls me closer, her hand trembling as she grabs my suit coat, taking it slowly off.

"So you and I agree? We can wait until later?" I whisper in her ear, and goosebumps rise on her soft skin.

"Sure, later," she whispers, leaning toward me.

"We should probably stop now."

Her breath, warm and sweet, ghosts over my lips. "Yes, let's stop."

Ada's back hits the granite wall with a thud as we crash into it; the bathroom stall next to us slams. We both freeze, waiting to see if another person is in the bathroom with us, but as soon as 5 seconds go by, we are safe.

My belt, pants, and boxers are pushed to my feet, leaving my bottom half completely naked.

Ada bites her lower lip while her hands sweep over my chest. Her eyes are filled with desire. Craving. Need.

I shove my hands under her arms as I wrap her legs around my waist. I hoist her up to me, bunching her dress. "Definitely not later," I growl against her neck, trailing wet kisses up the columns of her throat, nipping the edge of her jaw, lingering at her ear. "This is going to be fast and rough, but I promise later, I can show you my sweet lovin'."

With that, I dive forward, taking one nipple into my mouth and sliding my hand up her dress.

Jesus. There is nothing between my fingers and her pussy, but a pair of lace underwear. With my finger over her slit, she whimpers, causing moisture to flow out of my cock. I am going to lose it and come before we even get started.

Releasing her nipple, I lean back to gaze at her, drinking her in. Her wild hair, the rise of her high, full breasts. Her face is flushed, but she still looks beautiful. It drives me wild. I roll my fingers over her slit again.

"Yes, Lincoln," Ada hisses, using her heels to pull me closer until the tip of my stiff cock lines up with her wet spot on her panties. We both shudder. Driven by need. I drag the head of my cock between the lips of her sex. Up and down the lace of her thong.

"Oh my God," she chants. "Oh my God, Lincoln."

As I guide my aching cock through her silky, soaking folds, I want to go slow, savor this moment between us. But my body has a mind of its own as my hips give a short, hard thrust right into Ada.

"Linc, please give me more."

"Hold on to me." It is more a command than a plea. Her eyes lock on mine, as I continue to thrust into her, her body trembles against mine.

"More, Linc, more."

With every hard thrust I deliver, her walls tighten around me, and I can't stop. "Fuck. Fuck. Fuck, Ada."

Heat streaks down my spine and up my shaft as I let go of my release. My head falls forward onto Ada's shoulder, hearing her heartbeat just as fast as mine.

5 minutes later, I am setting Ada down on the floor as she moves toward the mirror, fixing what she thinks is a mess.

My beautiful mess.

Glancing at our reflection, Ada says, "That was, well, ama—"

I cut her off, "Amazing? Fucking hot?"

While biting her thumbnail, she giggles, looking adorable as hell. "Yeah, it was."

Suddenly nervous, she stares down at the sink, fiddling with her fingers.

Taking her by the hand, I tilt her chin up and say, "Hey. Look at me. Are you okay? Did I hurt you? Are you mad that just happened?"

Laughing, she wipes a tear from her cheek.

"Please tell me those are happy tears, Ada."

Nodding, she smiles. "Yes, they are tears of joy. No, I am not mad at you, because that was probably the hottest thing I have ever done."

"If that's the case, then there's more to come," I say, wiggling my eyebrows.

In a chuckle, she lays her head on my chest and murmurs, "I feel like I am finally home, Linc. I know we still have much to figure out, but I am here in your arms, my favorite place to be, and I couldn't be happier."

"Me too, baby, me too," I say, placing a kiss on her forehead.

Chapter Thirty-Seven

Ada

In the blink of an eye, the night passes, drinks are poured, speeches are delivered, dances are entertaining, make-up sex certainly occurs, maybe even a few times. We kiss and hug and whisper sweet nothings until it is time to go home, and I feel content, knowing that, despite all our differences and the adversity that has threatened us, he still chooses me.

Chooses me over his mom.

Chooses me over everyone.

Chooses to love me.

Chooses to accept me.

It is almost like a wake-up call for me. I had been so afraid of relying on someone else that I had closed myself off from the world and was unable to see how much I was missing out on. With Lincoln, I am reminded of the significance of having someone who is on my team and supports me unconditionally. He shows me that

I am capable of being vulnerable and trusting someone with my emotions, and that life is so much better when you have someone to turn to and share life with.

Something I don't want to ever lose.

Lincoln shifts in bed as his lips trace a path up my neck and whispers, "What are you doing awake, Ada girl?"

He already has me in a trance, and I'm powerless to his touch as I melt into him, giving a whisper, "Nothing, just thinking of you." My arms wrap around his neck as I pull him closer to me. "I'm just thinking how lucky I am to have second chances."

He hugs me tight, wrapping his arms around my waist.

"I never imagined I would see you again, let alone have the opportunity to love you all over again, Linc. But here we are," I murmur into his chest, feeling nothing but contentment as I finally feel like everything will be okay.

With a gentle sigh, he draws back and rests his forehead against mine. "I missed you," he confesses.

I continue to stare at him, listening to his steady rhythm of breathing, slow and deep. "I thought I lost you." His voice so serious.

"But you didn't."

"I know. I just never imagined that we would see each other again, let alone reconnect in this way." He turns his head as he continues, "I know I have made so many mistakes with us, with my mother, with everything."

Coaxing his gaze back to mine, with my hand on his jaw, I say, "Hi, I'm here. Don't stop talking. I know this is difficult for you, well, for the both of us, but I am here." I brush a kiss across his lips.

In a gentle nod, he kisses my collarbone. "I know I've made mistakes in the past, but I don't want to repeat them. I want to be enough for you. I want you to know that you can come to me and not run. I want to be the person you tell everything to, to be the one who helps you with whatever you're battling, even if it's my mother. I want to show you I can be the man you need, not the one you have to deal with," he murmurs, holding me close.

Be still my heart . . . This man is so sweet.

"I love you, Lincoln."

"Do you really mean that?" His eyes sparkle. "You mentioned it, but I felt like maybe we were caught up in the moment, ya know?"

Nodding my head, I move myself over to his hips. My eyes locked on his. "You know, I'm not sure I ever fell out of love with you. Back then, I thought it was easier for me to run away from all my problems, and even now, I know that's so easy to do, but I don't want to. I don't want to do it alone anymore. I want you, Lincoln, and I want to share everything with you, all the ups and downs, the good and bad."

With an adorable Lincoln smile, he sweeps his thumb across my jawline and asks, "Are you sure? Are you positive you want this? Want us?"

A smile spreads across my face as I grab his hand and move it right to the top of my beating heart. "Can you feel that?" I ask.

He nods his head.

Suddenly, my eyes well up with tears. I can't even describe how freeing it is to give my whole self to someone again, after all this time and heartache. I've finally made my way back to the person I was meant to be with.

"That's how I feel every time I see you, every time I am near you, every time I think about our future. My heart beats only for one person, you."

"But what about your job? The partnership at the firm? New York? You live there, I live here? Now that I just got you back, Ada, I don't think I could handle a long distance relationship."

Putting a finger on his lips, I quiet him. "Well, I don't have a job, which means I am not a partner at Sullivan & Rothman Law Firm anymore. As far as me living in New York and you in Blue Haven, well, that can work itself out, right? We have all the time in the world."

His eyes widen as he pushes onto his elbows. "What do you mean you don't have a job? Or that you didn't get the partnership?"

I shrug my shoulders. "After I went back to New York, I won the M&A case I had been dedicating all my time and effort to, which led me to receiving the partnership I wanted within the firm."

Looking him dead in the eyes, I say with a laugh. "And yes, 'Scotty' I did go out with all my friends and coworkers that night to celebrate. That was all it was."

His eyes widen in surprise as a laugh bubbles out of him. "Let me guess, Jewels said something about my fabricated Instagram account?"

I laugh. "Yeah, something like that."

"Anyway, after all that was said and done, I decided to take a step back from everything. For a few days, I realized that my career isn't everything. Due to the demands of my career, I knew I couldn't do what my heart and soul really needed, to live in the moment, enjoy life, and be present.

"Plus, being back in Blue Haven reminded me of all the reasons I missed the small town vibes. New York was great for me at that time in my life, but now? Not so much."

His eyebrows raise. "So, what are you saying?"

Pushing him back down on the mattress, I say, "That I am a free woman who is about to enjoy this next incredible chapter of her life. With you, Linc."

Lincoln

Ada is so strong and confident. She's certain about so many things in her life, and the only thing I've ever been so sure about is, well . . . her. Just a week ago, I had been dying to hold her, kiss her, and give her the space she needed. I am so thankful I did, because right now, well, it's the fucking best. The best feeling in the world, one I don't want to put an end to, nor do I have to. Everything feels so incredibly right.

In the midst of rolling, I tightly clutch Ada to my chest. Looking down at her, I whisper, "I fucking missed you so much."

In a goofy smile, she curves a finger toward me, clearly indicating her desire to have me closer. "Make love to me, Lincoln St. James. Make me yours."

I cover her mouth with mine. Ada's fingers sink into my hair, pulling me closer, as her tongue glides against mine. My hands creep beneath her back, skimming the arch, pressing into her smooth skin, holding her to me.

Her blue eyes lift to mine, and the love that is there, well, it's enough to knock the breath out of my lungs. "Ada St. James, sounds pretty good, don't you think?"

Ada giggles adorably as she says, "Oh, is this you proposing to me?"

I gently push a piece of hair behind her ear. "Definitely not, but you will become Mrs. St. James very soon."

She raises an eyebrow. "Soon, huh? How soon are we ta—"

My lips cover hers as I cut her off, "Doesn't matter how soon; either way, you will be my wife someday."

My woman smiles and bites her bottom lip. "Oh, you think so, do you?"

My grip tightens on her waist as I say, "I know so."

Ada nudges me forward and my lips come crashing down on hers. My mouth slides over the swell of her tits, loving each rosy nipple before continuing my path down, watching as her stomach flexes, nibbling the inside of her thigh. "Mine," I whisper. She's whimpering, begging, barely breathing.

"Lincoln," she cries when I lick her swollen slit. She struggles against me as her feet press into the mattress and she lifts, pushing herself closer to me. When I suck her into my mouth, her head falls back with a short gasp.

"Fucking Mine," I say with a growl.

"My man is so possessive," she says, peering down at me.

Hooking my arms around her thighs, I yank her closer. "You bet I fucking am. Now that I know what it's like to live without you, I never want to go through that again."

She's already close, shaking, toes curling, and when I plunge two fingers inside her, she cries out. I'm obsessed with her, and the way she's addicted to watching me get her off, like the sight itself is enough.

But it will never be enough. I kick the power straight up when I move toward her, wrapping her legs around my waist.

"Holy shhh—" Her words dissolve as I push inside her.

"Jesus Christ," I hiss as my forehead meets hers.

She cups my face in her hands, kissing me with such passion and love, making me want to come right there.

"Mine," I tell her, pressing my lips once more to hers. I grip her hips, thrusting forward. Her head rolls, as do her eyes, locked on mine. Her fingers curl around my biceps.

"F-f-f-fuuuck. I-I . . . " Her head lolls forward, wide eyes, as she says, "I'm gonna . . . I'm gonna come."

And we both do; my own orgasm starts barreling down my spine, my balls tightening, and when Ada whimpers my name once, then twice, I clutch her hips and thrust forward as hard as I can, over and over, until we both fall off the edge of the cliff, together, free falling into the sky.

Breathless, I collapse onto my back, dragging Ada overtop of me. Bringing her hand to my lips, I kiss her soft, small palm.

Briefly closing her eyes, I whisper, "Thank you so much for giving me a second chance to love you again, Ada girl."

Epilogue ♡
Ada

6 Months Later

"This is really going to be the last time we step foot in this house, isn't it?" Noah asks behind me.

I nod my head, silently holding back the tears that I know will eventually come. This house comes with a lot of hate, sadness, and resentment, but it also is filled with love, happiness, and warmth. Ever since I got closure with my mom, my past, and Lincoln, this place feels different. Light, freeing somehow, and thinking of letting it go has my stomach twisting in knots.

In the aftermath of Lexie's wedding, I moved back to New York to pack up my life. Several months after I moved back to Blue Haven, someone bought the house, and now it is time to vacate it and say our final goodbyes.

I take in everything one last time as I walk around the kitchen island, running my fingers along it. It is empty, bare, containing nothing of what it once was. Boxes line the stairs with our last possessions.

As soon as I had stepped inside the house, I was unsure what to think, but it wasn't this; I chalked it up to the house being meticulously staged, as the real estate agent told us it would be, but Noah had better ideas. Like letting the new homeowners envision what they saw in this house with their own personal belongings.

Having decided what I wanted for myself, my life, Lincoln and I'd future, I decided that it was time for me to start moving forward with what brought me happiness, one of which has been something I have dreamed about for a long time.

A. Collins Law.

A little someone, aka Lincoln, inspired me to start my own law firm about two months ago. While I was happy to be back in Blue Haven, spending time with family, friends, away from my career, enjoying the things that brought me joy, I soon realized my career could do the same thing for me. But because I let it get out of hand in New York, I've set boundaries, so I have the best of both worlds.

Lincoln made it his goal to always point out the little shop on Ivy street, reminding me that it was there if I wanted it. Yes, that sweet man bought the damn shop without consulting me; he was just waiting for me to come to my senses, that I didn't have to live a life without my career, that people, just like me, needed my help. Needed guidance, because I never had that growing up.

My career was supposed to help others, and I lost sight of that, but not anymore. Being in Blue Haven, and already seeing the clients I have, has shown me that.

Walking over to the staircase, I hear a loud noise coming from the entry table. Moving over to it, Noah's phone lights up with Elena's name.

Hmmm, so they did actually get together? Are they dating?

No, no way. Noah would have told me.

Elena would have said something, right?

You're right; it's probably some other woman named Elena.

"Sorry, got to take this," Noah says as he swipes his phone. His face turns crimson red. "I will be right back," he replies, running straight outside.

Shaking my head, I murmur, "Yeah, sure you will be."

"It's a real shame that we won't be able to just walk in here and give each other shit anymore."

Turning my head, I see Lexie and Josh walking into the house.

I smile, walking toward them, giving Lexie a bear hug. "What are you doing here?" I ask.

With a huff, she laughs. "Me," she points to her chest, "well, I did know this house very well too, so it was only right that I said my goodbyes."

I let out a chuckle. "Mhm, sure."

"So, we throwing a goodbye party in this place or what?" Garrett asks, tossing his hands in the air, followed a moment later by Mayra splaying him on the head with her hand.

"Garrett, not every goodbye has to be accompanied by a party. Some of us are just normal people."

The five of us begin laughing hysterically as Lincoln enters my view.

His handsome face smiles at me.

In a pinstripe gray suit and loafers without socks, he looks delicious enough to eat. His pants are tight around his thighs, but loose around his calves and ankles, where the fabric stops.

Okay, this is not my Lincoln.

Baseball caps and mesh shorts are his usual attire.

He has styled his hair to the side, in a messy manner, giving him a seductive look; something I was not expecting on a day like this.

Am I missing something? Did we have a date planned?

I peek at my own clothing: a pair of lululemon joggers, tennis shoes, and a tank top covered with a jacket.

Hmmm, yeah, I think I would have remembered if we were going out.

Lincoln

Shit, shit, shiiiit.

Lincoln, snap out of it, you got this.

As I approach Ada, I wipe my now sweaty palms as I touch the velvet box. The ring has been in my possession for several months. Lexie and my sisters helped me pick out some designs they thought Ada might like.

Oh, yeah, can't forget Garrett being with us; his face beaming with glee, like he knew what was coming.

As I draw closer to Ada, my heart thuds. She is absolutely stunning, especially when she is wearing no make-up and her hair is in a bun that resembles a nest. High-waisted joggers and a tank top, all natural, all mine, and about to be forever, if I have my way.

I'm not nervous, not at all, and not in the way she probably thinks, as she gives me a concerned look.

It's more of an anxious excitement.

I'm ready for this. I have known this since the day I laid my eyes on her. I love her, and I want to start our lives as husband and wife.

Interlacing my fingers with Ada's, I whisper in her ear, "Come with me."

Her chin touches my shoulder as she leans into my side. "What's going on, Linc?" she asks.

Ada

As he stares down at me, Lincoln asks, "Do you trust me?"

My head nods as we continue to walk to the kitchen.

"Open this for me," Lincoln says as he hands me an envelope written in the cursive script of Ada.

"What is this?" I ask, holding the letter out in front of me as I look up at him.

A smirk spreads across his face; that damn sexy St. James smirk.

Melt my panties, why don't ya.

"Fine, I will open it." Using a gentle tear, I open the letter without ripping it. My eyes scan the first line and I take a deep breath, steeling myself for the emotion I know the words will bring.

Dear Ada girl,
Where do I even begin? We have been
through so much. The ups and downs, the good
and bad, but we have made it through it all.
Our hardships in life made us who we are

today and led us back to each other. Something I will be forever grateful for. I get to wake up to you every day, call you mine every chance I can, love you every single second the way you deserve. Something I never thought I would have a second chance at doing. I don't know if you remember, but, one day, when we were lying in bed, you said that you were happy that second chances existed, and so am I, baby.

Because, without second chances, I wouldn't have had the opportunity of having you read this letter in front of me, or showing you every day that you are enough, that you are worthy, that you don't need others' opinions to tell you how great you are, because you're the best damn thing out there.

Laughing happily, I continue reading.

And most importantly, baby, I wouldn't have been able to give your childhood home back to you, where it belongs, and I wouldn't have been allowed to call you, Ada Jean St. James.

Let's start forever, baby, right here, right now. What do you say? Give us a second chance in Blue Haven?

When my eyes meet his, my heart tightens as I see this man on his knees before me. The man I know I was always meant to be with, the one I love so wholly, so endlessly.

"Ada, I was afraid," he says, as he grasps my hand and gives it a tight squeeze. "God, I didn't think I would get so emotional," he says, wiping at his tears as he runs his fingers through his hair.

Dropping to my knees, I face him directly and cup his face in my hands. The intensity of the moment is palpable, and my heart races. His expression is one of pure emotion, a mix of love and desire that I have never seen before.

"I was terrified. Watching you walk away from me the second time, and me not being strong enough to stop you in that moment, killed me. I didn't feel like I deserved another chance with you, that you deserved more than me, that you were already living your dream life.

"I thought I lost you forever, and I . . . " Fear steals his words, as he shakes his head slightly. "I . . . "

He blinks as I stroke two fingers down his cheek and dry away the tears. "I couldn't, Ada. I can't. I won't. I won't ever lose you again, Ada." He smiles, overflowing with love. "I love you, Ada. Through the perfect moments, and there are plenty of them, but I promise I will always love you through the imperfect moments as well. You're my best friend, baby."

"And you are mine." I wrap my palm around his

neck, guiding him to my body as I attempt to stand.

"Wait, wait, only you stand."

A chuckle escapes me as I give him a kiss and stand; he kneels, his beautiful ocean blue eyes lock on mine.

"Ada, I got the chance to fall in love with the young girl I knew years ago, but I also got a second chance to re-fall in love with the playful, courageous, and stunning woman standing before me. A chance that I'll never forget. Over the past few months, you've shown me so many reasons why I love you. From how you sleep diagonally in our bed, the way you work with your heart to help others, to opening up to me and letting me see you. The day Ginger came running into this house, knocking you on your ass, I knew the love I had for you hadn't dissolved. It was still there, Ada girl, and it always will be as long as you are mine."

He whistles as Ginger runs into the kitchen, holding a paper sign with a bow tie around her neck that says, "Will you marry us?"

"What do you say? Will you be mine forever? Will you build a life with me in this house?" Lincoln asks as he reveals a black velvet box.

Appearing in front of my eyes is the most gorgeous ring I have ever seen. It's an oval sapphire, more teal than blue. The gold band that it sits on is vintage. The three small marquise diamonds frame each side, making it look like flower petals.

My *dream* ring. He remembered what I liked in a ring from all those years ago.

My heart pumps wildly and my stomach starts to do flip flops. "Is this seriously happening?" I whisper.

"Yes, baby, this is happening," Lincoln says with a

chuckle.

A laugh escapes my lips as I cover my mouth. "Shit, I didn't realize I had said that out loud."

Waiting patiently for my answer, Lincoln raises a brow.

Perhaps I should tease him a bit, make him wait a little longer. Yet, who am I kidding. I can't allow another day to pass without him by my side.

My voice is filled with excitement as I shout out, "Yes! Yes, I will marry you!"

With his wide blue eyes, Lincoln stares at me, clearly not registering what I have said. "Really, you will be mine forever, baby?"

Nodding my head, I allow tears of happiness to run down my cheeks. Picking me up by my waist, he spins me around in a circle. "I knew you could not live without me."

With a hearty laugh, I let my head fall back out. "Did you really mean it, building a life here? But how? I don't understand? I thought the real estate agent said somebody else bought the house," I ask.

"I was the anonymous buyer, baby. I bought this house the day after my Little League game. When we were at Safe Harbor, it wasn't something you mentioned, but more of the way you reacted when you said you had to let this house go. It held so many memories for you, even if they weren't all that great, and I could tell you weren't ready to let it go. I just told the agent to keep it a secret until today."

He smiles at me as he continues, "I knew how much it meant to you, and to your mom; it's why I helped her with the renovations in the beginning."

My heart stops. "You're the one who did all this?" I

lift an eyebrow.

He did that?

All for me?

For my mother?

He brushes his fingertips against my cheek. "Yeah, I did, baby. Your mother did not have the funds, so I helped her devise a solution. I had her fill out a Home Improvement Grant, which she got accepted for. It was a win-win for me. I was able to use my handy hands, learn more about you, and get to build a relationship with the mom of the woman I love."

Oh.

My.

God.

This man, I tell you what.

My heart could fly out of my chest right about now. I never knew a person could hold this much love, let alone my own heart could love like this, but this man has given me so much to care for.

He seriously has the biggest heart I know.

While peering down at him, a cheer comes from the dining room, and I see everyone: Noah, Elena, Lucy, Lexie and Josh, Garrett and Mayra, as well as all of Lincoln's sisters.

They all smile and laugh, as they say in unison, "Congratulations, it's about time!"

My eyes turn to Lincoln as our foreheads meet. "To Second Chances, Linc," I say as he puts the ring on my finger.

"To Second Chances, Ada girl."

Acknowledgments

It is impossible for me to adequately express how grateful I am to all those who have made my dream a reality.

Brittani, thank you for encouraging me to accomplish my dream of becoming an author.

Thank you, Dillon, for always being by my side and listening to me vent about the process of becoming an author.

Most importantly, I am grateful to Chelsea, my publisher, for pushing me forward.

All of you were instrumental in my ability to write this book. Your courage and faith in me made this possible.

About the Author

A true romantic, Charli Cotner enjoys wearing a stylish pair of high heels with a spicy margarita in her hand. Her books cover everything from sweet to sexy, including A Second Chance in Blue Haven.

When Charli isn't writing, you'll find her reading, golfing, or spending time with her husband and three kids. She loves hearing from her readers, so please feel free to stop by and say hello.